WHIPPED BY THE LAW . . .

Longarm's gorge was rising. He felt that he'd stood all he could. Morton was almost unconscious now, hanging limply by his bound wrists. Still the wet, ugly splat of new blows sounded with monotonous regularity. In spite of his resolution not to interfere, Longarm had had a bellyful of the spectacle. He elbowed through the packed crowd until he stood in the front rank of spectators. Spud was raising the whip for another cut at Morton's bloodstained back when, without seeming to aim, Longarm fired. The heavy rifle slug ripped into the ground between Spud's feet. Spud leaped back, letting the whip drop from his hand.

"That's enough," Longarm announced. His voice was flat; he did not need to raise it to be heard in the stillness that hung like a shroud over the plaza. "The show's over."

Also in the LONGARM series

LONGARM

ON THE BORDER

TABOR EVANS

A JOVE/HBJ BOOK

Copyright © 1978 by Jove Publications, Inc.

All rights reserved. No part of this publication may be reproduced or transmitted in any form or by any means, electronic or mechanical, including photocopy, recording, or any information storage and retrieval system, without permission in writing from the publisher.

Requests for permission to make copies of any part of the work should be mailed to: Permissions, Jove Publications, Inc., 757 Third Avenue, New York, NY 10017.

Printed in the United States of America

Library of Congress Catalog Card Number: 78-19525

First Jove/HBJ edition published November 1978

Jove/HBJ books are published by Jove Publications, Inc. (Harcourt Brace Jovanovich) 757 Third Avenue, New York, N.Y. 10017.

Chapter 1

Even before he opened his eyes, in that instant between sleep and wakefulness, Longarm knew it had snowed during the night. Like the hunter whose senses guide him to prey, like the hunted whose senses keep him from becoming prey, Longarm was attuned to the subtlest changes in his surroundings. The light that struck his closed eyelids wasn't the usual soft gray that brightens the sky just before dawn. It had the harsh brilliance that comes only from the presunrise skyglow being reflected from snow-covered ground.

Opening his eyes only confirmed what Longarm already knew. He didn't see much point in walking across the ice-cold room to raise a shade at one of the twin windows. The light seeping around the edges of the opaque shades had that cold, hard quality he'd sensed when he'd snapped awake.

Longarm swore, then grunted. He didn't believe in cussing the weather, or anything else he was powerless to change. He was a man who believed that swearing just wasted energy unless it served some purpose besides relieving his own dissatisfaction.

Last night, when he'd swung off the narrow-gauge after a long, slow, swaying trip up from Santa Fe to Denver, he'd noted the nip in the air, but his usually reliable weather-sense hadn't warned him it might snow. For one thing, it was just too early in the year. It was only the first day of September, and the Rocky Mountains' winter was still a couple of months away.

Longarm hadn't been thinking too much about the weather last night, though. All that had been in his mind was getting to his room, taking a nightcap from the bottle of Maryland rye that stood waiting on his dresser, and falling into bed. On another night, he'd probably have followed his habit of dropping in at the Black Cat or one of the other saloons on his way home, to buck the faro bank for a few turns until he relaxed. He'd started to cut across the freightyard to Colfax instead of taking the easier way along Wynekoop Street. What he'd seen happen in New Mexico Territory had left a sour taste in his mouth that the three or four drinks he'd downed on the train couldn't wash away.

There was little light in the freightyard. The acetylene flares mounted on standards here and there created small pools of brightness, but intensified the darkness between them. Longarm was spacing his steps economically as he crossed the maze of tracks, sighting along the wheel-polished surface of the rails to orient himself, when he sensed rather than saw the man off to his left. He couldn't see much of anything in the gloom, just the interruption of the light reflected on the rail along which he was sighting.

"Casey?" Longarm called.

He didn't think it was Casey, who was the night yard super, and more likely to be in his office, but if it was one of Casey's yard bulls patrolling, the fact that he'd called the boss's name would alert the man that Longarm wasn't a freight car thief.

A shot was his answer, a muzzle-flash following the whistle of lead uncomfortably close to his guts. Longarm drew as he was dropping and snapshotted as he rolled, throwing his own lead at the place where he'd seen the orange blast. He didn't know whether or not he'd connected. He hadn't had a target; his shot was the equivalent to the buzz a rattlesnake gives when a foot comes too near its coils.

Faintly, the sound of running footsteps gritting on cinders gave him the answer. Whoever'd tried to bushwhack him wasn't going to hang around and argue. For several seconds, Longarm lay on the rough earth, sniffing coal dust, trying to stab through the dark with his eyes, straining his ears to hear some giveaway sound that would spot a target for him. Except for the distant chugging of a yard mule cutting cars at the shunt, there was nothing to hear.

Longarm didn't waste time trying to prowl the yard. Being the target of a grudge shot from the dark wasn't anything new to him, or to any of the other men serving as Deputy U. S. Marshals in the unreconstructed West of the 1880s. Longarm guessed that whoever'd been responsible for the drygulch try had been skulking in another car of the narrow-gauge on the trip up from New Mexico. God knows, he'd stepped on enough toes during his month there to have become a prime target for any one of a half-dozen merciless, powerful men. Any of them could've sent a gunslick to trail him to Denver and waylay him. The attack had to have originated in New Mexico Territory, he decided. Nobody in Denver had known when he'd be arriving.

Brushing himself off, Longarm had hurried on across the freightyard and to his room. He'd hit the sack without lighting a lamp, dropping his clothes to the floor as he shed them, bone-tired.

On the dresser, the half-full bottle of Maryland rye gleamed in the light trickling around the windowshade. Its invitation was more attractive than the idea of staying in the warm bed. Longarm swung his bare feet to the floor, crossed the worn gray carpet in two long strides and let a trickle of warmth slip down his throat. As he stood there, the tarnished mirror over the dresser showed his tanned skin tightening in goosebumps raised by the room's chill air.

Crossing the room to its inside corner, Longarm pulled aside a sagging curtain. He grabbed a cleaner shirt than the one he'd taken off, and a pair of britches that hadn't been grimed with coal dust from the cinders he'd rolled in last night at the freightyard.

He wasted no time in dressing. The cold air encouraged speed. Longjohns and flannel shirt, britches, wool socks, and he was ready to stomp into his stovepipe cavalry boots. Another short snort from the bottle and he turned to check his tools. From its usual night resting place, hanging by its belt from the bedpost on the left above his pillow, Longarm took his .44-40 Colt double-action out of its open-toed holster. Quickly and methodically, his fingers working with blurring speed, he swung out the Colt's cylinder, dumped its cartridges on the bed and strapped on the gunbelt.

He returned the unloaded pistol to the holster and drew three or four times, triggering the revolver with each draw, but always catching the hammer with his thumb instead of letting it snap on an empty chamber and perhaps break the firing pin. Each time he drew, when Longarm had returned the Colt to the holster he made the tiny adjustments that were needed to put the waxed, heat-hardened leather at the precise angle and position he wanted it to ride, just above his left hip.

Satisfied at last, he dripped a bit of oil on a square of flannel and swabbed the Colt down before reloading. He checked each cartridge as carefully as he did the fresh round he put into the cylinder to replace the one he'd fired last night. Then he checked out the .44 caliber derringer soldered to the chain that held his pocket watch on its other end. He put on his vest, dropped the watch into its left breast pocket, the derringer into the right-hand pocket. Longarm always anticipated that trouble might look him up, as it had in the freightyard. If it did, he aimed to be ready.

Longarm's stomach was growling by now. He quieted it temporarily with a short sip of rye before completing his methodical preparations to leave his room for the day. These were simple and routine, but it was a routine he never varied while in civilized surroundings. Black string tie in place, frock coat settled on his broad shoulders, Stetson in its forward-canted angle on his close-cropped head, he picked up his necessaries from the top of the bureau and stowed them into their accustomed pockets. Change went into one britches pocket and jackknife in the other; his wallet with the silver Federal badge pinned in its fold was slid into an inner breast pocket. Extra cartridges went into his right-hand coat pocket, handcuffs and a small bundle of waterproofed wooden matches in the pocket on the left.

As he went out of the room, Longarm kicked ahead of him the soiled clothing that still lay on the floor. Hoh Quah, his Chinese laundryman, would pick it up and bring it back clean that evening. He closed the door and between door and jamb inserted a broken matchstick at about the level of his belt. His landlady wasn't due to clean up his room until Thursday, and Longarm wanted to know the instant he came home if an uninvited stranger might be waiting inside—somebody, for instance, like the unknown shadow who'd failed to pick him off last night. Anybody who knew his name was Custis Long could find out where Longarm lived.

Not only the roominghouse, but the entire section of the unfashionable side of Cherry Creek where it stood was still asleep, Longarm decided when he stood on the narrow veranda looking over the street. The night's unexpected snowfall, though only an inch or less, made it easy for him to see whether anyone had been prowling around. He took a cheroot from his breast pocket and chomped it between his teeth, but didn't light it, while studying the white surface.

There was only one set of tracks visible. They came from the house across the street, and the toes were pointed in the safe direction—for Longarm—away from the house, toward the Cherry Creek bridge. Just the same, Longarm didn't step off the porch until he'd flicked his gunmetal-blue eyes into the long, slanting shadows between the houses. He didn't really expect to see anyone. The kind of gunhand who'd picked the safety of darkness once for his attack would be likely to wait for the gloomy cover of hootowl time before making a second try.

His booted feet cut through the thin soft snow and crunched on the cinder pathway as Longarm walked unhurriedly to the Colfax Avenue bridge. He turned east on the avenue. Ahead, the golden dome of the Colorado capitol building was just picking up the first rays of the rising sun.

George Masters's barbershop wasn't open yet, and Longarm needed food more than he did a shave. He didn't fancy the cold free lunch he knew he'd find at any of the saloons close by, so he went on past the barbershop another block and stopped at a little hole-in-the-wall café for hotcakes, fried eggs, ham, and coffee. The cheroot went into his pocket while he ate. The longer he held off lighting it, the easier it'd be to keep from lighting the next one.

Leaving the restaurant twenty-five cents poorer but with a satisfactorily full stomach, Longarm squinted at the sun. Plenty of time for a shave before reporting in at the office. He walked at ease along the avenue, which was just coming to life. The day might not be so bad in spite of the weather, he decided, feeling the warmth from his breakfast spreading through his lean, sinewy body. He grinned at the bright sun, glowing golden in a crystal sky. Deliberately, he took a match from the bundle in his pocket, flicked it into flame with a thumbnail, and lighted the cheroot.

Smelling of bay rum, his overnight stubble removed and his brown mustache now combed to the angle and spread of the horns on a Texas steer, Longarm walked into Marshal Billy Vail's office before eight o'clock. It gave him a virtuous feeling to be the first one to show up; even Vail's pink-cheeked, citified clerk-stenographer wasn't at the outside desk to challenge him. The Chief Marshal was already on the job, of course, fighting the ever-losing battle he waged with the paperwork that came from Washington in an ever-mounting flood.

Vail looked pointedly at the banjo clock on the wall. "This'll be the day the world ends," he growled. "What in hell happened to get you here on time for once?"

Longarm didn't bother answering. He was used to Vail's bitching. He felt his chief was entitled, bound as he was now to a desk and swivel chair, going bald and getting lardy. Deskwork, after an active career in the field, seemed to bring out the granny in a man, and Longarm decided he might bitch about life, too, under the same circumstances.

Vail shoved a pile of telegraph flimsies across the desk. "I guess you know you raised a real shit-stink down in New Mexico. You better have a good story to back up the play you made there. I've got wires here from everybody except President Hayes."

"Don't go feeling lonesome," Longarm replied mildly. "Chances are the word ain't got to him yet. Maybe you'll get one from him, too, before the day's out. You want me to tell you how it was?"

"No. In fact, I'm not sure I want a long report in the file telling exactly what happened. Think you can write one like you handed in after that Short Creek fracas a few years back?"

Vail was referring to a report Longarm had turned in about his handling of another political hot potato that had consumed a month of time, resulted in eight deaths, and upset a hundred square miles of Idaho Territory. The report had read simply, "Assigned to case May 23. Completed assignment and closed case July 1."

"Don't see why not." Longarm considered for a moment before he went on. "I figured things might be hottening up down around Santa Fe, at the capitol. Some gunslick tried to bushwhack me when I got off the narrow-gauge last night."

"Hell you say." Vail's tone held no surprise. "You get him?"

"Too dark. He ran before I could sight on him."

"Well. Keep your report short, so I won't have to explain things I don't know about. Besides, I want you out of this office before that pot down there boils over clear to Washington."

"Suits me, chief, right to a tee. There's snow on the ground and more in the air, and you know how I feel about that damned white stuff."

"If it'll cheer you up any, the place you'll be going to is just a little cooler than the hinges of hell, this time of year." Vail pawed through the untidy stacks of documents on his desk until he uncovered the papers he was after. "Texas is yelling for us to give them a hand. So is the army."

"Seems to me like they both got enough hands so they wouldn't need to come running to us. What's wrong with the rangers? They gone to pot these days?"

Vail bristled. As a one-time Texas Ranger, he automatically resented any hint that his old outfit wasn't up to snuff. Huffily, he said, "The rangers got more sense than to bust into something that might stir up trouble with Mexico. Here's what Bert Matthews wrote me from Austin." He read from one of the papers he'd uncovered. "He says, 'You see what a bind we're in on this one, Billy. If one of my boys sets foot across the border and gets crossways of Diaz's rurales, we'd risk starting another war with them. Whoever goes looking for Nate Webster's got to have federal authority back of him and can't be tied to Texas. That's why I'm looking to you to give us a hand.'"

Longarm rubbed his freshly shaved chin and nodded slowly, "I hadn't looked at it thataway. Makes sense, I s'pose. Who's this Nate Webster fellow and what'd he do?"

"He's a ranger, and as far as Bert knows he didn't do anything except drop out of sight somewhere on the Mexican side of the Rio Grande. Bert don't think it was by accident, because just a little while afterward two black troopers who deserted from the 10th Cavalry and the captain of their outfit, who went looking for 'em, all three disappeared across the river too."

"Wait a minute now. That Rio Grande's a damn long river," Longarm observed. "It's goin' t'take a while to prowl it all the way down to the Gulf of Mexico. I got to have some place to start looking from."

"You have, so simmer down. I wouldn't be apt to send you if it wasn't that all four of them men disappeared from the same place. Little town called Los Perros. Dogtown, I guess that'd translate into. You ever hear of it? I sure as hell never did, but it's been a spell since I left Texas."

Longarm shook his head. "Name don't ring a bell with me, but you know about the only time I was in Texas, how long I spent there, and all. Where's this Los Perros place at, in general?"

"It's supposed to be about where the Pecos River goes into the Rio Grande."

"Rough country, in that part," Longarm said thoughtfully. "If it's there, though, I reckon I can find it. Only, I aim to take the long way gettin' there. I better circle around New Mexico instead of going the straightest way. I show my face in old Senator Abeyeta's country before the old man wears his mad off, I'd have to fight my way from Santa Fe clear to El Paso."

"You steer clear of New Mexico Territory, and that's an order," Vail agreed. "You've stirred up trouble enough there to last a while."

"Now, don't get your bowels riled up, chief. I'll figure me out a route. Just let me think a minute." He leaned back in the red morocco-leather chair, the most comfortable piece of furniture in the marshal's office, and began thinking aloud. "Let's see, now. I take the KP outa here tonight and switch to the MP at Pueblo. That gets me to Wichita, and I make a connection there with the I-GN or the SP to San Antonio. Pick me up a horse and some army field rations at the quartermaster depot there, ride to Fort Stockton, or whichever other fort's nearer to Los Perros. That'll beat jarring my ass on the Butterfield stage, and it'll get me to spittin' distance of the border a lot faster."

"Tell my clerk," Vail said impatiently. "He'll write your travel vouchers and requisition your expense money. Here. Take these letters and read 'em on the train. They'll give you the whole story as good as I can. Now get the hell outa this office before I get a wire from the attorney-general or the president telling me to suspend you or fire you outright."

"Which you can't do, if I ain't here," Longarm grinned. "All right, chief. By the time I close this case and get back, things ought've cooled down enough to get me off the political shit list."

During the three train changes and four days and nights it took Longarm to reach his jumping-off place deep in Texas, he spent his time catching up on lost sleep and studying the letters Marshal Vail had gotten from the Texas Rangers captain and those sent to ranger headquarters by the post adjutant at Fort Stockton. He was looking for some sort of connection that might tie the four disappearances together, but there didn't seem to be any.

Ranger Nate Webster had been working on a fresh outbreak of wholesale rustling involving what had come to be called the "Laredo Loop" along the Texas border. Cattle stolen from central Texas ranches were hustled across the Rio Grande's northern stretches, their brands altered, and bills of sale forged to show that the steers had been Mexican-bred and bought from legitimate ranchers in the Mexican states of Chihuahua, Cohuila, or Nuevo Leon. Then, driven south through Mexico, the rustled herds were brought back across the river at Laredo and sold there to buyers. As Laredo was the only point on the border except El Paso, nearly a thousand miles north, where a railroad crossed the Rio Grande, it had long been a center for livestock sales. Even with Mexican cattle selling well below the market price for Texas beef, the profits were huge. Nate Webster's investigation had led him to Los Perros. He'd been heading there when he'd last reported to ranger headquarters in Austin. That had been early in July, and he hadn't been heard from since.

Soon after the ranger made his last report, the two troopers from the all-black 10th Cavalry, the "buffalo soldiers," as they'd been named by the Indians, who saw in the blacks' hair a resemblance to buffalo manes, had deserted from Fort Lancaster. This small outpost was one of a string of almost a dozen forts, a day's ride apart, that had been built paralleling the Rio Grande to forestall the threat of invasion during the U.S.-Mexican War in 1846. The two men had left a trail that the Cimarron scout summoned from Fort Stockton had had no trouble following. He'd followed it to Los Perros. Captain John Hill, the Charley Troop commander, had gone with the scout. Hill had sent the Cimarron back to report and had himself followed the deserters' trail across the Rio Grande. Like Webster, like the deserting troopers, Hill had vanished on the Mexican side of the river after leaving Los Perros.

"Dogtown," Longarm muttered to himself, drawing on four-year-old memories of the last case that had taken him to Texas. "Los Perros. Mouth of the Pecos. Wild country. Big enough and rough enough to swallow up four hundred men, let alone just four, without a trace being left. I better start trying to remember what little bit of the local lingo I learned."

Then, because it was his philosophy that a man couldn't cross rivers before he tested them to see how deep and cold they ran, Longarm ratcheted back the rubbed plush daycoach seat, leaned back and went to sleep again, the smell of old and acrid coal dust in his nostrils. A little stored up shuteye might come in handy when he hit the long trail on horseback from San Antonio to the Rio Grande.

At the I-GN depot in San Antonio, Longarm swung off the daycoach and walked up to the baggage car to claim his gear. He'd left everything except his rifle to the baggage handlers; it would have been tempting fate to leave a finely tuned Winchester .44-40 unwatched in a baggage car or on a depot platform between trains. The rifle had ridden beside him all the way from Denver, leaning between the coach seat and the wall.

As always, he was traveling light. He swung the bedroll that contained spare clothing as well as a blanket and groundcloth over one shoulder, draped his saddlebags over the other, and picked up his well-worn McClellan saddle in his left hand to balance the rifle in his right. Then he set out to find a hack to carry him from the depot to the quartermaster station.

"All the way to the quartermaster depot?" the hackman echoed when Longarm asked how much the fare would be. "That's a long ride, mister. Cost you fifteen cents to go way out there. It's plumb on the other side of town and out in the country."

"We got to go by Market Plaza to get there, don't we?" Longarm asked. When the hackman nodded, he went on, "I'll pay the fare, even if it does seem a mite high, provided you'll stop there long enough for me to eat a bowl of chili. I got to get rid of the taste of them stale butcher-boy sandwiches I been eating the last few days."

"Hop in," the hackman said. "It's my dinnertime, too. Won't charge you nothing extra for the stop."

Counting time taken for eating, the ride down Commerce Street and then north on Broadway to the army installation took just over an hour. The place was buzzing with activity. After more than five years of debating, the high brass in Washington had finally decided to turn the quartermaster depot into a large permanent cantonment, and everywhere Longarm looked there were men at work. Masons were erecting thick walls of quarry stone to serve as offices; others were busy with red bricks, putting up quarters for the officers. A few carpenters were building barracks for the enlisted men on a flat area beyond the stables, where the hackman had pulled up at Longarm's instructions.

Not until he'd been watching the scene for several minutes did Longarm realize what had struck him as odd. There was only a handful of soldiers working around the quadrangle the buildings would enclose when all of them were completed. The hackie lifted Longarm's saddle and saddlebags out of the front of the carriage; Longarm got out and paid the man. He stood with his gear on the ground around his feet until the hack drove off. Then he slung his saddlebags and bedroll over his shoulders, picked up the saddle, and started for the nearest uniforms he could see, a clump of soldiers gathered around a smithy's forge a few yards from the stable buildings.

Longarm singled out the highest-ranking of the group, a tall lantern-jawed sergeant. "I'm looking for the remount duty noncom," he told the man.

"You found him, mister. That's me. Name's Flanders."

"Mine's Long, Custis Long. Deputy U. S. Marshal out of the Denver office. I need to requisition a good saddle horse for a case I'm here on."

"Be glad to oblige, Marshal. Soon as you show me a badge or something to prove you're who you say you are."

Wordlessly, Longarm took his wallet from the pocket of his Prince Albert coat and flipped it open. The sergeant studied the silver badge pinned in the fold for a moment, then nodded. He measured Longarm's muscular body with his eyes.

"How far you going to be traveling?"

"To the border."

"You're a sizable man, Marshal Long. You plan to pack much more gear than what you've got here?"

"Nope. This is all the horse'll have to carry."

"Follow along, then. I guess we can fix you up."

Longarm followed the sergeant around the stable to a small corral where a dozen or so horses were milling. The rat a tat of carpenters' hammers nearby was obviously making some of the animals nervous, for they were walking around the corral's inner perimeter. The others stood in a fairly compact group near the center of the enclosure. Most of them were roans and chestnuts, but there was one dappled gray a hand taller than the rest. It stood out like a peacock among sparrows.

"Don't try to palm off any of them walking nags on me," Longarm cautioned the sergeant. "Last thing I need's a nervous mount."

"Maybe you'd rather do your own picking," the man suggested.

"Maybe I better, if it's all the same to you."

Longarm was still carrying his Winchester. He tilted the muzzle skyward, levered a shell into the chamber and fired in the air before the sergeant knew what he intended to do. Two of the horses at the corral's center reared, three others bolted for the fence. Most of those that had been fence-walking either shied or bucked. The gray was among the handful that did not react to the shot. Longarm studied the dapple through slitted eyes. A light-coated horse made a man stand out, more than a roan or chestnut would, but he told himself that could be good as well as bad. He pointed to the animal.

"I'll take the gray, if he stands up to a closer look. Bring him over here and let me check him out," he told the sergeant.

"Now, I'm real sorry, Marshal Long. That's the only one I can't let you have."

"Mind saying why? Is he an officer's private property?"

"Well, yes and no."

"Make up your mind, Flanders. Either he is or he ain't."

"He ain't officer's private property, Mr. Long. Thing is, Miz Stanley, that's Lieutenant Stanley's lady, she's took a liking to Tordo, there. Rides him just about every afternoon. She'd be mighty riled if I was to—"

Longarm interrupted. "This lieutenant don't own the horse?"

"No, sir. Except, we was going to ship Tordo up to Leavenworth for their bandsmen, seeing we got no band here, and the lieutenant stopped us because his lady'd took a shine to the nag."

"I suppose Miz Stanley'd be just as well off if she took her exercise on another horse, wouldn't she?"

"No, sir. Begging your pardon, Mr. Long, she'd want Tordo."

"Happens I want him, too. He's the best-looking of that bunch out there. Now, bring him here and let me check him over. You can give the lieutenant's lady my regrets next time she wants to ride."

Longarm's tone carried an authority the sergeant was quick to recognize. He opened his mouth once, as though to argue further, but the deputy's blued-steel eyes were narrowed now, and the soldier knew he was looking at a man whose mind was made up. Reluctantly, the sergeant walked over to the gray and put a hand on its army-style clipped mane. He started back to where Longarm waited. The horse, obedient to the light pressure of the man's hand on its neck, walked step for step with the sergeant.

"Seems to be real biddable," Longarm commented.

"Tordo's a good horse, Mr. Long. Can't say I blame you for picking him out."

Longarm checked the gelding with an expert's quick, seemingly casual glances and finger-touches. Teeth, eyes, spine, cannons, hooves, were all sound. His inspection lasted barely three minutes, but when it was finished Longarm was satisfied with his choice.

"He'll do, Sergeant. Make out the form for me to sign while I saddle him. Or is this the kind of post where commissioned men do all the paperwork?"

"No, sir. Most of the officers are out on a field exercise, anyhow. I've got the forms over yonder in the stable. I'll have 'em ready by the time you're fixed to ride. If you don't want to bother saddling him yourself, I'll call a trooper to do it for you."

"Thanks, but I'd as soon do it myself, Flanders. You go on and take care of the forms."

Longarm saddled the dapple with the same economy of motion that marked all his actions. He'd finished cinching the girth, had sheathed his Winchester in the scabbard that angled back from the right-hand saddle fender, and was knotting the last rawhide saddle string around his bedroll when a woman's voice spoke behind him.

"I don't know who you are, but that's my horse you're saddling."

Without turning around, Longarm replied, "No, ma'am. It's the U. S. Government's horse."

"Don't be insolent! Now, take that saddle off at once and find yourself another mount! I'm ready for my afternoon canter."

Longarm finished knotting the saddle string and turned around. He doffed his Stetson as he spoke. "Beg pardon, ma'am, but I ain't about to do that. I need this one in my work."

"Really? Just who are you? And what sort of work do you do?"

"I'm Custis Long, ma'am. Deputy U. S. Marshal from Denver. And I'm on a case, which is all I need to say, I guess." Longarm realized he was speaking arbitrarily, which wasn't his usual way with a woman, but this one was being just too damned high-handed.

His abrupt manner surprised and puzzled her, that was clear from the expression on her face. Longarm took the moment of silence to inspect her. He wondered if she kept one full black eyebrow higher than the other when she wasn't angry. He couldn't give her a good mark for beauty, he decided, her features were a mite too irregular. Her nose arched abruptly from the full brows down to wide nostrils now flared with displeasure. Her lips were compressed, but that didn't hide the fact that they were on the full side. Her chin was thrust out aggressively. Her eyes were dark, and her hair was dark, too. It was caught up in a bunch of ringlets that dropped down the back of her neck to her shoulders.

She was wearing a cavalry trooper's regulation campaign hat, though it didn't have the regulation four dents in the crown. A soft, plain white blouse was pulled tightly over upthrust breasts. Her feet, in gloss-polished riding boots, were spread apart to show she had on a split skirt that dropped nearly to her ankles. Her hands were planted on her hips, and from one wrist a riding crop dangled by its looped thong.

Longarm's unconcealed inspection didn't cause the woman to drop her eyes, or even seem to embarrass her. When she found her voice, she said firmly, "Mr. Long, there are ten or fifteen other horses over there in the corral. One of them will be just as satisfactory as Tordo for your use."

"I'm sorry if it makes you mad, ma'am, but the plain fact of it is, where I'm heading for, my life might depend on my having the best horse I can throw my saddle on."

As though he hadn't spoken, she went on, "I'll find Sergeant Flanders and tell him to get you another horse. Meanwhile, you will take that saddle off Tordo at once!"

"I ain't about to do that, ma'am. Let's see, you'd be Lieutenant Stanley's wife, I guess?"

"What difference does that make?"

"Not one bit, Miz Stanley. Except it ain't going to do you no good to call the sergeant. He told me you'd be mad, after I'd made up my mind which horse I wanted. It didn't matter to me then, and it don't matter to me now."

She stamped a booted foot. "Mr. Long, if you don't take that saddle off Tordo right this minute, I'll—"

"You'll do what?" Longarm had held his temper, but he was getting angry, too, now. "I need this gray for my business. You just want him for funnin'. It's a government horse, and I figure my claim's a lot better'n yours is. Now, I can't waste my time arguin' with you. I got my job to tend to."

As Longarm turned to mount the gray, she moved cat-quick, raising the riding crop to slash at him. As fast as she acted, Longarm reacted faster. He caught her arm as it came down and held it firmly while he took the crop off her wrist and tossed it to the ground. She brought up her free hand to slap his face, but Longarm grasped it before the blow landed. For a moment they stood there with arms locked, anger flowing between them like an electric current where flesh touched flesh. Then she relaxed, and Longarm released her.

They were still glaring, eye to eye, when Sergeant Flanders came hurrying up. His arrival broke the tension. He said, "Now, let's don't you and the Marshal go having words, Miz Stanley. I hope you won't blame me, but Marshal Long can carry his claim for whatever he needs clear up to Colonel Tompkins. I told him—"

"It's all right, Sergeant," she broke in. "Mr. Long's explained to me that you told him I always rode Tordo."

"Looks like I've convinced the lady I need him more'n she does, Sergeant," Longarm said. "Now, if you'll give me that form you got, I'll sign it and be on my way." He took the requisition Flanders had in his hand, rested it on the saddle skirt and scrawled his name on the proper lines. Handing the form back to the sergeant, he said, "Now, if you'll show me where the commissary's at, I'll swing by there and pick up some rations and be on my way."

Flanders pointed to a sprawling warehouse-like building a short distance away. Longarm nodded and swung into the saddle. Touching his hat brim to the woman, he rode off, leaving them looking at his back as he made his way to the commissary. He didn't turn to look at them.

Chapter 2

While waiting for the rations he'd drawn to be assembled, Longarm had gotten directions to help him find the road he'd take out of San Antonio. After he'd reached the end of the town, he'd have to rely on the army ordnance maps he'd picked up at the same time. He rode due west from the quartermaster depot. The houses of San Antonio lay to his left; the city was just changing the direction of its expansion from west to north. The line of closely settled streets stopped nearly two miles from the depot, though there were a few scattered dwellings, mostly small truck farms, between the body of the town and the military installation.

Longarm was taking his time, getting acquainted with the habits of the gray horse. Tordo had been trained well. The animal responded to the pressure of a knee and the touch of a boot toe with as much readiness as it did to the rein. For the most part, after he'd satisfied himself that the dapple could be trusted, Longarm let the horse pick its own way across the grassy, tree-dotted, saucerlike plain that sloped gently to the banks of the San Antonio River, which now lay just ahead.

He'd reached the riverbank and was looking for signs of a ford when thudding hoofbeats caught his attention and he turned to look behind him. Mrs. Stanley, mounted on a roan that must have been her second choice of the horses in the corral, was overtaking him fast. Subconsciously, Longarm noted that she sat the horse well, holding easily to the saddle as the roan loped toward him. He reined in and waited. She drew alongside and brought her mount to a halt.

"If you're looking for a ford, the best one's only about two hundred yards upstream," she said. "If you don't mind company, I'll ride with you a little way."

"You'll be wasting your time, if you're scheming to talk me into swapping horses," Longarm warned her.

"Otherwise, I'll be right pleased to have you ride alongside me for a spell, Miz Stanley."

"I promise that I won't try to persuade you." She seemed to have gotten over her fit of anger; her voice was light and pleasant. "I really rode after you to apologize for the way I acted back at the corral. I don't usually behave so thoughtlessly."

"Wasn't no need to come apologizing, ma'am. I don't hold grudges over things that don't amount to a hill of beans."

"Just the same, it was childish of me. I understand why you'd need the best horse you can find, in your job. It must be a dangerous one."

"I reckon it is, sometimes." Longarm wasn't given to dwelling on the danger of his work. In his book a job was a job, and a man did it according to his best lights.

"Here's the ford," she said, pointing to the spot where the river's olive-green water took on a lighter hue as the stream spread to run wide and shallow over a pebble covered underwater limestone shelf. Turning their horses, they splashed through water only inches deep and rode up the shallow bank on the opposite side.

"Guess you must ride this way pretty often," he suggested after they'd covered a few hundred feet on the west bank of the river.

"Almost every day. Riding's about the only relaxation I have in this dull little town. Especially now, when my husband's away on a training exercise."

"Funny. I never figured San Antone was so dull."

"I don't suppose it would be, for a man. You've got the gambling places and dance halls and saloons. But all I've got is the company of other army wives, and we get bored with one another after a few gossipy afternoon teas. At home, now, it's a different thing."

"Where's home to you, Miz Stanley?"

"New York. It's never dull there. We have the Broadway shows—musicals or dramas—tea dances at the big hotels, receptions, opera, always something interesting."

"I can see it'd be different. Can't rightly say much about New York; I never visited back there, myself."

"You should, sometime. It's a different world." She

pointed to a thickly wooded area that lay just ahead of them, where trees in closely spaced groves dotted a wide stretch of grassland that ended on their right, at the foot of a high white bluff. "Of course, you won't see things like that in New York. The nearest thing to open country there is Central Park. Somehow, that area ahead reminds me of it; perhaps that's why it makes me feel at home when I see it."

"Seems like I recall this place from when I was in San Antonio before. San Pedro Springs, they call it, don't they?"

"Yes. It's one of my favorite spots. On Sundays and holidays it's overrun with families having picnics, but on days like today it's as deserted as the Forest of Arden."

"Can't say I been there, either. Matter of fact, I never got out to San Pedro Springs but once, when I was here last time."

Mrs. Stanley seemed compelled to talk. "Sometimes I bring my lunch out here and stay all day. I've found arrowheads and pieces of old Mexican army equipment from the Texas-Mexican war of fifty years ago."

"You interested in history, then, Miz Stanley?"

"Not especially. But it gives me something besides garrison gossip to think about."

They were approaching an especially large grove of hackberry and pinoak trees bordered by a heavy growth of low-branched chinaberry trees that formed a wide, dense belt around the taller growth. Longarm kneed the dapple to turn it and skirt the edge of the grove, but the lieutenant's wife was reining in.

"There's the most beautiful spring in the middle of this grove," she said. "I just can't pass by it without stopping for a sip of water."

Longarm thought the excuse was flimsy, almost as thin as her story of having ridden after him to apologize. His work took him to army posts quite regularly and he'd met bored, restless army wives before. Almost from the time they'd crossed the river he'd been getting the groin-twitches he felt whenever he was with an attractive woman who was obviously making herself available to him. He pulled rein and swung out of his saddle before she was quite ready to dismount.

"I'm pretty thirsty myself," he told her. "We'll just go get some of that spring water together."

He moved to help her from her horse. She was riding sidesaddle, with her right leg hooked over the horn, and had to swing the leg high over the pommel to free it. Longarm caught her booted foot in one hand and steadied her to the ground. His free arm passed up the backs of her thighs, over the soft bulge of her buttocks to her waist. She was beginning to tremble before both her feet were on the ground. The trembling increased as he pulled her to himself and sought her lips. They locked together, tongues entwined. Longarm felt himself growing erect as she rubbed her hips against him.

She felt the swelling beneath his britches, pulled away, and panted, "Hurry! Let's go into the grove! I want you right now, this minute!"

Taking him by the hand, she pulled him into the shelter of the brush. They'd taken only a few steps into the screening growth when she stopped and began fumbling with the buttons of her riding habit. The thought flashed through Longarm's mind that this was going to be clumsy and uncomfortable, but the woman had other ideas. She let the skirt fall, slid her drawers down to follow the skirt, and went to her knees on the soft, cushioning grass.

"From behind!" she urged. "Like a horse mounts a mare! Be my stud! Now, right now!"

She dropped to her elbows. Her inviting, round, white buttocks gave speed to Longarm's fingers as he worked the buttons of his fly free and knelt behind her. He penetrated deeply, to his full length, withdrew until he almost lost her, then slammed fiercely to her again. The novelty of the situation was almost as exciting to him as it seemed to be to the woman. He thrust lustily, ramming hard, not trying to tease her or hold back. She whimpered deep in her throat, a sound like the whinnying of the mare she was pretending to be. The whimpers became moans and the moans changed to groans of pleasure. Longarm grasped her with a hand on each side of her hips, callused fingers digging into soft flesh. Her buttocks writhed against him as he drove fiercely into her, stroke following quick, full stroke. Then, in a sudden, gasping crescendo of quick, sharp cries, he felt her body sag and grow limp. Longarm held her up as he pounded home the few thrusts he needed, and pulled her firmly against him until his own climax pulsed and passed.

He lowered her gently to the turf. She lay on her side for a moment, ribs heaving. When she rolled over on her back to look up at him, kneeling there by her, she saw his frock coat gaping open to show the holstered Colt above his left hip.

"That's the first time I've been made love to by a man wearing a pistol and a long coat," she grinned. "But I loved it!"

"Me, too," he agreed. "Maybe it was a mite hasty, but it was sure fine."

"Damn it, I couldn't wait. The minute I felt your hands touching me when you helped me dismount, I started itching for you."

"We won't be in a hurry, next time," he promised. "You get out of that tangle of clothes you're in. I'll go get my bedroll, and we can stretch out and be comfortable together."

When he'd tethered the horses and returned with the bedroll, Longarm found Mrs. Stanley standing a little deeper in the shelter of the trees, in a clearing where a spring bubbled gently to form a small, grass-edged pool. Except for her boots, the lieutenant's wife was naked. Her clothes were hung neatly over the bottom branch of a spreading pinoak.

"I couldn't get my boots off," she told him. "You'll have to help me."

"I'll be pleased to help you do just about anything, ma'am."

"Start out by calling me anything but 'ma'am,' then."

"I damn sure ain't going to call you Miz Stanley, not now. But that's all of your name I know."

"It is, isn't it? My name's Cynthia. My best friends call me Cyn, which tells you something about me, I suppose."

"Unless I disremember, I told you my name when you was giving me hell back at the corral."

"Yes. Custis. Custis Long," she sighed happily. "And I'll admit, you're long where it counts the most."

They spread the bedroll and Cynthia sat down while Longarm yanked off her boots. He hung his coat and vest on the pinoak beside Cynthia's garments, and deposited his holstered pistol within easy reach, at the edge of the spread blankets. Then he worked his own stovepipe boots free and sat beside her. She offered her lips, and when the first clinging kiss exhausted their breath, Longarm began moving his mouth and tongue across her shoulders and down to her full, upthrust breasts, seeking the dark puckering aureoles that were thrusting up at him. She stopped him with a hand under his chin.

"Not fair, Custis. You've still got most of your clothes on. Here, I'll help you undress. That'll be part of my pleasure."

His undressing was prolonged, interrupted by kisses that started as soon as Cynthia had helped him shed his shirt and pulled down the top of his longjohns. At once she sank her teeth like a cannibal into his shoulder, biting almost hard enough to draw blood. Longarm's calloused hands caressed her breasts roughly. She began to moan again. Cynthia fumbled loose the strained buttons of his fly to release the erection she'd been helping along by passing a squeezing hand along its swelling length. He kicked off his longjohns and britches and rolled on top of her. She spread herself to receive him, legs raised high, hips rolling and rising to meet his slow deliberate thrusting. Longarm was not hurrying now, but prolonging the sensation. Twice when he felt her nearing climax he slowed to a stop, plunging full into her hot, wet depth, holding her tightly and pushing hard, but without motion. Each time after her breathing eased and her moans slackened to silence he began thrusting again, controlling himself, until the third time she began to cry and quiver. He knew she was ready now, and speeded his tempo, bringing her up with him until they exploded together in the long, dazed bursting of ultimate sensation that left them both limp and motionless.

After they'd begun to breathe normally, she whispered, "If you think I'm a shameless bitch, you're right, Custis. But not with everybody. It takes a certain kind of man to bring out the bitchiness in me, and you're that kind."

"Can't say I'm sorry, Cyn. You're some armful of woman. But I reckon you know that."

"I like for you to tell me." Her hand, exploring his chest, hesitated and stopped at a puckered scar. She sat up, looked, and said with a gasp of surprise, "My God! What kind of life do you lead?"

"About a normal one, for a man in my line of work. But we don't need to talk about them souvenirs. Let's just lay back and rest awhile. We've got plenty of time."

Cuddled together, they grew warm and dozed, sprawling languidly as the shade from the towering trees that surrounded the clearing and hid them crept across the grass.

Cynthia awoke first. Longarm became aware of hands moving warmly over his skin, exploring his body, of the moist tip of her tongue tracing his eyelids and ears and trailing along his cheek, before it slid into his mouth. Her busy hands had already brought him to a half-erection before he was awake, and when he became aware of her soft stroking the erection peaked. He rolled to face her, his movement pinning one of her legs under him. She brought the other leg high up on his ribs and guided him into her, squirming with sensuous pleasure as he entered slowly and went deep deliberately. When he began to move his hips, she clamped her legs tightly around him to stop him from moving.

"No," Cynthia said. "Not for awhile yet. I just want to feel you in me—all of you. Just to hold you here without moving, while you kiss and fondle me."

"I always try to oblige a lady."

"You still think I'm a lady, Custis?"

"Sure. Only you're a woman, too. Ain't often you'll find both of 'em together."

He lay still as she'd requested, except for the movements of his hands over her breasts and belly and along her hips and down them, to knead and squeeze her soft cheeks. The caresses she gave him in return, long deep kisses, sharp nips on shoulders and chest, had their effect. Longarm could feel himself building to a tremendous orgasm. He moved his hips experimentally, questioningly. She relaxed the grip of her thighs enough to let him make a few short beginning thrusts. He moved to rise on top of her, but she pushed her hand against his chest.

"Please, Custis. The way we did the first time. Be my stallion again while I'm your mare. Only slower, take longer."

Cynthia went to her hands and knees again and Longarm mounted her as she had asked him to. He went in fast, with one single, brutal stab. She whimpered and shuddered and came almost at once, but Longarm was in full control of himself now, and so of her. His back arched over her quivering body and he gave her no time to relax from her first quick orgasm, but set a rhythm, easy at first, pounding home hard, neither slowing nor stopping, until her limp muscles tightened and she came to life again beneath him. He felt no urge to hurry; she'd asked him to take longer. Even when Cynthia began moaning, her juices flowing freely, running down his thighs as well as hers, he neither hurried nor stopped. He was holding her tightly, as he had the first time, a hand clamped on each hip, but when she started to whimper again, deep in her throat, he leaned forward and grabbed her full breasts, using them like reins to ride her hard, to pull her back against him. Groans began to pulse from her throat, and Longarm felt himself getting close. Cynthia's writhing stopped, her body tensed under his, and now he went faster for a few tremendous lunges, before his own spasm took him, lifting him out of awareness of anything but the woman under him and the flow he was gushing deep inside her.

Awareness returned as they lay curled together, spoon-fashion, on the rough blanket, her back to him. The sun was red and low, and could be seen only through the treetops now as it neared the horizon.

"If you're going to get home tonight, we better be stirring," Longarm said. "It'll be dark in another little while."

"What're you going to do, Custis? Travel on tonight?"

"Nope. I aim to camp right here and start fresh at daybreak."

"Then I'll stay with you. If you'd like for me to, that is. All I've got to go home to is an empty house and a lonesome bed."

"I'll be real proud if you want to stay. It'll be a dark

camp, though—no fire, and hardtack and jerky for supper."

"Who cares about food? We'll be too busy to miss supper."

Cynthia proved as good as her word. They slept when they'd exhausted one another, and awoke to come together again in the bright silver light of the full moon. The night passed quickly. When false dawn showed, Longarm got up, leaving Cynthia asleep, and groped into his clothes in the half-light. His movements woke her, and when he came back from the edge of the grove, where he'd gone to check the horses and relieve the pressure on his night-filled bladder, he found her lying on her back, gazing at the sky.

"Why didn't you wake me up one last time?" she asked.

"Figured it'd be better if I didn't. It's time I left."

Cynthia sighed. "I guess I knew you'd say something like that. Damn you men, anyhow. You've always got some kind of duty that spoils a woman's pleasure."

"It's how the world was made. Nobody's been able to change it."

"Will you be coming back this way?" Cynthia stood up and walked to the tree where her clothes hung. "And when?"

"Can't say to either one. When I do come back, I'll find you."

"No goodbyes, now, Custis. You go ahead. No kisses, no last waving. Look back at me if you want to, but that's all. I'm superstitious about saying goodbye."

While they talked, Longarm had been folding and rolling his bedding, a tight, neat roll of blankets protected by a waterproof ground cloth with his slicker on the outside, where it'd be handy. He stood up and threw the roll over his shoulder. At the edge of the clearing, he turned once to look back. Cynthia stood with her shoulders squared, breasts high and proud in the dawn light. He smiled, and she smiled in return. Then Longarm turned and pushed through the high, whipping growth of chinaberries to where the dapple stood, saddled and ready to ride.

Tordo was feisty with morning freshness, and Longarm let the animal trot, stepping high, until he'd settled down to the day's work, and slowed to a walk. The sun grew warm on Longarm's back and sent the shadows of man and horse in long black streaks ahead of them. They moved across the rising lip of the saucer-like depression in which San Antonio lay. The long, hot days in the saddle that lay ahead were as far as Longarm planned. There seemed no use in making schemes until he got to Los Perros, the town that was still a mystery to him, and found out more about the border jumpers.

Chapter 3

Dusk found Longarm a long ten miles from the Butterfield stagecoach station at the Medina River, where he'd planned to spend the night. He hadn't wanted to push Tordo on his first day out, and the big dapple was still stepping high when Longarm decided to make a dry camp instead of stumbling through the dark until moonrise to reach the river. In rattlesnake country, he'd learned it wasn't a good idea to choose a sleeping place in pitch blackness, and he'd seen plenty of big rattlers sunning themselves that day. He scouted around to make sure there weren't any rattler dens close by before hobbling the gray and spreading his bedroll.

After he'd fed Tordo, he sat Indian style on his blankets while he chewed leathery jerky and crumbly hardtack and washed it down with a few sips of water. While he puffed the one cigar he was allowing himself every day, he used the last remnants of light to read the ordnance map, memorizing his route and studying the area of the Rio Grande where he was going. Before turning in, Longarm changed the plan he'd framed in Denver. Instead of going to Fort Stockton and backtracking from there, he'd bear farther south and go directly to the outpost from which the soldiers had departed—Fort Lancaster. Satisfied that he was on the trail at last, Longarm crawled under the top blanket. At least, he told himself as he dozed off, he wouldn't have to fight bedbugs all night, as he'd probably have done in one of the bunks at the stage station.

Midmorning breakfast at the Butterfield station on the bank of the Medina, and a good ration of grain for the dapple, set Longarm and Tordo back on the trail in high spirits. He pushed the horse into a lope for a mile or two, then nudged it into a run, testing its gait and wind and responsiveness to his commands. This was something he hadn't taken time to do the day before, while he was still getting acquainted with the animal. When he'd reaffirmed his opinion that he didn't have to worry about the gray, Longarm slowed their pace to a walk. He got to the Sabinal stage depot in time for a twilight supper, and pushed on across the stream before stopping for the night.

On familiar ground now, thanks to intensive study of his map, Longarm began cutting his time by leaving the road when it made curves and zigzags and pushing across country. In this way he could beat the time the stagecoaches made. The vehicles had to swerve to avoid hills and valleys; he could cross them. On the afternoon of the third day, with the Frio River behind him and the Edwards Plateau looming against the skyline to the northwest, Longarm rode into Uvalde. As he'd suspected it would be, the sheriff's office was in the back of the courthouse. He walked in and introduced himself to Sheriff Frank Purdom.

"I know your backyard don't exactly reach to the border," he told the sheriff, "but I was wondering if you'd heard anything about a little town right on the Rio Grande, somewheres close to the mouth of the Pecos. It's called Los Perros."

Purdom stroked his sideburns. "Los Perros? Can't say I recall it, but that don't signify much. There's plenty of squatter towns along the river that don't have names anybody's ever heard of, ten miles away from 'em."

"Figures," Longarm nodded. "Figures, too, if the place had a bad reputation, you'd likely have heard it mentioned."

"I imagine so," Purdom agreed. Then he added, "I'll tell you something, though, Marshal Long. We got enough mischief to handle right here in our own county, so we don't reach out for trouble."

"Sensible. That mischief—would it include a fresh rash of rustling?"

"There's always a certain amount of cattle thieving, you know that. I will say that here lately there's been bigger herds than usual drove off. Why? You onto something I oughta know about?"

"No. I was just wondering if you might've got an idea the old Laredo Loop's at work again."

His question surprised the sheriff. "Where'd you hear about the Laredo Loop? You never said you was from Texas, and I know all the old boys in the marshal's force around here."

"Now, I don't lay claim to knowing anything. Far as being from Texas, the only time I was here was on a gold smuggling case a few years back, but that was way south of here. I was just curious. I heard about the Laredo Loop then, and I got to wondering about it."

"I see." Purdom shook his head. "I just don't know. We don't work the Mexican side any more. Back in old Juarez's day, us and the rurales got along pretty good. With that bastard Diaz running things there now, it's all changed."

"So I've heard." Longarm stood up. "Well, I still got riding to do between here and dark. Anything special to watch out for between here and the border?"

"Nothing that comes to mind." Purdom surveyed his visitor's well-worn boots and skintight britches, his eyes stopping for a moment at the slight bulge made by the holstered pistol in the left side of his frock coat. "You look like you can handle yourself. If I was you, I'd shed that coat, though. You say you're strange to these parts, so just keep in mind you're going into right dry country, when you head west. Don't pass by any good water without letting your horse drink, and topping off your canteen. Do that, and you'll make it."

As he rode out of Uvalde, Longarm discovered the sheriff had neglected to tell him that besides being dry, the country was also about ten degrees hotter than hell's hinges. Even though he'd taken time before leaving the town to fold his coat and tie it neatly inside his slicker, he'd been on the road only a short time before sweat began welling out. The sun was like a bright gold coin that had been heated in a furnace until it was almost at the melting point. The character of the land changed suddenly. Grass and bright green foliage gave way to bare, stony earth, olive-hued mesquite, and gray-green cactus. The sparse plants looked as though the beating sun had bleached out all their color. The month might well have been July instead of September.

He looked at the baked countryside, at the low humps of the Edwards Mountains to his right, and wondered why they were named on his ordnance map as mountains. Nobody who'd ever seen the Rockies could call those little chunks mountains, he was sure of that. He rode on after fishing his bandanna from his pocket and folding it into a triangle, which he tied loosely around his neck to catch the drops of sweat that trickled off his chin. The heat leached out his energy, and when he reached the Nueces River just as the sun was turning to bright orange above the horizon's jagged rim, Longarm decided to stop for the night. The map told him this would be his last sure water before he reached Fort Lancaster, still 80 miles ahead.

"Tordo," he told the dapple as he tethered the horse by the rockstrewn riverbank, "you better drink good tonight and before we hit the trail in the morning. We got two damn dry days ahead."

Dry they were, indeed. The autumn rains hadn't started yet, and the only watercourse shown on Longarm's map was Sycamore Creek, which had neither sycamores along its bank nor water in its bed. Longarm had expected that, because the map also bore the notation, *dry in summer*. He poured water from the canteen into his cupped palm and sloshed it into Tordo's mouth, let the horse rest a short while, then kept pushing on at a carefully measured, energy-saving gait that brought him in sight of Fort Lancaster late in the afternoon of the third day out of Uvalde.

"You men are sure as hell out in the middle of nowhere, here," Longarm remarked to the fresh-faced young lieutenant who'd found himself in command of the fort when Captain Hill had disappeared.

"It's desolate, all right," Lieutenant Bryant agreed. His eyes followed those of his visitor in scanning the bare, beaten earth of the parade ground outside the orderly room window. Distorted by heat-shimmer from the earth, the U.S. flag hung limp on the flagpole, its thirty-eight stars hidden in its folds. On both sides of the hoof-pocked center area, on worn adobe walls of the narrow barracks buildings, the sun picked out seams and water-cut runnels that had turned the hardened clay into a jigsaw puzzle of lines, like those on the faces of very old men. A few troopers, with the sleeves of their gray flannel field shirts rolled high, lounged in the scant shadows at the ends of the structures.

"If a man was stuck here long at a time, I'd bet he'd get right randy," Longarm suggested. "Want to go find himself a woman."

"It happens. Makes problems for us when it does."

"Like them two that skipped?"

"I'll tell you something odd, Marshal. Those are the only two outright desertions we've had during the two years I've been here. Oh, there've been some who wandered off without authorization—overnight, a day or two. Most of them are men who go looking for a woman in one of the shanty towns along the river, or maybe at the Apache resettlement camp south of here."

"Only them two didn't come back, and when your captain went looking for 'em, he disappeared, too."

"You're certainly not suggesting that Captain Hill deserted?" Lieutenant Bryant sounded horrified.

"Don't get miffed, son. I didn't mean it that way." Longarm judged that this was the time to ask the question that had been puzzling him since he'd been assigned to search for the missing cavalrymen. "You got any ideas why them two troopers took off like they did? And wasn't it sort of funny your captain felt like those two men were important enough for him to go chasing himself?"

Lieutenant Bryant thought for a long time before he replied, "I'm sure you need to know this, Marshal, but I hope you'll keep it confidential. Captain Hill didn't want to cause any scandal, or do anything that'd harm the way the ranchers feel about our troopers."

"Go ahead and spill it, Lieutenant. If you knew me at all, you'd know I don't flapjaw. It's my business to find things out. If you don't tell me what you're trying to set on, I'll just go dig it up anyways."

"Yes, I suppose you will. Well, Captain Hill felt he had to bring those men back to face court martial. The troopers deserted because they'd raped a rancher's wife."

"White woman, of course?" When Bryant nodded, Longarm went on, "And I bet down here in Texas, your black buffalo soldiers ain't exactly what you'd call popular."

Bryant retorted sharply, "They're damned good

soldiers, Long. I don't care what civilians might say or think about them."

"Nobody said they wasn't. And rape ain't exactly something that comes with the color of a man's skin. But I can see you got a real problem. Don't worry. I don't aim to make it worse."

"Thanks. Now, how can I help you, Marshal?"

"About the biggest help you can give me is to trot out that Cimarron scout that went down to the border with the captain."

"Sorry, sir. He was called back to Fort Stockton. By now, he's out in the field somewhere."

"Well, hell!" Longarm didn't try to hide his disgust. "How'm I going to find out what Captain Hill was aiming to do when he went border-jumping? He must've had some idea in his head about where them two troopers was heading for."

"He did. I can help you there. Tinker reported to me—Tinker's the Cimarron's name—when he came back from Los Perros alone. He said the captain had found out, I don't know how, that the troopers were going south into Mexico until they got far enough from the border to feel safe. I suppose they thought we wouldn't follow them or try to bring them back, with conditions as they are now in Mexico."

"Um. How'd the captain find all this out?"

"From asking around Los Perros, Tinker said."

"It's for sure all three of 'em dropped out of sight after they left Los Perros, then?" Longarm rubbed his face. The sweat was making his stubble itchy. He reminded himself that he'd have to find out if there was a barber at the fort, and, he remembered, if the sutler there had his kind of cheroots; he was down to three. He said, "I guess that's my next stop, then. What d'you know about the place, Lieutenant?"

"Los Perros?" Bryant shook his head. "Not much. I've stopped there a few times, when a patrol took me close to it. Captain Long didn't like the men to go there, so I tried to set an example."

"Suppose you tell me as much as you can. Whatever you seen's pretty certain to be a help to me. I like to know what's in a hole before I jump in."

"There's not much to tell, Marshal Long. The place isn't really a town, just a bunch of shanties. Jacales,

37

they call them around here. Shacks made out of scrap wood and tree limbs and tin, whatever the people can pick up, I suppose. Two or three houses built of good solid lumber. A saloon, of course, with gambling tables."

"Whorehouse upstairs?" Longarm broke in to ask.

"Strangely enough, no. I think there was at one time, but when Captain Hill started discouraging the troopers from going to the town, the girls scattered out."

"I've traveled around some," Longarm observed, "and I've found out it's got to be a real piss-poor town that can't support a whorehouse."

"That's Los Perros," Bryant smiled thinly. "As far as I can see, it doesn't support anything except the saloon. No stores, nothing."

"How big a place is it, then?"

"Not big at all. Only perhaps twenty or twenty-five Americans and a couple of hundred Mexicans and border breeds."

Longarm nodded. He'd seen a few border settlements such as the one the lieutenant had described when he was breaking the gold-smuggling case. He said, "That really ain't what I'm after. What kind of people are they? They go by the law, or what? And this fellow I heard runs things, what's he like?"

Bryant thought for a moment. "Marshal, I can't tell you a lot about the people. Some of them have little truck gardens, not big enough to be farms. They sell produce to the ranches and to the fort, here. Some have little goat herds or they keep chickens. They scrape out a living, somehow. And I don't know what the Americans do, if they don't work at the saloon or for the sheriff."

"That's one I'm interested in. He's the big boss, ain't he?"

"Yes. Tucker's his name, Ed Tucker. And I don't think he was ever elected sheriff, he just took over the job."

"Got any idea where he's from?"

"I'd guess from the South, judging by the way he talks."

"Is he old enough to've fought in the war?"

"Oh, yes. I'd guess he's pushing fifty, maybe past that."

"Mean, or easygoing?"

Again the young officer hesitated before answering. "Maybe not mean, but he's sure not easygoing. I mentioned that Captain Hill unofficially discourages our men from going there. Since the captain began doing that, anybody in an army uniform gets a cool reception."

"How many men has he got backing him?"

Bryant shook his head. "That's something I can't tell you, Marshal. I've only seen Tucker two or three times. I'd say he's got a lot of curiosity, or maybe it's suspiciousness."

"How's that?"

"Well, I went to Los Perros once looking for the Mexican who supplies the fort with eggs. Tucker stopped me, asked what I was doing, and when I told him, he tagged along with me until I left. The next time, I was in the saloon. It was a hot day, and getting late, and I was going to bivouac my patrol a little way out of town. I thought if I let them stop for a beer or two, they wouldn't be so tempted to sneak back at night for a drink." Bryant looked earnestly at Longarm. "It wasn't exactly according to the captain's ideas, but there weren't any official standing orders—"

"I understand about the army, Lieutenant," Longarm broke in. "Go ahead."

"Tucker came into the saloon while we were there. He came up to me and said I'd better keep my men on a tight rein, that their uniforms wouldn't keep them out of his jail if they made trouble. That was about all."

"Damn it, you must've noticed something more, or heard talk. It'd be a big help to me if I knew whether the sheriff had two or three men to back him, or two or three dozen. I'll remind you about something. When I go into a place, I'm by myself. I don't have a squad of troopers with carbines and sabers to back up my play."

"I wish I could help you more, Marshal Long. The plain fact is, I just don't know any more to tell you."

Longarm sensed the young officer's disappointment. "Guess if you don't know, you don't. It ain't your fault. Wasn't your job to go prying into what goes on in Los Perros. Leastwise, it wasn't the times you was there."

"What're you planning to do, Marshal? About Captain Hill and the deserters?"

"Whatever I got to do to find 'em. And to find me a Texas Ranger that dropped out of sight about the same way they did. Last place he was heard from was Los Perros, too."

"You think there's some kind of connection?"

"Don't know yet, son. Might be, might not be. All I can say right now is about what you told me a minute ago. I just plain don't know. But I sure as hell intend to find out, soon as I can get to Los Perros and start digging."

"If there's anything I can do—"

"Just happens there is." Longarm smiled. "I been eating outa my saddlebags the past few days. I washed as best I could when I made a stop where there was water, but I ain't fond of shaving with cold lather. If you was to offer me some cooked supper and a hot bath in a tub, and maybe dig up one of your troopers who knows how to shave a man without cutting his guzzle in two—"

"Of course. I—I suppose it'd be all right if you stayed in the captain's quarters. His orderly can look after you. And you're more than welcome to join us at our mess, such as it is."

"I'd appreciate that, Lieutenant. Man's going out looking for trouble, he always feels better if he goes clean-shaved and with a full belly. And I can smell trouble waiting for me in Los Perros."

Chapter 4

Longarm reined in at the edge of the sandy draw and looked across the white expanse at Los Perros. Remembering the lieutenant's description, he had to agree that the young officer had been right when he said it wasn't much of a town. The Rio Grande dictated the settlement's shape: long and narrow. Los Perros stood on a sandspit, and Longarm could see that when rains upstream swelled the river, the sandspit would become an island. Now, the sandy wash on the Texas side of the river was dry. Beyond the town, the green current ran in a narrow channel, and Longarm judged it was both deep and swift.

Los Perros stretched out, a long, thin, straggling shamble of houses. Most of them were patchwork jobs, put together from spliced short boards. Some of the planks bore the faded imprint of words: "Silver's Cuban Tobacco Twist," "Aunt Miranda's Dark Molasses," "Winchester Arms Co.," showing that they'd come from salvaged packing cases. Some of the shanties were pole-shacks, made by driving tree limbs into the ground in a square and nailing to them sheets of metal made from straightened-out kerosene containers, or the red-painted metal cannisters in which army gunpowder was once shipped. The roofs of most of the houses were rusted sheets of metal that came from only God knew where, to wind up on a sandspit on the Texas border.

A few structures were solidly constructed from planed boards, and even these were in need of paint. Longarm spotted the saloon at once; it was Los Perros's biggest building, two low stories tall, with a false front that made it look higher than it really was. A short distance from the saloon, another solid house rose above the low roofs of the jacales. This one had been painted, though there were patches of bare wood showing now where the paint was peeling off. Another decent house stood on the opposite side of the saloon, and a third could be seen behind the bar's false front. On the near side of the sandspit a new house had been started, though no one was working on it now.

There were no streets that Longarm could see. The houses stood higgledy-piggledy, and sandy trails wound between them. A few people were moving in the town. Most of them seemed headed in the general direction of its center. All but a few were on foot, though the hats of three or four who rode burros or horses could be seen bobbing along at a higher level than the heads of the pedestrians.

Instead of crossing the draw at once, Longarm nudged the dapple with his heel and turned to move along the sandy margin. He wanted a look at the town from one end, and wanted as well to get an unobstructed view of the river channel that divided Mexico from Texas. At the end of the sandspit he reined in and looked back. Now he could see the place from another angle, and decided it was a bit bigger than he'd thought at first; there were houses on the sloping western side that had been invisible from his earlier broadside vantage point.

Sloping ground led to the river. A lone fisherman, his pole propped in a forked stick, sat at the shore's edge. In its channel the Rio Grande rolled smoothly, its water an opaque greenish brown. The surface, unbroken by ripples, told Longarm the water was both deep and swift. The bank on the Mexican side rose sheer from the water. The rough, stone-studded rise was crowned with a thick growth of chamizal, a mixture of scrub mesquite, catsclaw, and broad-leafed pear cactus. It looked tangled, impenetrable, and unfriendly, as scrubby and shabby as the town itself.

"Well, old son," Longarm muttered under his breath, "It sure as hell ain't much to look at, and I don't reckon it'll improve when I get closer."

He angled across the draw to the humped center of the sandspit and rode into Los Perros, moving in the general direction of the saloon. Before he reached the building's tall false front, Longarm entered an open space, not a formal square or plaza typical of so many Southwestern towns; this one had no well-defined perimeter. The buildings that marked its roughly circular area were set askew, at odd angles to one another, giving the enclosure a ragged, unplanned look. The saloon, across from the spot where Longarm sat on Tordo, seemed to be the area's chief focal point; the second was a well, located a bit off-center, and half a dozen yards from the well a single, man-high post a foot in diameter had been set in the hard earth. The plaza, if it could be called that, was obviously about to be the scene of some kind of public occurrence. People kept arriving to join the crowd already stirring within it.

Longarm was less interested in the buildings and other permanent features of the place than he was in the people standing and moving around. Most of them were men, though a handful of women clustered at one side, shrilling at children who darted like so many small, brown, active beetles between the legs of the men. It was not a prosperous-looking group. The men were generally dressed in the loose raw cotton blouses and trousers of borderland peons; their heads were covered with wide-brimmed straw sombreros, their feet stuck sockless into huaraches of braided leather. Black was the predominant color among the women: black dresses that swept the ground and black rebozos that covered the wearers' heads and shaded their faces so that Longarm couldn't tell which were young, which middle-aged, and which old and wrinkled.

Against clothing dominated by monotones, the few men wearing charro outfits stood out like peacocks in a flock of pigeons and crows. The charro suits glistened with gold or silver embroidery on waist-length, fawn-hued jackets and on towering felt sombreros, and along the seams of skintight pants that were tucked into tall, shining, high-heeled boots. Equally conspicuous were the men, fewer in number, who wore the regulation outfits of border ranch hands: tight Levi's faded from indigo to sky blue by repeated washing with lye soap, denim shirts of blue or gray or tan, stitch-traced high-heeled boots, and broad-brimmed Stetsons, creased Texas style, a single deep dent running up the front from brim to crown.

Longarm was suddenly very conscious of his Prince Albert coat and his cavalry-style, forward-tilted Stetson. He was also aware that the eyes of just about everybody in the plaza seemed to be watching him. He looked around for a hitching rail and saw only one, in front of the saloon, and guided Tordo at a slow walk around the edge of the plaza, twitching the reins when necessary to keep the dapple from breaking up a group of people.

He noticed now that here and there around the plaza's rim, tiny threads of smoke were beginning to rise from the improvised stoves of food vendors. Longarm recalled that any event in a settlement along the border drew food stalls to feed the crowds, as well as vendors carrying trays of sweets, buns and candied cactus and sweet potatoes. It had been a long time since breakfast. Longarm watched for a tray bearer, spotted one and reined up. For a nickel he got three puffed buns crusted with colored sugar on top, and munched them as a prelude to the lunch he'd look for later. He sat Tordo long enough to finish the last bun after he got to the hitching rail, then dismounted and looped the gray's reins around the crossbar.

He'd taken three or four steps away before he remembered the Winchester in his saddle scabbard. In almost any place except Los Perros, Longarm would have left the gun where it was. Nowhere in the West would a saddled horse or its gear be touched by anybody except its owner. Los Perros impressed Longarm as being a town where normal rules and customs were ignored. He went back, slipped the rifle from its scabbard, and tucked the butt into his armpit. Then he joined the crowd that by now had grown to sizable proportions. The center of interest seemed to be near the well. He dodged his way in that direction and stopped eight or ten paces from the well.

One of the men wearing the clothes that identified him as a ranch hand stood alone, a short distance from where Longarm stopped. The marshal stepped up to him and asked, "What's the fuss about?"

"Everybody's waiting for the whipping to commence."

"Whipping?"

"Sure. Sheriff Tucker's got the right idee. Instead of lockin' a lawbreaker in jail, havin' to feed him and keep him, the ol' sheriff sees he gits a good whipping, then he's turned loose."

"Who's getting whipped today?"

"Don't recall his name. Some saddle tramp that pulled a knife on one of the sheriff's deputies and cut him a little bit."

"Maybe I'm wrong, but I thought public whipping was outlawed in the United States," Longarm observed. "Seems to me that was done when the slaves got freed."

Turning, the stranger faced Longarm squarely. "Mister, here in Los Perros nobody gives a billy-be-damn for the U.S.A. If you're a Yankee bluenose, this ain't no place for you."

Longarm was more interested in getting information than he was in protesting an implied insult. He let the comment slide by and asked, "I suppose this drifter stood trial, didn't he? And the judge said he was guilty?"

"Sure. It was all handled legal and proper."

"Who was the judge that tried the case?"

"Hell, we ain't got but only one judge in Los Perros —Sheriff Tucker. If you wasn't a stranger here, you'd know that."

"Seeing I am a stranger who don't know beans about your town, maybe you can tell me how come a man can be sheriff and judge all at the same time."

"Maybe you better ask Sheriff Tucker about that. It's just the way things has always been here, I guess."

"I see."

Before Longarm could ask another question there was a stir in the crowd and a murmur of voices. Longarm and the stranger craned their necks to see what was happening. A knot of men was coming around the corner of the saloon building. Their leader was an imposing figure. He stood high and wide in fancy, heeled boots with colored stitching and wore a tall-crowned Stetson creased in a Dakota peak, but his width competed with his height and detracted from his overall appearance. His stomach hung over his trousers-top and rolls of fat forced him to wear his gunbelt too low. Even then, the fat crowded the butt of the old-fashioned ivory-handled revolver that dangled in a tooled leather holster. A gold badge was on the big man's left shirt pocket.

Longarm realized he was getting his first look at Sheriff—and apparently, Judge—Ed Tucker, the man who occupied the catbird seat in Los Perros. Longarm would have been more impressed if Tucker had been a bit on the lean side, and if he hadn't reeled ever so slightly as he strode in front of the little group that trailed him. Still, Longarm thought, he'd reserve judgment until he'd had a chance to study Tucker's face, which was concealed by the shadow his broad-brimmed Stetson cast in the noonday sun.

One of the four men walking behind Tucker was obviously the prisoner. He was shirtless, and wore handcuffs that caught the sun and reflected silver. Longarm paid less attention to him than he did to the other three. Each of the two men flanking the prisoner held one of the handcuffed man's arms. The one bringing up the rear carried the whip, a broad leather thong, over his shoulder. All three of the men, who could only be sheriff's deputies, had the cocky walk of hard cases. Longarm knew the breed, he'd seen them and tangled with them before.

Old son, he told himself silently, looks like you're going to be on the short end of the odds, if it comes out them fellows had anything to do with the army men and the ranger who dropped out of sight.

By now the sheriff and his men were pushing through the suddenly thickened crowd in the center of the plaza. They wasted little time in ceremony when they reached the cleared area around the well and post. The two who'd escorted the prisoner lashed the man's hands high on the post and stepped aside. The sheriff stepped forward.

"Jed Morton," he proclaimed loudly, "you been tried and convicted of attemptin' manslaughter. You been sentenced with mercy, because the man you tried to kill didn't die. Instead of hangin' you up by your neck till you're dead, the court's been good to you. All you're goin' to git is fifty lashes." He nodded to the man holding the whip. "All right, Spud. Go ahead and lay it onto him."

Stepping aside, the sheriff made room for the man carrying the whip to move into position beside the prisoner. He whirled the lash experimentally, the wide leather thong whistling through the still air, then brought it down on the prisoner's back with a loud, flat thwack. The man flinched, but did not cry out.

Though he'd never heard of Jed Morton and didn't know whether the man was innocent or guilty, Longarm twitched in sympathy as the whip fell. He'd heard of fifty-lash whippings in the old days, and knew they usually meant death to the one receiving them. He made no move to protest. He knew any interference he offered might get in the way of carrying out his assignment. He'd reminded himself sternly during the few seconds before the whip-wielder began the punishment that this was no business of his.

Again the whip whistled and landed, but as before, Morton did not cry out. The third blow brought a sigh from deep in his throat, though, and the fourth lash, landing on the weals raised by the earlier blows, produced a louder sigh, a moan of pain. Spud, the whipper, continued the punishment. Longarm, his stomach muscles tightening, lost count of the blows after the sixth or seventh had fallen. Morton was moaning steadily now, a throaty monotone that rose only slightly in volume as each new slash cut into his tattered back. His skin had split after the first few lashes, and blood spattered each time the whip swung. The spectators nearest the whipping-post pushed back to avoid the flying drops.

There was an unearthly air hanging over the plaza. The crowd was deathly silent. The only sounds heard were the whip's whistling, the wet, flat noise as it splatted home, and the fading moans of the man tied to the stake.

Longarm's gorge was rising. He felt that he'd stood all he could. Morton was almost unconscious now, hanging limply by his bound wrists. Still the wet, ugly splat of new blows sounded with monotonous regularity. In spite of his resolution not to interfere, Longarm had had a bellyful of the spectacle. He elbowed through the packed crowd until he stood in the front rank of spectators. Spud was raising the whip for another cut at Morton's bloodstained back when, without seeming to aim, Longarm fired. The heavy rifle slug ripped into the ground between Spud's feet. Spud leaped back, letting the whip drop from his hand.

"That's enough," Longarm announced. His voice was flat; he did not need to raise it to be heard in the stillness that hung like a shroud over the plaza. "The show's over."

He shifted the rifle, bringing its muzzle high enough to cover Sheriff Tucker and the two deputies beside him. All three men had started forward when the shot rang out. Now, as the Winchester's muzzle stared into their faces with its single menacing, unblinking black eye, they took a step backward.

"Who in hell you think you are?" Tucker called.

"I'm the man who stopped this sorry damned circus," Longarm replied levelly. He raised his voice only a little. "That's all you need to know right now."

"You got no right!" Tucker's throat and jaws worked with repressed fury. "You're interferin' with the law's due process! I can put you in jail for this!"

Still in the same low, level tone, Longarm invited, "Come ahead." He shifted the rifle to swing it in a short arc that menaced the sheriff and his two deputies in turn. "If you're ready to pay what it'll cost you."

None of them moved. Tucker repeated his question: "Just who are you, anyhow?"

"I told you once, that's enough." Longarm still kept his voice at a conversational pitch. He might have been discussing the weather, or the price of steers. Addressing the deputies, he said, "You two. Get that man down off the post."

There was a steeliness in Longarm's tone now that the men recognized as the voice of authority. They neither argued nor made any threatening gestures as they moved to obey. Rather, they very carefully kept their hands in front of them, at chest level, while they walked to the stake and untied Morton. When they'd freed him and were supporting his unconscious form, they looked questioningly at Longarm, waiting further orders.

From the moment the Winchester's blast had shattered the silence of the plaza, the crowd had been frozen and motionless. Now people began to stir, those closest to the whipping-post pushing back to widen the circle in which Longarm held the sheriff and his men. The spectators remained silent, though, and now the eerie quiet was making itself felt, stretching the nerves of the little group in the plaza's center.

Longarm felt the tension building and moved to

take charge before it broke. He ordered, "Take that poor devil someplace where his back can be tended to."

For the first time, the deputies looked to Tucker for instructions. He said, "I guess the jail's as good a place as any. Haul him over there, boys. Tell Wahonta I said to take care of him."

When the deputies turned to Longarm for confirmation of the sheriff's instructions, he nodded. "Do what he told you to. We're going to be right in back of you, me and the sheriff, to make sure nothing happens to him on the way there."

Spud, the man who'd handled the whip, asked sullenly, "What about me?"

"You come along with us," Longarm replied. "And bring that whip with you." He turned to Tucker. "All right. Let's march. You lead out."

Silently, the crowd parted to make an aisle for the group. The deputies carrying the unconscious Morton led the way, with Spud behind them. Behind the three deputies came the sheriff. Longarm walked just far enough to the rear to keep the muzzle of his Winchester out of Tucker's reach. He didn't want gunplay on the crowded plaza. The deputies in the lead headed for the saloon, and for a moment Longarm wondered if the jail and sheriff's office were part of that building, but they veered around one side of it and went to a smaller structure the saloon building had hidden from view. It was built of the sturdiest timbers Longarm had seen in Los Perros.

As an afterthought, when they started around the saloon, Longarm called to Spud. "You. That gray over at the hitch-rail's my horse. Get him and lead him along with us. The rest of you hold up right here till he brings the critter up."

As in most of the towns he'd seen wherever his cases took him, Longarm found that the Los Perros jail also included an outer office for the sheriff and a lean-to or ell for his living quarters. As they entered, Sheriff Tucker let out a bellow.

"Wahonta! Git out here with some hot water and rags! There's a hurt man I want you to tend to!"

Judging by her name and appearance, Longarm placed the girl who responded to the summons as an

Apache. She looked surprisingly young, though as was always the case with women of the Southwestern Indian tribes, her age was hard to judge. She had the Apache stockiness of build, short legs, wide hips and shoulders, and the square tribal face that would broaden and flesh out as she grew older. Yet she had about her the bloom of extreme youth as well as the quick, springy step of the very young. Longarm guessed what her relationship with the sheriff was, and made a mental note to confirm his hunch when he had time. Right now there were more important things to do.

He said to the men carrying the prisoner, who was beginning to twitch and moan, but still wasn't fully conscious, "One of you at a time, take off your gunbelts and hang 'em on those pegs on the wall." In sullen silence, the deputies obeyed. Spud wore no gunbelt. "Now all three of you take that fellow back in the jail and put him on a bunk." Tucker, after a moment of indecision, started to follow his men. Longarm said, "Not you, Sheriff. You stand right where you are." To Wahonta he said, "You go in, too. Fix up that man's back as good as you can." The Apache girl looked questioningly at the sheriff, who nodded. Then she followed the men into the first cell.

Longarm swung the Winchester's muzzle in Tucker's general direction. "Lock 'em up."

"Now, wait a minute—" Tucker began.

Longarm cut him short. "Lock 'em up, I said!"

Tucker glared, but took a key ring from the wall peg on which it hung and locked the cell door. It was crowded in the cell, even with Morton stretched out face-down on the cot that was the cubicle's sole piece of furniture. Longarm held out a hand for the key ring. The sheriff handed it over.

"Now, then," Longarm told the thin-lipped Tucker, "let's you and me go in there—" he indicated the door by which Wahonta had entered, "—and have us a little private confab."

Chapter 5

Sheriff Tucker pushed his hat back on his head as he and Longarm went into the ell attached to the jail building, and Longarm got his first really close look at the man's face. It wasn't one to inspire confidence. Tucker's eyes were narrow slits set in puffs of fat. His lips were a wide, crooked slash that turned down at the corners above a once-firm chin that was now half-buried in a set of double chins bulging below it. He wore a Burnside beard—a heavy mustache that crept around his cheeks and clean-shaven jaw to merge with full, flowing muttonchop whiskers. His nose veered back and forth between brow and tip, evidence that the sheriff had at one time been a man prone to indulge in fistfighting. Longarm revised Lieutenant Bryant's estimate of Tucker's age. He'd bet the man would never see fifty again, and might well be past fifty-five.

Tucker asked again, "Who in hell are you, to come bustin' into town like you did and get in the way of the law bein' enforced?"

"I might just argue with you about that whipping being according to law," Longarm replied. "Fellow I was talking to before it got started said you're sheriff and judge both, here in Los Perros."

"Well? What if I am? Somebody's got to keep the damn town in line."

"Makes me wonder just whose laws you're talking about, though. Your own, or the state's, or the U.S.'s."

"We don't worry about little things like that around here. We do what we got to, to keep things quiet."

"What kinda things?"

"Damn it, man, you know what I'm talkin' about. Lawlessness in general."

Choosing his words carefully, Longarm said, "The way I look on it, laws made up to suit special cases is worse'n no law at all."

"An expert on the law, are you?" Tucker challenged.

"Nope. Never claimed to be that. Let's just say I got my own ideas. And when push comes to shove, I figure my ideas are as good as the next man's."

"You still ain't told me who you are."

"Name's Custis—"

Before Longarm could finish, the sheriff spoke quickly. "Custis? Now, that's a real fine old Virginia name. Fought on the side of right during the war, I suppose?"

"I suppose." Longarm didn't need to ask which side Tucker meant. The sheriff's Southern accent told him that.

"Who'd you fight under?"

"Depends on when. I rode with more'n one, while I was serving."

"Did you now? You want to name me names?"

"I disremember things like names, sometimes. Especially when I figure somebody's getting too nosy."

"Look here, Custis, it ain't nothing to be ashamed about, being on the side that lost. Hell, I'm real proud to say I rode with Quantrill, back then."

Tucker's naming of the notorious guerrilla fighter, far more outlaw than soldier, told Longarm perhaps more than the sheriff had intended. It also changed his mind about revealing that he was a Deputy U.S. Marshal, at least for the time being. Letting Tucker think he was a bullying opportunist with more brass than brains might serve his purpose better. Instead of commenting on the sheriff's revelation of his past history, Longarm merely nodded.

"Now, you might wonder why I told you about myself," Tucker went on. "Fact is, I got a good thing goin' here, have had for a pretty fair spell, and I don't aim to let some owlhoot drifter mess things up for me. Which is what you come close to doin' when you busted up that whippin'."

"Maybe my stomach ain't as strong as it used to be," Longarm offered mildly.

"I don't know about your stomach, but I got to say I like your nerve. Ain't many men'd have enough sand in their craw to call a play the way you did."

"That wasn't much, Sheriff. I didn't look for sensible men to argue with a cocked and loaded Winchester, no matter how fast they might be with a Colt."

"You feel like tellin' me why you showed up in Los Perros?" When Longarm said nothing, but just continued to look at the sheriff with his steel-blue eyes, Tucker asked, "You're on the dodge, ain't you? Law's after you someplace up the line—San Antone, maybe, or El Paso. Fort Worth? Galveston?"

"Now, seeing as you're the law here, or say you are, you don't expect me to answer a fool question like that, do you?" Longarm was curious to find out how far he could prod the sheriff before he'd balk.

"Not unless you got less brains than I give you credit for." Tucker paused, studying Longarm closely. "If it'll make you feel any better, I ain't interested enough to find out. But it's got to be that, or you're lookin' for somebody that's got your dander up, on the prod to gun him down."

"Let's leave it stand that I'm just traveling."

"If that's how you want it." The sheriff frowned thoughtfully. "It could be something else, a-course. You might be carrying a badge. Or you might've been with a bunch that got busted up, and lookin' to make a new connection."

"Like I said, Sheriff, let's say I'm just traveling."

"You'll be plannin' to move on then." Tucker wasn't asking a question. Longarm understood that, and got the warning message that the statement implied.

"Sooner or later," he said.

"I guess you know you only got two choices."

"Which are what?"

"Move on, or throw in with my boys and me."

"You saying you'd pin a deputy's badge on me, after what I done out there a while ago?"

"Shucks, Custis, I'm a big enough man to overlook that. I was about to tell Spud to hold up, anyhow. It wasn't in my mind to let him kill Morton. Except he had to be give a good lesson to."

"Fellow I was talking to, the one told me about Morton's trouble, he didn't say it wasn't a fair fight that got your deputy hurt."

"That don't signify." Tucker's voice hardened. "Thing is, my man got cut so bad I had t' send him clear down to Laredo for him t'be doctored. Most people in Los Perros, they know they can't hurt one of my boys without they pay for it. Them as don't got t'be reminded. That goes for you too, Custis."

"Join up or move on? Is that the way of it?"

"Clear as I can say it. You do one, I take good care of you, money and all the rest. You do anything else, then you better keep on travelin'. For your own good."

"Suppose I tell you I'd like to sorta nose around a little bit and see what Los Perros is like before I make up my mind?"

Tucker thought about this for a moment, then nodded slowly. "All right, that's fair enough. You stay around a few days, see what you see. Only don't go pullin' no more stunts like the one I'm lettin' you git away with."

"Now I didn't come here to get crossways with you, Sheriff. Or with anybody else, far's that goes. I got mighty tender toes, though. I'd imagine you're smart enough to tell them deputies of yours not to step on 'em."

"Don't worry about that. They're my boys, they do what I tell 'em to. Nothing else." Tucker frowned, then added, "Except maybe for Spud. He's been actin' a little bit uppity, now and again. Not enough so I got to whip him into line, but he'd be the only one that might give you a bad time."

"That's my problem, though, ain't it?"

"I'd say so. Don't look for me to take sides, though, Custis. Even if he is my boy, when I tell him to leave you be and he don't, that's his lookout."

Longarm marked down the possible ill feeling between Tucker and Spud as a hole card that might fill a thin hand for him if it was needed. He said, "Looks like we understand how it stands between us, Sheriff. Now let's go see what's happening to that poor devil your man Spud just about beat to death. And I guess all of 'em oughta be glad to get let out of that cell. They'll be getting a mite restless by now."

Longarm's guess was a good one. The Apache girl, Wahonta, was still tending to Jed Morton's back; Morton lay face-down on the cot, groaning now and then. The three deputies were crowding up to the bars, impatient to be released.

"Took you two long enough to settle whatever it was you went to talk private about," Spud grumbled as the sheriff unlocked the cell door.

54

"Cool off, Spud," Tucker advised. "You wasn't hurt a bit, no more'n Ralston or Lefty." The others grunted, but said nothing. Tucker led them to the office area, where he sat down behind the battered desk and motioned for the others to find seats, too. "Now," he said, "this gentleman here's Mr. Custis. He's made a right handsome apology to us for gittin' hisself crossways of our law, and him and me have settled any differences there might've been."

"Now just a minute—" Spud began.

Tucker cut him short. "You shut up, Spud. If you hadn't been so damn heavy-handed with that whip, this dust-up never would've happened."

Spud glowered, but kept quiet.

"Mr. Custis figures to stay in Los Perros for a little while," the sheriff continued. He shifted his eyes from Longarm to Spud as he spoke. "He ain't lookin' for trouble with nobody, and I told him we wasn't goin' to hold no grudges for him buttin' in on us. You all understand what I'm tellin' you?"

All three of the deputies had their gaze fixed on Longarm. He kept his face impassive, meeting their stares without flicking an eyelid.

Tucker concluded, "Now. That's all I got t'say."

When it was clear that none of the deputies was inclined to argue with their boss, Longarm spoke up. "I aim to get along with everybody. Now, if you gentlemen feel like you want to join the sheriff and me, I'm standing the drinks."

It didn't appear that the general population of Los Perros could afford saloon prices, Longarm thought. Except for Tucker, the deputies, and himself, the cavernous, shabby place was echoingly empty. The scarred floor gave indications that booted feet did walk on it in numbers at times, however, and the array of bottled goods available, as shown by the display in front of the mirror behind the bar, seemed adequate. From inside the building, the exterior outlines of the structure made sense. The bar area covered about two-thirds of the available space. A small enclosed area—offices, maybe storerooms, Longarm thought—filled the rear portion. Above this was a balcony, and though the stairs to it ended in a blind turn, Longarm was sure there were rooms opening onto a corridor over the offices or storage area. He absorbed the layout in one quick, sweeping glance as the group crossed to the bar. An aproned barkeeper appeared from nowhere. Longarm tossed a gold eagle on the scarred pine that in Los Perros substituted for the mahogany or walnut of more civilized places.

"Name your pleasure, gentlemen," he said.

For himself, Longarm ordered his standard Maryland rye, and realized as he sipped it with relish that this was his first drink since he'd gotten off the train in San Antonio, just a week ago. He felt for a cheroot to go with the drink, and remembered that the sutler at Fort Lancaster hadn't been able to replenish his dwindling supply. There were only three left in his pocket. It seemed to him the occasion called for celebrating, so he fished out one of them and lighted it. The heavy smoke and sharp tang of the whiskey did a lot to make him feel more at home in the alien surroundings.

Ralston, the deputy standing at Longarm's right, asked, "You going to be around Los Perros for a while, Custis?"

"A while. And I aim to stay out of trouble while I'm here."

"Hell, I don't blame you much for butting in today. I was just about sick, listening to that poor son of a bitch groan, and them whacks Spud was dealing with the whip."

"It didn't seem to bother Spud any," Longarm commented, carefully keeping his voice neutral.

"Nothin' like that bothers Spud." Ralston looked down the bar. He was standing on Longarm's right. Lefty, the other deputy, stood on his left, and beyond Lefty was Tucker. Spud, the last man in the line, was engaged in a whispered conversation with the sheriff. Dropping his voice, Ralston said to Longarm, "I'd look behind me when I was out at night, if I was you, Custis. Spud took that deal today right personal. He was saying some pretty ugly things he'd like to do to you while we was all locked up together."

"Thanks, Ralston. I'll remember that. Maybe I can return the favor someday."

"Ah, forget it. I didn't say nothing, anyhow."

Raising his voice, Longarm called, "There's another

56

round or two of drinks to come out of that eagle on the bar. Sing out for refills."

He thought about Marshal Billy Vail, back in Denver, and could imagine his chief's face changing color if he was to see government expense money being spent on whiskey for a bunch of toughs in Los Perros. His thoughts were interrupted by Sheriff Tucker calling his name.

"Custis! Come on back to the office with me. I just saw Miles Baskin stick his head outa his door. He's a man you'll want to know, if you're goin' to be in town a while."

Baskin turned out to be a somewhat colorless individual. His lean face was adorned with the walrus mustache that was the trademark of a saloonkeeper, but this was the only outstanding feature of an otherwise nondescript face. His eyes were colorless, his nose unremarkably straight, and what his lips looked like was a secret guarded by the overhanging mustache. As he hadn't been involved in the dispute that had flared in the plaza, Baskin greeted Longarm pleasantly enough.

"I don't know what brings you to Los Perros, Custis, but any new customer's welcome in my place," he said. "Hope you'll drop in often."

"I was hoping I might do better'n drop in. I see you got some rooms upstairs, and I'm going to need a place to sleep. You happen to have one vacant, or are they all full up?"

"I don't keep whores in them, if that's what you're getting at," Baskin said. "You can have your choice for two bits a night. We don't get many travelers stopping off here."

"Fine. I'll pick one out later on. I don't guess there's a livery stable in town, is there? I got a horse that's going to have to be stabled and fed."

"No," the saloonkeeper said. Then, as an afterthought, "Ed, seeing Custis is a friend of yours, why don't you let him put his animal in the corral with your spare ones?"

"Well, I—" Tucker stopped, smiled, and went on, "I guess it'd be all right. One more nag won't work old Joselito to death."

"Looks like I'm all fixed up then," Longarm said.

"That calls for a drink, if you gents feel like stepping out to the bar."

"No need for that," Baskin told him. He opened a wall cabinet and took out a bottle. "I keep enough back here to take care of my friends when they drop in. What's your pleasure, Custis?"

"Maryland rye, if you got it handy."

"Just happens I do." The saloonkeeper reached in and brought out a second bottle. He put the bottles and glasses on the table that he used for a desk. "Drink up, gentlemen."

After his first sip, Longarm decided that the quality of Baskin's private stock was a lot better than that of the liquor sold over his bar. He remarked, more to fill the silence than for any other reason, "Looks like business is slack for you today."

"It's quiet," Baskin agreed. "Things will liven up tomorrow, though. Ed'll tell you that."

"Oh? What's the occasion?"

"Why, it's the big Mexican holiday," Tucker said. "*Dieciséis de Septiembre*, their Independence Day. They'll be swiggin' mescal and pulque and dancin' in the plaza out there till all hours. But my boys'll be on hand to keep things from gittin' too wild."

"Now, wait a minute, Ed," Baskin interjected. "Did you forget—"

Tucker said quickly, "No, damn it, Miles, I ain't forgot. We can talk about that later on."

"If you gents need to talk private business, I'll excuse myself," Longarm offered.

"It's nothin' important," the sheriff assured him. "Just a little somethin' I told Miles I'd give him a hand with." He turned back to the saloonkeeper. "And I'll take care of it, don't worry."

"You go on and settle your business," Longarm told them. "I'll step on back to the bar and finish my drink with your deputies, Sheriff."

Spud, Lefty and Ralston were standing where he'd left them, and Longarm noticed that the ten-dollar gold piece he'd put on the bar had disappeared. The thought passed through his mind that with bar whiskey a dime a shot, the three must've done some real two-fisted drinking during the few minutes he'd been with Tucker and Baskin, but he didn't say anything. It was worth a lot more than ten dollars to him to wash away the anger the plaza incident had sparked.

He said, "Well, it looks like I'm all fixed up. Room upstairs, a place for my horse in the sheriff's corral. Now, if one of you gentlemen'll just be kind enough to show me where the corral is, I'd better unsaddle him and get settled in."

Ralston, the friendliest of the three, volunteered, "Come on, Custis. It's just a step or two. I'll show you the layout."

"I'd appreciate it."

Longarm followed Ralston out of the saloon and around the building to the sheriff's office. Tordo stood at the hitching rail. Just outside the office door, the Apache girl was wiping out the basin in which she'd brought the water to minister to Jed Morton's back. She paid no attention to the two men.

As he slipped the dapple's reins free of the rail, Longarm asked the girl, "How's the man you were tending to?"

"Him all right." Her eyes, turned to Longarm as she spoke, were jet black and opaque. "Him be sore four, five days. Not hurt bad."

"Thanks for fixing him up, Wa—Wawayna, is it?"

"Wahonta." When she corrected him, Longarm thought the girl almost smiled. She added, "You welcome," and turned to go back into the office.

Ralston warned, "Don't get no ideas about the 'Pache gal. She's private property."

"Yours?"

"No. Times when I get horny, I sorta wish she was. Well, hell, you'll find out soon enough. She's Ed's girl. So be smart and keep outa her way." They started around the building to the corral. Ralston added, "Keep outa Spud's way, too. He holds onto a mad a long time."

"But you and Lefty don't?" Longarm was loosening Tordo's saddle girth. He didn't look up from his job.

"I can't say about Lefty, but I already said I don't hold you no bad feelings because of today."

Longarm set his saddle where some others rested on the top rail of the corral, tossed his bedroll over one shoulder, his saddlebag over the other. He chalked up his purchase of drinks for the deputies as a wise investment, one that was already paying dividends. The return he was getting from Ralston alone was making it worthwhile. He said, "You mentioned it. Don't worry about Spud. I'll be careful not to let him get behind me. Especially in the dark."

"You've got his style tagged, all right. You take the way he's trying to cut—" Suddenly, the deputy seemed to realize he was letting his mouth run away with his good sense. He stopped short.

Longarm was curious to know what he'd started to say, but decided it'd be better to wait instead of prodding. He could get the man talking again, later on. There was also a growing void in his stomach that was yelling to be filled up. He remembered that he'd had only those three buns at noon, and lunch had slipped his mind in the general ruckus.

"I'll pick up my rifle from inside, and go see about that room," he told Ralston.

"I'll walk on back with you, I guess. Nothing else to do right this minute."

Side by side they walked back to the saloon. Lefty and Spud no longer stood at the bar; except for the aproned barkeeper the place was empty. Longarm said, "Hate to leave you by yourself, Ralston. You been real helpful. I'll remember it. Right now I'm going to see if this place has got such a thing as a bathtub. I need to soak the trail dust off my hide. When I'm dirty, I feel about as mean as your friend Spud acts. See you around town, tonight or maybe tomorrow."

As he went up the stairs, Longarm could feel Ralston's questioning gaze on his back.

Chapter 6

There was still daylight in the western sky when Longarm glanced out the window of the room he'd selected. He felt a lot better now, more like going downstairs in search of food. For a dime, he'd been provided with a big wooden tub of hot water in which he'd soaked and soaped away the travel grime. He'd felt so good that he'd tipped the mozo who'd brought the tub another dime.

Fresh underwear and socks and a clean shirt added to his well-being. The porter who'd attended to the tub had assured Longarm that his wife was *"una lavandera maravillosa,"* who'd be glad to wash the dirty garments Longarm had removed and return them the next day. After the mozo left, Longarm wasted no time getting ready to seek his supper. He dressed quickly, though not so fast that he neglected his invariable routine of checking his Colt and derringer. He'd had the foresight to bring a bottle of Maryland rye up from the bar; he had enjoyed a few sips while he was soaking, and another as he dried himself, and the whiskey had whetted his growing appetite.

As always, hunger took second place to safety. Longarm paused long enough after locking the door to his room to break a match and wedge half the stick between door and jamb. He didn't want to risk being surprised on his return by Spud or one of the surly deputy's friends.

One look at the free-lunch counter that stood at the end of the saloon's bar only confirmed what his quick glance earlier had hinted. The slices of darkening curled-up bologna, discolored rat cheese, brine-scummed pickles and hardboiled eggs with chipped shells was enough to stop a man's appetite dead in its tracks. Baskin's free lunch offering not only didn't compare with those of the Windsor Hotel bar or the Black Cat Saloon, but were less appetizing than most of those he'd seen when cases had taken him into the cheap, shoddy bars in Denver's Lowers.

Recalling the food stalls that had been setting up for business at the time he'd first entered the Los Perros plaza, he stepped through the batwings onto the narrow veranda that ran the width of the saloon's front and looked around the almost deserted open area to see if any of the native vendors were still in operation at their stalls.

Old son, he told himself, maybe you're in luck. Looks like you don't have to depend on that slop inside to fill your belly. That grub out there might not be much better, but it'll at least be hot.

Though the plaza wasn't nearly as crowded as it had been when Los Perros's residents were gathering in anticipation of the whipping, there were still a few people around. Taco and tamale vendors stood beside the small charcoal fires that kept their iron pots hot. In addition, a half-dozen stalls—bare planks supported on trestles to make rough counters—dotted the margin of the plaza. People stood at most of them, eating. Longarm stepped to the ground and strolled idly around, going from counter to counter, trying to find the one at which the food looked most appetizing. As he walked, the tang of stewing hot red peppers mingled with the fainter smells of beef and garlic to set his juices running.

All the stalls seemed to be family affairs, operated by women. All of them offered about the same menu: chili con carne, tamales, frijoles, enchiladas, and steaming tortillas, served in thick ironstone plates that held the heat in the food. While the patrons stood at the counters, the women cooked and served them. The distribution of labor, he noted, was very consistent. The younger girls filled the plates from pots that rested on improvised stoves bent from metal sheets; the older girls served the food; the mothers cooked the tortillas; the grandmothers made them, starting with small balls of moistened cornmeal, slapping the balled meal into thin round sheets, rotating the meal cakes between wrinkled palms until they were paper-thin and ready to be cooked, greaseless, on the top of the metal stove. The very youngest children worked at one side of the serving area, grinding raw dried corn kernels on stone *metates* into a meal almost as fine as flour.

Approaching darkness was bringing out lanterns on the counters of the stalls before Longarm finished his leisurely inspection tour. He hadn't found anything different at any of the stalls; all he'd succeeded in doing was making himself hungrier by watching others eat. He stopped at a counter where a girl was trying to get a lantern lighted. Darkness had brought a breeze, and every match she struck fizzled out before she could touch it to the wick. Longarm took one of his waterproofed matches from his pocket and thumbnailed it into flame. Cupping the match expertly in his hands, he touched the wick with it. The kerosene-soaked fabric ignited, and he guided the girl's hand in lowering the glass chimney quickly, before the wind whipped the flame out.

"*Ay!*" the girl breathed. "*Muy bueno! Gracias, señor, por su ayudo.*"

Longarm scraped up enough of his scanty Spanish to reply, "*De nada, señorita.*"

"*Pues, habla Español?*" the girl asked, bringing her eyes up to meet his. "*Ve que esta extranjero.*"

"*No hablo mucho,*" Longarm replied. "*Conoce Inglés?*"

"A little bit, I speak," she said. "You are stranger, no?"

"I'm a stranger, yes, and hungry."

"*Porqué no come? Mira—*" she indicated the pots on the stove behind the counter, shook her head and said, "Excuse, *señor*, I forget. Look, we got good *chili colorado, chili verde,* we got tamales and frijoles, and *mi abuela,* her *tortillas* they very fine. So, what you wan' to eat?"

"Everything you just said sounded pretty good. Maybe you can fix me up a plate with a little bit of everything on it?"

"*Un poco de todas? Sí.* I fix you."

She moved back to the stove, almost dancing, Longarm thought, her steps were so light and graceful. Moving with unconscious poise, she ladled food from the pots crowded together, peeled the cornmeal husks from four tamales and put them on top of the beans and chili con carne swimming on the plate. Finally, she grabbed a stack of smoking tortillas from the cloth-covered platter where they were being laid by the woman cooking them—obviously, Longarm thought, her mother. She laid the tortillas on the other food and danced back to where he waited.

"You eat now," she commanded with a smile that showed flashing white teeth between firm crimson lips. "Is no good when it get cold."

Longarm looked for utensils. There was no fork, no spoon, no knife. He asked, "How'm I going to eat without tools?"

"Tools?" She frowned, then her eyes widened. *"Ah, sí, cuchara, tenedor. Pues, señor, no tenemos."* Seeing that he didn't understand her, she added, "Here, I show you."

Picking up a tortilla, the girl pulled a strip off one side and folded it between her fingers and thumb to form a scoop. She pushed the edge of the tortilla into the food, lifting meat and beans in it, and held it to his mouth. Longarm was too surprised to do anything but make a single bite of the tortilla strip and the chili and beans it contained.

"You see?" the girl giggled. "Is easy, no?" She handed him the remainder of the tortilla. "You do, now."

Longarm's fingers were as dexterous as any man's, but he had trouble forming the strip he tore off into a scoop of the proper shape. He made a try or two, but the tortilla always opened out and let the food drop back on the plate before he could lift it.

"No, no," she said. "Do like so. Here."

She took his hand in both of hers and bent his fingers into the proper curves to support the thin tortilla while he scooped up a portion of chili and beans and got them in his mouth. Her hands on his were warm and light, and reminded him somehow of a butterfly he'd caught many years ago, when he was a boy in West Virginia. All at once he was aware that the girl was less a girl than a pretty young woman. He became purposely clumsy, so that she had to keep helping him.

"What's your name?" he asked. After being helped to several bites, he'd picked up a tamale and was eating it.

"Lita."

"Let's see, that'd be short for—Adelita, maybe?"

She smiled. "No, *señor*. Guess some more."

"Carmelita?"

"*No, no! Ay, nunca advenirse. Mi nombre completa es Estrellita.*"

"Now, that's a right pretty name, I'd say."

"*Y usted? Que se llama?*"

Longarm remembered how the sheriff had shortened his name in time to reply, "Custis."

"Cos-tees?" she tried, frowning.

"No. Custis." He stressed the "u," which she'd turned into an "o".

"*Ah, sí!* Coos-tees. Is nice."

Lita's mother had been keeping an eye on the pair. From her place at the stove, she called, "*Lita! Paradese hablando con el gringo!*"

"*Callate, mama!*" the girl replied. "*No daname hablar un poco con un extranjero!*"

"*Cuidado, chica!*" the woman said. "*Los gringos quieren solamente una cosa de mujeres!*"

"*No hay que tal!*" the girl shot back. "*Dejame in paz!*"

Longarm's rusty and slight knowledge of Spanish kept him from understanding the exchange, but he caught the woman's warning. He thought, all women are alike wherever a man goes. They see a fellow making up to their daughter, they're damn sure all he wants is to get in her drawers.

Lita didn't seem bothered by the scolding, which stopped as soon as her mother saw she was wasting breath. She went back to cooking tortillas, casting an occasional suspicious look over her shoulder while Lita continued to help Longarm eat his dinner.

He wasn't sure which he enjoyed most, the food or the girl's help in eating. He found Lita a delight to watch. She was at that point when a girl has just become a woman, with a woman's awareness of a man. Lita was small, but fully rounded in all the right places. Her full gathered skirt didn't hide a saucy pair of buttocks when she danced from counter to stove, and her blouse was cut low; its rounded neckline gave Longarm a view of the valley between full breasts each time she leaned toward him across the counter.

Her cheeks were high in a face that was neither oval nor triangular, but a blending of the best of both. Dark eyes, full lustrous brows, and dark red pouting lips under a straight flared nose completed his picture of her.

"You like?" she asked, when his plate had been cleaned of the last peppery trace of chili sauce.

"Yep. It was real good. *Muy bueno.*"

"You wan' some more? Is plenty on stove."

"No, thanks, Lita. I'm as full as any man's got a right to be."

"Maybe you come back, some time?"

"You just bet I will. Now how much do I owe you?"

"Ah, quince centavos, Coos-tees. Like you say, feefteen cents."

"It's worth double that." He dug into his pocket and passed her a half-dollar. "Here. You keep whatever's extra, for helping me."

"Gracias, Coos-tees. I think you a nice man."

"And you're a right pretty girl. I'll be back to eat with you again, real soon. Maybe tomorrow."

"I think I will like that. *Vaya con Dios,* Coos-tees."

There being no place else to go in Los Perros, Longarm went back to the saloon. The place had lost the deserted look it had had in the afternoon. Poker games were in progress at two of the four felt-covered tables, and there was a respectable lineup along the bar as well as a scattering of men sitting at the round tables that dotted the floor. Most of the men had on the clothes that marked them as ranch hands: faded Levi's, boots, wide-brimmed felt hats. He found a place at the bar at the edge of a knot of men and ordered his usual rye. He sipped it slowly while listening to the backwash of gossip from the group beside him.

To Longarm's disappointment, gossip was all he heard. Much of the chatter consisted of complaints: bedbugs in the bunkhouse, hard beans in the cookshack. He listened until he'd finished his drink, then ordered a refill and wandered over to watch the poker games. So far, he'd heard nothing useful. Rustling had been mentioned once or twice, but casually, not in terms of a major new outbreak. Nothing had been said about either the army or the Texas Rangers.

That wasn't too unusual. Longarm had worked before at picking up cold trails. He'd learned that as time went by, incidents that were prime conversational fodder when they happened were forgotten. Captain Hill had been missing since June, Nate Webster since July. If their vanishing had been discussed then, it had been forgotten by September. Questioning would refresh memories, but Longarm wasn't quite ready yet to start asking questions.

Standing between the two poker tables that were busy, Longarm watched silently. Spud was in the game at one of the tables, and although he'd seen Longarm, he'd ignored him. The game at the other table was uninteresting, a friendly affair with two-bit antes, bets of fifty to seventy-five cents, and raises about as big as the bets. The game at the table where Spud sat was for blood, and small change wasn't being mentioned by any of the players in it.

There was room for six, and all seats were filled. Spud was at the dealer's left, and after he'd begun paying attention to the game, Longarm thought there was something vaguely familiar about the house man. He couldn't associate him with any case he'd handled, or match his face with the descriptions or pictures on any of the "wanted" circulars he'd looked at lately. He heard the other players call the man George, but that didn't ring a bell, either.

Three of the other men at the table were ranch hands, judging by their clothes. Two were in their thirties, old enough to have cut their teeth on poker in bunkhouse and trail-ride games. The third was a fresh-faced young cowboy who wore the expression of one who'd been sliding deeper and deeper into the hole that waits for gamblers trying to buck a game out of their depth. The remaining two players were Mexicans, dressed in embroidered charro suits; they played with skill, folding when their cards didn't justify a draw, raising moderately but not extravagantly when they stayed in the pot.

There was no friendly banter or "dealer's choice" about the game these seven played. George, who was banker as well as dealer, stuck to five-card draw, the game that demands the greatest skill and judgment from a player. The house man wasn't a fast-shuffle artist, Longarm decided after he'd watched a few hands, nor did he use the standard gaffs such as rubber- or spring-loaded sleeve holdouts, palmed cards, or other devices professionals use to give themselves an unbeatable edge. As far as Longarm's skilled eyes could tell, it was an honest game, for which he gave Miles Baskin good marks. He hadn't expected a straight game in Los Perros.

During the short time Longarm had been looking on, the pile of chips in front of the young cowhand had shrunk steadily, and the young fellow had been getting nervous in inverse ratio to the diminishing of his stake. Now, as the dealer flicked cards around the table, the youth grabbed each one as it hit the felt in front of him, looked at it quickly, and added it to the fan forming in his hand. He'd begun growing tense after he'd picked up the third card; his nerves tightened visibly after he'd seen the fourth, and then he relaxed after looking at the final card.

"Openers?" the dealer asked the table at large.

Shaking his head, Spud put his cards face-down on the table. The man to his left, one of the charro-suited Mexicans, also passed. The ranch hand who had the next call opened for a modest dollar, "Just to keep the deal from being wasted," he remarked.

Wordlessly, the second Mexican tossed a white chip into the pot. After a moment's hesitation, but before the play passed him by, he added a second white chip.

"Cost you two dollars, Billy-Bob," George announced. "Spud, if you and Gonzales want in, you better be making up your mind."

"Plenty of time," Spud remarked. "I'll see what Billy-Bob does."

Billy-Bob put in his two whites; so did the other ranch hand in his turn. The dealer followed suit; after he'd fed the pot he riffled the depleted deck and looked questioningly at Spud and Gonzales. Both of them tossed their second white chips into the growing pile in the table's center.

"Who wants cards?" George asked.

"It ain't worth it, but I'll take the two I paid to see," Spud said. He got the cards, looked at them, and stacked them on the table in front of him.

"One," Gonzales requested. He threw his discard

on the pile Spud had started before sliding the new card into his hand.

"Two for me," said the ranch hand who'd opened. He tossed out his discards, looked at the new ones without comment or change of expression, and squeezed the fanned-out cards into a stack that he cradled protectively in his hands.

Instead of speaking, the Mexican held up two fingers, tossing his discards out and sweeping the new ones into his hand in a single motion. He laid his cards down, his face bland and unruffled.

"I—I'll play what I got," Billy-Bob announced. His voice was a bit higher-pitched than usual and he was clenching his cards tightly between pressed palms.

"Luke?" the dealer asked the last man.

"Since I paid for 'em, you better gimme two." He got the requested cards, looked at them, added them to his hand, and tossed all the cards on the discard heap.

"I'm drawing two," George announced. He did so, discarded and stacked the discards neatly, then looked across the table. "You bought the bet when you raised, Gonzales."

"Five." Gonzales tossed a red chip in the pot.

The ranch hand and the second charro followed suit.

"And five," Billy-Bob said as soon as their chips had clattered to the table. He tossed in two reds from the small stack of chips he'd been clicking nervously.

There weren't enough chips in the young fellow's stake to drag the betting out, Longarm thought.

"Ten to me, then, gents," George said. "And you, too, Spud. If you're staying in, that is."

"Oh, I'm in," Spud replied. He threw in the chips, then leaned back in his chair, smiling to show that he hadn't a worry in the world.

George raised his eyebrows at Gonzales, who added another red chip without speaking. Then the dealer's eyes moved to the next player. "Fiddler?"

"Reckon I'll just cut my losses before I get tempted." The ranch hand slid his hand to George, who added it to the deadwood.

"Aleman?" George asked. The Mexican shrugged

and fingered his chips for a moment. Impatiently, George repeated, "Aleman?"

"I find myself forced to raise," Aleman announced. "But only a small amount. Five more dollars, *señores.*"

Defiantly, Billy-Bob tossed in the red chip, then added his last blue. "And ten more," he said, making an almost visible effort to keep his voice steady.

Wordlessly, George tapped the tabletop with his five stacked cards and added them to the discards. In equal silence, Spud added a red and a blue chip to the pot. Holding up two fingers, Gonzales dropped a red and two blues in the table's center. Aleman threw in two blues, his face still bland and unreadable.

Longarm hadn't been keeping close track of the betting, but it had registered subconsciously. He estimated that there was something just over a hundred dollars in the pot, three or four months' wages for the young cowhand whose raise had escalated the betting.

"Damn it!" Billy-Bob said. "I wanta raise, but all I got is enough to call!"

On impulse, Longarm flipped a double eagle onto the table in front of Billy-Bob. The youth looked up, startled. He identified Longarm as his unexpected benefactor and said, "Thanks, mister. I'll pay you back outa the pot."

"Win it first," Longarm told him.

Billy-Bob tossed the twenty-dollar gold piece in the pot. "I guess I don't need to buy chips with this." Then he added his last two reds to the growing heap on the table. "And up ten more."

"I got too much in there not to look, now," Spud observed. He fed the pot a pair of blues. "But all I'll do is call."

Gonzales announced regretfully, "That will not be good enough, *señor.*" He put in three blue chips. "The game becomes more costly."

"*Sí, amigo,*" Aleman agreed. "I also raise. Ten more dollars."

"Hell's bells!" Billy-Bob exploded. "You men are freezing me out!" He looked at the house man. "Unless I can play the pot short."

"Not a chance." George shook his head. "There's a house rule against short-played pots. Baskin says they give him too much trouble."

Billy-Bob looked pleadingly at Longarm.

"Sorry, friend," Longarm said. "I kept you in the game once, but that's as far as I go."

"Come look at my hand," Billy-Bob invited.

Longarm shook his head. "Nope. I didn't mean to, but I seen what one of these other men's holding, after I staked you. If I look at your cards now and put up money for your bet, it'd be just like you was playing with a marked deck."

"He's right," George said approvingly. "But there's sure not any house rule that says the rest of you can't make a side-pot, if you want to. High hand out of the three'd take the side pot, Billy-Bob's hand would just count in the main pot."

"I won't get sucked into a three-way pot with them two greasers," Spud announced angrily.

Gonzales straightened up at the insulting word, but subsided when Aleman hissed a remark in a voice too low for Longarm to hear.

Gonzales said, "If the *caballero*—" he made the word sound like the sort of insult Spud had hurled at him as he indicated the deputy—"if the *caballero* objects, then the *joven* must find the chips with which to call or raise."

"Damn it, I got too much in that pot to be raised outa it," Billy-Bob protested. He appealed to the man on his left. "Luke, will you stake me? You know I'm good for it, if I happen to lose."

Luke sighed. "I guess it's only money. All right, Billy-Bob. I'll stake you if you promise you won't do nothing but call from here on in. You make any raises, I pull out."

Billy-Bob started to object, but caught Longarm's headshake out of the corner of his eye and settled back into his chair. "We got a deal, Luke. All right. I'll just call any raise that's made."

Somehow, the dispute had shattered the game's mood. Spud glared angrily at the two charros and they glared back. He looked with equal anger at Billy-Bob, who raised his chin defiantly.

George tried to make peace. "Billy-Bob's called your raise, Aleman. Luke, you owe the pot two blues for Billy-Bob. Spud, you're short two blues, and Gonzales is shy one, if you're going to let the call stand."

"I'm damn sure goin' to see what everybody's been bettin'," Spud said. He tossed the chips in.

"That will satisfy me, also," Gonzales said.

Aleman shrugged. "I would not want to be the only one who disagrees." He added a blue chip.

"Show 'em down, then, gents," George ordered.

Gonzales said, "These I would like better if they were in sequence, but with an ace at the top, I think they will get respect." He spread out a heart flush.

"They ain't good," Spud told him. "Not against my four tens."

"Qué lastima!" Aleman murmured. "I have put too much trust in three treys and two queens."

As Billy-Bob watched the hands being displayed, the grin on his face grew bigger and bigger. Trying to match the calm of the other players and not quite succeeding, he laid his cards down one by one, all spades, in sequence from the five to the nine.

"I guess I got all of you topped," he said, exhaling gustily.

Spud exploded. He kicked his chair aside and swiveled to face Longarm. "Damn you, Custis! You begun this! If you hadn't staked that little cowpoke, he'd've been froze out and I could've run that pot up to a good one!"

"Cool down, Spud!" George commanded. "The gent didn't do anything that was out of line."

Longarm said nothing, but faced Spud with an expressionless face.

"That's twice today you butted into my business," Spud went on. "And that's just about two times too many!"

Longarm remained silent. He kept his features frozen, his hands still.

George was out of his chair by now, moving between Longarm and Spud, saying, "Hold yourself down, Spud! You know the boss don't like dustups in here!"

Over the house man's shoulder, Spud grated, "This ain't the time to settle with you, Custis. But stay outa my way! You hear?"

"Loud as you're yelling, I'd have to be deaf not to," Longarm replied quietly. When Spud began to sputter, he added, "I judge you ain't got any more to say, so I'll bid all you gents good night."

Deliberately turning his back on Spud, but watching the deputy in the flyspecked bar mirror, Longarm walked away.

Chapter 7

Before Longarm got to the bar, Billy-Bob caught up with him, waving the twenty-dollar gold piece that had gotten him over the hump in betting up the pot he'd just won.

"Mr.—Custis, ain't it? I don't know how to say thanks for helping me out. I'd be right proud to buy you a drink if you'll let me," the young cowhand said, handing Longarm the double eagle.

"You don't need to thank me. It'd be a hell of a sorry world if a man couldn't do something for somebody besides himself, once in a while."

"Just the same, I'd be proud to stand up and drink with you."

"Well, I won't say no to your invitation, Billy-Bob. What's the rest of your name, anyway?"

"Larkin. I work for the Bar Z Bar, down on Devil's River."

"That's to the southeast, ain't it?" Billy-Bob nodded and Longarm asked, "Your friends Luke and Fiddler work there, too?"

"No, sir, they're from the next spread south, the Arrowhead."

"You been around here long?" They'd reached the bar; without asking, the barkeep set a bottle of Maryland rye in front of them.

"About two years." Billy-Bob cocked an eye at the bottle's label and asked, "Is this what you always drink, Mr. Custis?"

"Yep. I guess it's what folks call a cultivated taste."

"If it's good enough for you, it'll sure do for me." The young hand poured the whiskey into the glasses the barman had put beside the bottle.

"Not a lot of ranches down this way, are there?" Longarm asked.

"No, sir. Not too many. The range is so poor, a
74

spread's got to be mighty big around here. The Bar Z Bar foreman says it takes fifty acres to feed a steer."

"You folks bothered by rustlers much?"

"Haven't been since I got here. There's an awful lot going on up to the north, I hear. Up along Howard Creek and the South Concho and the Cemeche country."

"That so?" Longarm sipped thoughtfully before he put the next question. "You heard any talk about the Laredo Loop working again?"

Billy-Bob frowned. "I've heard it mentioned, is all. But didn't the Laredo Loop start someplace up above the Pecos?"

"It all began there." Longarm had been recalling, since he'd left Denver, all the stories he could remember about the across-the-border-and-back operation. "On up north from that place they call Vinagaroon. Then this fellow that's made himself a judge, Roy Bean, moved into Vinagaroon and set up some kind of six-shooter law. I got an idea the Loop's back in business, but it crosses into Mexico quite a way south of where it used to."

"You wouldn't be working for the cattleman's association, would you, Mr. Custis?"

"Nope. That kinda job wouldn't suit me a bit. I'm just sort of curious. Billy-Bob, you can do me a favor, if you will. Keep your ears open, and if you hear any talk about the Loop, or about rustlers, pass it on to me."

"Anything I can do to help you, I sure will," Billy-Bob promised. "Will you have another drink?"

"Guess not, but I thank you." Longarm looked across the room toward the poker tables. George, the house man, was sitting by himself, dealing solitaire. The two-bit ante game was still going strong, but the men who'd been sitting in the money game had gone. He told the young cowboy, "I need to go talk to George a minute. Then I'm going to turn in. I had a right early start and a busy day."

"I'll look for you next time I'm in town," Billy-Bob promised. "Maybe I'll hear something that'd help you. And thanks again for staking me."

"You needed it. I don't suppose you've played as much poker as I have, but for what it's worth, I'll tell you something I've found out. Learning the game's just like eating an apple. You take one bite at a time."

"I guess I see what you mean."

"Sure you do. Just remember to chew every bite up good, and don't bite off more'n you can gulp down without choking. I'll see you later on, son."

I'd be a sight better off if I took my own advice about biting and chewing, Longarm thought as he crossed to where George was sitting. For a while there, today, I came close to getting a bigger mouthful than I could swallow.

George looked up at Longarm's approach and said, "If you're looking for a game, this is about all that's going right now."

"Thanks, but poker's not on my mind tonight. I just wanted to say I'm sorry I busted things up for you a while ago."

"I was glad to see Billy-Bob get some help. That game was too rich for him, anyhow. No, I don't blame you a bit. That Spud's got a real hair-trigger temper. If he didn't work for Ed Tucker, I don't think I'd let him sit in on any game I was dealing."

"Well, he's been building up a real mad at me all day."

"I know. I watched you face down him and Ed's bunch in the plaza earlier today. It didn't surprise me when Spud blew up." George frowned and looked closely at Longarm. "Say, don't I know you from somewhere else?"

"You might. I've got around a little bit. Seems like I've seen you someplace, too."

"I move around. Most of us do; it's part of the trade. And we might've run into one another if you've been in Cheyenne or Helena or San Francisco or Denver in the past few years."

Longarm's memory clicked. "Sure. Denver. You ran a faro table at Big Jim Little's place, just down Holiday Street from Jennie Rogers's whorehouse."

"That I did, for damn near a year. I guess that's where I remember you from. But I can't recall your name. You a miner? Cattleman? You don't look like the kind that sits at a desk or stands back of a ribbon counter."

"I'm traveling now as Custis." Longarm knew that

in the half-world of the professional gambler he needed only to use this phrase to warn George that he didn't want his identity revealed if the house man should remember him more clearly.

"I see." George nodded understandingly. "Well. Denver. It's a long way from Los Perros. I don't mean to pry, but the way you acted out on the plaza today, you sure didn't seem bashful."

"Now, I didn't say I'm on the dodge, did I? There's other reasons a man might have for changing handles."

"Sure, sure." The gambler dropped his voice. "I'll just tip you that if it's the law you're bothered about, you're safe in Los Perros as long as you stay on Ed Tucker's good side."

"I gather he's all the law there is here. How'd he work that out, you know?"

George shook his head. "I haven't been here all that long. From what I've heard, he just grew into the job. Had a few men behind him, more or less took over the town."

"That's about how I figured," Longarm nodded. "Tucker and your boss get along pretty good, don't they?"

Suddenly, the gambler's face stiffened and he dropped his confidential tone. "I suppose they do. Baskin would have to, wouldn't he, the business he's in?"

"Oh, I wasn't prying," Longarm said hastily. He stood up. "Well, now that I know I was right when I figured I'd seen you before, I'll sleep easier."

"Oh, come on, the night's early. Stay a while, and we'll hash over Denver, and Big Jim and Jennie and Mattie Silks, and Vesta King, and all the gorgeous girls they had."

"Maybe tomorrow night, or the next. I started riding before sunup, and it's getting on for late."

"Sure. Later on, then, Custis. Sleep good."

"I almost always do."

Longarm made his way across the saloon's main floor, unworried. He wasn't sure George's memory would put a badge on him, but even if it did, the gambler would almost certainly keep quiet unless it came to a hard-rock showdown with Baskin standing beside Tucker. He started up the stairs, being glad that the place didn't have a gaggle of women taking customers up to their rooms through the night. He hadn't been exaggerating when he'd told George it had been a long day.

Habit kept his feet quiet as he walked along the uncarpeted hall to the door of his room, fishing the key from his pocket as he moved. The habit of walking silently was by now almost an instinct. So was the habit of checking the broken matchstick that he'd wedged between the door and jamb. Longarm looked for the sliver of wood before inserting the key. His hand stopped in midair when he saw the matchstick half was missing. He'd shifted the key to his left hand even before he looked down and saw the splinter of white pine gleaming, a little speck of brightness on the dark wood of the floor.

A half-dozen possibilities flashed through Longarm's mind in as many seconds while he studied the closed door.

It could be Spud, he thought—bushwhacking's about his speed. Or somebody Spud put on me, to do what he don't want to face up to. Tucker, maybe, he'd send a gunslick instead of coming himself.

No, Tucker was doing his damnedest to butter up to me today, as soon as he saw I wasn't going to crawfish.

Might be Tucker's looking for somebody to handle Spud for him—he hinted at that—but Tucker wouldn't wait in my room, he'd wait till we got by ourselves in private, on his grounds.

Spud's still the one it's most likely to be.

One of the corners, I'd say. Or setting on the bed, it's right even with the door. No. That'd put the window in back of him. If he's smart, not the bed.

Me, I'd be along the wall just inside the door, the side it opens along.

Whoever's there, it ain't that big of a shucks, now I know.

Longarm inserted the key delicately, careful not to scrape metal against metal. He recalled that the lock worked easily, and took a full minute, turning the key with infinite patience to engage the wards and pull the lock's square bar out of the strike-plate without it scratching. If he made a noise, it was inaudible to his own ears, and he was satisfied that whoever was inside couldn't have been warned.

Leaving the key in the lock, Longarm drew. He turned the knob with his left hand, quickly, and flung the door wide open. As soon as it had swung wide enough to admit him, he dove into his room, rolling when he hit the floor, winding up against the wall away from the bed. His eyes had been sensitized to darkness by his walk down the unlighted hall and his moments of deliberation outside the door. He had no need for the Colt that was ready in his hand. Except for himself, the room was empty.

Well, now, he told himself, leaning against the wall in the darkness, guess I better be glad there wasn't nobody here. Now I'm the only one who knows what a damn fool I looked like, diving in ass over appetite. But it's a hell of a lot better to look foolish than to be dead.

He got to his feet and closed the door, locking it automatically. He started for the dresser in the dark, groping for the bottle of rye. His fingers encountered cloth. In the darkness, he stood laughing silently, thinking, I plumb forgot that I sent out my clothes to be washed; it was that porter come in to deliver 'em while I was gone. He crossed to the window and pulled down the shade before lighting the lamp, then pushed the lamp as far back on the bureau as it would go, resting against the mirror, so it would cast no shadow on the windowshade. Only then did he pick up the bottle and have a nightcap.

Hanging his gunbelt on the bedpost at the left of his pillow, Longarm emptied his pockets quickly, undressed even faster, and was in bed within five minutes from the time he'd entered the room. He went to sleep instantly, and slept like a baby.

Though he was by nature an early riser, Longarm didn't wake up until the sun was shining yellow against the drawn window shade. He snapped awake instantly and sat up in bed. Though he'd checked the sheets and mattress on moving into the room the day before, he'd learned through unhappy experience that bugs that bite by night have an uncanny way of making themselves invisible during daylight hours; before leaving the room he had spread his own groundcloth and blanket over the bed without turning the linen down. If there'd been any miniature bloodsuckers that his inspection had missed, they hadn't found him to disturb his rest.

Throwing back the blanket, he rolled to his feet and snapped up the shade. He stretched hugely in the sunlight, the solid muscles of his body flexing the last vestiges of drowsiness from his system. Fishing the chamberpot from under the bed, he arced a golden stream until the morning pressure on his bladder was relieved, then padded on bare feet to the dresser for a wakeup shot of rye.

Ten minutes later, his routine of dressing finished, his Colt and derringer checked thoroughly, he strode down the stairway to the bar.

"What does a man do for breakfast here in Los Perros?" he asked the barkeeper. It wasn't the same man who'd been tending bar the night before.

"Help yourself to hardboiled eggs and whatever else strikes your fancy." The barkeep jerked a thumb at the free lunch table.

Longarm went over and looked at it. The same food he'd seen there the evening before was spread on the same chipped platters.

"Thanks," he told the barkeep. "Maybe later on."

When he stepped through the batwings and looked at the plaza, Longarm was surprised to see an even bigger crowd milling around than had gathered for the whipping yesterday. Then he remembered the sheriff telling him about the fiesta, Mexican Independence Day. He noticed, too, that it wasn't the same quiet, almost sullen crowd he'd seen the day before. Today, the people of Los Perros wore their best and brightest clothes, and were laughing and happy.

A few streamers of colored paper dancing in the light breeze on the far side of the plaza caught Longarm's eye; he wondered if the food stalls might not be setting up early. He started toward them, pushing through the throng. Somewhere close by he heard a mariachi band tuning up. Before he reached the streamers, Longarm thought he saw a remembered figure. He changed direction, and when the crowd in his way no longer blocked his vision, he saw that it was indeed Lita's family, setting up their trestles and counter.

Lita saw him when he was still a yard or so distant. She was wrestling with a plank twice as long as she was tall, and let it rest across one shoulder to greet him. "Coos-tees!" she exclaimed. "You come to eat again, no?"

"If you got something ready, Lita. But I'll give you a hand with that board, first."

"I can do it. I am strong."

"But I'm stronger." He took the plank and settled it into place across the trestles, completing the serving-counter. "Now then. I hope you got something besides chili and frijoles. They're a mite too spicy for breakfast."

"Is not cook yet, the chili. We got bizcochos that *Mamacita* bake just a little while ago. And we bring hot coffee from our kitchen at *la casa,* so we don't lose customers who don't wait for it."

"If that's what you got, that's what I'll have."

"You wait, I fix."

In a moment, she'd produced three of the same kind of round, sugar-crusted buns that Longarm had eaten the day before, together with a cup of steaming coffee. Longarm bit into one of the buns. He hadn't paid much attention to those he'd had the previous day, there'd been too much else on his mind. This bun was still hot and moist, and tasted of spices and seasonings strange to him. Accustomed to flat-tasting baked foods—bread, biscuits, and soda crackers—he thought it was odd, but excellent.

"You like *Mamacita's* bizcochos?" Lita asked.

"They're right tasty. I guess I could stand 'em for breakfast now and again." He sipped the coffee. It was laced heavily with chicory, and reminded him of the French-type brew he had been served when he was in New Orleans.

Mamacita came up to the counter and expressed her disapproval of Lita's attention to Longarm's breakfast needs in rapid-fire Spanish that was beyond his ability to follow. He didn't need a translation, though; the expressions on the faces of both Lita and her mother were easy for him to read. The exchange lasted only a few moments before Mamacita turned away with a disgusted shrug.

Lita said, "I got to work now. You come to the *baile* tonight, Coos-tees?"

"Sure. It's the only dance in town, ain't it?"

"Maybe I dance with you then, if you ask me."

"Oh, I'll do that." He swallowed the last bite of the last bizcocho, drained his coffee cup, and handed Lita a quarter. "That enough money to pay for breakfast?"

"Is plenty. You pay too much, like last night."

"Well, like I told you then, anything extra's for you." Longarm touched a forefinger to his hat and said, "See you at the dance." Then he started back to the saloon. He wanted his Winchester for the scouting trip he planned to make.

When he went to the corral for Tordo, he avoided the sheriff's office. He didn't want to start the day with a run-in with Spud, and for all he knew the deputy might be on duty. Going directly to the corral, he saddled Tordo and started south along the river channel. He wasn't sure what he was looking for, but knowing the lay of the land was often an insurance of survival. Longarm intended to survive.

By midafternoon, he'd covered the area near Los Perros on the U.S. side of the Rio Grande as well as the bank of the channel along which he'd started. That left the northern, upstream, end of the sandspit. He was forced to ride back almost to the center of town in order to avoid the lagoon formed by the backwater where the sandspit split the river. Going north on the spit, the houses of Los Perros straggled to an occasional lonely shanty more quickly than he'd realized they would. He'd thought there would be dwellings all the way to the northern end of the spit that rose like a whale's humped back above the river; the south end was thickly built up. Beyond the northernmost of the hovels, though, the sandspit stretched for at least two miles. He saw why when he'd left the last of the dwellings behind. High-water marks began to show almost at once.

Longarm continued to the point where the river split. Here, the Rio Grande now ran wide and sluggish at low water, over a sandy bottom. Might even be some quicksand here and there, he thought as he surveyed the point from the height of Tordo's back. He recalled that Texas rivers running in sandy beds were notorious for their quicksand. At the place where he'd pulled up the dapple, there was water on both sides of him: the lagoon on his right, the channel on the left. On the Mexican side of the channel the bank began a steep rise that quickly became a steep bluff; under the bluff the water deepened and the current ran as fast as it did along the downstream end of the sandspit.

Longarm could easily see why Los Perros was a no-man's-land, a place where an unscrupulous pusher like Ed Tucker could set himself up a miniature kingdom. In the rainy season, when the Rio Grande ran in flood, Los Perros stood as an island which could be claimed—or disclaimed—by the U.S. or Mexico. It was, he thought, like places he'd encountered elsewhere in the West. He remembered spots in Indian Territory where there were similar no-man's-lands, created by careless or inexpert surveyors who'd mistaken a natural landmark or guessed at longitude and latitude lines instead of making a star-sighting to establish them correctly.

Anyhow, Longarm told himself, there wasn't going to be any argument about which country had jurisdiction when the time came for him to produce his badge, as long as there was dry land on the U.S. side of Los Perros.

Tordo tossed his head and snorted, and Longarm read the message; the horse was thirsty. Stopping to let him drink every time there was a wet spot on the ride from San Antonio had imprinted in the animal's mind the notion that he had to drink every time he saw water. Longarm slacked the reins and touched the dapple's side with his toe to wade him out into the river where he could drink easily. The gray waded out, testing the sand underfoot before each step, his instinct telling him that such bottoms could be treacherous. Tordo stopped in knee-deep water to drink.

There was no current to ripple the surface; the river's rushing water passed to Longarm's left. Idly, he looked over the dapple's bent head and gazed at the bottom, clearly visible through the shallow water. For a moment, he didn't take in what he was seeing. Then it sank home that the sand under the surface was covered with a pattern of dents that could have been caused by only one thing: the hooves of steers being waded across the stream.

Waiting until the dapple had drunk his fill, Longarm nudged the horse ahead. The bottom dropped gradually for a distance of at least two hundred yards. Until it started there to slant, Longarm's stirrups had stayed several inches above the surface. He went on until he felt wavelets slapping his bootsoles, then reined in. The water wasn't as clear here, roiled a bit by the current, but he could still make out hoofmarks in the sand.

To his left, the Mexican bank of the Rio Grande was low. The upward slope began at a point opposite the sandspit's end. To his right, the calm surface of the lagoon lapped at land that was almost level with the water. There were no hoofprints in the sand that stretched back from the lagoon; its surface rippled in windswept ridges.

To Longarm's trailwise eyes, the story was completely clear. Even a light breeze would smooth the loose, soft sand, and beyond it the baked soil was too hard to take prints. The bank on the Mexican side shelved gently from the water, here. At this one point, there seemed to be no quicksand. Driving a herd of cattle across, even at night, would be no trick at all.

Old son, Longarm told himself as he sat on Tordo's back surrounded by the green sun-dappled water, looks like you just fell headfirst into the place where the new Laredo Loop starts out.

Chapter 8

Standing on the veranda of Baskin's saloon, Longarm looked out across the plaza. Los Perros had turned out in full for the fiesta. He was sure that every man, woman, and child was crowded into the irregular circle that served as the town's public arena.

Music from a mariachi band in front of the saloon almost drowned that from a *banda Guadalajara tapatia* on the other side. The twanging of the strings and bell-like marimba notes of the mariachis at times clashed sourly against the brasses and cymbals of the *Guadalajareños,* but if there were discords where the music blended in the plaza's center, this didn't seem to bother the dancers. They twirled and stomped to the rhythm of the music that was being played closest to them.

"I really do like to see my people having a good time," said a voice at Longarm's elbow.

He turned. Sheriff Tucker had come out of the saloon behind him. Longarm agreed, "They're whooping it up, all right."

"Didn't see you at the barbecue at noon today," Tucker said.

"Maybe that's because I didn't know there was one."

"Well, doggone that Lefty! I told him to make sure you got a special invitation. Man like you, Custis, comin' from outside, don't generally find much t'do in a little place like this."

"Oh, I manage to fill up the time. Tell me something, Sheriff. How many ranches would you say there are in a day's ride to the north, up along the Pecos on both sides?"

Tucker pursed his thin lips. "Not too many, that close. There's such poor range hereabouts that most of the spreads have got to be so big it'd take you a day just to ride across one of 'em."

"That's about the way I figured," Longarm nodded.

"There sure as hell ain't much grass anyplace I looked at around here so far."

"Sounds like you been sizin' up the range, Custis. You lookin' for anything special?"

"No. Just interested in seeing the lay of the land around these parts, is all."

"You interested in ranchin', then? Funny. I didn't take you for a cattle rancher. Guess I'm goin' to have to change my mind again."

Longarm finally realized that Tucker's sudden expansiveness didn't mean he was getting friendly. The sheriff was drunker than usual. He asked, "How's that? I didn't know you'd made up your mind about me in the first place."

"Well, I did. When you took on Spud and the boys that day you showed up, I put you down in my book as a gunslick on the owlhoot trail. But after I'd thought a bit, that didn't make sense. If you was on the dodge, you'd've laid low, not called no notice to yourself."

Longarm wasn't going to waste the man's loquaciousness. He threw the logical question. "After that, how'd you tab me?"

"I didn't, till now. You had me plumb puzzled. Right now, though, it's popped into my mind you might just be a land agent for one of the big railroads. I keep hearin' there's two or three of 'em that wants to run a line down to the Gulf. If you're interested in land, but not in ranchin', that's all the reason I can see."

Longarm wasn't too surprised at Tucker's conclusion. Everywhere in the West, railroads were adding lines to supplement their major routes, and right-of-way agents were thick. Dropping his voice, he said, "I won't say yes or no. But suppose I was, now. Think you might help me pick up some land on the quiet?"

"You're damn right, I can! What I say is law, anywheres inside of a hundred miles of here." Tucker looked around. "Listen, this ain't the place to talk about a deal, Custis. Let's go back to the office. The boys are all out, keepin' an eye on the fiesta. We can talk private there."

In the sheriff's office, with the outer door closed, Tucker shouted, "Wahonta! Bring the whiskey bottle and some glasses!" When the Apache girl came in with a half-filled bottle and some thick tumblers, he told her brusquely, "Now, go tend to whatever it is you're doin'. We got business to talk."

Longarm's eyes followed the girl as she left. Tucker noticed him watching her. He said, "Maybe she don't look like much to you, but that little 'Pache gal's the sweetest piece of ass I run into in a long time. Acourse, I broke her in right. I was the first man ever rode her. She wasn't but only fourteen when I bought her off the resettlement camp south of here, a couple years ago."

"She's a right nice-looking girl," Longarm commented neutrally.

Tucker had poured, now he passed Longarm a glass across the desk. "Now, then. Like I told you, I'm the law here—sheriff, judge, and jury. When I say frog, people jumps. I can get whatever land you're after, Custis, water and mineral rights throwed in. You call the tune, I make 'em play it." He waited for Longarm to take the bait, and when no response followed he added, "Understand, now, I'd look to git a little something for my trouble. A sort of commission, we could call it."

"We could call it that," Longarm agreed. "But I got a better deal than that."

"I'm listenin'."

"Let's just suppose I was after land for a railroad right-of-way. Think you could push the price I'd pay down low enough so I could double what I'd charge the railroad? That way, we'd have a real big piece of cash to split up between us."

Tucker grinned. "That'd be easier'n pissin' in a dishpan. I can set my own price on what land you'd want. And there's ways to fix up deeds and papers so the railroad never would catch on."

"I know all about deeds and papers," Longarm said. "There's one thing that bothers me, though. How about your boys? Spud and Lefty and Ralston, would you have to cut them in on the deal?"

"Hell, no! I let them pick up what they can, cut 'em in on my deals when I feel like it, but you can leave them to me to handle." Tucker splashed more whiskey into his glass.

Longarm said, picking his words carefully, "Meaning no offense, Sheriff, but are you including Spud in that? I guess you heard I had a little run-in with him in the saloon last night, after you told him everything was supposed to be nice and friendly."

"Well, I hadn't heard, but you got to remember, Spud's hotheaded. He's got a real quick temper."

"I noticed that yesterday. Times I wondered if you had him on a real tight halter. He was just about sassing you."

Tucker nodded, his blubbery lips twisted angrily. "I ain't forgot that, Custis." He thought for a moment. "Look here now. You've laid it out straight with me, I'll do the same with you. Spud's been gettin' uppity of late, I got a hunch he's feelin' too big for his britches. Gittin' idees, if you follow me."

Longarm nodded. "Like taking things over, here in Los Perros?"

"Somethin' like that," Tucker agreed unhappily. He drained his glass and refilled it. "Listen, Spud was just a lard-ass boy when I talked Quantrill into lettin' him ride with us. And I put him in as my *segundo* when I took over here. I made him, and I can bust him."

"Suppose you can't?"

Tucker winked across the desk. "You recall I told you I had you tabbed for a gunslick at first? One reason I let you off so light, let you stick around, is so I could watch and see if you might be a man who c'd he'p me handle Spud, when the time's right."

Longarm leaned back in his chair. "Well, now. I could handle him, but whether I would handle him, that'd depend." He decided it was time to get on another track. When Tucker sobered up, he'd remember their talk, and might just regret it. He asked, "How'd you get to be boss man here, anyhow? I bet it took some doing."

"Sure it did, and here's how I done it." Tucker slapped the heavy ivory-handled Schneider & Glasswick revolver that hung from his gunbelt. The old-fashioned pistol had caught Longarm's eye the day before. He'd noticed it had been modified to handle cartridge loads, and had wondered why the sheriff still carried such an outdated weapon when new Colts were so cheap and plentiful.

Tucker continued, "I used this as free as I had to, just like I did in the war. This is the same gun Quantrill give me, you know that? Had it worked over, but I still hold to it. Maybe because it's the gun I killed my first man with."

Longarm saw that the sheriff was growing maudlin. It was time to cut off their talk. He said, "You let me think about what you've told me. We'll get down to cases later on."

"Wait a minute! Have we got a deal, or haven't we?"

"Maybe. I got to sleep on it. My tail'd be in a worse crack than yours would, if what we was doing leaked out."

"Don't worry about that." Tucker slapped his holster again. "I can shut up anybody that starts to give us trouble."

"I still want to think about it some. We'll talk some more tomorrow." Longarm stood up. "You going back to watch the fiesta?"

"No. I think I'll just stay here and lay up with Wahonta for a while." As Longarm went to the door, Tucker said, "One more thing, Custis. If we get in this deal, it wouldn't do for us to act too friendly. Them railroads swing a lot of steam. If they get a hint there's somethin' funny going on, they might even get them damn federal marshals in here to check up on us."

"Sure. I'll keep that in mind." Longarm opened the door and waved. "Enjoy yourself, Sheriff. We'll talk about things tomorrow."

Walking back to the plaza, Longarm took stock. He was beginning to make tracks to where he wanted to be. He'd found what was pretty sure to be the crossing of the new Laredo Loop, and his hunch was that it would somehow lead him to Nate Webster's trail. He was getting on terms with Tucker that should open the trail leading to information about Captain Hill and the 10th Cavalry deserters. Best of all, just by keeping quiet and letting Tucker's crooked imagination do his work for him, Longarm had repaired the damage done by his impulsive move in stopping the whipping the day he'd arrived in Los Perros. On the bad side, his snap decision to keep his real identity covered might hinder him from asking too many open questions. In a place like Los Perros, there'd be gossip aplenty. Everybody in town probably knew what was going on, and they'd be leery of answering questions put by a man who had no authority to do so. Still, in very little time, he'd made a pretty fair start, good enough for him to take the evening off and spend a little time at the fiesta with Lita. He had mixed feelings about Lita. There were times when she seemed to be little more than a child, and times when a woman showed through. Maybe how he'd act would depend on which side of her showed up strongest when the time came, if it came.

Things had gotten quieter and noisier both, Longarm thought when he entered the plaza. The two bands had reached some kind of truce, and were both playing in the plaza's center, taking turns instead of competing. The sun was low, and the uneven edges of the big open area were already deeply shadowed. Flickering hachones, bottles or funnel-capped cans filled with kerosene into which rag wicks had been inserted, were mounted on poles here and there, turning the plaza into a patchwork of bright spots and shadows.

Longarm started for the stall where he'd had breakfast, thinking he'd probably find Lita somewhere close to it, but before he could push very far through the crowd he was hailed by Lefty, the sheriff's deputy.

"Hey, Custis! I got a bottle in my pocket, come have a drink with me!"

Longarm didn't especially want a drink after the heavy slug he'd downed while talking with Tucker, but he didn't want to do anything that would stretch the taut truce that had been patched up among himself, Lefty, and Ralston. He said, "Don't mind if I do."

Lefty hauled a flask out of his pocket, and Longarm managed to swallow a light swig while appearing to take a heavy one. He gave the bottle back to Lefty, who tilted it and smacked his lips.

"Ah! That's prime stuff!" Lefty pocketed the bottle. "Listen, you don't need to be all by yourself, Custis. Want a partner to dance with? Hell, just ask any of these little greaser gals, they don't care who swings 'em around, long as he's got pants on."

"I'm just walking, Lefty, trying to stay out of trouble.

Looks to me like the easiest way to do that is not to horn in on somebody else's girl."

"They ain't goin' to be no trouble," Lefty assured him. "Ed's put the fear o' God in this Los Perros bunch."

"Just the same, I'll walk easy and keep quiet."

"Ah, what's a fiesta, if you don't have a dance or two?" Lefty scanned the crowd, saw a young girl and her escort a few feet away and waved to them. "Hey, Luis! You and Tina come here a minute!" As they started to obey, he said to Longarm, "I'll tell the gal to dance with you. Luis won't mind."

"Now, wait a minute—" Longarm began, but before he could go any further the couple had joined them and Lefty was making the arrangements he'd insisted on.

"Luis, this is a friend of mine, *Señor* Custis. He's a stranger here, wants to dance a round or two. You don't mind if Tina obliges him, do you?"

"If it is her wish," Luis replied. "I do not own her, *Señor* Lefty."

Lefty turned back to Longarm. "See? It's all fixed. Tina, this *señor* wants to dance with you a little while."

"*Porqué no?*" the girl shrugged. "A *baile* is for dancing, no? Come, *señor*. If you do not know the steps, I show you them."

"Now, hold on," Longarm protested. "When it comes to dancing, I got two left feet. I'm afraid I'd step all over you. But I thank you kindly for offering to show me, *Señorita* Tina."

"*Qué pasa?*" Tina asked Lefty. "*Dice el hombre quiere bailar, ahora el dice no. Qué chiste es?*"

This time it was the deputy who shrugged. "*Por supuesto, es un engano. El me diga quiere bailar.*"

"*Qué cosa!*" Luis exclaimed. "*Bastamente esta tontería! El gringo insulta mi Tina!*"

Longarm caught the gist of this exchange, and said to Luis, "No, *amigo. La senorita es—*" he sought the word he couldn't remember and finally found it—"*es muy linda.*"

"*Cagado!*" Luis exclaimed.

Lefty intervened. "*Cállate, Luis! Hablamos mas tarde. Véte, tu y Tina!*"

Muttering, Luis took Tina's arm and led her away.

Lefty said to Longarm, "Damn it, Custis, you like to've fixed yourself with that greaser. He was real put out, claimed you insulted his girlfriend."

"I got the general idea," Longarm said. "Don't blame it all on me, Lefty. I told you, I ain't interested in dancing. Thanks for your trouble, anyhow. Sorry I rubbed your friend the wrong way."

"Ah, he's just a spic I know," Lefty replied. "I guess I was a little too previous. Here, have another swig, and we'll forget it."

To placate him, Longarm took a token swallow, thanked Lefty, and walked on as soon as he could without offending the man further. He was still looking for Lita; the girl Lefty'd tried to get him to dance with couldn't hold a candle to her, he thought as he pushed toward the food stalls. He wondered why the deputy had suddenly become so friendly; the day before, he'd been standoffish, not as hostile as Spud, but a lot less amiable than Ralston. Maybe he'd been told by Tucker to be cooperative, maybe Ralston had talked him around, or maybe he'd just changed his mind by himself, Longarm thought. Whatever the reason, Lefty's solicitude had come as a real surprise.

As he'd half expected her to be, Lita was near the spot where her family's food stall had been earlier in the day. The stall was dismantled now, with trestles, planks, stove, and pots piled up ready to be carried home. A short distance away, Mamacita was gossiping with a group of women who, like her, were draped in black rebozos; two of the younger children had curled up at her feet and were sleeping. Lita stood off to one side, laughing and chattering with a few girls of her own age. She saw Longarm and tripped, light-footed, to greet him.

"Coos-tees! I think maybe you forget we going to dance."

"Don't count on me doing much dancing, Lita. Stomping around to music ain't right in my line."

"Is nothing, to dance. Come on, I show you. You learn real fast." She tucked her arm in Longarm's and led him to a space where there was room to maneuver. "Now. You listen to *la musica* and look how my feet they go. Then you see is easy."

Lita began to dance, facing Longarm and holding

his hands, arms stretched out. To humor her, Longarm began moving his feet, but they kept getting tangled up. It wasn't as much his clumsiness that was to blame as it was the sight of Lita's firm young breasts bouncing unconfined under her thin, scoop-necked blouse. She stopped and stamped a foot in mock anger.

"Coos-tees! You don' look at my feet, you watching my *tetas!*" she exclaimed. "Is not good you look so here! *Mamacita* might see."

"I told you I wasn't no dancer," he said. "Why don't we forget about dancing, and find some place where your mama can't watch you?"

"No!" Lita's eyes flashed and her smooth round chin set stubbornly, though she was still smiling at him. "We don' go nowhere till you dance with me! You look, now, I show you *mas despacio,* slow."

Longarm hadn't lied to either Lita or Tina. Though he'd done a little square dancing as a boy in West Virginia, he'd decided early that dancing was a time-wasting substitute for the real activity it imitated, and a lot less enjoyable. After making up his mind on that point, he'd lost interest in becoming skilled on the dance floor.

He said, "All right, if that's what you want. But you're just wasting your time, trying to turn me into a dancer."

Just as Lita began her second effort to teach him, Longarm saw Tina and Luis dancing their way toward them. Luis was trying to look unconcerned, but Tina's face was cast in a glowering frown. Longarm smelled trouble, and he wasn't disappointed. As soon as the other couple had gotten within a yard or so of him and Lita, Tina broke away from Luis and ran up to Longarm. Without any preliminary scolding, she brought up her hand and slapped his face.

"*Gringo cabrón!* You make *insulta* to me!" she cried loudly.

Around them, the other dancers stopped to watch. Luis took a step that brought him closer to Longarm. He demanded loudly, "What you do, *Tejano zopilote?* You wan' to take *mi querido* away from me? Just because you big gringo, you think you better as me, no?"

Longarm knew better than to respond to Luis's

insults either with words or with action. In that particular crowd, whatever he did could be wrong. The people would help Luis if it came to a fight, whether Luis attacked him or he struck the Mexican youth first. He felt a surge of relief when Lefty appeared from nowhere.

"All right!" the deputy called, *"Ningunes hace maleza!"*

His shout quieted the angry murmurs that were rising, and those nearest shoved back a bit. The spectators in the rear, who hadn't heard Lefty, and knew only that trouble was brewing, kept pushing in, though, trying to see what was going on.

Longarm said quickly, "Look, Lefty, this ain't no fight I picked. All of a sudden, this girl begun yelling, and slapping at me. Said I'd insulted her."

"He call me *puta!*" Tina said loudly.

Her voice low and angry, Lita spat, "You are *puta!*"

Longarm thought Lita was even prettier when she got mad than when she was just having fun.

Lefty asked him, "That right, Custis? You call this girl a whore, right here in front of her friends?"

"I never called her anything!"

"Mientrador!" Luis shouted. "I hear him say it! You get out of my way, Lefty! I wan' to fight him!"

"That's a pretty serious thing to do in these parts, Custis, insult a young lady. Looks to me like I got to do what Luis says, git outa the way and leave you two go at it."

Longarm had seen the setup coming. He wasn't worried about a fight with Luis, but he knew what Luis's friends would do—and, he thought, those friends include Lefty. I can put Luis down with a punch or two, but the minute we start mixing it up, his friends start closing in and out come the knives. Then Lefty can play it any way he wants. He can let 'em carve me, or he can shoot me and say he had to do it, or it was an accident while he was trying to break up the mob. And if I draw on this bunch, five shots won't stop 'em.

He said to Lefty, "You guarantee to stand by, see it's a fair fight? Just Luis and me, none of his compadres buttin' in?"

"Don't worry, Custis. You know these Mexicans

ain't no good with their fists. I'd say you can put him down with one punch, and that'll be it. But if I don't let him have a chance at you, this crowd's gonna git outa hand. Hell, you can see that yourself."

"All right. I'll take him on."

"You'll have to shed that gunbelt first. They wouldn't figure it was a fair scrap if I let you keep it on."

"Figured I'd have to do that." Longarm opened his frock coat and unbuckled his gunbelt. He handed the belt and holstered Colt to the deputy. "You take care of it for me."

"Sure. I won't let nobody grab it. The fight won't last but a minute anyhow, if you're the man I take you to be."

When Longarm shed his pistol, the tone of the crowd's rumbling changed. It was no longer as angry and threatening as it had been. There was a sudden jostling in the circle that enclosed Longarm and the others. He looked around to see several very sullen-faced men shoving into the front ranks of the onlookers. If Longarm had any doubt left that the deputy had set him up, it vanished at that point.

Oh-oh, he said to himself, here come the knife-hands.

Aloud, he said to Lefty, "Guess I better skin out of this monkey-coat, too. If I'm going to fight, I'll do it in style."

Slipping out of the sleeves of his Prince Albert, he folded the coat into a neat square. When he pushed it at Lefty, the deputy instinctively held out the hand with which he wasn't holding Longarm's gunbelt. Longarm shoved the coat against Lefty's chest, forcing him without seeming to into bringing up his entire arm to clasp the coat securely.

"What about your vest?" Lefty asked.

"Oh, I'll just keep it on. But I'll ask you to look after my watch. Don't want it to get busted."

He lifted the watch out of its pocket and ran his fingers along the chain to the pocket on the opposite side. Lefty's eyes were caught by the glitter of the watch. He didn't see the derringer until it was in Longarm's hand. Before the deputy could free his own loaded hands, the muzzle of the ugly little double-barreled derringer was pushing, cold and menacing, into his temple.

"There's two .44 slugs in this little thing." Longarm's voice was low, almost a whisper. "One of 'em will blow whatever you use for brains right outa that ugly skull of yours."

"You don't have to shoot me!" Lefty said. "I'll do just what you tell me to!"

"Good." Raising his voice, Longarm said, "Lita! Get over here, quick!" The girl ran to stand beside him. Longarm said, "Take his gun out and hand it to me. Soon as you do that, strap my gunbelt on me."

Lita moved without hesitating to follow instructions. He held out his free hand and she slid Lefty's pistol into it, butt-first. Then she relieved the deputy of Longarm's gunbelt.

Events had moved so swiftly that the crowd hadn't had time to grasp exactly what had happened. Those closest to the action were frozen into silent motionlessness, their eyes trying to follow everything. The angry mutterings from the more distant spectators began to subside as mob instinct transmitted the feeling that something was going on that should be heeded. In the momentary silence, Lita got Longarm's gunbelt around his waist. The pressure of her soft body, the warm scent that wafted up from the valley between her breasts, all registered on Longarm, but he put them out of his mind and concentrated on the job at hand.

He replaced the watch and derringer in their pockets and settled the gunbelt to his liking. He looked at Luis and said, "I don't like people that lie to me, Luis. I know this *hombre* here put you up to trying to get me. You better tell me about it."

Luis was eager to talk. "*Sí, señor*. It was hees idea. He say so soon you and me start to fight, then my *compañeros* they help out, with they knives."

"About what I figured. You ready to tell the sheriff that?"

"*El jefe?* Señor Tucker?" Luis hesitated only a moment. "*Sí.* I tell him, just like I say it to you."

"Good." Longarm turned to Lita. "You better come along, too. This crowd's going to be upset. After I'm gone, they might take their mad out on you."

"I go where you say to, with you, Coos-tees."

"Now, then." Longarm looked sternly at Lefty. "You're going to walk in front of me and Lita, and shoo people outa our way. If you got an idea I'm too good to backshoot a man, you're right, but I don't count rats like you as men. Now, march!"

With the deputy leading the way, motioning the onlookers aside, a path opened like magic. Longarm kept Lefty in front, Lita on his right, Luis and Tina on his left, as they moved quickly through the crowd of silent spectators, around the saloon, and into the sheriff's office.

Chapter 9

As Longarm had suspected he would be, Sheriff Tucker was still in bed with Wahonta. Tucker came in from the ell in response to Longarm's call, tugging his trousers up over his longjohns. His eyes snapped open wider than anyone had ever seen them do before when he saw the little group.

"Just what in billy-blue-hell's this all about?" he demanded.

"It ain't very important, Sheriff," Longarm answered. He took his Prince Albert from Lefty and slid his arms into the sleeves as he was talking. "Just figured you might want to explain to this deputy of yours that he can go to jail on charges of attempted murder and stirring up a riot, if I feel like pushing charges on him."

"Lefty?" Tucker was incredulous.

"He's the only deputy of yours I see here."

"Now, damn it, Custis, I let it pass by when you begun a ruckus with my men yesterday. I ain't so sure I'm of a mind to be as easy on you, if you're tryin' the same stunt again."

"Maybe you better listen to what this young fellow here's got to say, before you blame me for starting anything," Longarm suggested.

Tucker glared at the young Mexican. "All right, Luis, what you got to say about all this?"

Luis shuffled his feet, head hanging. "He tell you the true, *Señor Jefe*. *El Señor* Lefty, he wan' me and Tina, we make *alboroto*, and he wan' me I have some *toscos* ready, they should *matarle apuñalados* so soon we start."

"He tellin' the truth, Lefty?" Tucker demanded. "You put him up to startin' a ruckus with the crowd? And havin' his tough friends ready to knife Custis in the fracas?"

"It wasn't my idea, Ed," Lefty pleaded.

"I don't give a hot-pepper shit whose idee it was! I'm askin' you did you do it the way Luis told me?"

"Yeah, but it was Spud's idea!" Lefty confessed. "After Custis cost him that big pot in the poker game last night, and after he'd made fools outa all of us at the whippin', Spud figured we had a right to git even!"

"So you and Spud framed up this scheme to do it," Tucker nodded. "Well, I'm the one who tells you and Spud what you do and what you don't do! You don't get no wild hairs up your ass and go off on your own! And both of you knows that, by God!"

"What the sheriff's trying to tell you, Lefty," Longarm broke in, "is that we settled whatever differences there might've been between us, when we had a private talk a few hours back."

"Is that right, Ed?" Lefty asked.

"Yes, damn you, it is! And you and Spud come close to—" Tucker caught himself before he'd said too much. He changed the direction of his words. "You boys been with me long enough to know that I'm the one that gives orders who you're to take after or let alone."

Longarm had to compress his lips to keep from laughing. When he was sure his voice wouldn't give him away, he said, "Looks to me like your boys are getting outa hand, Sheriff. I'd say they need a good lesson."

"What'd your idea be of a lesson?"

"Is this one here any good with this gun I had the girl take off of him?" Longarm held Lefty's pistol out to the sheriff. "If he is, and you'd want to look the other way, I'm just about mad enough to face off with him."

"Well . . ." Tucker sounded doubtful. "That'd be a quick way to settle things, I guess. You sound pretty sure you can take him."

"If he can't use this any better'n he can hang onto it, I don't guess I'd have much to worry about." Casually, Longarm nudged aside the lapel of his coat and rested a hand on the butt of his Colt. He had an idea that both Lefty and Tucker would recognize the professional's touch shown by his gunbelt and holster. His guess was correct; Lefty took one look and started shaking his head.

"That's a shooter's rig if I ever seen one, Ed. I'd just the same as suiciding myself if I went up against him."

"Now, you can count on me to see it's a fair and square showdown," Tucker told the deputy. It was obvious to Longarm that the sheriff was enjoying watching a man squirm, especially since it wasn't costing him anything.

"No, Ed. I ain't fool enough to take on a deal like that."

Tucker's voice showed his disgust. "You're a damn sorry turd, Lefty. Now, in case you'd forgot, you got a job I told you to do tonight. Git the hell outa here and git on it! When you git back, you and me and Spud will set down and have a little private talk ourselves." He took the pistol that Longarm still held and handed it to Lefty. "Maybe you better practice up with this, just in case you make another mistake like the one you just did."

After Lefty had gone, Longarm told Tucker, "You might as well send these other two kiting." He indicated Luis and Tina. "All they done was what your man told 'em."

"What about the other girl?"

"I'll take care of her."

"I'll just bet you will!" the sheriff chuckled. He waved a hand at Luis and Tina. "Git! Vamoose!" As they left, he took Longarm by the arm and led him to one side, where Lita couldn't overhear. In a half-whisper, he said, "Look here, Custis, Lefty and Spud stepped outa line, but I didn't put 'em up to it. Fact is, you was more'n half right earlier, when you said they was gittin' uppity. After we wind up the deal with your railroad, how'd you like to settle down here and throw in with me?"

"I'd have to think on it, just like I'm still thinking about the other deal." Longarm stared into Tucker's little pig eyes. "I guess you'd look for me to help you get rid of Spud? Maybe Lefty, too?"

"Well, it'd even things up if you was around backin' my play, when the time comes for me to make it."

"We'll talk about it more, later on." Longarm turned to Lita. "Come on. I'll see you get back to where you belong."

When he closed the door of the sheriff's office behind them, Lita said, "I think you a very brave *hombre*, Coos-tees. I like you, *mucho muchissimo!* You better kiss me now." When he hesitated, she asked, "You think maybe I'm still *niña*, leetle girl? You don' look at me like that when my *tetas* jiggle when I show you the dance, no? All right, I show you more!"

Lita pulled Longarm's head down and her mouth found his. Her lips were soft and firm in turn, pulsing and alive. Her tongue darted into his mouth, hot, seeking, probing. He felt the pressure of her breasts on his chest as she clung to him. Then, before he'd expected her to, Lita broke off the kiss.

"So, what you think now, Coos-tees?"

"I think we oughta find a better place than this. Come on." He led her to the corral. There was a new moon, hanging high; it gave little light, and in three hours, four at most, it would be gone. Still, it was bright enough to see Tordo's gray form in the corral.

"You ride a horse?" he asked.

"No. I don' know about a horse. Better I ride with you."

Longarm didn't waste time cinching on his McClellan. His saddle blanket hung over the corral rail beside the McClellan and his bridle; he took the bridle, ducked through the pole fence, and slid the bit into Tordo's mouth. He led the dapple out of the enclosure, tossed the blanket over his back, and lifted Lita on. He leaped on behind her. He'd never ridden the gray without a saddle before, but he trusted Tordo's instincts. Besides, they weren't going very far.

During the short ride to the sandspit north of Los Perros, far enough beyond the last of the houses to insure privacy, he held Lita close to him. He left the reins slack, guiding the dapple with the pressure of his knees, while his hands explored her breasts under the thin, low-necked blouse. He bent his head now and then to nuzzle her neck and bare shoulders. There was a smell of spice—cinnamon or cloves, he thought, or perhaps something he couldn't name—that clung to her skin. Her hair, long and black and shining in the moonlight, brushed back across his cheeks as Tordo moved over the last stretch of hard earth before the thudding of his hooves was swallowed by soft sand. They rode almost to the end of the sandspit before Longarm reined in and jumped to the ground.

He reached up and lifted Lita from the dapple's back. His hands spanned her waist, and he felt the quick pulsations of her breathing as he held her briefly while lowering her to the ground. Her head came only to his shoulders; she had to stand on tiptoe to bring her mouth up to meet his. He felt her hands travel across his shoulders, slipping off his coat and vest, then she was fumbling at his gunbelt. He let go her soft buttocks to help her, and eased the gun carefully down to his coat, where it would not touch the sand. Then his hands went back to pull her close to him once more, her soft body nestling close, her hips undulating as she felt him grow hard against her.

"Chíngame!" she urged, whispering. "I think I die if you don't!" Her hands became busy with Longarm's britches, freeing his belt, fumbling open the buttons below it. She sensed his hesitation. "Don' worry, Coos-tees, I been with men before." She'd liberated his erection now, and added with a sigh, "But not a man like you!"

Her hands flashed swiftly in the soft moonlight, grasping her full skirt and pulling it high. She wore nothing underneath it. Longarm got a glimpse of her dark pubic hair as she brought a leg up to straddle him, squeezing her thighs around him tightly. Holding him between her moistly warm thighs, she moved her hips gently back and forth. Longarm began to believe that Lita was, as she'd insisted, no longer a little girl.

For a few moments they clung, kissing, while Lita moved her hips, rubbing him slowly. She began to gasp. Longarm picked her up by the waist and lifted her off the ground. Lita spread her legs and guided him into her hot throbbing depth, wrapped her legs around his waist and locked them behind his back, to pull him into her fully. She screamed then, a light, breathy cry of delight. Longarm braced his legs by spreading them and supported her buttocks with his hands, squeezing their soft, firm muscles. Her body twisted, her gasps became a sobbing laugh of pain and pleasure as with his hands he moved her back and forth. He felt the vibrations begin deep in her body.

They spread, her muscles undulating, until she was trembling. Her head fell back, the laughing sobs rising from her taut throat as she let ecstasy take her and shake her until, still trembling, she gave a final gasp and went limp in his hands.

He supported her gently, still buried deeply in her, still rock-hard and unsatisfied. "Hold on around my neck," he told the girl as soon as he felt her muscles become firm again. Lita clasped her hands behind his head, and Longarm moved with short careful steps to where Tordo stood, only a few feet away. Whisking the saddle blanket off the gray's back, he managed to unfold it and after a fashion to spread it on the sand.

Longarm's britches had slipped down when he took the few steps needed to reach the blanket and place it on the ground. He sidled along its edge, Lita still locked close to him, her hot wetness urging him to hurry. He was holding himself back, not wanting to enjoy his orgasm alone, giving Lita as much time as he could manage to be ready to share it with him. He dropped to his knees on a corner of the blanket and in the same unbroken motion lunged forward, pinning her beneath him, stabbing even deeper into her than he'd been while they were standing up.

"*Madre de Dios! Que verga!*" she cried out. "*Qué cosa maravillosa! Es mas qué chorizo, es un grifo de caballo! Dame todo, Coos-tees! Ándale! Ándale!*"

Longarm obeyed her demands. Although he didn't understand the words, her tone told him that Lita needed no more time. He thrust fiercely and she splayed her legs wide to engulf him, her hips rocking. Her trembling began almost at once. Longarm was past being ready, but after the interruption of moving, it took him a few minutes to reach a peak again. He rocked faster and faster, racing Lita's beginning orgasm, until he caught up and pushed hard one last time, and held himself deep within her while her cries broke the cool night air, until his shaking ended and he fell aside, leaving the girl sprawled on the rough wool beside him, both of them limp and spent.

They lay, not moving or talking, watching the moon as it waned imperceptibly, then began playing the game of undressing one another. The night breeze was soft on their naked bodies. Lita lay with her head cradled on Longarm's shoulder. Now and then she'd rub her cheek on his skin, or he'd raise a hand to caress her breasts, his hard fingertips gentle as they traced the puckered tips of her dark rosettes. As their vigor returned the kissing began again, and their hands on each other grew more inquisitive. Longarm rubbed his palm down the smooth warm flesh of Lita's stomach and combed his fingers through her brush to feel the fresh moisture stealing out between her thighs. She spread them for him, and his fingers explored more deeply. Lita's hands were cradling and hefting him, curling around, weighing, feeling his erection begin to grow.

"*Es muy hermoso, su grifo,* Coos-tees. But I like it more inside me, not in *mis manos.* You wan' I show you how I like?"

"Sure. If you like it, I will, too."

Her hand went to his hip, lightly pulling, and he responded by turning on his side. Lita was lying on her back; she threw her legs across his body and used her heels to pull herself close, then to pull even closer when he was inside her. She moved with measured slowness, sighing now and then, a small healthy gust of breath, and Longarm lay quite still, contented to feel her inner pulsing wrapping him in soft sensation. She shuddered gently, relaxed, and lay motionless for several minutes. Then she began a slow rotation of her hips, digging her heels into his back, and moved this way until another shudder seized her, quicker this time than before. Once more she lay quiet. Longarm stretched a hand and grasped her breast, its firm smoothness resilient and alive under his palm. He cupped his hand gently, moving it to find the other breast and caress it.

Lita began to quiver. She pulled away and brought her legs up in the air. In the brush between them the waning moon caught glints like dewdrops. "Go in me, Coos-tees!" she gasped. "*Al frente! Con su grifo de caballo! Chíngame duro, presteza! Duro! Duro!*"

Longarm didn't know all the words this time either, but no interpreter was needed. He lunged into her swiftly and fiercely, ignoring her cry of pleasure or pain, arched his back above her and pushed hard, driving deep, the flood building in him forcing him to speed, to thrust, until it crested and burst and Lita's cries of *"Duro! Duro!"* faded to a long, choking moan, and then to silence.

Longarm relaxed, lying heavily on top of her, too spent to move. Lita did not object, but bore his weight with little breaths of pleasure. The moon had gone by now, and the night lay dark and still around them. After a long while, he rolled off and lay by her.

"Tu es mucho hombre, Coos-tees," she murmured, nibbling at the lobe of his ear. "You still think I am *niña,* now?"

"If I ever mistook you for a little girl, I sure know better," he replied. "You're *muy mujer,* Lita."

"I make you feel good, no?"

"You make me feel good, yes. How you feel?"

"You wait a little while, I show you."

Longarm's chuckle was cut short before it got out of his throat. Distantly, the quiet was broken by an irregular thudding of many hooves and the muted blats of cattle protesting being night-driven. He sat up quickly, there was no mistaking the sound.

Lita sat up, too. "What is it, Coos-tees? What you hear?"

"Hush a minute. I'm trying to figure which way they're coming from."

"They come from the *nordeste,* from *los ranchos grandes de Tejas,"* she said casually, as though surprised that Longarm didn't know such a simple fact.

"How do you know?"

"Por supuesto, Coos-tees, everybody know this thing. Is happen *muchos veces.* Maybe three, four weeks was *otro hato de ganados* go *sobre del rio."*

"You mean everybody in Los Perros knows there's cattle being drove across to Mexico pretty regular?"

"De verdad. Porqué?"

"Because them steers are rustled, Lita. They're stolen from ranches up along the Pecos and above there."

"Sí. Esta conozco. Why you don't ask me, you wan' to know?"

"Because I didn't realize you knew about it." Longarm stood up, pulling Lita to her feet. "Come on, put your clothes on. We got to get out of here."

"Porqué? You tired *hace chinga?"*

105

"No, I ain't tired. If I had my druthers, I'd stay here all night with you. But I got business to look after."

By now, the movement of the cattle herd was much louder. Longarm judged the first riders hazing the steers would be getting to the ford within fifteen or twenty minutes. Dark as it was, there'd be no chance of him and Lita being seen, but the rustlers might have guards, outriders, ahead of the herd, or flanking it, and there was no place on the sandspit for them to hide.

He told Lita, "I'll carry you back to town. I got to go pick up my gear anyhow, get the horse saddled proper." He was pulling on his clothes as he spoke.

"Coos-tees. You go away, now?"

"For a spell. I don't know how long."

"But you come back, no?"

"Sure. I'll be back, soon as I can. You ain't seen the last of me yet, Lita." Then, in sober afterthought, he added, "At least, I hope you ain't."

Longarm dropped Lita off at the spot she pointed out, a shanty a short distance from the plaza. He rode to the corral and in swift silence, working by feel, saddled Tordo. Then he made short work of collecting his bedroll, saddlebags, and rifle from his room. Within little more than half an hour he was back at the sandspit, in time to hear distantly the splashings of the last few steers being driven across the river.

There wasn't enough light for him to tell how many men were riding herd. By the same token, the rustlers wouldn't be able to see him, either, sitting at a safe distance from the crossing, getting his clues from sounds alone. He waited until the hoofbeats and splashings and blattings subsided, and the rustlings in the chamizal on the Mexican side of the border were barely audible. Then he nudged Tordo ahead and across the Rio Grande, in pursuit of the stolen herd.

Chapter 10

Following the rustlers was easy, even in the dark. The cattle cut noisily through the belt of chamizal that extended only a mile or two beyond the river, then angled south and west. Longarm stopped in the brush to let the steers and their drivers get safely ahead of him, for after the chamizal ended there was no cover. Past the strip of brush, the land ran level for a score of miles before it rose at the beginning of the foothills of the Serranias de Burro, further west. It was a harsh plain, as Longarm saw when daybreak came, a place of scanty vegetation, rolling gently between river and foothills, dotted by groves of mesquite scrub and cactus, cut by dry arroyos and an occasional shallow canyon in which there might run a thread-thin stream, more creek than river.

For once, Longarm was pleased with the glacial slowness shown by the army's procurement branch. The ordnance map he carried in his saddlebags dated from the U.S.-Mexican War of 1846, and had been prepared for troops being staged to invade Mexico from the Texas border. It covered the area he was traveling through in very good detail. Studying it, he could figure what he'd do if he was driving a stolen herd to Laredo, and was able to ride unworried at a distance from the rustlers.

There were no settlements within more than sixty miles of the Burro foothills, no people to see the moving cattle—or the lone rider following them. Somewhere to the south, probably along the Zarro or San Carlos River, he was pretty sure there'd be a ranch used by the ring that ran the new Laredo Loop. They'd need such a place, where brands could be altered and bills of sale forged to allow the cattle to be returned to Texas and sold at the Laredo railhead without questions being raised.

As he'd expected, the rustlers turned the herd almost

due south after angling in from the border. Longarm's map had led him to the most likely place ahead of the slower-moving herd; he'd gotten to the shallow valley he'd guessed would be their path just before sunup. Finding a cut in which to hide the dapple, Longarm had waited an hour before the steers passed by, a good three-quarters of a mile distant, too far to see anything except the dust cloud they'd raised in passing. He'd leaned back, resting against a convenient rock, while he chewed jerky and hardtack and sipped from the canteen. He'd given up wishing for a cheroot. After having failed to find any at Fort Lancaster or Los Perros, he'd reminded himself philosophically that he'd intended to give up the damned things, anyhow.

Stomach filled, he'd dozed. There was no great hurry. The herd would leave an easy trail to follow, and he'd had a busy day and night. When he woke up, he was sweating; the sun was blazing clear in a bowl of cloudless blue. The trail ahead promised to be a hot one, and his map told him it led through a baked, water-scarce land. He was splashing water from his cupped hand into Tordo's mouth when the riders passed. Sunlight glinting from a bit or strap-buckle, or perhaps from the silver conchos of a hatband, alerted him to their approach. Their path was too close for comfort, he thought. He led the gray deeper into the narrow arroyo and clamped a hand over his muzzle. He wasn't sure whether Tordo had the habit of whinnying at the approach of strange horses; he'd never been with the gray in a situation like this before. The restraining hand eliminated a needless risk.

There were four riders. Longarm watched their backs as they loped their mounts in a direction that would take them straight to the ford, and wished he could've seen their faces. Old son, he told himself, those hombres backtracking has got to mean just one thing. They've left the steers with two or three men up along the trail, and there'll be another herd crew taking over to push the critters on to their headquarters. And that's the place I want to find.

Mounting, he set Tordo to a trail-burning lope, picking up the broad path of droppings and faint hoofprints that the steers had left. He kept a close watch for dust ahead of him, but saw none. Instead, after he'd covered four or five miles, he saw the thin line of smoke from a small fire rising from a canyon half a mile ahead. Neither riders nor steers were visible. Longarm risked riding almost to the rim of the canyon before dismounting. He looped Tordo's reins over a mesquite limb and took his rifle from the scabbard that hung slanted in front of the saddle. Dodging from one area of scant cover to the next, he worked his way slowly to the rim.

A small creek, little more than a series of bathtub-sized pools connected by a trickle that in places narrowed to a hand's width, ran through the canyon. Steers straggled along the creek. Some drank from the pools, some looked for graze on the barren soil, others just stood staring vacantly into nowhere. Longarm couldn't see all the brands, but he noted that at least five were represented in the herd. It was a typical rustler's herd, small enough to be moved quickly and quietly by just a handful of men.

At one of the pools upstream from where the herd milled, two men squatted beside a tiny campfire. A tin skillet sat canted on a boulder near them, beside the tiny blaze that had drawn Longarm to the spot. Their horses were unsaddled, tethered to a bush a few paces from the fire. The men were eating from tin plates.

Their backs were to him, so Longarm took his time studying the way the land lay. There were no boulders or rock outcroppings near the fire big enough to give the two any kind of cover. Their rifles were with their saddles, beside the tethered horses. He had the advantage of both position and surprise, and the need for information outweighed the easier alternative of dogging the rustled herd to the gang's headquarters. Longarm sighted quickly and sent a slug from the Winchester into the skillet.

Amid splinters of rock and with a metallic clanging that started the steers jumping and running aimlessly, the skillet bounced three feet into the air. The men dropped their plates and leaped to their feet, hands reaching for revolver-butts.

"Get your hands up! First one that touches his gun's a dead man!" Longarm shouted. He was still hidden by the boulder behind which he'd crouched to survey the camp.

His call stopped the rustlers' hands in midair. Slowly their arms went up, and they turned carefully to face the direction from which the command had come. Longarm wasn't too greatly surprised to see that one of the pair was Lefty. He'd been very sure, after Lita's revelation of the night, that Sheriff Tucker was involved in the rustling ring, and Tucker had sent Lefty off with a reminder of a job that waited for him.

When he was sure that both men were frozen into position, Longarm stood up and stepped from behind the boulder. Keeping the men covered by his Winchester, he began to pick his way across the bare, rockstrewn ground down the sloping canyon sides.

Lefty's companion said something to the deputy when Longarm had closed half the distance between them, but Longarm was too far away to hear the remark or Lefty's answer. He called, "Keep your mouths shut! If I get the idea you're framing to jump me when I get close, my trigger finger might get sorta nervous!"

There was no more conversation between the two. Longarm was within thirty yards of them when the steer locoed. He hadn't noticed the animal in particular, all along the creek there were cattle running and snorting, disturbed by his shot. The one that panicked hadn't done anything to attract attention; it just reacted in the way half-wild range cattle do at the sight of a moving man on foot. The steer pawed the ground, bellowed, and charged Longarm from a distance of less than fifty feet.

Longarm swiveled and dropped the animal with a single quick shot, but the diversion gave the unknown rustler the chance for which he must've been watching. The instant Longarm swung his rifle to shoot the locoed steer, the rustler dropped his arms and drew.

Longarm caught the move in the corner of his eye and dove for the dirt. He rolled twice before snapshooting. The rustler's slug kicked up dust where Longarm had recently been, but the man dropped before he could get off a second shot. Longarm lay still, his rifle ready. The downed outlaw didn't move. Neither did Lefty. He'd seen Longarm shoot before, and kept his hands safely in the air.

Keeping the deputy covered, Longarm rose to his feet. He walked slowly toward the men, his eyes darting from one to the other. Ten feet from the campfire, he stopped.

"All right, Lefty. Seems like I sorta got in the habit of taking your gun away from you. Lift it out easy, and toss it over here."

Lefty obeyed. When the pistol lay on the ground at Longarm's feet, he said, "I told that damn fool not to try it. He got itchy, soon as he saw you was by yourself. Wanted both of us to throw down on you, but I told him I wanted to live a while longer."

Longarm nodded. "You was smart, for a change. Who's your friend?"

"Name's Sanchez, and that's all I know. Never heard anybody call him anything else."

"Is he dead?"

Sanchez answered the question with an involuntary twitching. Longarm took two quick steps and kicked the fallen rustler's pistol out of reach. He took his eyes off Lefty long enough to glance at the downed outlaw. Blood was seeping through Sanchez's shirt. The rifle slug had taken him in the side, between his belt and bottom rib. Sanchez was beginning to groan.

"You better see what you can do to help him, Lefty," Longarm ordered. "Probably he ain't worth saving, but maybe he'll live long enough to hang."

Lefty bent over Sanchez, loosened the man's belt, and pulled his clothing aside to uncover the wound. "He's lucky," Lefty said, then added, somewhat doubtfully, "I guess."

Longarm's bullet had plowed through the flesh just above Sanchez's hipbone. It was too shallow to have hit a vital spot. The wound would hurt and perhaps disable the man for a while, but it was a long way from being fatal.

"Put some kind of bandage on him," Longarm told Lefty. "He'll live long enough to tell me a few things I'm curious to know.'"

While Lefty worked over the wounded man, Longarm collected the rifles and pistols belonging to the pair and carried them far enough from the fire so they'd be out of diving distance. There was a coffee pot propped on a stone behind the boulder off which he'd shot the frying pan. He set the pot on the dying fire and rinsed out one of the tin cups that lay by it while he waited for the coffee to heat.

Lefty stood up. "I guess I got him stopped bleeding. He's gonna be sore as hell for a while, though."

"It's his own fault," Longarm said unemotionally. "Only a damn fool tries to draw on a man who's got him covered with a rifle."

"You are wrong, *gringo*." Sanchez's voice was weak, but his tone was positive. "Is better a bullet under the sky with my hands free than a rope in a jailyard."

"Can't say I'd argue that," Longarm replied. "Except that a man's better off not setting hisself up for a rope to start with."

"Look here, Custis," Lefty broke in, "just who in hell are you? You damn sure ain't some drifter that just happened to wind up in Los Perros accidental-like. I'm guessing you're either an enforcer from the cattleman's association, or a lawman of some kind."

Longarm had decided the time had come to begin working on his primary assignment. To get Lefty started talking, he'd have to tell him who he was, and that revelation couldn't be delayed much longer. If he had to keep the word from being passed to Tucker, he'd hustle the deputy past Los Perros on the Mexican side of the river and put him in Roy Bean's jail up to the north, or even haul him to Fort Lancaster.

"That's a good guess," he told Lefty. "You just know the first part of my name, for openers. Custis Long is the full handle, and I'm a Deputy U.S. Marshal working out of Denver." He took out his wallet and showed his badge.

"You're a hell of a ways from home base."

"Not so's you'd notice, or that it'd make much of a never-mind. Los Perros is like a lot of places, it ain't organized by the state, so that leaves it under federal jurisdiction."

"You checking out the rustling? Or hot on Ed's trail?"

"What I'm really here for is to run down a cavalry captain named Hill, who took off from Fort Lancaster after a couple of his troopers who deserted. And there's a Texas Ranger missing, too, name's Nate Webster. That's what got me interested in your rustling ring; Webster was checking to see if the Laredo Loop was working again when he dropped outa sight."

"Jesus! Ed thought him and his partners over here in Mexico was too smart for anybody to catch up with so quick. They figured they'd be able to go five or six years before the law come noseying around, and here it ain't been quite two years."

"Tucker didn't fool anybody. I had him figured for one of the kingpins in the rustling after I'd talked to him for ten minutes."

Lefty sighed. "Yeah. Ed's got sorta careless of late. He ain't the man he was, six, eight years ago."

"That's why you and Spud began scheming to push him out, I'd imagine," Longarm said.

"It was mostly Spud's idea."

Longarm remembered Lefty's efforts to shift the blame for the attempted attack by Luis onto Spud. He recognized Lefty's value as the weak link in Tucker's outfit and pressed on. "This is as good a time as any for you to tell me about the whole setup," he told the deputy. "And I mean all of it, including the Mexican side."

"Sanchez can tell you more about that than I can. He knows it better."

"How about it?" Longarm asked the wounded Mexican. "You ready to talk?"

"Chinga su madre, federalista! You don' get nothin' out of me!" Sanchez spat.

Longarm tried reason. "I'll find out soon enough without you helping me, Sanchez. But if you talk, it might save you from hanging."

"No soy graznido, hombre! No dice nada, nada, nada!"

"You might as well spill what you know," Lefty advised Sanchez. "I seen this fellow work. He'll find out what he wants, one way or the other."

"Cago en su boca, Lefty. *Ahorita, no hablo Inglés."* Sanchez turned his face away. Longarm knew he'd get nothing more out of the man until he'd had time to apply a lot more persuasion.

"I don't need you to tell me anything," he told the Mexican. "You and your friends left a trail a tenderfoot can follow." He turned back to Lefty. "You going to do like him, or you going to be smart?"

"What'll it get me if I tell you?"

"It might not get you much, except save you a stretched neck."

"Well, shit! I guess I might as well. Ask ahead."

"We can save the rustling part till later," Longarm said. "But you can start by telling me about those four men I'm looking for."

"Spud's the one that'll have to tell you about them nigger bluecoats," Lefty began.

"No. You better tell me, right now!"

"Hell, I don't know where they are!"

"Make a real good guess, then. But do it now. Don't waste my time, or I might run outa patience with you."

"Well." Lefty saw he was cornered. "You know how Spud and Ed is about niggers."

"No, I don't. I might guess, but I'd rather hear you say it."

"They're old Quantrill riders, and anybody who was with *him* ain't exactly what you'd call a nigger lover. Spud's worse'n most, though, I guess. Anyhow, them troopers made two or three real bad mistakes. They come into Los Perros, that's number one. They strutted into Baskin's saloon, that's number two. Then they sassed Spud, and that's number three. You ain't goin' to find them troopers, not ever, Marshal."

"You still haven't told me what Spud did."

"When they give him hard lip in the saloon, he cut one of 'em down, right then and there. He made the other one tote the body out in the brush somewheres. Don't ask me whereabouts, because Spud never told me, and I had sense enough not to ask him. Anyhow, the live one never come back."

"You're pretty sure Spud killed him, too?"

"Sure as God made little apples. He just as good as told me he did. Spud was havin' one of his mean spells right then, so I didn't wanta rile him by askin' questions."

"All right." Mentally, Longarm wrote off the two deserters. That left two men still missing. "What about Captain Hill? And the ranger, Nate Webster?"

"They both come through Los Perros all right. The ranger was the first one to show up, about a month before the army man. Both of 'em visited with Ed, but I don't know what they talked about. He never did tell me. Only thing I'm sure of, the ranger was in town one day and gone the next, and the captain was, too."

"You're not exactly a goldmine of information, Lefty," Longarm observed. "You'll have to do better than that."

"So help me, Marshal, I'm tellin' you all I know. I can't tell you things I don't know, now can I?"

"You were on the inside, Lefty. Put your mind to it. I'm right sure you'll remember a few things you've forgot."

"Well . . ." the deputy frowned. "I did hear Ed say he'd sent the ranger kitin' off on a wild-goose chase over the river."

"That's better. Where, over the river?"

"He didn't say where. Just Mexico, something like that."

"What about Hill? Did Tucker give him the same treatment?"

"Just about. Ed knew Spud had killed them troopers, you see. He had to get the captain outa town fast, before he could ask too many questions. So Ed made out the men had hightailed it right on through town and across the river."

"Then the captain followed the trail Tucker gave him?"

"Well, you couldn't call it a trail. He didn't aim the bluecoat in any special direction, the way I got it. And that's all I know, Marshal. It's God's own truth, that's all I can tell you!"

"It all hangs together," Longarm nodded. "And I don't think you're a good enough liar to make up a yarn like that, Lefty."

"If you was to string me up right here and now, I couldn't tell you no more," Lefty said fervently.

"All right. Let's get to this rustling business. Looks to me like you and your friend Sanchez are waiting for a bunch of hands to come and drive this herd on south. Is that right?"

Sanchez spoke for the first time since he'd disclaimed any more knowledge of English. *"Este hijo de puta, Esquivel! Es su tacha!"*

Longarm asked Sanchez, "Who's Esquivel?" When the man didn't answer, he said to Lefty, "I don't need to be told that, I guess. I'd say Esquivel's the fellow that was supposed to be here to meet you, ain't he? To take the herd on south?"

Lefty nodded. "Yeah. Him and his bunch was supposed to be here by sunup. Spud and our boys had to start back by then."

"What about you, Lefty? Were you going to collect Tucker's payoff here, or were you going to the headquarters place for it?"

"Lefty!" Sanchez warned. *"No mandaté esto!"*

"Hell, Sanch, it won't hurt to tell him," Lefty said. "I was goin' along with Esquivel. It's near enough so's I could be back in Los Perros early tomorrow."

Longarm didn't comment on the deputy's remark, though it pinpointed for him the location of the rustlers' headquarters. All he'd have to do was study his map and find a spot where there was plenty of water, within a four- or five-hour ride. Instead, he asked, "How many's coming with this Esquivel hombre?"

"I don't know. Four or five, I guess. Ed didn't say."

"Then, if you—" Longarm began.

A shout from the canyon rim interrupted him. He looked around, and saw four riflemen standing, shielded by boulders, their guns leveled.

"Damn!" he snapped. "Looks like I waited too long to start us heading back to the river! That'd be your pal Esquivel!"

Sanchez started to laugh, though the effort brought a grimace of pain to his face. "You a fool to waste time, *gringo!* Now it is you who will get *el tiro,* not me!"

Longarm looked at the opposite rim of the canyon. Two more men were posted there, rifles covering the camp. His own Winchester was leaning against the rock where he'd put it when he heated the coffee. He estimated his chance of surviving if he tried for it, and gave up the idea. Suicide wasn't in his plans.

A horseman appeared behind the men on the south rim of the canyon. Motioning them to follow him, he walked his horse down the slope. When he'd gotten close enough for Longarm and the others to see him clearly, Sanchez let out a despairing moan.

"Sangre de la Virgen! No es Esquivel! Ahora todos tomen el tiro! Ellos son rurales!"

Chapter 11

When he heard Sanchez's words, Longarm felt better about everything. The *rurales,* the Mexican Federal Rural Police, occupied a position similar to that of the federal marshals in the United States. They operated out of a number of strategically located field headquarters scattered throughout Mexico, and answered only to the national government. He watched the mounted rurales approach with the feeling that after he'd identified himself and explained everything, they'd give him what help was needed to capture the rustler force that was now on its way and long overdue.

Lefty said in a whisper, "God a-mighty, Marshal! If Sanchez is right, we're in trouble up to our assholes now!"

"You and Sanchez, maybe. There ain't no way that bunch your man Esquivel's bringing along can stand up to these fellows."

"Is that how you figure?" Lefty shook his head, and with a sincerity that Longarm knew couldn't be put on, said, "Don't fool yourself for a minute. They won't help you. Shit, they won't like you because you're a gringo and in Mexico. I tell you, the only thing the rurales gives a fuck about is the rurales."

"What're you driving at, Lefty? They're federal police; so am I, only from another country. If you're trying to spook me, get me to help you outa this jackpot by telling them you and me are working together, you're about to be disappointed."

"You ever run up against the rurales before?"

"Sure. About four years ago, when I come down here on another case. They were real helpful. I tagged 'em as a pretty good outfit."

"Four years ago, they was. That's before Diaz got to be boss of Mexico again. The rurales is his boys now, just like me and Spud and the rest of our bunch is Ed Tucker's men. And if you think he's a bad one, you don't know what bad is, yet."

Longarm wasn't convinced that the deputy could be believed, but told himself that he'd find out soon enough. The rider coming down the slope was almost within speaking distance. He carried a pistol in one hand, but a rifle was slung across his back. His men were still only halfway down from the rim; they were moving cautiously, keeping their weapons ready. The horseman reined in and looked at Longarm, Lefty, and Sanchez for a moment before speaking.

"*Qué tenemos aquí?*" he finally asked. "*Quien hace tiros oíagamos un momento pasado?*"

"He wants to know who was doin' the shooting a while back," Lefty translated for Longarm. "What you want me to say, Marshal?"

"I'll do my own talking," Longarm replied curtly. He asked the rurale, "You speak English, mister? *Habla Inglés?*"

"*Sí, un poco.* A little bit, I speak."

"It was me done that shooting." Longarm spoke slowly and distinctly; in a situation like this he didn't trust his slight knowledge of Spanish, even though a lot of it had come back to him since he'd arrived on the border. "I'm a U.S. Deputy Marshal. Same kinda job you got, understand?" The rurale gave no evidence that he was following the explanation, so Longarm went on, "If you won't get trigger-nerved, I'll reach in my pocket and show you my badge."

His brow knitted, the rurale said, "*Un federalista de los Estados Unidos?* You can prove this thing you say?"

Moving very slowly indeed, Longarm pulled his coat lapel aside and took out his wallet. He flipped it open to show the badge pinned in its fold. "Here. Look at it."

"*Dameló,*" the man commanded. "Give me to it."

Longarm stepped up and handed over the wallet. The rurale took it, examined the badge carefully, opened the folded wallet, and looked at the money it contained.

"*Muy interesante,*" he grunted. A grin began to form on his face. "Anybody can carry a badge, *hombre.*" He put the wallet in his pocket. "I keep this for now."

"Wait a minute!" Longarm protested. "That's my badge and my money you got there!"

"No apasarse, hombre. I weel take good care of it. And your gun, too." He turned, saw that his men were now just behind him, and ordered one of them, *"Tóme su pistola."* He indicated the rifles that were off to one side, the pistols lying on the ground near them. To another of his men, he said, *"Los fusiles y pistolas ayá, ponerles."*

Both men moved quickly to obey, one starting for Longarm, the other to collect the rest of the guns. When the rurale who was taking Longarm's Colt saw the gold watch chain snaked across his vest, the man reached for it greedily. The commander saw the move.

"Cuidado, Felipe! Este botin toca al Capitán Ramos! El no le gusta si tome el reloj del gringo!" he called.

His threat was enough to cause the rurale to pull his hand back as if the watch chain were red-hot. Longarm caught enough of what the commander said to deduce that he wasn't going to be searched thoroughly until he was in the presence of the captain himself. He reminded himself to try to find an opportunity to drop the watch into the pocket that held his derringer, so the chain wouldn't be so highly visible.

There was a moment of inaction while the men who'd taken the guns showed them to their leader. He hefted Longarm's Colt, but didn't find it to his liking, for he waved the weapons away with a disgusted grunt. Longarm used the pause to study the mounted rurale.

He didn't really like what he saw. The commander wore a gold-embroidered charro outfit, short jacket, tight pants, high-crowned felt sombrero, calf-high boots. This seemed to be the uniform of the rurales, though none of the men wore garments as elaborately decorated as that of their leader; what braiding their jackets and hats showed was predominantly silver with an occasional golden accent-stitch. It wasn't the commander's clothing that stirred Longarm's concern, but the man's face. He had the cold, slitted eyes that Longarm had seen in the faces of killers who enjoyed their work; he'd looked into eyes like that too many times to misread their significance. The rurale's face was razor-thin, with a long nose and jutting jaw punctuated by an untrimmed mustache. Longarm bet himself that the man's lips were even thinner than his nose, though he couldn't see them.

"*Bueno,*" the commander said, after his men had bundled the captured weapons for one of their number to carry. He turned his gaze on Longarm. "You say you are *Tejano*—"

"No," Longarm interrupted. "That ain't what I said. My office is in Denver, Colorado, it ain't in Texas at all."

"*No significa, hombre.* You tell me you are *federalista de los Estados Unidos,* you show me badge, *verdad?* So, now you tell me what you do in my country?"

"I was trailing them stolen steers you're looking at. Them two fellows there, along with some others who've already left, were driving the animals from the U.S. side of the Rio Grande to someplace south of here."

"*De verdad?* And you make the shootings my men and me we hear while we ride by on our patrol, yes?"

"Yes. That one on the ground cut down on me and I had to wing him. The hole I put in him ain't going to kill him, but if you aim to save him for hanging, you better get him to a doctor to fix it up."

Looking down at Sanchez, the rurale asked, "*Es verdico, el gringo? O es mientrador?*" Sanchez said nothing. The rurale frowned. "*Cabrón! Repuestamé!*"

Lefty spoke for the first time. "Sanchez wouldn't know if the Marshal was lyin' or not. He's tellin' you the truth, though."

"*Es posible. Es posible tu es mientirador también. Díme verdad, hombre, tu es otro ladron de ganados, no?*"

"No, I ain't no rustler! And I ain't lyin' about the Marshal. And I'm a law officer, too. Outa Los Perros!"

With a wolfish smile, the leader shook his head slowly. "*Ay, Los Perros! El jefe Tucker, no?*"

"Yeah, Sheriff Tucker. I guess you know who he is?" Lefty retorted.

"*Sí. Tan mas bueno.*"

"He's one of Tucker's men, all right," Longarm said. "But he was working with the rustlers."

"He is not with you?" the rurale asked.

"Hell, no! He was with the bunch I was trailing!"

"*Pues, es ladron de ganados.*" Over his shoulder, the commander called, "*Pónese las manillas, esto y el herido.*"

Longarm watched Lefty being shackled. He half wished he'd felt able to trust the deputy, but he'd learned by bitter experience that it was a fool's game to depend on a born liar, and a weakling to boot. He felt a little better when the commander didn't order him to be handcuffed. There's a good chance the captain at his headquarters will understand things better, Longarm thought hopefully. Then, to try the leader's temper, he said, "Well, now you got things straight, suppose you give me back my badge and my guns. I'll ride to your headquarters with you, and tell your captain what this is all about."

"Is not so easy like that," the rurale replied. "If you are what you say, you have invade Mexico. This is serious crime, *hombre*. I take you to *mi capitán*, along with these two others."

Longarm snorted. "Like hell, I invaded Mexico! You act like I'm a whole damn army! I was chasing crooks that I guess broke Mexican laws, just like they did ours!"

"Mexico needs no help to enforce our laws from the *gringos*."

"Well, are you arresting me, or what?" Longarm demanded.

"*Quien sabe?*" The commander shrugged. "We see what Capitán Ramos want to do with you."

A cry from Sanchez drew the attention of both Longarm and the rurale. The man who was putting the handcuffs on the injured man was lifting Sanchez to his feet. When the rurale let go, Sanchez gave another cry and dropped to the ground.

"*Madre de Diós!*" he groaned. "*No puedo andar, no puedo cabalagar!*"

"*Otra vez!*" the leader ordered.

Again Sanchez was helped to his feet, and again he collapsed with a loud moan.

"*Creo que es verdad, no puede andar,*" the rurale said.

"*Pues, 'sta bien. Mátale,*" the commander ordered.

Without changing his expression, the rurale who'd

been helping Sanchez picked up the rifle he'd laid aside while putting on the handcuffs and shot Sanchez through the head.

Longarm stared unbelieving. "You didn't have to do that," he told the commander. "Where I come from, we don't execute people until a court finds they're guilty."

"In Mexico, we are not so soft," the rurale replied calmly. "We don' waste the time of a judge on a *pelado* like that one." He turned back to the executioner, who was taking off Sanchez's cartridge belt, and called, *"Ándale, hombre!"* Then, to Longarm, "We go now."

"Ain't you even going to bury him?"

"Porqué? Los zopilotes, they got to eat, too."

"What about them other rustlers? The ones that's supposed to come get the steers? Seems to me you'd wait and take them in, too."

"Hombre, you say they come. How I know you don' lie? So, we ride now. I take you to *el capitán."*

There was no chance for Longarm to talk to Lefty during the ride to the rurales' headquarters; the leader kept them separated. Nor did Longarm have a chance to talk further with the commander himself. The patrol leader rode ahead of his men, and Longarm was kept between two of the rurales who ignored or did not understand what he said when he made an effort to talk with them.

Longarm used his eyes instead of his mouth. He watched the route they took, which was not a road, but a narrow horse trail that led them southwest, across the low humps of the Burro Mountains foothills. He was pretty sure he could find his way back from the rurales' headquarters, a ride of almost two hours. The headquarters was not an imposing sight. The patrol pulled rein in front of a small cluster of buildings, low-walled adobe structures with vigas protruding little more than head-high. The vigas, beams made of tree trunks, supported roofs that were built up from layers of brush covered with packed layers of dirt. There were three large buildings in the cluster. A corral stood a little distance away, and still farther off, apart from the larger structures, was a straggle of shanties much like those which made up Los Perros.

Neither Longarm nor Lefty were allowed to dismount at once. The patrol's commander disappeared into the building by which they'd stopped while his men stayed on their horses, silently watching the prisoners. After what seemed a long wait, the commander came out. He pointed at Lefty.

"*Tómelo al cárcel*," he ordered. "*El capitán quiere hablar con el otro gringo.*" To Longarm, he said, "You come talk to *el capitán.*"

Longarm had to duck his head to get through the doorway as he followed the rurale inside. The interior of the building was no more imposing than the outside. Small, narrow windows were set high in the end walls of the big room that stretched across the entire width of the structure. In the wall opposite the entrance, doors led into other rooms, but they were closed, and Longarm could only guess that they might be a kitchen, a bedroom, a private office, perhaps. The inner walls, like the outer, were unpainted, covered with a thin coat of adobe plaster through which the outlines of the adobe bricks showed clearly. The place might have been a fort; indeed, Longarm guessed that it had been at one time, during one of Mexico's wars or revolutions, some kind of minor stronghold or outpost.

When he was shoved by the patrol commander into the front sala, Longarm's eyes were almost useless until they adjusted from the harsh outdoor sunlight to the room's dimness. The man sitting behind the wide, imposing table at one end of the room was a formless blob for a few moments. As Longarm's eyes adjusted, he saw the table first. It was an imposing piece of furniture, eight feet long and half as wide, with massive carved legs at ends and center. Its once glossy mahogany top still bore traces of a fine varnished finish, though now it was scratched and scarred to expose bare wood in places. He wondered how the table had found its way into such surroundings, and decided it must have been looted from some rich family's hacienda.

His voice a deep rumble in the quiet room, the man behind the table said, "*Sergento* Molina have tell me you say you are a *federalista* officer from the United States. Is true, what you tell him?"

"Sure it's true." Longarm blinked to speed the clearing of his vision. For the first time he could now see the captain clearly.

He saw a man who was grossly fat. Ramos's belly pushed out the cloth of the waist-length charro jacket he wore; his was even more ornately embroidered with gold than that of the patrol leader's. Tufts of black hair stuck through the gaps between his shirt buttons, and the shirt itself was grease-stained. His face was moon-round, his eyes encased in pouches of fat that squeezed them thin. Under a wide, scarred nose he sported the narrow, waxed mustache of a dandy. Above a round chin that was almost buried by two other chins beneath it, his mouth was like that of a frog.

Longarm's Colt and Winchester lay on the table in front of the captain. Longarm was tempted to grab for the Colt, but saw Molina watching him closely, and resisted the temptation. He realized that they were probably hoping for him to make just such a move. That, he thought, might be why they put the guns so handy—after they took all the shells out. He looked on the table for the wallet, but it was not there.

He told the captain, "My name's Custis Long. Deputy U.S. Marshal outa Denver, Colorado. Who in hell are you?"

"I am *Capitán* Ernando Ramos, of the *Policia Federal Rural de Mexico*. And you will speak respectfully to me, *gringo!*"

"No disrespect intended, Captain. I just like to know who's talking to me when I'm on official business."

"There is no such thing as a *federalista* of your country having official business in mine, unless he has the permit from my government. Do you have such permission?"

"Can't say I have. Didn't know I'd have to chase a bunch of cattle rustlers into your country, Captain. They started out in mine, and I just followed along. One of them thieves was Mexican, you see, and I don't expect he had official permission to be in my country."

"You can prove you are what you claim to be? You can prove what you say about the rustlers?"

"Well, I showed your sergeant the steers. They all had U.S. brands on 'em. They're still back in the canyon where your men jumped us."

Captain Ramos looked at the sergeant. *"Es verdad, Vicente?"*

Molina shrugged. *"Quien sabe, mi Capitán? Eran ganados, sí. No conozco que será estolada."*

"You didn't let me finish," Longarm said. "This sergeant told one of your men to kill the rustler who could've told you where his gang hangs out. He was the Mexican I was telling you about, if you're interested."

"Un pelado," Molina said with another shrug. *"Herido por este gringo. No puede andar o cabalagar. Tal vez, acerca de muerte."*

"You have hear what *Sergento* Molina say," Ramos told Longarm.

"I heard him, but I didn't understand him. I don't talk your language, Captain, outside of a word or so."

"He say you shoot this man first, and he is about to die."

"Oh, I winged him, sure. He was trying to shoot me, is why."

"To kill a man in my country is murder. Is not so in yours?"

Suddenly Longarm realized he might be fighting for his life. The shock of learning that the rurales, far from cooperating with a lawman from across the border, were treating him like a criminal, had clouded his thinking. Choosing his words carefully, he said, "I'd call it self-defense. A man's got a right to defend himself in any country I ever heard of."

"We will have to study this question, no? So. You say you are *federalista* from your country. You can prove this?"

"Your sergeant's got my wallet. It's got my badge in it." As he spoke, Longarm hoped the badge was indeed still in its usual place.

Again the captain turned to Molina. *"Tienes el mochila?"*

Stepping up to the table, the sergeant handed over Longarm's wallet. Ramos flipped it open to examine the badge, still in place. He studied the engraved legend carefully. Then he opened the currency compartment and found it empty. Longarm started to protest; he knew there'd been just over $200 in it when he'd surrendered it to Molina. Before he could object, he thought better of the idea. No use in muddying up the water over a little thing like money, when keeping his mouth shut might make Molina feel uneasy. It could work both ways, though, he reminded himself. If he gets nervous, he might want to get rid of you, instead of going easy because you didn't give him away for a thief.

"Does your government not provide you with money?" Ramos asked. He sounded disappointed.

"All I got to do is show my badge at a bank and sign for what cash I need," Longarm lied, gambling that Ramos wouldn't know.

"This badge you say is yours, it looks like it might be real," the captain said thoughtfully. "But how to prove it? Eh?"

"All you got to do is send a telegram to my boss in Denver. Or to Washington, if that's what it takes to satisfy you."

"*Ay, quá malo!*" Ramos sighed. "Our small outpost, it does not have the telegraph wire."

"Then send one of your men to the closest station. How far'd that be, anyhow?"

"Much too distant," Ramos frowned. Then he brightened. "Now. I will tell you what you must do. You must write the letter to your ambassador in our capital."

"Hell, he never heard of me," Longarm objected. "It'll save time to wire Denver or Washington. A letter'd take too long to get there. It'd be next summer before you'd get an answer."

"We will do it the way I say." Ramos's voice was firm. "I will tell you what to put down."

"I can write it myself," Longarm grumbled.

"Maybe it is that you do not understand. In this letter, the words must be chosen so your government will not make the mistake."

Longarm was suddenly suspicious. "Hold up. Just what kind of letter is it you want me to write?"

"You will see," the captain promised him. "Vicente! Bring a chair for this one." When Longarm was seated at the table across from Ramos, the rurale captain produced paper from a drawer, as well as an old-fashioned quill pen and inkwell. He slid the paper across to Longarm and placed the inkwell in front of him. "Now. You will write as I say you to."

Longarm dipped the quill in the ink and began writing. Ramos reached across the table, grabbed the pen from his hand, and crumpled the paper angrily. His face was livid.

"You will learn to obey my commands! Vicente! *Un gólpe en la cabeza por el gringo!*"

Before Longarm could move, Molina rapped him sharply on the head with his pistol butt. Longarm started to rise, but the sergeant flipped the pistol by its trigger guard and Longarm found himself staring into the muzzle.

"*Sientese!*" Molina growled, motioning with the pistol. Longarm sat down.

Ramos gritted threateningly, "If you need more lessons, you will get them!" He returned the pen to Longarm and shoved over a fresh sheet of paper. "Now. Write this time as I tell you! Not a word more, not a word less!"

"All right. I got the idea. Your man won't need to whop me again," Longarm said. On the fresh sheet, he wrote to Ramos's careful dictation:

"His Excellency, Ambassador of the United States. I am an agent of the federal government. I have murdered—"

Longarm threw down the pen. "To hell with that, Ramos! I ain't murdered anybody! It was one of your men shot Sanchez! All I did was wing him a little bit!"

Ramos studied the vigas in the ceiling. "How you would like it if I write your ambassador, to tell him I regret you have been kill by *los ladrones de ganados*? Do not forget where you are, *gringo!* Think a moment. If I tell Vicente, or any of my men, to take you somewhere from here and to shoot you, do you think they disobey me?"

Longarm remembered the instant obedience of the rurale who'd been ordered to kill Sanchez. He was beginning to see that he'd underestimated both the power and malevolence of the captain. It gritted on him to knuckle under, but it was better to do that than to die without a chance to fight back.

Still, he decided he'd balk at murder. He said to Ramos, "I'll tell you what, Captain. I'll write down I shot Sanchez, but damned if I'll say I murdered him, because I didn't."

Ramos thought about this for a moment. Then he nodded. *"Esta bién.* But the rest, it must be as I say."

When Longarm finished the letter, brushing up Ramos's wording a bit, it read:

> "I have shot a citizen of Mexico. Because I am an official of our country, the officers of Mexico where I am in prison do not wish to cause sorrow to the United States government by executing me for my crime. They will free me if the United States pays the expenses to which Mexico has been put in conducting my arrest and trial. The expenses are in the amount of 15,000 dollars in gold. You will send this money at once to Capitán Ernando Ramos, at the rurale district headquarters in the state of Coahuila. The money must be paid within one month, or I will be executed. Mr. Ambassador, I appeal to you to save me from this death."

As he wrote, Longarm's amazement increased. It was clear to him that Ramos hadn't the slightest idea how diplomats worked. Longarm didn't have very much of an idea himself, but once when he'd arrested a Canadian citizen up in Montana the man had appealed to his country's ambassador and the result had been a ruckus that the President himself had had to step in and settle. Longarm kept his grin inward, but he was pretty sure Captain Ramos was in for one damned big shock when this ransom demand was delivered.

"I will read every word before you sign your name," Ramos said, holding out his hand.

Longarm handed him the letter. "It's just what you told me to say."

Ramos read carefully, and finally nodded his satisfaction. He returned the letter. "Now, you will sign your name and put under it your official title. I will send it by a messenger. In three weeks, a month, when the gold is delivered, you will be free."

In a pig's ass, I will, Longarm thought. Once this bastard gets that gold, or gets an answer saying there won't be none coming, I'll get shot accidentally while I'm trying to make a getaway.

Forcing a cheerful smile, he said, "Well, I done what you said, Captain. Now, I guess you'll have a place for me to stay while we're waiting. And a good square meal'd taste mighty good right now."

Ramos smiled without sympathy. "You must have see when you get here, we have little space. But you will have a place to stay." He snapped his fingers in the direction of the sergeant. "Vicente. *Cerrase in el cárcel!*"

Chapter 12

If Captain Ramos's office had been dim, the jail was definitely dark. The squat, square adobe structure had only one window, which was at the end of a corridor onto which the two slat-steel barred cells on each side of the building opened. The cell into which Longarm was thrust stood at the end of the building near the door, so it was farthest from the tiny window. In the dim light that seeped reluctantly from the little opening fifteen feet away, Longarm couldn't see anything during the first moments after Molina clanged the metal door closed behind him and left through the main door.

From the darkness a voice said, "If we're going to be cellmates, I guess you better tell us who you are and what you're in here for."

"Damned if you don't sound like an American!" Longarm exclaimed, squinting through the gloom. He thought there were two others in the cell with him, but couldn't yet be sure.

"We're both Americans," a second voice spoke up. "I'm John Hill, captain, 10th Cavalry, U.S. Army."

"And I'm Nate Webster, Texas Rangers," the first voice said. "Now, who're you?"

"Custis Long. Deputy U.S. Marshal, Denver office. And you two men don't know how much trouble you saved me!"

"Listen to him talk about trouble!" Hill said dryly. "Wait'll you've been in here a while, Long. You'll find out what trouble really is!"

"I didn't mean it that way," Longarm explained. "You're the fellows I was sent down here to locate."

"Well, glory be!" Webster exclaimed. "It's about time somebody tumbled we were missing. Wait a minute, though. How come Bert Matthews went to the federals for help? Why didn't he send one of our own boys after me?"

"Same reason the army didn't send a cavalry troop

after the captain, here. You rangers and the army both fought the Mexicans in wars. I guess they figured if they sent one deputy marshal, it wasn't going to look like an invasion. On top of that, nobody on the other side of the Rio Grande knew where the hell you two had got off to."

"I'll tell you something," Webster said. "I wouldn't mind leading a ranger company against this bunch Ramos runs here."

"Amen to that," Hill said. "I'd like to have a platoon under me with orders to clean house here."

"It needs a lot of cleaning," Longarm agreed. "I never seen such a mess in my life. Ain't nobody in charge of things in this country got any brains?"

"Old Porfirio Diaz has brains enough," Hill said. "The trouble is, they're the wrong kind." When neither Longarm nor Webster had any comment, the army captain asked, "If you were sent down here to look for me and Webster, Marshal, you must be looking for those two deserters from my outfit, too."

"I was, but I'm not any longer. You don't need to look either, Captain. They're both dead."

"Hell you say." Hill didn't sound too surprised. "The rurales get them?"

"No. They got crossways of an unreconstructed reb in Los Perros. Deputy sheriff named Spud something. He killed 'em and hid their bodies. It's a safe bet you'll never find 'em."

"Well." The captain was taking the news philosophically. "They were pretty good soldiers until they got horny and raped that rancher's wife. I won't say I'm glad they're dead, but if I'd caught them, I'd have had to give evidence against them at a court-martial and watch them executed by a firing squad. I don't think I'd've enjoyed it."

Longarm could now make out details of his surroundings and see his cellmates' faces clearly. Nate Webster was tall, almost as tall as Longarm himself, but a bit thinner and rangier. His face was fading from the deep bronze he'd acquired in his job. Above his eyebrows where his hatbrim sat there was a band of white skin between the tan and his sandy hair. Hill was on the short side, with a baby-round face from which the fat was beginning to melt away. Both men were dressed in little more than rags, and neither wore shoes or boots. Their sockless feet were thrust into huaraches of braided leather such as Longarm had seen on the feet of Los Perros dwellers.

Webster saw Longarm eyeing their attire and said, "If you're wondering what happened to our clothes, we ate 'em."

"You did what?"

"I guess you've never been in a Mexican jail before," Hill said. It was a statement, not a question.

"Come to that, I ain't," Longarm replied.

Webster explained, "They don't feed prisoners in Mexico. If you've got food or something to trade, you eat. If not, you starve."

"So you traded your duds for grub," Longarm nodded. "I guess I'd've done the same thing. Guess I got off lucky, then. Don't know how it happened, but them bandits out there missed searching me. I got a little cash in my britches, even if that sergeant did lift $200 outa my wallet."

"I hope you're feeling charitable, Marshal," Hill said. "We've just about run out of anything to trade."

"You know you're both welcome to what I got. Only how do we go about getting grub? My belly's been pushing against my backbone for the last three, four hours."

"Sebastian will be around after a while, to see what kind of dicker we can offer," Webster replied. "If you don't mind a bit of advice, don't let him know how much money you've got, and don't pull off your boots when you go to bed."

"Who's Sebastian?"

"He's the jailer," Webster answered. "He looks too old to be worth much, but the son of a bitch is cagey. He'll steal you blind with your eyes open, and trade you outa your socks."

"Thanks. I'll remember. But I might be outa here before too long." Seeing the questions in his cellmates' eyes, Longarm explained about the letter. "It was a straight-out holdup, a ransom note, but when it hits Mexico City, it ought to bring some kind of action."

"Ramos got you on that, too, did he?" Hill asked. "You mean he had you write a letter like that?"

"He sure as hell did. He wants $25,000 in gold to let me go back across the river," Hill grinned.

"Well, I'm right took down," Longarm said. "He sure didn't put my price that high."

"You're both going cheap," Webster told them. "The price on me was $30,000. I guess the extra's a sort of revenge for whatever part the rangers took in whipping them at San Jacinto."

For a moment the three men looked at one another, then burst out laughing. In spite of their serious situation, the idea of a Mexican rurale who'd risen no higher than the command of an isolated, unimportant police outpost demanding ransom from the United States struck them as comical. It wasn't until their laughing spell died down that Longarm remembered Lefty.

"Hold up a minute," he said. "That patrol brought in somebody besides me. A deputy sheriff from Los Perros. How come he's not in here, too?"

"I wouldn't know," Webster said. "They haven't brought anybody else in, though. All the other cells were full until yesterday, but there were Mexicans in the others. The two across from us had a bunch of vaqueros in 'em, and I guess they got turned free. That one back of us had a bandit in it, but they hauled him out and shot him this morning."

Longarm said thoughtfully, "These damn rurales sure don't waste much time. Don't they ever give anybody a real trial in a court?"

"None that I've noticed," Webster replied. "But remember, Long, the rurales today're not like they were in Benito Juarez's time. They used to be a real crack police force, then. This bunch now's made up mostly of Diaz's hatchetmen and killers. They don't answer to anybody but him, and the only law they know is what comes out of a rifle or a sixgun."

Captain Hill added, "What they've got in Mexico today is what you saw in Los Perros, Marshal, only on a bigger scale. The army's got a few agents in Mexico, and the reports that trickle down to me in the situation bulletins from staff headquarters keep warning us field commanders to be careful as hell in our moves along the border. The army doesn't want to be responsible for starting another war."

"Too bad Mexico don't feel the same way," Longarm observed.

Their conversation stopped abruptly when the heavy door of the jail building creaked open. An old Mexican with a bent back and a pronounced limp came in. He stopped in front of the cell door and peered at the three prisoners.

"Quien quiere comida hoy?" he asked.

"Todos, los tres de nosotros," Webster answered. He turned to Longarm. "This is Sebastian. Wants to know if we want supper, which is his way of telling us we better have cash or something to swap. You said—"

"I remember," Longarm broke in. "You go ahead and dicker for all of us, you handle his lingo better'n I can. Best I can do is catch a word now and again."

"I'll get us off as light as I can," Webster promised.

He began bargaining in Spanish with the jailer. Longarm caught an occasional word, but most of the haggling went over his head. After about five minutes, Webster turned away from the door and winked at the others as Sebastian watched, trying to hide his eagerness.

"He'll give us meat and frijoles for a dime a head," Webster said. "That's about right, I think, Marshal."

"Sounds cheap enough, considering he's got a tighter monopoly than John D. Rockefeller. Tell you what. See if he'll throw in a cup of coffee apiece at that price."

Webster haggled again briefly, and reported, "He'll add the coffee for a nickel, that's for all three of us. I don't know what it'll taste like, but anything's better'n this horse piss he gives us for water."

"It's not that bad, after you get used to it," Hill explained to Longarm. "It gives you the trots for the first week."

"Them I can do without," Longarm said. "Tell him it's a deal, Nate. At that price, I got enough to feed us for a spell."

Before Sebastian came back with the food, the jailhouse door opened again and two rurales dragged Lefty in. The Los Perros deputy was unconscious, his face covered with blood, his clothes torn and stained. Longarm opened his mouth to protest, but before he could say anything, Webster clamped a restraining hand on his arm.

"Don't!" he whispered. "Just keep quiet. You get them mad, they might come in here and give us the same kind of treatment!"

Longarm subsided. They watched the rurales haul Lefty into the cell across from theirs. The rurales didn't bother to deposit the unconscious man on the low cot that stood in the cell. They dumped him on the floor, clanged the slat-iron door shut and locked it. Then they left, without a word or glance at Longarm and the others.

"Looks like they gave him a real working over," Longarm said.

"That the deputy from Los Perros you were wondering about?" Webster asked.

"That's Lefty. Or what's left of him."

"What'd he know that was important to them?" Webster wondered aloud.

"Beats me," Longarm answered. "Unless Ramos is figuring to go after that rustler ring Lefty was mixed up with."

"Yes, that could be it," the ranger frowned. "Or it could be he was trying to get the deputy to give him something more on you."

"That'd be my guess," Hill said. "A deputy sheriff's not quite as big a fish as a U.S. Marshal."

"Or an army captain or a Texas Ranger," Longarm added. He got as close to the cell door as he could and called, "Lefty! Can you hear me?" There was no response from the cell across the corridor.

"Wait until Sebastian comes in with our supper," Hill suggested. "Maybe we can get him to swab the man off with some cold water and bring him around."

"Not much else we can do," Longarm pointed out. "I ain't got much use for the worthless son of a bitch, but right now I'd give a hand to anybody Ramos hurts. Besides, I'm curious to know what they were trying to get out of him."

They didn't have to wait for the old jailer to revive Lefty. Before Sebastian returned with their supper, they heard moans coming from the cell across the way and when they crowded up to the door, Lefty was sitting up, holding his head between his hands.

Longarm called, "You all right?"

"No, damn it, I ain't! I hurt like hell, where them

greaser bastards kicked me in the balls and poked me in the belly with their rifle butts. But I ain't dead yet."

Longarm asked, "Why'd they whip you? You get crossways of Ramos? Or Molina?"

"Shit, I didn't do nothing. I guess all you need's to be from Texas for them greasers to start walloping you."

"Damn it, they must've asked you something," Webster said.

Lefty squinted through eyes that were swollen closed. "Who in hell are you?"

"Nate Webster. Texas Rangers."

"Now how in God's name did the rurales get hold of you?"

"That ain't important," Longarm told him curtly. "Even if it was any of your business, which it ain't."

"We're all in the same jail," the deputy reminded him. "I can make out somebody else in there with you, too."

"Name's Hill," the captain told him. "Captain, 10th Cavalry."

"Oh, sure. You're the one that come looking for a couple of your troopers that went over the hill. I recall the sheriff sayin' something about you."

"No thanks to him—or you, either—I found out what happened to them," Hill said brusquely.

"Damn it, you two quit butting in!" Longarm was irritated. "I need to find out things from this fellow." He faced the deputy again. Lefty had dragged himself up to the cot now. Longarm went on, "You better tell me what-all Ramos wanted to know."

"He was mainly interested in what you knew, and that's what I couldn't tell him, because I don't know myself. Then he got to askin' me questions about you."

"What kind of questions?"

"Why you come over the border. How long since you got to Los Perros. Who you was really after. If you was honest to God a federal marshal—*federalista*, he called it."

"What else?" Longarm was sure that Ramos's questioning hadn't stopped there.

"He tried to find out how much I know about what you've turned up so far." Lefty moaned, clutching his

136

groin. "Then, he wanted to make sure you set out from Los Perros. He had some idea you come from Mexico City, that you was a spy Diaz sent out to check up on him, or try to get somethin' on him."

"What'd you tell him?" Longarm demanded.

"Shit, Custis—Long, whatever your damn name is— what could I tell him? I spilled all I knew after they begun to beat on me, but how in hell do I know who you really are for sure?"

"That ain't what I asked you." Longarm's voice was hard. He'd seen Lefty crawfish more than once, trying to save his own skin at the expense of somebody else. "In my book, you're down as a damned liar and a crook. I don't put it past you to lie to Ramos, just to make it easy on yourself. Now, what'd you really tell him?"

"So help me God, Marshal, I didn't make nothin' up! I can't help whether you believe me or not. I told him what I knew certain-sure, and that was all!"

Longarm saw he'd gotten all there was to get out of Lefty for the moment. He still didn't know what to believe of what the deputy had told him. He said, "All right. If you remember anything else, you pass it along to me. If you do that, I just might help you."

"Help, my ass!" Lefty snorted. "You're in the same fix I am!"

"Maybe. Did the rurales shake you down good? Take all your money and everything else?"

"What'd you think they'd do? They stripped me clean."

"You know about Mexican jails, I guess?"

"Sure." Lefty stopped short, then sighed. "Oh, sweet Jesus! I ain't got a dime to buy a meal with! Not a lousy fuckin' penny!"

"I'm better off than you are," Longarm told him. "They forgot to clean me out. I already promised to help these fellows in here with me; they traded off all their duds for grub."

"Listen, Marshal Long," Lefty pleaded, "I didn't know anything to tell that rurale, and I didn't make nothin' up. You got to give me a hand!"

"I don't figure I owe you one damn thing, Lefty. Now, I might feel different, if you remember anything you forgot so far."

A rattling of the jailhouse lock put an end to their conversation. All four men fell silent when Sebastian appeared. He had a small pot in each hand. The jailer set the pots on the dirt floor outside the cell where Longarm, Webster, and Hill were confined, then went outside and brought in a cloth-wrapped bundle and a steaming coffeepot.

"*Su comida, gringos,*" the jailer announced. "*Dame treinte-cinco centavos, si quieren comer.*"

Being careful not to let Sebastian see that he had other coins in his pocket, Longarm dug out the thirty-five cents and passed the money through the bars. Sebastian unlocked the cell door, opened it just wide enough to slide the food inside, and locked it again. He'd already started to leave when Lefty called to him.

"Hey, *amigo! Donde es mi comida?*"

"*Tienes dinero?*" Sebastian asked.

"*No. Esta cosa tu conoces.*"

"*Pues, no dinero, no comida.*"

"Try trading your boots," Longarm suggested. He felt a small twinge of conscience, but smothered it. If Lefty knew anything more, there was only one way to get it out of him. He went on, "My friends in here swapped their clothes to get fed. You're no better'n they are. Your clothes ain't much more'n rags, but maybe you can get him to swap you a meal or two for your boots."

Pressed up to the bars, the cellmates watched while Lefty dickered with the jailer. Where cash wasn't offered, Sebastian proved to be a very tough bargainer. He and Lefty argued for a good quarter-hour before they came to terms. The deputy passed one of his boots through the bars. Sebastian went out and brought back a battered tin plate on which red beans swam in a redder sea of chili con carne. A small stack of tortillas lay on top of the mixture. Lefty grabbed the plate and started eating. Longarm and his companions ate their own meal, taking turns scooping food from the pots with strips of tortilla.

They all finished at about the same time. Longarm called across the corridor, "Well, you got fed tonight, Lefty."

"Yeah." The deputy's voice was surly. "No thanks to you."

"I said I'd make you a deal. You better think about how long you're going to eat on that one boot you got left. All you got to do is tell me everything you know about the deals your boss is into, and I'll see you keep eating, such as it is."

"What good would it do me? Ain't neither one of us likely to walk outa this trap we're in."

"Maybe. While I'm still alive and kicking, I got a job I'm paid to do, and I aim to go on doing it. The way I see it, a man's good as long as he's alive, but he can't stay that way if he don't eat. What're you going to do when you've ate up your other boot?"

"Damn you! You really know how to squeeze a man when he's down!"

"You just don't know how hard I can squeeze, when I got a mind to. Well, I offered you the deal. If you don't see fit to take it, that's your loss."

"Now, don't be in such a hurry—" Lefty started.

Longarm cut him short. "I got to be in a hurry. I don't aim to stay here, Lefty. Right now, I don't owe you nothing. If that was to change, I might see a way to help you go along when me and my friends go outa here."

"You're bluffing me. You got no more chance of walking outa this place than I do."

"You go on and think that, if you've a mind to. And you think how quick I changed a few things in Los Perros. And you think about that when your belly gets empty again."

There was a long silence from the other cell. Finally, Lefty said grudgingly, "All right. You win. I'll talk."

Chapter 13

Lefty talked for more than an hour. The beating he'd gotten from Ramos's rurales had battered his body and spirit and weakened his will enough for Longarm to break it, but his instinct for survival was still strong. Parts of his rambling confession only repeated what he'd told Longarm earlier, though he did reveal a few new details about the murders of the 10th Cavalry troopers and the operations of the rustling ring that ran the Laredo Loop.

There was a small amount of new information concerning the activities of Sheriff Tucker: frameups of enemies, beatings, and other intimidations of Los Perros inhabitants perpetrated for money or for extorting free labor or participation in criminal activities of minor sorts. Little of this was much of a surprise to Longarm, who'd seen towns or counties taken over by crooks of Tucker's stripe in other areas. One of Lefty's admissions was news, though.

"You think you're so damn smart," he said to Longarm. "You got Ed Tucker tagged as the boss of Los Perros. Shit, you ain't even come close to guessin' who the real boss is."

"Well, then, suppose you tell me," Longarm suggested.

"It's Miles Baskin, that's who. He's the real brains behind just about everything that goes on there."

"Baskin? The saloonkeeper?" Longarm was genuinely surprised. Baskin, the one time he'd talked with the man, had left an impression of being a mild, inoffensive type of man, one who'd walk around trouble instead of into it. At the same time, the revelation settled a nagging question that had been in the back of Longarm's mind. From the very beginning of his prodding in Los Perros, he'd been wondering how Tucker could appear so smart at times and so stupid at others.

He asked, "You and the other deputies ever get your orders direct from Baskin?"

"No. Not unless it was some little thing, like we was doin' him a favor. He liked to work through Ed."

"Did Baskin lean more toward one of you than the others? Did he like you or Spud or Ralston best?"

"Well . . ." Lefty hesitated. "Spud, maybe. But just a little bit. He was pretty careful not to set one of us up above the others."

"Lefty," Longarm said solemnly, "you better not be lying to me, or trying to save your skin, or Tucker's. Because if you are, I'll sure as hell find it out."

"Honest to God, Marshal, it's the truth," Lefty insisted. "It was Baskin that give Ed most of his ideas about how to make money outa Los Perros after Ed begun to take over the town. And this new Laredo Loop business, it was mostly his idea, too."

"All right. If it's the truth, I'll dig up evidence to back up what you've said."

"I reckon you can at that. Only one hell of a lot of evidence has got buried in them quicksand sinkholes along the river shallows."

"There'll be more," Longarm promised. "And it'll come out. I'd say you've earned your grub, Lefty. You'll eat along with the rest of us. Hell, I might even buy your boot back from Sebastian, if I can get Nate to do the jawbone work for me."

"Be glad to," the ranger said. "Aside from one thing that's kept bothering me, I've been right interested in hearing what that hombre across the way's been telling you."

"That's bothering you?"

"Well, it appears to me like Lefty was right a minute ago. He said he didn't see it'd do any good if he did tell you everything he knew, long as we're all in this place together."

"Nate's got a point," Captain Hill agreed. "He and I have done a lot of talking about how to break out of here, but it's always looked to us like a case of out of the frying pan, into the fire. There're twenty-five or thirty rurales outside, with pistols and rifles. All we have is our fists. That's not good odds."

"Let's jaw about that later on," Longarm suggested. "I didn't get a wink of sleep last night, and I rode pretty hard most of today, until the rurales shanghaied me here. I don't know about the rest of you, but I aim to curl up and get some shuteye. Tomorrow, we'll see what we can work out."

It was still dark in the jail when the sleeping prisoners were awakened by the clinking of the lock on the outside door. It swung open and the flickering light of torches blinded them briefly. Two unshaved rurales came in, their bootsoles scraping on the packed dirt floor. Marching to Lefty's cell, the rurales dragged the sleepy deputy into the corridor and through the outer door.

When they left the building, the men did not close the outside door. From their cell, by straining hard against the front bars, Longarm and his companions could see a slice of the torchlit area outside. Captain Ramos came into view; he carried a pistol in his right hand. The rurales who'd hauled Lefty out of his cell swung the deputy around to face the captain. The distance was too great for those inside to hear what was said, they could only watch and imagine what passed between Lefty and Ramos.

Whatever the rurale captain said or asked brought only vehement headshakes from Lefty. Each time they could see Ramos's lips move, and each time the deputy's head shook in the negative. Even when Ramos slapped Lefty's face, there was no difference in the response he gave. Ramos was obviously growing angry. He brought up the pistol and shoved it hard against Lefty's forehead. Lefty tried to drop to his knees, but the men holding his arms kept him erect.

After a moment, Ramos brought the pistol down. He talked for perhaps a minute. Watching the dumb show, Longarm guessed that Ramos was trying to force Lefty into confessing to something—he couldn't figure out quite what—that would suit the rurale's private purposes, while Lefty kept pleading that it was impossible for him to do what Ramos wanted.

None of those in the cell were prepared for the finale of the pantomime. Ramos pushed the muzzle of his pistol into Lefty's neck, just under the deputy's jaw, and pulled the trigger. The shot sounded thin inside the jail, but Longarm and his cellmates could see Lefty's head shatter in a spray of blood and brains bursting from the top of his head. The deputy slumped and this time the rurales holding him let his lifeless body fall to the ground.

Even men as accustomed to violence as Longarm, Webster, and Hill, were shaken by the brutality of the killing. They looked at one another in stunned silence, half aware that outside the two rurales who'd held Lefty were dragging away his body, leaving a wide blood trail on the hard-packed ground. The slamming of the outer door and the metal rasping of its lock brought them back to the reality of the moment.

"Jesus!" Longarm muttered. "Them rurales sure don't believe in things like courts and trials, do they?"

"Not this breed, no," Webster said soberly. "That's the Diaz way, though. Like I told you, the rurales aren't a police force any more. They're Diaz's revenge squad, his executioners. It's one of the ways he keeps Mexico under his thumb."

"You realize that what we saw could happen to any of us," Hill reminded them in a quiet, matter-of-fact voice. "Marshal Long, you said just before we turned in that we'd see what we could work out, and I suppose by that you meant getting out of here. Well—" Hill motioned toward the single window at the end of the corridor, which was gray with the dawn light—"it's today, and I'd say it's time we started working."

"You said just what I was thinking," Longarm agreed. "Let's just squat down and have us a powwow. We'll hear soon enough when that jailer comes to see about breakfast."

"He won't be here for a while," Webster said. "Usually, just a little before noon. This jail doesn't serve but two meals a day."

They sat on the floor, ignoring the hard cot, so they could lean together with their heads close and talk in low voices.

Longarm said, "It didn't occur to me we had to hurry until I watched what they did to Lefty. That changed my mind fast. Now, you men have been here longer'n I have. What've you found out about the way they run things outside?"

"Damned little," Hill replied. Webster nodded agreement, and the army man went on, "You see, Nate and I thought just like you did, Marshal. We talked things over, and decided we had plenty of time before we started to worry."

"How'd you figure that out?" Longarm asked.

"Oh, you know what's happened to those ransom demands Ramos has sent to our ambassador. They're going through channels. Probably our man sent them to Washington for instructions before he said anything to the Mexican government. Those things take time."

"I know my chief's always bellyaching about how long it takes for his bosses in Washington to answer a simple question like what's two and two," Longarm smiled. "But I never was in a situation just like this one before."

"Neither was I," Hill said. "But I did a tour with our embassy in Haiti, right after the war. I was brevetted a colonel during the fighting, but the minute Lee surrendered, I went back to my regular rank, and there were so damned many lieutenants that they shipped a lot of us out as military attachés to get us out from underfoot."

"John tells me that ambassadors don't know their tails from a hot rock most of the time, and the regulars who run our embassies are afraid to pee without asking Washington first," Webster put in.

"Most of those nervous Nellies in the State Department squat to pee, anyhow," Hill said sourly. "But that's beside the point I'm trying to make. I don't think the Mexican government's heard yet about what Ramos is trying to do. Ramos seems to think all he has to do is send a letter to the U.S. ambassador, and wait for the gold to flow. It's not that simple."

"I guess I'm following you," Longarm said. "But go on, spell it out for me."

"Sooner or later, either in Washington or Mexico City, there's going to be a protest made to the Mexican government. When that happens, Ramos is going to find himself up shit creek. And he's likely to panic."

"He sure don't seem bothered now," Longarm pointed out.

"No. I tried to get across to him that he'd have to be patient," Hill explained.

"John and I figured we were safe until the Mexican government got the word we're being held illegally, and that one of their police officers is trying to hold up the U.S.," Webster added.

Hill said, "That's when the real squeeze will come. Diaz isn't stupid. Crooked, mean as hell, unscrupulous, but not stupid. From what I know about him, which isn't much, he'd be likely to send one of his execution squads up here to get rid of us and Ramos both. Then he'd play innocent; he'd say, 'No, we haven't got any American prisoners, and Captain Ramos was killed in a fight with bandits.'"

Longarm took his time analyzing the captain's conclusions. He nodded slowly. "I'd say you've done a pretty good job of figuring things out. And if you're right, then we don't have a hell of a lot of time left for getting outa here."

"Getting out's not going to be a big job," Webster said. "We know how that can be done. It's what we'd do once we were out of this jail, facing that bunch outside without any kind of weapons to give us a chance."

"We don't even know whether they post regular guards, or whether the whole outfit turns in at night," Hill told Longarm. "And until they killed that deputy today, we haven't felt like we needed to tip our plans by showing too much interest in their operational procedures. But as Nate says, the main thing that's held us back is lack of weapons."

Longarm started to tell them about his derringer, but decided that holding the news until just before they finished their plans would give the morale of his cellmates a bigger boost at a time when it'd be needed more.

Hill had been thinking, too. He said, "Weapons or not, I'd say the time's come to do something. And I mean immediately."

"I'm with you there," Longarm assured him. "I guess you've had the same idea I got, looking at the roof up there?"

"We decided it's the weakest point," Webster said. "Breaking through shouldn't be a big job. But then what? Do all of us go, and if we do, where do we go? To the corral and grab horses? Or prowl around looking for some guns?"

"I'd say the first thing we got to decide is whether we all go out at the same time, or if one of us gives it a try by himself."

"One man has a better chance than three of moving around without stirring up an alarm," Hill observed.

"Sure does," Webster agreed. "Well, I'll volunteer. I've done enough scouting so's I can get around quiet in the dark. And I talk the lingo enough so if a guard challenges me I can throw him off long enough to get close to him and shut him up."

"I was about to offer," Hill said. "I'm not what you'd call the world's best scout, but I've done my share of night fighting."

"Now, look," Longarm said, "I don't mean to put myself up to be a hero, or feel like I'm a bit better'n either one of you, but I figure it's my job to get out there and bust us all free."

"I'd like to know how you figure it," Webster said dryly.

"Yes, so would I," Hill chimed in.

"It's real simple," Longarm told them. "First off, you fellows have been in this damn place a lot longer'n I have. Nate, you been here how long? Close to three months?"

"Give or take a week or so," the ranger agreed.

"And you been here a month or more, John." Hill nodded. Longarm went on, "All the time, you been getting more starved out, cooped up in this little cell without a chance to stretch your muscles or loosen up your joints. I'd say you're both a mite rusty; it stands to reason. My muscles are in better shape than yours are, which'd give me a little bit of an edge."

"There's nothing wrong with my muscles," Webster protested.

"Nor mine," said Hill. "Both of us have tried to keep in shape, you know. Give us credit for that, Marshal."

"Oh, sure. But there's one little thing I been thinking about that might make more difference than anything else."

"What's that?" Hill and Webster spoke almost in unison.

"Your feet. Look at them things you got on. How're you going to run in 'em? Or sneak in 'em? They go shush-shush every step you take. But I still got my boots."

"We could draw straws to see who'd wear them," Webster suggested.

"We could," Longarm nodded. "What size you wear, Nate?"

"Elevens."

"John? How about you?"

"I take size nine."

"And I wear tens. Now, nobody can move right, whether he's sneaking or running, in boots that don't fit. Am I right?" Reluctantly, both the others nodded. "Well, then, I guess I win the job by a toe. Or maybe a heel. Anybody object?"

"As far as I'm concerned, it's settled," Webster said. "We'll be ready to back you up, Marshal."

"We damned sure will!" Hill nodded. "Now, then, how can we help you form a battle plan?"

"Well, you're getting over my head, John," Longarm replied. "I was just aiming to bull ahead by guess and by God, and hope I do the right thing."

"In the service, we'd call that setting out to look for targets of opportunity," Hill smiled. "In this case, I'd say it's about the only battle plan we can make."

"I got one ace I've been keeping in the hole," Longarm announced. He fished his watch and derringer out of his vest pocket. "Ramos got so interested in the letter he made me write that he didn't get his men to clean out my pockets. So there's two shots here that might make the difference between us getting out, or going the way Lefty did."

Webster chuckled. "You're like old Captain McNally, who used to run my outfit, Marshal. He always says some men are born lucky, some are born unlucky, but good men make their luck as they go. I don't suppose you made that piece of luck, but it's sure going to help all of us."

"Gentlemen," said Hill, "I'll make a suggestion. If I'm taking troops into an engagement, I try to give them a good rest before the battle starts. We might as well follow the same tactics."

Relaxation came hard during the day's long hours, but they somehow managed to rest and to doze a bit. When Sebastian came in to bargain over their meals, Webster went through the usual routine of dickering. He complained of the price they paid as well as of the quantity and quality of the food they'd had the evening before. The haggling didn't improve their luncheon, but for supper they got a big helping of roast *cabrito*. It was a bit strong, really more goat than kid, but it was a lot more substantial than the soupy chili con carne and frijoles they'd had the previous evening and at noon.

After the jailer had gone out, while they were eating, Longarm told his companions, "I been thinking about this deal off and on all day, whenever I couldn't sleep. Appears to me like I got a choice of two times to make a try. One's right now, while them bastards is eating, maybe swigging a little mescal or pulque. The other's late tonight, after they bed down."

"If you're asking for an opinion," Hill said, "I'd imagine they won't be as alert while they're eating. And we still don't know whether they keep sentries on duty at night."

"Strikes me John's right," Webster said quickly. "I'd bet they do have some kind of night patrol, but when the grub's served, all the pigs rush to the trough."

"I sorta favor now, myself," Longarm agreed. "If we move quick, I can get through that roof and be on the ground outside before they finish their supper."

To keep Longarm as fresh as possible, Hill and Webster took on the job of breaking through the jailhouse roof. The ceiling was low, but still high enough to make it necessary for one man to stand on the other's shoulders while they took turns pulling aside the saplings that had been laid across the vigas to support the layers of brush and dirt that formed the foot-thick roof. The bottom layers gave way easily, but the topmost layer had baked hard, and formed a crust four inches thick. They used the tin plates from their supper as scrapers and prods, bending them into triangles that provided pointed ends for gouging at the crust and wide sides for scraping the dislodged pieces away.

Both roof-breakers were grimy from head to foot before the job was completed. Longarm estimated they'd taken less than an hour to finish the job, and the sight through the hole they'd opened, of the clear sky deepened into after-sunset blue, gave encouragement to all three of them.

"Well, let's don't lollygag," Longarm said. "Boost me up as far as you can. Once I get armpit-high through that top layer of 'dobe, I'm home free."

Webster and Hill each took hold of one of his feet

and Longarm held his body stiff while they lifted him straight up. The hole wasn't as big as it looked; they'd worked fast and kept their digging to a minimum in cracking through the hard top crust. His shoulders almost stuck, but Longarm managed to raise his arms up straight above his head and scrape through the opening. For a moment, he rested on his elbows, forearms on the roof, head and shoulders protruding through the escape hatch. The adobe wall of the building was only eight or ten inches above the rooftop. Longarm pulled himself out slowly, bending forward, hauling his body ahead with his forearms and elbows, until his booted feet cleared the hole and he lay flat in the scant concealment of the wall.

For a few seconds he lay motionless and listened, trying to locate the rurales who might be on the ground by the sound of their voices. Most of the noises came from a distance. He risked raising his head above the parapet of the wall to check the evidence of his ears and saw that the men were about where he'd placed them mentally. Apparently, the rurales weren't provided with a mess hall. They were clustered around a spit suspended over a bed of coals beside what he guessed was their barracks. The almost-stripped skeleton of a young goat was suspended on the spit.

Several rurales were by the cooking fire, carving strips of meat off the cabrito and eating it where they stood. A few had taken plates to sit on the ground, leaning against the wall of the barracks. Most of the rurales had jugs or bottles; Longarm was reasonably sure these contained either pulque or mescal. He didn't think the average rurale could afford even the lowest grade of tequila or aguardiente. There were no rifles to be seen, but all the men he could see clearly still had on their pistols.

Give 'em a little time, old son, he told himself, long enough for it to get full dark. By then, they'll be full of meat and pulque and won't be able to hit the side of a barn if they shoot, let alone a spry man running.

At one side of the barracks building, thirty or forty paces distant, stood the headquarters. Lights glowing through the high-up horizontal slit-windows told him that Captain Ramos must be sitting down to enjoy his own supper inside. Through the deepening dusk he could see other structures, a cluster of jacales beyond the barracks and some distance away from the larger buildings. The huts were even more primitive than the jacales of Los Perros. Fires twinkled in front of most of them, and women as well as men moved around the shanties. Longarm realized that these must be the quarters of married rurales, or the dwellings of the lavanderas, the camp followers who were to be found with every Mexican military force, and who were given with Latin courtesy their title of "washerwomen."

Whatever men are back at those shanties, or around 'em, won't be paying much mind to what goes on around the barracks or jail, Longarm thought. They'll have their women to keep 'em occupied.

On the opposite side of the barracks from the headquarters, he saw the corral. Even in the dimness of the rapidly fading light, Longarm could make out Tordo's gray shape; it stood out among the roans and chestnuts that plodded aimlessly around inside the pole enclosure. On the corral rail, saddles were lined up; Longarm tried to count them, but the light was too bad. He guessed there were about thirty, which was the figure he and Hill and Webster had estimated as the number of men stationed at the outpost. He didn't really like the location of the corral. To get to the horses, they'd have to pass by the barracks.

Don't worry about that now, he commanded himself, wait and see how this damn stunt comes off before you start saddling up to ride.

By the time Longarm had finished his cautious survey of the area, darkness was almost complete. From the jacales, a guitar plinked; if it accompanied a singer, his voice was lost in the distance. Another sound drew his attention to the barracks. There, a group had gathered around a man playing the concertina. Singly and in twos and threes, voices began rising in the melancholy strains of "La Borrachita."

"Marshal!"

Nate Webster's whisper behind him almost sent Longarm jumping out of his skin. He turned to see the ranger's head sticking out of the escape hole.

"Damn it, Nate! You like to scared the shit outa me!"

"We didn't hear any ruckus, so we figured you must've made it," Webster whispered.

"Had to get the layout of this place in my head, first." Longarm wiggled backward so they could talk more easily. "Looks like it's all clear. I'm going to see if I can get us some guns and a bunch of shells. These two shots I got won't help much if they take after us."

"You sure it's safe?"

"If I wanted to live safe, I'd be selling calico back of a store counter. I did think of one thing—Sebastian."

"John and I did, too. We're going to grab him through the bars and hold him till you come let us out." He breathed deeply. "God, this fresh air smells good!"

"We'll all enjoy it more, ten miles from here."

"Sure. Well, good luck." Webster's head disappeared.

Longarm belly-crawled to the side of the jail opposite the barracks and lowered himself over the wall. Hanging by his hands, he dropped the few feet between his feet and the ground. He landed running, crouching low, heading for Ramos's office.

Chapter 14

Darkness, sweeping in rapidly, was his friend. Longarm slowed his run almost as soon as he'd started it when he saw there was no sentry posted at the door of the headquarters building. He ambled lazily across the bare area, keeping himself from hurrying, now. Any of the rurales who saw him would, he hoped, think he was just another of their group reporting to the captain.

He reached the deep shade of the building walls. Standing on tiptoe, he could just see inside the big sala. A vigil light flickered in its glass container in a niche near the door. Its flame was so tiny that the circle of light it cast reached barely to the edge of the huge table Ramos used as a desk. There was no one in the room, but another blade of light gleaming along the floor gave him the location of a door; Ramos must be in the room behind that door, he thought.

Hugging the building wall, he made for the door. It was latched with a simple lift-lever. Longarm tested it cautiously. The lever lifted easily; the door was neither locked nor barred. Across the narrow room the knife-edge of light became his goal. He lightfooted toward it. As he went, he snaked the derringer from his pocket and freed his watch from it by feel. He'd operated the snap on the chain in the dark so many times that the job was automatic. Dropping the watch back in his pocket, he cocked the derringer before knocking on the door. He tried to make the light tapping sound apologetic.

"*Qué pasa?*" asked Ramos's voice from the adjoining room.

"*Solamente mí, Capitán.*" Longarm had rehearsed the phrase in his mind so often that he had no fear of stumbling over it, in spite of his rusty Spanish. "*Es necessario que habla con usted.*"

"*Mañana, hombre. Vólves temprano, y hablamos.*"

Longarm had expected to be told to come back tomorrow, and had the next phrase ready. *"Anoche, por favor, mí Capitán!"* He tried to make his voice humble and pleading.

A muffled grunt of disgust came through the thick door, then a rustle of movement. Longarm stood aside, hugging the wall, turning his head away so he wouldn't be blinded by the sudden glare of light when the door opened. He counted on Ramos's eyes being used to the bright room beyond; the rurale would be almost blind for the first few seconds when he looked into the dark sala. The door opened and Ramos's bulk filled the lighted opening. He wore only a pair of trousers and was barefoot. Stepping across the threshold, he peered ahead into the darkness.

"Quien es?" he grumbled. *"Quien estorbame in mi recamera?"*

In one swift move, Longarm jammed the cold barrel of the dérringer into Ramos's temple and with his other hand clamped the man's mouth closed.

Coldly, he hissed, "You make a noise, and you're dead. I'll spatter your brains the way you spattered Lefty's this morning."

He kept his hand over Ramos's mouth until the look in the rurale's eyes told him it was safe to let him talk.

"El gringo federalista!" Ramos gasped. *"Como entre por aquí?"*

"Talk English," Longarm commanded.

"How do you get in here?" Ramos asked. "You are in jail!"

"Maybe I'm twins," Longarm suggested, his voice without mirth. "I got tired of your jail. Me and my friends are ready to say goodbye to your place here, but we're taking you along for the ride."

"You think you can take me from my brave men?" Ramos blustered. "Only I call once, and they will come!"

"And they'll find your corpse, if you yell. But maybe you are stupid enough to make some noise, even if it kills you. Back up, into your bedroom." He emphasized the command with a push on the derringer's barrel. Ramos obeyed.

Longarm gave a quick glance around the room. He

was so surprised when he saw the woman in the bed that took up most of one wall that he almost pulled the derringer's trigger.

"Who in hell are you?" he asked.

Ramos said, "She is—"

"I didn't ask you!" Longarm snapped. He looked at the woman. "Well? You going to tell me?"

"My name's Flo Firestone. Oh, not really, that's my stage name, but I'm more used to it than my real one. I know who you are, and am I ever glad to see you!"

Longarm shook his head, unbelieving. "You talk like you're an American."

"You're damned right, I am. And it's a real treat to see you standing there with a gun at that bastard's head!"

"Well, whoever you are, we'll save the palaver until later. I guess you're on my side, from what you just said, so why don't you find me some rope or something to tie this hombre up with. Then we'll try to get things straightened out."

She got out of bed, giving Longarm a glimpse of smooth pink thighs as her long legs kicked the covers aside. She stood up; he was surprised that she was almost as tall as he was. She was a blonde, full-lipped, round-chinned, and her sheer nightdress revealed that she was a true blonde. The almost transparent material of the nightgown hid nothing of her figure, which was statuesque, though the erect pink-tipped nipples of her generous breasts pushed the sheer fabric out so that it fell straight to her bare feet. When she moved, the gown clung to her, emphasizing her smoothly rounded stomach, wide hips, and tapered legs. In spite of her size, she was large rather than fat. Longarm had to work at keeping his mind on Ramos while the woman scurried around looking for rope or cord. Finally, she settled for ripping a bedsheet into wide strips.

She handed these to Longarm. "These'll have to do, I guess. If you twist them when you tie him up, they'll hold tight enough."

"Give me a hand," he said. "Put a gag on him first, in case he gets a fool idea about yelling for help." Ramos glowered while she obeyed, pulling the twisted cloth tight through his mouth. Longarm told the rurale,

"Now then. You just march over and sit down in that chair. Don't forget, this gun's cocked, and I got a nervous trigger finger."

Ramos could see the derringer at full-cock in the mirror of an ornate dressing table that stood opposite the bed. He obeyed without hesitation. Longarm sat him down in the armless boudoir chair and after the woman had bound his hands, helped her to tie the rurale's feet to the chair legs. He checked the lashing that held Ramos's wrists around the back of the chair, and found them as tight and secure as they'd have been if he'd put them on the man himself. Longarm tucked the little gun back into his vest pocket.

"Now," he said to the woman, "you wanta tell me how you got here, and why?"

"I got here because this two-bit *cholo*—I don't know what that means, except that it's some kind of Mexican insult—decided he wanted to keep me around after his men wiped out the bandits that had kidnapped me off the train that I was taking back to the states."

"How long ago'd this happen?"

"Let's see. I've just about lost track of time, but I guess it was about three weeks ago that Charley—" she pointed to Ramos—"I call him Charley because it makes him mad—ambushed the train robbers. And I don't know where it was, because I rode a day and part of a night with the bandits, and two days with Charley and his crew."

"And how'd you know who I am?" Longarm asked suspiciously.

"Marshal, when you're shut up all the time in a bedroom you don't much care for, you listen at the keyhole and you work out the things you can't see happening. I just about gave up when Charley told them to toss you in the pokey, and you'll never know how glad I am you got out. How did you, anyhow?"

"That'll wait," Longarm replied curtly. He wanted to satisfy himself that the woman was what she seemed to be. "This train you were on, how'd you happen to be riding it?"

"I was trying to get back home. Look, Marshal, I'm an actress. Well, I guess burlesque's acting, in a way. Our troupe got stranded, but we scraped up enough money between us to take the train from Monterrey to Laredo, wherever that is. We thought once we got back across the border, we could work our way back to New York. You know, hitting the tank towns, performing wherever we could pick up a booking."

"What happened to the rest of the people in your outfit?"

"God might know, but I don't. You ever been on a train that ran off the rails because a bunch of robbers dynamited the track? It was a mess—shooting, dark, people all mixed up. I don't know what happened, because I had a sack over my head. I could tell daylight from dark, but that was about all. I could tell you a lot more, but don't you think we'd better save it until later?"

"You're right, Flo. You did say Flo, didn't you?" She nodded, and Longarm went on, "Sounds like a real interesting story, but there's two more fellows waiting for me to get 'em out of jail, and I got to work up some kind of scheme to do it."

"You're going to include me in the getaway party, I hope?" Flo asked.

"Sure, now that I know about you, which I didn't before. But there's something like thirty of Ramos's rurales between us and a clean break. There ain't a way I can see to bull through that many. They'd cut us down fast, we'd be so outgunned if we tried to just bust through."

"If you're looking for guns, there's a whole closetful in a little room off the one Charley uses for his office."

"Ammunition for 'em, too?"

"I wouldn't know what bullets fit which gun. Let's go look. I'll show you where they are."

"Just a minute. Is there anybody in this place except you and him?"

"No. Charley didn't want any interruptions, if you know what I mean. Some woman comes in to cook and clean up, but she won't be here until time to fix breakfast."

"All right. Let's have a looksee. And I'll bolt that front door, so in case anybody does come around they won't just walk in on us."

Flo seemed unconscious of her body gleaming through the filmy nightdress as she led Longarm through the sala to a little storeroom lined with cabinets.

She pointed out the one that held the weapons. Longarm opened it and found it crammed with rifles, shotguns, pistols, and boxes and bags of ammunition. There was enough firepower in the cabinet to fit out an army, he thought, and for a moment wished he had one behind him.

Apparently, Ramos kept for himself the best weapons captured by his men from the bandit gangs which were supposed to be the chief targets of the rurales. The guns were all in good condition, most of them relatively late models. Among them, Longarm found his own Colt and Winchester; he checked to be sure they were loaded before putting the Winchester aside and strapping on the Colt. For the first time since it had been taken from him, he felt fully dressed.

"These'll fix us up real good," he told Flo. Then the relief drained out of his voice as he added, "But they won't be a damn bit of use until I pass 'em on to Nate and John."

"They're your friends who're in jail?"

"An army captain and a Texas Ranger. They was both here before Ramos brought you back, I expect."

"I knew there were prisoners out there, I didn't know who."

Longarm was frowning, concentrating on completing their escape. He thought aloud, "About all I can see to do is wait until all those rurales turn in and get sound asleep. Flo, you know whether they set guards out around this place at night?"

"No. Charley's kept me busy at night, or tried to." She sighed. "Too bad there's not some kind of medicine, like laudanum, in one of these cabinets, something that'd put the men out there to sleep real fast."

"You can say that again," Longarm told her.

"I said—"

"Never mind, I was just talking. Listen, Flo, is Ramos a big drinker?"

"He does pretty well. I guess he grabs liquor whenever he gets a chance to; that cabinet right there's loaded with it. French brandy, Scotch whisky, bourbon, rye, and a lot of Mexican stuff like habanero and tequila. There's enough in there to stock Rector's bar. Look." She crossed the room and opened another of the cabinets, showing shelves crammed with bottles.

"Liquor's as good as laudanum for putting a man to sleep," Longarm said. "It just don't work as fast. I'm beginning to get me an idea. See if you can dig a bottle of Maryland rye outa there, Flo. I need something to stir up my brains while I scheme."

Flo rummaged and came up with the bottle Longarm had requested. A corkscrew hung on a nail inside the cabinet door. She used it expertly and passed him the bottle. He tilted it and let the warm, nippy whiskey slide down his throat. Immediately, he wished for a cheroot to follow, but reminded himself he'd better be grateful just for the bottle.

"Don't you offer ladies a drink in the crowd you travel with?" she asked. He extended the bottle to her and she took a swallow. Her eyes watered. "God! That's a man's drink!" she exclaimed. "I guess I'd better stick to something mild, brandy or Scotch."

"We better leave it alone for now," he cautioned. "I got the start of a scheme worked out. I'm going to have to ask you to help me some, if you don't object."

"Object! Listen, you tell me what you want me to do. There's not much I'd balk at, if it'll get me out of this place and on a train back to Broadway again."

"Well, what you'd do ain't much. Pay attention now, and I'll tell you what I got figured."

Longarm outlined his plan. Flo listened attentively, nodding now and then, as he explained what she'd have to do. When he'd finished she chuckled throatily.

"My God, you've missed your calling, Marshal! Belasco'd pay you a fortune to write plays for the Lyceum. That's a real fine scene you've worked up, and I'll do my best to ad lib it. Don't worry, I won't blow my lines. Most of the shows I play in are half off the cuff. I'll play it to the hilt!"

"It's both our necks if you mess it up," he warned her. "All right. You go get on a wrap. I'll see if I can rummage out some bags or bottles from the kitchen."

Longarm searched until he found a big, sturdy basket and two burlap bags. He filled them with bottles from the liquor cabinet, choosing the strongest spirits: tequila, habanero, rum, hundred-proof bourbon. Flo came from the bedroom in time to help him. Together they carried the basket and bags to the door of the sala, and put them down just inside the room. Longarm looked at Flo. She'd put on a negligee over her nightdress. The effect, he thought, was just right.

"Glad you like it," she said when he told her this. "I was lucky enough to hold on to my dressing case when I jumped off the train. This night stuff and a suit is all I've got to wear."

"Remember, now, don't overdo things," he cautioned her. "Let Sergeant Molina look, but don't let him get near enough to grab you. Just be sure he'll come back, is all."

"Don't worry. I've had more experience dodging stage-door Johnnies than you know about. They only catch me when I want 'em to. Well, if we're ready, let's ring up the curtain on act one."

"Might as well. Get going."

Flo went out the front door. Longarm followed a step behind her, and when she continued toward the barracks he stopped in the deep darkness at the corner of the building. He'd brought his Winchester to cover her, if trouble developed. If there's a ruckus, he thought, the damn scheme's ruined before it gets started good.

A dozen paces from the barracks, Flo stopped. She called, "Sergeant Molina! Captain Ramos wants you! Right away!"

Longarm had chosen Molina as his target not only because he was Ramos's second in command, but because the sergeant was the only rurale he was sure understood enough English to make the plan work. He waited while the men still seated around the fire scurried to look for Molina. Just before Longarm was beginning to think he'd come up with a bad idea, the sergeant came around the corner of the barracks building. He peered at Flo, who was still standing where she'd stopped.

"What does *mí capitán* want?" Molina called.

"He has a reward for you and his brave men," Flo called back. "He wants you to come and get it."

She turned at once, without waiting to see whether Molina would follow her. The sergeant hesitated only a moment before doing so. Longarm slipped through the darkness along the wall to the headquarters door and slid inside before Molina got close enough to see him. He crossed the sala and went into the closet, leaving the door ajar and swapping his Winchester for his Colt.

Straining his ears, he could hear Flo open the door and come into the sala. There was a moment of silence before Molina spoke.

"Where he is, *mí capitán?*"

"In the bedroom," Flo replied. "He doesn't want to be disturbed. He told me what he wants you to do."

"Qué es?" Molina sounded suspicious. "Why is the *capitán* not here himself?"

"He's resting," Flo replied. She dropped her voice to a low, confidential tone that to the listening Longarm seemed dripping with honey. "I'll tell you the truth, Sergeant. The captain's a little bit, well—a little bit drunk."

"Ah. *Un poco borracho.*" Now, Molina's voice held the verbal equivalent to a shrug. "So. What he is want me to do?"

"Look here." Another silence; this time, Longarm visualized Flo showing Molina the liquor. "Captain Ramos says you and the men have earned a reward, a treat. He wants you to share the bottles with the men."

"Sangre de mi vida! Que admirable!" Molina chuckled. "I should go thank *mí capitán* for his gift, no?"

"No. I—he's asleep." She sighed. "And I'm all by myself."

After a long pause, Molina took the bait. "You are lonely, *señorita?*"

"I had expected Captain Ramos—" She sighed again, more deeply. "You know what is said about men who drink too much, Sergeant."

"Ay, sí!" Then, philosophically, "It can happen to any man, *señorita*. Tomorrow, the *capitán* will be himself again."

"But that doesn't help me tonight," Flo said seductively. "Now, if there was only some big, fine man—"

Longarm thought she was overdoing her act a bit. He risked peering around the closet door, saw that Flo had let her negligee fall open and that Molina's eyes were fixed on her body.

"You would like me to return, no?" Molina whispered. "After I take the bottles to the men? But what would *mí capitán* say?"

"He's sleeping so deeply, he'd never know."

"Ay, las rubias!" Molina chuckled. *"Todavia bus-*

canda un hombre!" He chuckled again. "What *mí capitán* don' know won't hurt us, you and me? No? *Pues,* I take the bottles quick, and come right back."

"Hurry, then!" Flo urged. "I'll be waiting for you!"

Not only was Flo waiting for Molina when he came back. Longarm was, too. The sergeant rushed eagerly through the door into the *sala*. Flo had stationed herself a few feet inside, and Molina saw only her. Longarm stepped from behind the door and shoved his Colt hard against Molina's bare neck.

"Stop right where you are, hombre, and keep quiet, or you're dead."

Molina was as startled as Ramos had been. "*El gringo federalista!* Why you not in jail?"

"I reckon because I busted out," Longarm said. "Take his gunbelt off, Flo. Then we'll put him in with Ramos."

While Flo was relieving Molina of his pistol belt, he asked, "*Mí capitán,* he is not *borracho?*"

"No, but I'll just bet he wishes he was," she told him.

"*Rubia perfidia!*" Molina snorted. "You and the *gringo cabrón* have plan this!"

"You finally figured that out, did you?" Longarm grinned. To Flo, he said, "Come on, we'll put him in where him and his boss can look at each other."

There was plenty of material left in the bedsheet Flo had torn up when Ramos was being bound to provide strips with which to tie Molina to another chair. Longarm kept his gun trained on the sergeant while Flo gagged and tied him. Ramos and Molina sat facing one another, glaring angrily across the few feet that separated them. It was obvious that each would try to blame the other for their plight.

Longarm guffawed. "I'd sure like to be around when they start jawing. I bet a man could pick up a bunch of brand-new Mexican cusswords about that time."

"What I hope is that we'll be a long way from here when they get loose," Flo said. "I've seen all I want to of rurales and Mexican bandits, both."

"It's going to be a while before we can take off," Longarm reminded her. "It sure won't be safe to show our heads outside this place until the whole bunch down by that barracks is blind drunk."

"How long do you think we'd better wait?"

"An hour. Maybe two. I'll look out now and again, to keep an eye on how their party's going. We can tell when the time's right."

"I suppose I can wait that long. But let's go somewhere else, in the big room, where we can have a drink and relax."

"Sounds fine to me. Might as well make the best we can of waiting, since there's no way we can cut it shorter."

"I'll get the only other clothes I've got," Flo said. "This nightgown's comfortable, but if I'm going for a horseback ride, I'll want something more than it between me and the wind."

She groped behind the dressing table, brought up a small portmanteau, and busied herself throwing into it the cosmetics that were on the dresser and the dark dress that hung beside it.

"There. I guess that'll fix me up," she told Longarm. "Now let's get out of this damned room. I don't like the things it makes me remember."

Chapter 15

Longarm stayed in the bedroom long enough to blow out the kerosene lamp on the dressing table. He told the gagged rurales, "It just wouldn't do if one of you was to work your chair over and manage to knock that lamp off. Setting fire to this place'd be a sure way to bring your gang kiting up here, now wouldn't it? So, you'll just have to put up with being in the dark, I guess."

He followed Flo into the sala. She'd dropped her portmanteau and was making a beeline for the liquor cabinet. "I need something to wash the taste of that rye whiskey you favor out of my mouth." She found a bottle of Otard and looked at the label. "This is the best liquor I've seen since a rich stage-door Johnny took me to supper after the show at the Astor House, a week before I left to come down here."

"I'll stick to my own," Longarm told her, tilting the bottle of rye. Flo was using the corkscrew on the brandy bottle; Longarm idly began looking into the other cabinets that lined the room's walls. He found one packed with small valuables of various kinds: rings, watches, bracelets, table silver; his idea that the rurales under Diaz behaved very much like the bandit gangs they were supposed to control was confirmed by the sight of the loot. The next cabinet he opened was packed with clothing, and the garment that lay on top of the heap was the frock coat that had been taken from him the day before. He slid his hand into its pockets. Except for his wallet, their contents were untouched.

Flo said, "Unless you just want to keep on looking around, we might as well go in and sit down at that fancy table in there. It's going to be a long wait, isn't it?"

"Times when a couple of hours seems like a week," Longarm said. "But you're right, we might as well be comfortable."

They moved back into the sala. Flo set the bottle of brandy on the big table and pulled a chair up in front of it. "I'm not a lady drunk," she told Longarm. "But this is a time when a girl needs a little comforting. Don't worry, I won't overdo."

"I ain't worrying." Longarm sipped from the rye. "Talking about drunks gives me an idea, though. I'll just step outside and see how that bunch is doing with the liquor we sent 'em."

He tossed his coat on the table and, more as a precaution than because he thought he'd need it, picked up his Winchester. As he stepped out the door, Longarm heard music coming from the direction of the barracks, and saw the bare ground between the headquarters and jail flooded with firelight. He slid along the headquarters wall until he could get a clear look. The fire at the barracks had been rekindled. Its dancing flames spread over the entire outpost area. Around the fire, an impromptu fiesta was being held. The lavanderas had joined the rurales at the barracks; men and women were dancing around the fire to the music of guitar and concertina. The flames glinted on bottles being passed, lifted, waved.

Longarm watched for several minutes. As his eyes adjusted to the light, he could see that the liquor had already taken a number of the rurales out of action. A half-dozen sprawled forms lay beside the barracks wall, or were propped against it. While he was watching, another man who'd overestimated his capacity, or underestimated the potency of liquor strange to him, staggered and went down. His dancing partner helped another rurale to drag the drunk man to the wall, then she and the man who'd helped her rejoined the dancers around the fire.

Things ought to quiet down soon, Longarm told himself, when there's just enough men left sober to pair off with the women.

He slid back along the wall and into the sala. Flo had given up her chair and was sitting on the edge of the big table. She was sipping from the brandy bottle again. Longarm could see from the smile she turned to him when she took the bottle from her lips that she was feeling good, not from the lift of the liquor, but the euphoria of having her freedom again. It occurred to him that he felt pretty much the same way she did.

"How's the orgy going?" she asked him.

"Oh, they're whooping it up, if that's what an orgy is. Makes me sorta wish I could join 'em, they're having such a good time."

"How long before things will be quiet enough for us to sneak your friends out of the pokey and get away?"

"About another hour, I'd guess. Maybe a little longer. I'd go get Nate and John right now, except that they've built up their fire, and the damn place is just about as bright as noontime outside. Can't risk moving around, they might notice us."

"You might as well have another drink, then," Flo invited.

"I was just going to." Longarm stepped to the table, picked up his bottle of rye and sipped. Flo raised the brandy bottle in salute and sipped, too.

"I don't remember even saying thank you for getting me out of this mess," she said.

"You better save your thanks. We ain't out yet. Most anything could happen after we leave here, and it's still a long ride to Los Perros after we get started."

"Where in hell's Los Perros?"

"About a two-day ride. You never heard of it, Flo. It's a little shantytown on the border. I still got unfinished business there, so has Nate Webster. And John's cavalry post's not too far from it."

"Is there a train I can take out of it for New York?"

"Flo, there's no train tracks inside of two hundred miles of Los Perros. There's a stagecoach that passes by Fort Lancaster, though. I'll see you on a stage that'll get you to San Antonio. You can take a train back East from there."

"How far's San Antonio?"

"About a week on the stage."

Her eyes widened. "You know, God must've had one hell of a lot of spare space on His hands when He created Texas."

Longarm grinned. "There's been some questions asked whether it was God or the devil that's responsible for Texas. Me, I don't take either side. I get along wherever I might happen to be."

Flo looked at him narrowly. "You know, I believe you do. You're quite some man, Marshal."

"Thanks. But I'd feel better if you'd call me by my

name, which I guess we been too busy for me to tell you. It's Custis Long."

"Sure, Custis. Look, before we get off the subject, I was starting out to thank you for getting me away from Ramos and all the rest of this."

"I didn't do it for thanks."

"You've got mine, whether you want them or not. And just to show you I mean it—" She broke off, threw her arms around Longarm's neck, and pulled him to her. Before he knew what was happening, she was pressing her lips on his. He thought it was going to be a friendly thank-you kiss until he felt her tongue pressing his lips apart.

Longarm responded predictably. Flo hadn't yet changed clothes, and the gauze-thin nightgown she wore could hardly be felt when he brought his hands up to cup her generous breasts. His fingertips were hard on her budding nipples as he caressed them. The scent of her body, all aroma of woman not lately soaped or perfumed, filled his nostrils. He broke the kiss and bent to take her nipples in his lips, nipping them gently, pulling them into his mouth and feeling them roughen, swell and grow firm as his tongue's tip flicked them through the thin nightgown.

Flo leaned back, bracing herself with her arms, hands flat on the tabletop, her body upthrust to give Longarm free access to it. His face still buried in the soft flesh of her bosom, he rubbed a hand slowly down over her voluptuously rounded stomach and caressed her blonde pubic hair. She gave a dancer's kick to send the skirt of her gown flying upward, baring her legs and thighs. Longarm let his fingers stray deeper; she opened to them and he felt her beginning moisture on the soft lips between her thighs.

Flo was leaning back on only one arm, now. Her free hand was rubbing Longarm's crotch, feeling his erection grow. She worked at the buttons of his fly and tried to slip her hand in, but his britches fitted too closely. With a muttered "Damn it!" she unbuckled his belt and tugged at the waistband until she'd pulled the britches down over his hips and freed him.

"I'm as ready as you are," she said softly when she felt his hard springiness under her fingers.

"No use us waiting, then."

He moved between her legs and went in full and deep. Flo was on the table, Longarm standing in front of it. She lay back and brought her legs up, locked her ankles around the back of his neck.

"Ride me, now!" she commanded. "I want to feel you hit bottom!"

Longarm obliged. He pulled away from her, not leaving her totally empty, but nearly so. Then he thrust deliberately, deeper than he'd been able to go before.

Flo shrieked, a cry in which pain and pleasure mingled. "Oh, God, you did hit bottom! Do it again, faster!"

After a dozen deep, shattering thrusts, Longarm felt Flo's juices begin to ooze. Her cries of excitement, the heat of her body, the dangerous surroundings, were having their effect on Longarm. He was moving fast to orgasm. He pounded harder, bringing animal yelps from deep in Flo's throat. She became rigid for an instant. Her inner muscles tightened around him and he pressed hard for the instant before both of them were seized with a shuddering that ended in a blissful outpouring and a total relaxation. Longarm fell forward, pushing Flo's knees down nearly to the tabletop and penetrating her even more deeply than ever for a shattering instant before he relaxed.

Neither of them moved for several moments. Flo found breath enough to whisper, "I didn't know, a minute ago, just how much man you really are."

"You're a right smart bundle of woman, Flo. But we're a couple of damn fools, you know that?"

"After the past few weeks, it feels so good to be able to let go completely that I don't mind being a damn fool. It didn't last nearly long enough, though."

"We'll have more time, later. After we get away from this damn place."

"I think you're telling me something. We'd better get ready to run the gauntlet, is that it?"

"Something like that."

He pulled away from her reluctantly. Flo sat up and Longarm began to button his britches. His sense of timing told him they'd better be thinking of the men in jail instead of one another.

"Get into your traveling clothes as quick as you can," he told her. "I'll go see what things look like outside."

Longarm looked back across the sala before he went out the door. In the dim light of the vigil candle, he saw Flo in half-silhouette. She was standing beside the table, naked, the light dancing on her tall body, outlining its features. Her upraised arms, stretching luxuriously, pulled her breasts high and taut. Her rounded stomach flowed into flared hips, her pubic fringe matching the hair that fell in glowing gold, long, down her back. Her long legs seemed even longer as she rose on tiptoes in her stretching. For an instant he wanted to turn back, but common sense said no. He went through the door and out into the darkness.

This time, it was true darkness. The fire that had flared a half hour ago was dying down. Only a handful of dancers now moved their feet in time to the thin melody of guitar strings. The concertina was silent. There were more figures lying on the ground and leaning against the barracks wall. A wide belt of deep shadow lay between barracks and jailhouse. Longarm felt a twinge of guilt because he'd made his cellmates wait such a long time. It was, he decided, safe now to risk making an effort to leave.

Flo was wearing a flared skirt of dark material, a man-styled blue silk blouse, and a short jacket. She'd twisted her hair into a bun low on her neck. She saw in Longarm's face that it was time for them to go.

"I'm ready," she told him. "Just tell me what you want me to do."

"Stick close by me. We'll mosey slow across the open space. Most of the rurales and their women are sleeping-drunk, and the ones that're still on their feet are about ready to fall over."

"What if they see us?"

"Don't pay any attention until one of 'em starts to holler, and then let me handle things. Can you use a gun?"

"God, no, Custis! The only gun I ever shot was a toy popgun I used in one of my dance routines."

"Then you'd better carry the ones we're taking for Nate and John. Think you can tote 'em?"

"Dancers have to keep in trim. I'm pretty strong, you ought to know that."

He remembered her arms pulling him down to her, her legs clasping his body. "You are, at that." He picked up the rifles he'd taken from Ramos's collection and helped her balance them in her hands before draping a gunbelt with a holstered revolver over each of her shoulders. He'd looked until he'd found guns of the same caliber as his own Winchester and Colt, and had gathered up all the .44-40 ammunition he could find. This he'd put into bags, which he slung over his own shoulder.

"Just move slow and steady," he cautioned her. "And don't fret. We'll make it, all right."

Their passage through the belt of darkness between the headquarters building and the jail drew no attention from the dancers still twirling by the waning fire. Longarm hadn't expected it to. The minutes of danger lay ahead, when they'd be working with the horses at the corral. They got to the jail and found the door swinging wide. Longarm slipped inside. It was pitch black.

"Nate? John?" He kept his voice low.

"We're all right." It was Webster's voice.

"What in hell's name happened that took you so long?" Hill asked.

"Had to wait until the liquor I fed them rurales put most of 'em under. All but a few's passed out now. But we'll still have to tiptoe when we go outa here." His eyes could penetrate the gloom of the jail's interior now. He saw a white form spreadeagled across the door of the cell in which Webster and Hill waited. "What happened in here?"

"We had to throttle old Sebastian." Hill spoke without emotion. "Hated to do it, but he started yelling when he noticed you were gone. Before we could stop him, he threw the keys down the corridor. We couldn't reach them to let ourselves out."

Longarm reached into his coat pocket for a match, thought better of showing a light in the jail, and said, "I'll scrabble for 'em."

While he was groping around on the floor, Webster said, "We heard all the music and laughing, and I shinnied up to look outa that hole in the roof. By then, it was too light from their fire for us to try a sneak."

"We didn't know you'd arranged their party," Hill said. "If we had, we wouldn't have been so nervous, waiting."

Longarm finally located Sebastian's key ring. He said, while he unlocked the cell door, "It was the only way I could figure to put most of 'em to sleep. If we're lucky, we can get away without raising a ruckus."

He led the way outside. When Webster saw Flo standing by the door with the guns, he made a leap for her and would've wrestled her down if Longarm hadn't grabbed him.

"She's with us," he said. "Flo's been a real help. I might not've been able to swing it without her."

"Where the hell did you find her?" Hill asked.

"Ramos grabbed her away from some bandits who'd kidnapped her off a train. She can tell you about it later. She's American, just like us."

"And ready to go home," Flo said.

"She's American, all right," Hill agreed. "Easterner, I'd say."

"New York, New York," Flo told him. "And if I ever get back there, nobody's going to get me west again, not even across the river to Jersey."

"We better be thinking about another river," Webster reminded them. He gestured toward the two or three couples still dancing around the embers of the fire. "If that's all of Ramos's crew that's still able to stand up, we won't have much trouble."

"Let's try to do it without no trouble at all," Longarm suggested. "Here's what I'd like to do: we go down to the corral real quiet, so's not to spook the horses. That gray of mine's the easiest to spot, so I'll pussyfoot in and lead him out while you fellows get us some saddles. We'll load the saddles on the dapple, just any which way, and I'll lead him off. Then you sneak your animals out the same way, one at a time. We'll get far enough so nobody can hear us, then we'll saddle up and be off free."

"Wait a minute," Webster said. "Miss Flo, you know how to sit a horse?"

"I guess Mexican horses are pretty much the same as the ones I ride in Central Park. I had a friend who was—" She broke off. "That's neither here nor there. Yes, I can ride enough to get away from here. I'd ride an elephant, if I had to."

Circling to stay within the increasingly wide zone of

darkness, they walked slowly and steadily until they were within a few yards of the corral.

Longarm said, "All right. Everybody knows what we'll do. I'll leave Flo to hold my gray after we're far enough off, and come back to get a nag for her."

Groping along the corral's top pole, Longarm located his saddle by feel. He knew it was taking time, but he hated to part with the old McClellan and have to break in a new one. He tossed three other saddles to the ground and followed them with a heap of saddle blankets, then bridles. He whistled low, and Webster and Hill moved up to untangle the gear. Longarm located the gate pole and ducked under it. One or two of the horses shied and whinnied, but none of them cut up too badly or made a lot of noise. He found Tordo and rubbed the dapple's nose.

"Easy, boy. Come along."

Tordo followed him readily through the gate. With nose-pats and low-voiced words, Longarm kept the gray standing while Webster and Hill piled the saddles loosely on his back.

"I'll head straight north," Longarm told them. That was all he needed to say. He knew both men were trail-wise and would sight on the North Star and stay on a straight course until they reached wherever he'd decided to stop. "Come on, Flo." She joined him and they moved off.

When they were out of earshot of the corral, she said with open amazement, "Those men acted like it was the most normal thing in the world for me to be here, a million miles from nowhere. Why, Custis, they didn't ask more than two or three questions."

"They're both good men. They know when it's time to talk and when it's time to do. Back at the jail, we had to do, not stand palavering all night."

"How far will we have to ride now?"

"Tonight we'll just push far enough on to get a good lead on the rurales. When we come to a good place, we'll stop and rest a while, and move on at dawn."

"You think Ramos will come after us, then?"

"Damn right he will. He can't afford to let even one of us get away. He likely won't start, though, till it's light enough for his trackers to read trail. We got a little time. Not much, but a little bit."

They walked on in silence for a while. Finally, Longarm said, "I guess this is far enough. I'll saddle Tordo while we're waiting; as soon as I hear John or Nate coming, I'll start back."

"I'm not afraid to wait in the dark, if that's keeping you here." Flo put her arms around Longarm's waist. It wasn't a sexual gesture, but more as though she needed comforting. "But I'll admit, it's a lot nicer to have you to wait with."

"Maybe it's just this wild country bothering you." Longarm was holding her gently. "People that live in places like New York get spooked when they're out away from everything."

"It's not that. I'll tell you, Custis, New York's just a different kind of wild from this place here. And I'm used to looking out for myself."

Longarm had known theatrical women before; he had enjoyed their breeziness and the uninhibited approach to living that characterized those with stage backgrounds. He'd seen them tear through danger, as Flo had earlier, without turning a hair, and then be caught up, just as she was now, in a reaction. Her need for reassurance didn't really surprise him.

"We're going to be fine, Flo. You think about how much better off we are now than we were a few hours ago."

"Like hell we are. A few hours ago, you and I were having one of the best damned fucks I've ever enjoyed. Now, we're out here in the middle of some big black nowhere, don't know where we are, whether those murdering rurales are after us, or what."

"But there's twice as many of us now," he pointed out. "We got guns, and don't you think for a minute we're lost. You settle down, now, keep on kicking for a day or two, and before you know it, you'll be on your way back home."

She leaned back in his arms, and in the starlight he could see that she'd cried a little bit, but was smiling now. "Sorry, Custis. I don't usually act like a baby. I keep telling myself I'm a big girl and don't need anybody to pat my ass and tell me I'm going to be all right. But I guess all of us do, sometimes."

"You'll be fine now, though."

"Sure I will. As long as I can hold on to you for a minute or so, once in a while."

"Whenever you want to. I'll see you're safe."

Hoofbeats told them that either Hill or Webster was approaching. Longarm whistled softly, to help whoever it was in finding them. In a few minutes, Hill came up.

"Nate'll be right along," he said. "Everything was quiet when I left, so it looks like we've pulled it off."

"Now you're here, I'll go cut out a horse for Flo," Longarm said. "It oughtn't to take me long."

He had no trouble at the corral. In front of the barracks building, the fire had died to a few stray red coals and all the dancers had gone. Longarm thought he could see some forms still sprawled against the building's walls, but couldn't be sure. The headquarters was dark; so was the jail. He made quick work of cutting out a horse, wasting a few minutes patting necks and noses, hoping to find one that seemed gentler than most of the Mexican horses he'd seen so far. He wasn't sure whether Flo could really ride, or was just claiming she could for fear of being left behind.

Hill and Webster had the other horses saddled by the time Longarm got back. The fourth was quickly fitted, and Longarm was satisfied when he saw Flo mount easily and with confidence that she'd be able to stay on. He swung onto Tordo's back.

Hill said, "Well, gentlemen—and lady, too, of course—I don't see any reason to stay here. Since we don't have a bugler to sound commands, I'll give them myself. Route pace, ma-arch—ho!"

Chapter 16

A raw September breeze from the low peaks of the Burro Mountains was in their faces as the little group skirted the foothills, riding through the darkness. Without discussion, the men fanned out ahead, calling out when a barrier such as a steep canyon cut across their path, or when the way ahead of one or the other seemed easier. They followed no trail because there was none to follow, but set their way by the stars, bearing consistently northeast. The going was slow and rough on the horses. They circled the deeper canyons, slid down the slopes of shallow arroyos, and pushed through brushy patches that tore at their legs. It was country that called for both chaps and tapaderos, but they had neither.

After four hours of steady but slow progress, Longarm called a halt. "We better let these animals rest," he said. "Far's that goes, I guess we need a breather ourselves. It's still a while before daybreak, and I don't figure the rurales are going to start after us until they can see our sign."

"They'll be moving faster, though," Webster warned. "And some of those cholos are part Indian. They'll know the land better, too."

"We haven't left that much of a trail," Hill protested. "But I'll agree, we do need to rest. I just hate to lose our lead."

"After daybreak, we'll make better time," Longarm pointed out. "I'd say to stop at the first good place we come to, and start out fresh with first light."

"If you're worrying about me," Flo said, "I'm tired, but I'll sure keep on going as long as you men want to. Don't do me any favors just because I'm a woman."

"We ain't," Webster assured her. "It wouldn't be any different if you weren't along, Miss Flo."

They pushed on, moving more slowly now, until they came to a brush-covered slope over which a handful of tall ocote pines towered, their night-black limbs breaking the deep blue sky. Longarm called for the others to stop and urged Tordo into the fringe of the brush that surrounded the trees. The dapple pushed through the shrubs without hesitating. Longarm leaned down to feel the vegetation and found that the stalks of the bushes and their leaves were smooth and free of thorns. He reined Tordo lightly, to turn him, but the animal resisted, wanting to go ahead. Longarm let him. The gray broke into a clearing, and moved faster. Then he stopped. Longarm heard the splash of running water, and then saw the little pool made by a spring reflecting the stars. He let Tordo drink sparingly and went back to tell the others.

"Damn horse had more sense than me, for once. I ought to've known when I felt them huisache leaves that there'd be water, they're thirsty plants. If everybody agrees, this is as good a place to rest as we're likely to find."

There was no dissent. They pushed into the clearing and dismounted. After all of them had drunk and wiped the cool, faintly salt-tasting water over their dusty faces, they let the horses drink, and tethered them with slacked girths at the edge of the clearing.

Hill's military training showed. He asked, "Don't you think we ought to take turns at sentry duty? We don't really know that the rurales aren't on our trail right now."

"Makes sense to me," Webster nodded.

"Me, too," Longarm agreed.

"Since it was my idea, I'll take the first watch," Hill offered. "If we stand an hour each, that ought to take up what's left of the night."

Webster spoke up. "I'll relieve you, then, and the Marshal can stand the wake-up watch."

"What about me?" Flo asked. "I'll do my share, too."

"No need, Miss Flo," the ranger said. "You've had a real hard day. You get what sleep you can."

"But—" Flo began.

Longarm interrupted her. "Listen to what Nate says. He's got a reason maybe you don't understand. It's not because you're a woman, but because you're a tenderfoot. All three of us'd know if we heard a horse or maybe a deer or goat in the dark. You wouldn't."

"I hadn't thought of it that way," she nodded. "All right, if that's your reason."

There was a brief time of settling down. Hill took his rifle and pushed through the brush, following the trail they'd broken on their way in. Webster, an old hand at impromptu bivouacs, found himself a patch of green weeds far enough from the spring to be on dry ground. He curled up and was snoring in two minutes. Without exchanging a word, Flo and Longarm threaded their way through a patch of brush to the base of one of the ocote pines. They sat down together.

"I wanted to—" she began.

Longarm put a finger across her lips. "No need to talk about it, Flo, honey. I wanted to, too. There's better things in life than just sleeping, ain't there?"

She turned her lips to him. They sank back on the short, curly growth that carpeted the ground where it was shaded by the ocote. Flo shrugged out of her jacket and Longarm began to rub her breasts.

"It was fine, back at the rurales' place, but it was over too quickly," she murmured into his ear.

Instead of answering, Longarm began kissing her. His hands wandered over her body and hers were exploring his. She broke their embrace long enough to slide her short silk knickers off, and he ran his hand along her smooth, tapered thighs. Flo began working at freeing Longarm's erection; feeling it grow in quick pulses set her to breathing faster. She stirred, rolled on her side, and pulled him to her. She took him between her thighs, squeezing him tightly, pushing against him, until the moist heat spreading upward from his groin and the incessant movement of Flo's tongue in his mouth brought Longarm up full and swollen.

"Let me in you now," he told her, and Flo obeyed.

"But slow," she whispered in his ear. "I love the feeling of you going in. I want to enjoy it as long as I can."

Longarm penetrated her as she'd asked him to, slowly and deliberately, and for what seemed a very long time they lay simply enjoying the sensation of their intermingled bodies. Flo began to contract her inner muscles in a gentle rhythm that brought Longarm to an orgasm that was as quick as it was unexpected. There'd been few women he'd known before who'd mastered use of the muscles Flo was employing. She didn't stop her inner contractions while Longarm rested, still hard inside her, and she teased him with gentle nips of her sharp teeth on his neck and ears and lips.

Longarm recovered quickly and rolled on top of Flo. She was as eager now as he was, and opened her thighs to let his slim hips drop between them to sink into her more deeply. He began rocking slowly, feeling her hips roll beneath him. Soft birdlike cries escaped Flo's lips. Longarm read the signal she was giving him and began thrusting faster to meet her growing frenzy. Time stopped for both of them for a while; they were aware of nothing but sensation.

"Faster, now!" she urged him. Her head began rolling, loosening the bun in which she'd caught her hair, and her long blonde locks spread over the dark ground.

Longarm began driving, his arms encircling Flo's neck, holding her mouth hard to his while they exchanged tongue-caresses. Her hips were bouncing frantically now, but she still controlled her motions, just as Longarm did his. They didn't need to exchange words. Instinct joined experience to guide their movements, hips drawing apart and coming together in unison, in perfect mutual rhythm, to send each of his strokes fully into her depths.

Then the moment came when Longarm felt his control slipping away. He speeded his thrusts, Flo matched his downward plunges, as they rushed together toward those few final seconds when their desire could no longer be denied and the climactic shuddering began that brought them both pressing together, passing through the little death that left them sprawled inert, helpless and almost senseless.

Panting, they rolled apart. Longarm said, "Damn! You really got it, Flo. If I wasn't a broad-minded man, I'd be jealous of anybody that ever got in you before me."

"Don't be, Custis. The first few didn't get much. Neither did I, for that matter. But I can't remember any man who had more than you've got, or knew how to use it better."

"I guess we've both had about the same amount of practice. I'll give you this, Flo: you know what you want, and don't let anything stop you from taking it."

"I needed somebody like you, after Ramos. He was so little and so damned fat that all he could do was make me want a real man. Besides, I enjoy giving, but I don't like being taken." Flo turned her head suddenly and spat, somehow making the unladylike action a maidenly gesture of utter contempt. "Ramos! *Paugh!*"

"Talking about Ramos, if we don't do more sleeping and less fucking, we're not going to be much good later on."

"I feel like sleeping, now. I didn't before." She stretched like an animal. Longarm could almost see the muscles under her silken skin rippling in the starlight. What he couldn't see, he imagined.

"You move like that another time, I'm going to be all over you again," he warned her.

"Come on. Any time." When he didn't move, she asked, "Sleepy?"

"Some. A mite tuckered, too. And beginning to think about what might happen tomorrow. If I'm feeling drawn-out, you must be, too."

"I'll sleep, if you'll hold me."

"You got a deal. But pull on your drawers, and I'll button up. If we don't, we'll be starting in again."

Cuddled together, they were asleep in a few minutes.

Captain Hill woke them. It was still dark. Hill said, "It's about time for you to relieve Nate, Marshal." He hesitated, and added, "But if the lady feels safer with you here to look after her, I'm still fresh. I'll take another watch."

"No you won't. It's my job, and I aim to do it. You'll be fine as long as you know the captain's here, won't you, Flo?"

Sleepily, Flo replied, "Sure. I'm not a baby any more." She closed her eyes again at once and was asleep again.

Longarm and Hill walked quietly away from her

until they were far enough to be sure their voices wouldn't disturb her. "Looks like she's fallen for you," Hill commented. "Not that it's any affair of mine what you and the lady do, but if it comes to a fight, and she keeps clinging to you, it might get all of us killed."

"I don't think you got anything to fret over. Flo's sensible. I seen that when she was helping me tie up Ramos and Molina. She'll carry her own weight, if it comes to a scrap."

"Good. Well, I'll go back to sleep, then." Hill lay down, using his arm for a pillow, in the manner of a man used to sleeping on the ground. He grinned up at Longarm. "Tell the bugler not to bother to blow reveille. I always wake up before he does, anyhow."

Chuckling, Longarm backtracked through the bent-down huisache growth until he found Webster. The ranger was sitting Indian style on a boulder, his rifle across his knees.

"Nothing so far," he greeted Longarm. "We didn't really expect there'd be, I guess."

"No. Still too soon. If we're lucky, we'll pick up another half-day's lead on 'em before they get to where we are now."

"We better be lucky, then. We're outgunned about eight to one, when they do catch up," Webster said thoughtfully. "Which wouldn't spook me much, if it wasn't for Miss Flo."

"That's occurred to me too, Nate. I got a hunch we can handle Ramos's bunch, though, if we don't make a bunch of tomfool moves."

"Sounds like you been doing some thinking."

"Some. Haven't you?"

"Oh, sure. Trouble is, this deal's a little out of my line. In the old days, you know, us rangers moved in companies, during the Indian-fighting and Mexican wars. The work we do nowadays is mostly single-handed."

Longarm carefully avoided suggesting that the ranger was old enough to've fought in the War Between the States. If Webster'd been in it, then there'd be the risk of stirring up bad memories. And Longarm knew just how bad those memories could be. He'd never rid his mind of the image of the dead rotting under summer rains at Shiloh. Then again, if Webster'd skulked out of the war, he wouldn't be proud of it. Longarm decided it wasn't a good idea to talk in military terms.

"I've got the glimmer of a scheme that might get us across the river without a stand-up fight, Nate," he said. "Tell you what, you go get your shuteye, and give me a little more time to think. I'll come in at first light and the three of us'll powwow."

Longarm's watch wore itself along uneventfully. He spent his hour sitting on the boulder that Webster had occupied, keeping his ears tuned for sounds that might give warning of pursuit and thinking of ways to keep the rurales at bay when they caught up. He had no doubt that they would catch up, sooner or later.

When the first faint threads of gray showed across the high mesas in the east, Longarm uncoiled, stretched the kinks out of his leg muscles, and walked back to the thicket. He found Webster and Flo still asleep, but Hill, true to his promise, was stirring around.

"I've tightened the girths and put the bridles back on the mounts," the cavalryman announced. "As soon as we mount up, we can move out."

"Let's stay here a minute or two, John," Longarm suggested. "Give Nate and Flo time to duck back of a bush and pee, and wash their faces. Then we'll have a little council of war, if everybody's agreeable."

When they'd assembled, he outlined the plan he'd worked out during his hour of sentry duty.

"We got to figure the rurales will come after us," he began. "We shoved their faces in a hot cow pie when we slipped away from 'em, and Ramos can't let us go free and make trouble for his bosses in Mexico City. Now we know we can't outgun 'em in a showdown fight. Them rurales look sloppy, and sometimes they don't seem right bright, but from what I've heard, they're damn tough fighters."

"They're that," Webster affirmed. "Our only chance would be to hole up in a place where they could only come at us a few at a time. But even if we found a place like that, all they'd have to do is starve us out. Our best chance is to keep ahead of 'em."

"It's our only chance," Hill said. "Not just the best one."

"Sure, all of us know that," Longarm agreed. "We've

got to take out of here running and keep running till we get to the border."

"But we can't afford to blow our horses," the cavalry officer cautioned. "They've got remounts, we haven't. Even if it loses time for us, we'll have to breathe them before they drop."

"I figured on that," Longarm said. "My scheme is for us to go like hell when we take off. When the horses need a rest, we'll stop. From there, we'll split up." He saw that Webster was about to object and held up a hand to stop him. "Just a minute, Nate. I'm not done. Far's I know, there's only one place you could call a town on the other side of the river that we'd have a chance to get to. That's Los Perros. Am I right about that, John?"

"Yes. There're a few other shanty settlements along the river, but Los Perros is the biggest one, the only place we'd have a chance to find enough men to help us. The others only have a dozen or so people living in them."

"That's what I'd guessed," Longarm said. "Now, then. When we split up, we'll do it someplace where two men can hold back Ramos's bunch for a while. It don't have to be for too long, just enough cover to stop the rurales for an hour or two. If the ones that leave ride hell for leather, they oughta get to Los Perros in time to pull some kind of crew together to beat the rurales back."

"What about the two who've fought rear guard?" Hill asked. "Do you think they can outrun the rurales all the way to the river?"

"If they make a sneak and get a start before Ramos's men know they've gone, I figure they can," Longarm replied.

Webster and Hill thought about the idea for a moment, then the ranger said, "It's about the best we can do, I'd say. We're sorta between a rock and a hard place."

"I'd give a lot to have just one squad of my men at the river," Hill said grimly. He smiled and added, "But I'd give a lot to have a Gatling gun along with us right now. All right, Marshal, it looks like we agree that your plan's our only chance. Nate and I will take the rear guard job, you and the lady ride ahead."

"I didn't figure it that way," Longarm said. "It looks to me like you're the man to get Sheriff Tucker into line and organize whatever kind of bunch he can help you put together in Los Perros."

"I'm not sure you're right about that, Marshal." Hill shook his head. "Tucker and I have had our differences. He propositioned me to be his silent partner a couple of years ago in a plan he'd come up with to turn Los Perros into a honkytonk town. Wanted me to give my troopers extra payday liberty to come in and spend their money at the whorehouses—excuse me, Miss Flo—and the gambling joints he proposed to put in. I read him off and told him I'd do my damnedest to keep my men out of his town in the future. And I have. I don't think he'd forget that."

"No. He ain't that kind," Longarm said. "Damn it! I was sorta counting on you to take care of that part of the scheme."

"I won't say I can't, but I won't say I can. You know army policy. We're not supposed to interfere with civilian government affairs unless we're asked by the authorities for help."

"I don't know you'd call Tucker an authority," Webster put in. "He never was elected to be, except by himself. But John's got a reason to be doubtful, just like I have. I had a run-in with Tucker when I first started looking into the Laredo Loop business. He just the same as told me to go to hell. I've got a hunch that it was Tucker who tipped off his partners in Mexico to get the rurales looking for me after he found out I'd crossed the border."

"That leaves you, Marshal," Hill said. "I think Nate and I both feel you're the man to do it. From what you told us while we were in that cell together, you've handled Tucker before, and you've got the lever on him to handle him again."

"John's right," Webster agreed. "Your scheme might just save all our butts—excuse me, Miss Flo—save our hides, if you can get Tucker to round up a couple of dozen men to cover the two of us when we get close to the river."

"I didn't plan to be the one to split off when I dreamed up this scheme," Longarm said. "But I can see you might be right in figuring the best way to work it out."

"There's only one weak spot I can see," Hill frowned. "Ma'am, can you handle a horse at a gallop over rough country?"

"I never had to, until now," Flo said. "But if I'm betting my life on whether I can or not, I'll do it one way or another."

"Flo's kept up so far," Longarm reminded them. "I ain't too worried about her staying right alongside of me."

"It's settled, then," Hill nodded. "We'll push on, and when the time comes, all of us will know what to do."

"And all we need to make things work," Longarm said, "is some nerve and good shooting and one hell of a lot of luck!"

Chapter 17

"How much farther is it?" Flo asked Longarm. They'd pulled up to give the horses a breather.

"Two hours. Maybe three." He squinted at the sun dipping now to the west, but still well above the humped tops of the Burro range. "You getting tired, Flo?"

"Some. But don't look for me to quit, Custis. I won't do that."

"Didn't figure you would, or you wouldn't be here."

They'd parted from Webster and Hill shortly after noon, at a rock outcrop that all of them agreed was the best defensive position they'd seen so far. The spot was on that single long spur of the Burros that pushes out far past the other rises of the foothills, and runs at an angle to the rest of the range. The spur, instead of lying generally north-south, slants off to the east, in the direction of the Rio Grande.

A fault in the rock had created a fortress in miniature that might have been planned by an engineer. Through the centuries, the crevasse had become filled with broken rock, then topped with rain-washed sand to create a firm, fairly level floor. The rock fissure was triangular, big enough to hold two horses and their riders and still leave room for them to move about. To the south and along the hump of the spur, the rock was unbroken, solid but slick. A horse could not keep its footing on it, and a man would be able to do so only with difficulty. The triangle that constituted the fort was deep enough to protect a horse or a standing man. Behind it, sheer, raw rock rose two hundred feet straight up. Except for the extension of the fissure that gave access to the triangle, there was no way for an attacker to approach it.

Captain Hill had been delighted from the instant they'd seen the place. "That's our spot, Nate! From behind that shelf, we can cover any approach the rurales might want to use."

"Except from behind us," the ranger pointed out. "If they get a man or two up above us, shooting down, we're wide open."

Hill squinted along the face of the cliff. "I think there's enough of an overhang to shield us. I'll take the chance, if you will."

"Oh, I didn't say I'd back away from it," Webster said quickly. "Time's running out, and this is about the only place we've come to where we'd have a better than even chance."

"You might not have to make a fight at all," Longarm reminded them. "We've kept ahead, so far. You stay here about two or three hours. If they don't show up, ride for the river."

"I wouldn't bet we're going to get off that light," Webster said. "And I wouldn't want Ramos's outfit to get off, either. After what happened to John and me, we're both ready to sting 'em."

"Win, lose, or draw, then," Hill said, "this is where we stay. Three hours, Marshal. We'll guarantee you that much time."

"No," Longarm shook his head. "Don't set a limit, John. Just do your best if they catch up, but don't let 'em get you. If it gets too hot, you and Nate pull leather for Los Perros. We'll try to be ready. Just remember, Ramos ain't Santa Ana, and this place ain't the Alamo."

He and Flo had started off, then, and had ridden as fast as they dared push their horses without crippling them. Longarm kept a close lookout for familiar country. The trailless foothills were strange to him. The path taken by the rustled herd he'd followed south had avoided the higher country and moved along the narrow strip of flat land between the Burros and the Rio Grande. He'd set a course on a long slant that he'd confidently expected would intersect the rustlers' route. Once on that trail, he'd planned to follow it to the ford above Los Perros. He didn't want to risk a strange crossing; the Rio Grande's reputation for horse-swallowing quicksand beds in its shallows and tumbling, unpredictable currents in its deeper stretches was something he remembered from his earlier trip there. So far, though, there'd been no sign of the rustlers' route.

Now, looking as far ahead as possible from the slight elevation of the ridgeline they'd been following, he still saw nothing that resembled the terrain he'd noted on his way south. He pressed his knees to Tordo's ribs, and found that the gray was breathing easily, no longer panting. Flo's Mexican mount seemed to have eased too.

"We've given 'em all the time we can spare," he told her. "We better be moving again." He picked up the reins from his saddlehorn and was just about to nudge Tordo ahead when he saw the thin column of dust below and behind them. He called to Flo, "Hold up!"

"What's wrong? Did you see something?"

"Dust devil, maybe. It's hard to tell what the wind's doing in country like this." He kept his eyes on the smudge that rose low into the harsh blue sky. The thin cloud wasn't acting the way a dust devil ought to. Those miniature whirlwinds rose fast, moved erratically, and died quickly. This one was moving slowly and kept hanging in the sky. There wasn't enough dust to mark a lot of riders, though, he thought.

Anxiously, Flo asked, "Is that the dust devil, right there?" She pointed.

"That's what I'm looking at. Only I'm damn sure now it ain't a dust devil. It's riders."

"How many?" she asked. Then, as soon as she realized how impossible her question was to answer, she added, "I'm sorry. That was a silly thing to ask."

"For all you know, my eyes might be sharper than yours. But whoever it is or however many, they're still too far off to see."

"You think they're Ramos's men, Custis?"

"Likely as not. Nate and John wouldn't be down on the flat there. They'd be trailing us." Then, as an afterthought, Longarm added, "Unless they're being chased. But if they were, there'd be two dusts instead of just one."

"It's sort of like a Chinese puzzle, isn't it?" Flo asked. "You've got to fit all the pieces together just right, to work it."

"I'm pretty sure I've worked this one. It's just about bound to be some rurales. Not many, only maybe three or four. My guess is that Ramos took up our tracks, figured where we was headed, and sent a few riders to cut us off."

"You think there are more, on the trail we left?"

"That's about the only way to figure. Now we got something else to work out."

"What?"

"Whether we want to let them hombres down there go on past us, or try to stop 'em." Longarm saw that Flo didn't understand. He explained, "We let 'em get by, we don't have a fight right here and now, but we'll have one later on. They'll go on to the ford and set up an ambush."

"Which would be the easiest? Now, or later?"

"It's six of one, half a dozen of the other. We've got a little better position now. Later we won't know where they might jump us." Flo didn't reply. She was, Longarm knew, waiting for him to decide. He made up his mind quickly. "Let's keep moving. Maybe we can find a place up ahead before they catch up that'll be better'n where we are now."

They started on down the slope. Longarm kept watching the dust cloud, which grew larger bit by bit as it came closer. He was also scanning the ground ahead, looking for a place that would offer them cover. The land across which they were passing was in the zone where the foothills merged into the narrow plain that almost at once became the river valley. There were no rock outcrops here, only a few shallow barrancas cut by rains cascading downslope during the wet season. The ground was baked hard, too hard for the hooves of their mounts to raise any dust, and while Longarm had no hope of finding a natural fortress like the one Nate and Hill had to shield them, he thought their presence might not be noticed while the approaching riders were still distant. Given time, he and Flo might find concealment.

He checked the dust cloud again. It hadn't changed direction. Their course and the one the unknown riders held to were still converging. He estimated that they'd come together within the next two or three miles. Then, the hump of the ridge down which they rode would no longer hide them from the other group. Somewhere before that distance was closed, he and Flo would have to find cover or risk odds he couldn't yet guess at in a standup fight. If he'd been alone, he thought, he'd have taken the odds, sight unseen. Having Flo with him changed things.

Down the slope just ahead, a little below the shoulder of the ridge, Longarm saw a strange angular patch. It was the only feature of an otherwise barren stretch of baked, arid earth. He glanced at the dust cloud again. As nearly as he could tell, their path and that of the unseen riders would intersect only a short distance beyond the strange formation ahead. He still wasn't sure what the patch was, but it was the only unusual feature in an otherwise featureless landscape. It might be an unusual rock formation, or even the foundation of a long-abandoned building. Whatever it was, it was the only thing he could see that promised cover.

Over the drumming of their horses' hooves, he shouted to Flo, pointing, "We'll make for that place there!"

She looked, saw what he was indicating, and nodded. Longarm turned Tordo and tried to get a bit more speed out of the dapple. Flo followed him as he led the way to the strange formation.

As they drew closer, Longarm could see that what had caught his attention wasn't a rock outcrop, but a heap of fallen trees. The water that had once nourished a grove had failed and the trees had died and toppled, crisscrossing one another. It wasn't much protection, only a half-dozen sunbleached trunks, but it was better than nothing at all. With luck, the windfall would hide them from the oncoming riders. At worst, they'd provide a breastworks he'd have a chance of defending.

They reached the trees only seconds before the other horsemen rounded the foot of the ridge and came into sight. The tree trunks lay too low on the ground to hide the backs of their horses, but Longarm hoped the rurales —he was sure now that the strange riders had been sent by Ramos to cut them off from the river—would pass by without looking too closely in their direction.

He and Flo dismounted with no margin to spare. As they led their horses into the fallen trees they saw the horsemen galloping across the plain at the bottom of the slope. There were only three of them. Longarm breathed an inward sigh of relief. Three to one were odds he might handle. For a moment, it looked as though the trio of riders would pass on without seeing them, but apparently they'd been pushing their mounts as hard as Longarm and Flo had been driving their own. The three reined in about two or three hundred yards distant from the fallen trees.

Longarm had taken his Winchester out of its saddle scabbard when they dismounted. He studied the three men, in clear sight now that a dust cloud no longer surrounded them. The look removed any doubt as to their identity. All three wore the charro suits that the rurales had adopted as a sort of unofficial uniform.

"Are you going to shoot them?" Flo asked, looking at Longarm's rifle.

"Not now. It might be smart if I did, though. It's either now or later, when we get closer to the river."

"It seems so—well, so coldblooded. I mean, to shoot them when they're not shooting at us."

"If they see us, they'll be banging away soon enough. And three to one ain't odds exactly in our favor."

At that moment, the question of who'd start shooting first was settled without delay or debate. The rurales, getting ready to move ahead, were scanning the area all around them. Longarm could tell when one of the men spotted him. He gesticulated to his companions. The others swung in their saddles and gazed at the trees. They may have seen the horses' heads and rumps sticking up above the windfall. The three whipped their rifles around to free them from their shoulder slings and lead slugs began to slam into the tree trunks that sheltered Flo and Longarm.

"Guess we were bound to come down to it," Longarm muttered.

He centered the sights of the Winchester on the midsection of the nearest rurale and squeezed off a shot. The slug went high. He saw it kick up dust beyond the riders.

"Damn it!" he swore.

"What's the matter?" Flo was suddenly alarmed.

"Ramos or somebody must've monkeyed with my sights." He spoke while he was aiming again, making allowance for the change. This time his bullet went home. The rurale dropped from his saddle and lay still.

A fresh volley from the other two splatted into the trees, and a stray slug or two whistled overhead. The rurales were firing as fast as they could lever shells into the chambers of their guns. Flo was trembling. Longarm grabbed her and pulled her to the ground. After another shot or two, the firing from below stopped abruptly.

"Do you think they've gone?" Flo asked. The sudden ending of the gunfire had its effect on her voice. Even though their attackers were too far away to hear her, she whispered.

"Not a chance. I stopped shooting. They figure they've put me down. Soon as they can see us, they'll start up again."

Longarm raised his head above the tree trunks for a quick look. The riders below had thrown the body of their companion over his saddle and were disappearing around the shoulder of the ridge.

"Smart sons of bitches!" Longarm growled.

"What're they doing?"

"Just what I'd do, if it was me down below there. Pulling back around the shoulder, where I can't see 'em."

"But they can't see us either, can they?"

"No. But they can cut up the other side of the hump and get above us. Or split up, one come at us from the shoulder, the other one from below. That'd catch us in a crossfire."

Longarm wasted no time making up his mind. While he shoved fresh shells into the Winchester's magazine, he told Flo, "Now you do exactly what I tell you to." She nodded, her eyes wide. "I'm going to take a sneak up that shoulder. Here." He handed her his Colt. "You keep watch down below, there where they were before. If you see one of 'em coming around the shoulder, let go one shot at him. Just one, you understand?"

"Custis, I've never shot a pistol in my life."

"That don't matter. The rurale won't know that. And I don't expect you to hit anything. I couldn't myself, with a pistol at that kind of range. All I want to do is keep him down there."

"What if he doesn't stay there, though?"

"Shoot again. But watch your shots, mind? Only one at a time; you only got five. If he keeps coming, you wait till he's close enough for you to count his whiskers. Then just point the gun at his belly, like you would your finger, and pull the trigger."

"Is that this little lever here? And don't I have to do something called cocking it?"

"No. Just pull." He placed the gun in her hands and showed her how to hold it. "Now. Think you can do it?"

"I can sure as hell try." She shook her head determindly. "No. I'll do better than try. I'll hit him!"

"Good girl! Now duck down and stay down except when you raise up for a quick look."

Longarm started up the ridge. He was pretty sure the two remaining rurales would waste a little time discussing what to do, and he figured he had an edge of two or three minutes on them. He didn't slow himself down by crawling, but ran up the slope and toward the hump, his bootsoles slipping now and then on the baked earth.

When he neared the crest of the shoulder, Longarm slowed down. He dropped flat and began snaking forward. At the top of the rising ground he moved even more cautiously, holding his rifle as ready as he could and edging ahead by inches. The ridge wasn't sharply defined. Its top was rounded, not angular, and when he reached the end of the rise, inches from the slope on the other side, Longarm took time to adjust his rifle in his hands so that he could fire instantly. Then he raised himself to his knees and looked.

He and the rurale saw each other at the same time. The Mexican was crawling up the opposite slope, just as Longarm had climbed up his side. The difference was that the rurale had chosen to sling his rifle across his shoulders and crawl up on hands and knees. The difference cost him his life. Longarm's Winchester was ready. His slug shattered the rurale's face while he was still trying to get his rifle free. The man lurched forward and lay still.

A shot from below kicked up dust inches from Longarm's side. He dropped flat and peered cautiously over the hump. The rurale trio had stopped in the shelter of the shoulder as soon as they'd gotten out of sight of the tree trunks where Flo and Longarm had holed up. Then the man Longarm had just killed had started up the ridge to get above the tree trunk bastion. Longarm's shot had wounded the man he'd hit, but hadn't killed him. The injured man lay on the ground, the third of the rurales bending over him, bandaging him. When they'd heard the shot that finished their companion, the unwounded rurale had started shooting, using his pistol. Now, Longarm saw, he was going after his rifle.

Before Longarm could get off a shot, the wounded rurale clawed his pistol out and began shooting. The range was too great for his slugs to carry, they fell short. By now, the unwounded rurale had his rifle in his hands. Longarm snapshotted without aiming, and though he missed, both men rolled behind the protection of their horses.

Longarm held his fire when his targets disappeared. The slope rose too abruptly for the rurales to fire from below the bellies of their mounts, but as long as they stayed behind the horses, Longarm couldn't put a slug into them. It was a standoff, but Longarm had been in standoffs before, situations where the first man who moved or exposed himself became an automatic target for his enemy's shot. Keeping his Winchester ready, Longarm studied the layout.

There wasn't much time for decision, he knew that. In just a few seconds the rurales would take advantage of their numbers. On count, both of them would step around the ends of the horses and present Longarm with two targets, giving him a choice of one, leaving him a target for the other man. The thought of retreating behind the ridge didn't enter Longarm's mind. He saw his only chance, and took it without hesitation.

Allowing for the change somebody'd made in the Winchester's sights, Longarm aimed at the rump of one of the horses and fired. Before the wounded animal had stopped bucking and started running, he'd levered a fresh round into the chamber and pumped lead into the hindquarters of another of the beasts. The third horse saved him the trouble of wounding it. When its companions began rearing and whinnying, it bolted, with the wounded ones close behind.

Longarm used the shell he'd pumped in the chamber to knock down the rurale who was raising his rifle.

The wounded man had just bent down to pick his rifle up from the ground when Longarm's next slug knocked him the rest of the way. Neither of the men gave any sign of movement, but Longarm waited with his rifle ready until he was sure they wouldn't. Then he reloaded.

His face grim, Longarm took careful aim at one of the prone men and squeezed off the shot. The body twitched when the slug hit. He stooped carefully, slowly, keeping his eyes on the other rurale, and picked up a cartridge case from the ground. Using it as a screwdriver, he adjusted the Winchester's rear sight. He lined up the buckhorn and the front sight on the form of the rurale who'd been wounded and saw the lead hit true. It wasn't a job he enjoyed doing, but he couldn't risk one of the men playing possum until he'd picked his way down the slope and surprising him with a belly-shot at pointblank range. He watched the two figures for a long moment. When neither of them moved, he started back to the windfall and Flo.

She was waiting, trying to look calm and hide her apprehension. "What happened?" she asked. "I heard the shooting, and then it stopped, and after a while there were some more shots, and I imagined all sorts of terrible things. I was afraid you might be—" She couldn't get the last word out.

"Dead?" Longarm asked her gently. She began trembling in delayed reaction to the strain she'd been under. He took her in his arms and held her for a moment until her shaking stopped. He kissed her before pulling out his soiled and wadded bandanna and wiping away the tears that were welling from her eyes.

"Come on. Let's sit down a minute. Everything's all finished. Don't fret yourself about it any more." He led her to one of the tree trunks and they sat side by side, Flo leaning on Longarm, his arms holding her. After a while she sighed and pulled a little away from him. But when she turned her face to him, she'd started to smile.

"I thought I was a pretty hardboiled dame," she said. "I guess you've figured by now that my life hasn't been a lot of creampuffs and talcum powder. Most of the time I can take a man or leave him alone.

193

If I want something bad enough, I can even put up with a man I don't much like. And even if I like him, I can kiss him goodbye without it bothering me. But damn you, Custis Long! You're different!"

"Now, you're just all upset, in a place that's pretty rough and strange to you. From what you've let on, you must've had a real rough time lately too. After you get used to me, you'll find I'm just as ornery as any other man that wears britches."

"Like hell you are." Flo kissed him hard. "You're not like any man I've ever met before."

"Look out, now. You're going to make me proud, and if there's one thing I can't put up with it's a man that's vain." Before she could continue the conversation, he went on, "We can't take time to visit, Flo. We've got to get on with what we set out to do. Now, I got one more chore to do down there at the bottom of this hill. You take your time about coming down there to meet me. What I've got to do's something you don't want to see."

He rode Tordo up the hump and down the other side to where the dead rurales lay, stopping at the midpoint of the downslope to pick up the rifle and pistol of the man he'd shot first. The unwounded horse that had bolted wasn't too far away; Longarm hazed him easily back to where the two dead men lay. He loaded their weapons and ammunition belts on the spare horse, tying them with its saddle strings. For all he knew, Ramos's main force might have wiped out Nate and John and be riding fast for the river.

With the captured horse on a lead, Longarm and Flo set off again at a gallop toward the Rio Grande and Los Perros. The clanking of the weapons that had belonged to the dead rurales rang in their ears, a constant reminder that the shooting wasn't over yet.

Chapter 18

"Well," Longarm told Flo, pointing across the slick, green, rolling surface of the Rio Grande, "there it is. That's Los Perros."

She grimaced. "It doesn't look like much."

"No. And when you come right down to it, it ain't much. But it's all we've got to lean on." Longarm nudged Tordo and the tired dapple moved slowly through the chamizal toward the ford that was still a short distance upstream. Flo followed after. Longarm said, "It's better'n nothing at all, I'd say. But we might still have to do a lot of leaning to get Sheriff Tucker to do what we got to make him do."

They'd hit the river at midafternoon, and with the stream as a landmark, Longarm had quickly located the rustlers' trail that led them to the ford. Nothing had happened after the brush with the rurales. They'd ridden across the plain that sloped gently down to the river, and though they'd looked back often, they'd seen no sign of Nate Webster and John Hill. They could only assume that before nightfall the two men would arrive, and that Ramos and his rurales would be there a little later.

Longarm led the way across the ford and turned south on the sandspit. When they reached the shanties and entered the town, the little procession they made drew stares from everyone who saw it. Longarm led on the gray, his chin stubbled with a week's beard, his frock coat ripped in several places and stained with the grime of the trail. The rurale horse was next, festooned with rifles and pistol belts and bandoliers. Flo brought up the rear, her blonde hair streaming down her back, her flared skirt draped over her horse, as badly stained as Longarm's coat.

As much as he felt like stopping at Miles Baskin's saloon for a comforting drop of Maryland rye, Longarm rode around the building and reined in at the hitching rail in front of the sheriff's office. Wahonta, the Apache girl, was standing beside the door. She looked at the riders with her opaque obsidian eyes, her face expressionless.

"Is Tucker inside?" Longarm asked.

"Yes. Him there," Wahonta said. She stood aside to let Longarm and Flo enter.

When he saw Longarm and Flo, Sheriff Tucker's eyes goggled. "Curtis? Where the billy-blue-hell you been? I've had Spud and Ralston out looking for you the past three-four days, now."

"Had to make a little sashay over the river," Longarm said shortly. "To save you asking, this lady's Miss Florence Firestone. From New York. Flo, this is Sheriff Tucker."

"Pleased to make your acquaintance, miss. You're a friend of Mr. Custis's, I take it?"

Longarm had briefed Flo on the situation they'd be stepping into at Los Perros. She didn't blink an eyelid when she replied, "I am now, Sheriff. He rescued me from a very unpleasant situation."

"Welcome to Los Perros, then, Miss Firestone. Any way I can he'p you, just call on me." Tucker laid the Southern gallantry on a bit thicker than Longarm remembered having seen him show it before. The sheriff returned his attention to Longarm. "You ain't the only one missing, either. You wouldn't happen to know anything about my deputy, Lefty? He dropped outa sight about the same time you did."

"Wish I could say I'd brought him back with me, Sheriff, but I can't. You'll have to find him yourself, I'm afraid."

Tucker's eyes narrowed. "If he don't come back soon, I'm goin' to be a man short. Remember what we talked about the other day? You was goin' to think on it."

"I've been too busy with my regular job to do much thinking."

"That railroad figurin' on building into Mexico, too, is it? You didn't mention that, Custis."

"Let's say I had my reasons." Longarm winked. He didn't know what reasons the sheriff's crooked mind would dream up, but that didn't matter much. He

196

went on, "Right now, we've got a spot of trouble that I'm going to ask you to help out with."

"I don't go back on my word. I told you that since we're going to do business together, I'd he'p you any way I can. What kind of trouble you talkin' about?"

"Well, in about two or three hours, maybe less, there's going to be a bunch of Porfirio Diaz's rurales come galloping up, and they'll be after my hide. Miss Firestone's, too."

Flo said sweetly, "And you said you'd help me too, Sheriff. Just a minute ago, remember?"

Tucker whistled. "Rurales? You mean you got crossways of 'em while you was over there?"

"Afraid I did. Now, my guess is that the rurales won't pay much attention to that river. They'll be mad and mean, and if you let them get into Los Perros, you're not going to have much of a town left when they get through."

"What d'you expect me to do? I got two men, with Lefty gone."

"You'll have to muster up a bunch of special deputies. If I was in your place, I'd deputize every man I could, and stop 'em cold on their side of the river."

"Hold on, Custis! Damn it, you're askin' me to start a war with Mexico!"

"No, I wouldn't put it that way. If you line enough men up on our side of the river, the rurales won't cross. I don't imagine they'd want it said that Mexico started a war, either. The thing is, you're the duly constituted authority here. It's your duty not to let those rampaging hombres come into your town."

Longarm could see that his cool, matter-of-fact way was baffling Tucker. That was what he'd set out to do. Getting the sheriff off balance, convincing him that his help was in his own interest and not a life-or-death matter to Longarm had been his objective from the beginning.

Tucker said, "Look here, Custis, I better find out what you been doin' over in Mexico before I start a fight with them rurales. For all I know, you might've broke some of their laws, maybe be a fugitive from justice. If that's so, the rurales might have some kind of right to come over here after you."

"Sheriff, your rights stop at the river, don't they?"

"Well, sure, I guess that's so."

"Then, damn it, theirs stop on the Mexican side. And, like I mentioned, if a bunch like that comes storming into town, you're not going to have a town left here. Now, if you don't—"

Longarm's argument was interrupted when the jail door swung open. Spud, Tucker's chief deputy, came swaggering out. He started talking before he saw Longarm.

"Ed, that little greaser bitch don't know a thing about Custis. I had to knock her around a little bit—" He saw Longarm and his words faded out. His eyes stuck out even farther than had Tucker's. "Damn you, Custis! Where you been? And what'd you do with Lefty? I know damn well—"

Tucker cut Spud short. "Shut up! I already asked him about Lefty. He don't know any more'n you and me does."

"I want to know something about who you've been knocking around back in that jail, though," Longarm told Spud coldly. "Far as I know, there's just one woman in Los Perros you might think'd know something about me." Spud didn't answer. Longarm raised his voice and called, "Lita! That you back there?"

"Coos-tees?" It was Lita's voice coming from the cells. *"Ay, que milagro!* I know you come when you find out I am here!"

Longarm turned to face Spud. "If I find you've hurt that girl . . ."

"You'll do what?" Spud challenged. He'd stepped into the office now, and stood facing Longarm across the room. "You know, Custis, I think it's time you found out I'm a better man than you are!"

"Wait a minute!" Tucker shouted. He let the air cool for a few seconds before saying, "You two banty roosters quit shaking your combs. Spud, Custis tells me there's a bunch of rurales on their way here to haul him back to Mexico."

"Let 'em!" the deputy snapped. "We'll be well rid of him!"

"Shut up, Spud!" Tucker ordered for the second time. "Bad feelin's between you and him is one thing. But if them rurales wants Custis bad enough to cross the river to git him, they're goin' to be in a mood to tear this town apart."

Spud obviously hadn't thought of this. He scratched his head. "Well, Ed, what d'you think we better do?"

"We better be ready to stand 'em off. Them rurales don't much listen to reason, unless there's guns backin' it up."

"For this worthless chawbacon? I tell you one thing, I don't aim to stick my neck out to save his!" Spud blustered.

"It ain't Custis worryin' me," Tucker said. "We put a lot of time into settin' ourselves up here. I don't aim to see it busted up. It ain't Custis we'd be helpin', man! It's us!"

"No, by God!" Spud shot back. "We don't have to fight them greasers! All we got to do is grab Custis and hand him over!"

"You figure to do the grabbing, Spud?" Longarm's voice was mild, almost casual. He might have been asking the deputy about the weather.

Lita's voice called again from the jail, "Coos-tees? Why you don' come help me? I don' feel so good."

Longarm took a half-step toward the jail door.

"Custis!" Spud yelled, "I warned you!"

As he spoke, the deputy's hand swooped for his revolver. He almost reached it before Longarm's Colt barked once. Spud crumpled. As he folded to the floor, Flo screamed and Tucker half rose from his chair.

"I'd sit right back down, Tucker, if I was you." Longarm's voice was suddenly as steely as his eyes.

"Jesus God!" Tucker breathed. He sagged back into his chair. "I thought Spud had a fast gun hand!"

Flo hadn't screamed after her first involuntary cry. Her eyes were fixed on the deputy's body. She said, disbelief in her voice, "You—you killed him!"

"He needed it," Longarm told her. To get Flo busy and keep her mind off the shooting, he said, "Do me a favor, Flo. Go back to the jail and see if that girl needs help. Tucker, where's the keys kept?"

"On—on a peg just inside the door."

Longarm continued, "If she's been beat up, get hold of that Apache girl we passed on the way in. Wahonta's her name. She'll get hot water and cloths and whatever else you need."

"You mean that man you shot was beating a helpless girl?" Flo asked.

"You heard him admit it."

"Well! If that's the kind he was, I'm glad you shot him!" Flo bounced across the room with long indignant steps and disappeared into the jail.

Longarm said to Tucker, "Well, make up your mind, man! Damn it, time's getting short!"

While Tucker was still grappling with his indecision, Ralston burst through the door. Miles Baskin was right behind him.

"Fellow run in the saloon," Ralston panted. "Said there was shooting here when he passed by!" He saw Spud's body. "Who done it, Ed?"

"Custis. But it was a square facedown. Spud wasn't fast enough."

Ralston looked at Longarm, who presented a face from which all expression had been carefully removed. After a moment, the deputy said, "Can't say I'm surprised. Spud didn't bother to keep it a secret that he was after you."

"A man's a fool to carry grudges," Longarm said by the way of a reply. "Sometimes they get in the way of his good sense."

Tucker said to Baskin, "Miles, I'm real glad you're here. Custis tells me we're due for some trouble."

Without appearing to be interested, Longarm took careful note of the interchange between Tucker and Baskin. It wasn't yet time to let the saloonkeeper know that Lefty had involved him in the rustling ring as well as tagging him as Tucker's secret boss. Getting the ground cleared for Webster and Hill to get safely across the river and setting up a defense against Ramos's men was the first order of business.

"What kind of trouble?" Baskin asked. "And how do I come into it? You're the sheriff, Ed. You're supposed to handle trouble."

"This is a sorta special kind," Tucker explained. "Custis got crossways of the rurales while he was across the river. There's a bunch of 'em ridin' here to take him back, he says."

"Well? Why tell me?" Baskin asked impatiently. He

seemed to be bothered by the sight of Spud's body; he kept looking at it and then glancing away quickly.

"You don't understand, Miles!" Tucker's voice now carried a note of pleading. "If the rurales bust in here, they won't stop till they find Custis, and if they don't find him right off, they'll rip Los Perros from asshole to appetite. And then the army'll be in, and maybe the rangers, and maybe federal marshals. It'll be one big stinkin' mess!"

"Um. I see what you're driving at," Baskin nodded with a frown. "Well, the answer's pretty damn plain, Ed. Arrest Custis and hand him over to the greasers. Then they'll go home and leave us alone."

"That's what Spud said," Longarm remarked quietly.

Baskin gulped. He looked again at the dead deputy, then at Longarm. He made no reply to Longarm's comment.

As though the saloonkeeper hadn't spoken, the sheriff told him, "Custis wants us to get some men together and keep the rurales on their side of the river."

"What men?" Baskin demanded.

Without giving Tucker a chance to reply, Longarm said, "You, for one, Baskin. I expect you can handle a gun well enough for a job like this. And we'll want everybody you've got working for you in the saloon: barkeeps, card dealers, swampies, everybody."

"Why should I put my people in danger?" Baskin challenged him.

"Maybe to save their own skins, Baskin. And yours, of course. You see, the sheriff's only got one deputy now, with Lefty gone and Spud dead. He's going to have to deputize a lot of men for this."

"Well, let him," Baskin bridled.

"You understand that if the sheriff deputizes a man who refuses to take on the job, that fellow goes to jail." Longarm was drawling his words out slowly, now, and Baskin was beginning to get angry.

"Fine. That's where they belong."

"Glad you think so." Longarm turned to Tucker. "Sheriff, you can start by deputizing me and Baskin, here. Then, if he balks at being sworn in, I'll arrest him for you."

Tucker had already started to rise from his chair

when Baskin's angry bellow froze him. "Ed! Why in hell are you letting this man take things over? You know, I've got a good mind—"

Tucker interrupted. "Now, Miles, don't say anything you might be sorry for. Custis ain't running things. I am."

"See that you do, then!" Baskin snorted.

Longarm suggested, "The sheriff might make you a deal, Baskin. If I was in his place, I would. Maybe if you let him have the men that work for you, he'll let you off from being deputized."

"Now that's fair enough, Miles," Tucker said. "How about it?"

Grudgingly, Baskin nodded. "If it'll get this fellow off my back, I'll send my crew over."

"With guns," Longarm stipulated. "I expect you got enough that your bouncer's took off drunks or that you've took in trade for drinks, to fit 'em out."

"All right, damn it! I'll see they've got weapons," Baskin growed. Then he said to Tucker, "Ed, I'll talk to you about all this later on!" He stamped out of the office.

"Well, there's the start of your posse," Longarm said to the sheriff. "Now if you and Ralston can round up a few more—"

Tucker was still too stunned to reply. Ralston answered, "Oh, we can find enough men, Custis. Guns, that's another thing."

"What d'you mean?"

"Well, you see, to cut down on gunplay and general meanness, we grabbed all the guns from the people a few years ago."

"And left your damn town wide open to any crew of gunmen who might ride by? Well, I've got three rifles and pistols and shells for 'em on that horse outside. You can start with those. And I'd guess the sheriff can dig up a few more, somewhere."

"I—I guess I can. We saved a few of the best ones," Tucker volunteered. "You go round up some men, Ralston. I better stay and swear in Miles's people, when they come over."

"Sure," Ralston agreed. But he looked to Longarm instead of to the sheriff when he asked, "How many you think we'll need, Custis?"

202

"How many will Baskin send over?"

"Well," Ralston said, then frowned. "He's got four barkeeps and three cardsharks and two swampies. Of course, the swampies is Mexicans—"

"That won't matter. That's nine. I'd say another dozen."

Ralston asked Tucker, "That sound right to you, Ed?"

"Yes. And get started, damn it! If Custis is right, we ain't got too much time!" When Ralston had left, the sheriff said to Longarm, "You damned near got us all in trouble, Custis. But I got to say, I admired the way you made Miles tucker down to you. Now, listen, you and me have got to work out a deal. I want you to take Spud's place, be my good right arm, so to speak."

"We'll talk after the rurales leave," Longarm told him. "But I don't mind telling you, what I say's going to depend on what happens when they get here."

"Now don't you worry. I'm goin' to put you in charge of the posse. How's that sound?"

"Good enough. When Baskin's men get here, you send 'em to the sandspit north of town."

"Where the ford is?"

"That's the place. I'm going there just as soon as I check up on Flo and Lita."

He went into the jail. Lita and Flo were sitting side by side on the low bunk in the last cell. There was a bruise on Lita's cheek, but otherwise she seemed unharmed. She jumped up and wrapped her arms around Longarm's neck.

"Coos-tees! I think you maybe don' come back! I am worry," she said, kissing him soundly.

"You take a look, you'll see I'm all here." Longarm smiled over Lita's shoulder at Flo, who was looking amused. "How is she?"

Flo replied, "She's fine, except for that place on her cheek. You know, Custis, I've really got to hand it to you. You beat any damned sailor who ever walked a deck."

"You mad at me?" he asked her.

"Oh, hell, no! Matter of fact, I think you're a pretty good picker. Lita saw you first; you might say I just came along accidentally." She cocked her head thoughtfully and added, "And it's one accident I don't regret. I think we're pretty much alike, you and me. No, I don't mind one bit."

"Good. I was hoping you'd see it that way." Now Longarm grew serious. He took the derringer out of his vest pocket and removed the watch from the chain. "Them rurales ought to be here soon, the way I figure it. I've got to be down at the river to meet 'em. This is about the safest place I know of for the two of you, so you stay right here." He handed the derringer to Flo. "Don't be afraid to use this, if you have to, in case there's trouble." He showed Flo how to use the weapon, kissed her and Lita soundly, and said, "I'll be back to get you after a while."

After he'd mounted Tordo and started for the sandspit, Longarm dropped the insolently calm attitude he'd been careful to maintain with Sheriff Tucker. His jaw was set; a furrow formed between his eyebrows. Somehow, there had to be a way to keep a shooting match from breaking out between Ramos's rurales and the posse that he hoped would be on hand to meet them. Longarm had seen enough of the ponderous mechanism of federal bureaucracy to know what would happen to a Deputy U.S. Marshal who'd created a serious border clash with a country that was technically friendly.

Old son, he told himself, they say that new federal pen at Leavenworth's a pretty fancy place, but I got no hankering to put in the next twenty years enjoying whatever view I'd get from a cell in it.

Except for a few long-billed herons looking for frogs in the lagoon on the U.S. side of the Rio Grande, the sandspit was deserted when he reined Tordo to a halt at the water's margin. He was getting edgy. The two-hour lead he and Flo had gained when Webster and Hill remained behind was all but gone. He began worrying about the ranger and the captain now, and out of habit reached into his pocket for a cheroot before remembering he'd been without for a week. It was, he thought, the only time he'd ever succeeded in quitting the damn weeds.

Even the arrival of Ralston with the score of volunteers he'd assembled didn't ease Longarm's worry about Webster and Hill. He carried it with him while he helped the deputy space out the men in the semblance of a skirmish line, putting those with the best rifles in the center, those with shotguns nearest the river, those with ancient single-shot Martini and Remington rolling-block rifles at the ends. He'd begun to think about crossing into Mexico himself and trying to backtrack in an effort to turn up Hill and Webster when a shout sounded from the men closest to the channel.

"Here they come! Get ready to give 'em hell, boys!"

Weapons were lifted to shoulders along the line. Longarm kept his eyes on the chamizal, which still hid the men on the horses whose hoofbeats were growing louder above the soft murmur of the Rio Grande's opalescent water. The riders burst through the brush and started down the bank. Longarm let go the deep breath he hadn't been aware he was holding.

"Don't anybody shoot!" he called. "These fellows are on our side!"

Webster and Hill urged their stumbling horses across the shallow ford. They saw Longarm and managed to persuade their mounts to make the few final yards necessary to reach him.

Hill surveyed the ragged line of men and said dryly, "You'd never make drillmaster in my outfit, Marshal. But I will say, I'm damned glad to see you've got a greeting squad."

"How far behind are Ramos and his bunch?" Longarm asked.

"Maybe a mile or two," Webster answered. "We been trying every trick in the book to shake 'em, but they've stuck like patent glue."

"How many men's he got?" Longarm tried to keep his voice as casual as Hill's had been, but his anxiety seeped through.

"He's down to about sixteen, now," Hill said. "That's four less than he had when he caught up with us."

"Flo and me took out three that he'd sent to cut off the river crossing," Longarm told him. "I'd say Ramos ain't too happy right about now."

A bit impatiently, the cavalryman asked, "Well, what's your battle plan? Do we shoot on sight, or wait for the rurales to get in the first volley?"

"I been telling these boys not to touch a trigger till

I say so," Longarm replied. "I guess that's about the best I've come up with. What's your idea, John?"

"Improve our position," Hill said promptly. "We're too exposed. The rurales can take cover in the chamizal and cut us to pieces. At least we can dig some rifle pits."

Hoofbeats sounding from across the river wrote an end to the captain's suggestion. Longarm said, "Sounds like we're too late for that. I guess it comes down now to who shoots first. What I'm hoping is that Ramos won't have any more of a mind to set off a war than we will."

"Calculated risk," Hill observed. "Worth taking, most times."

"I'd appreciate it if you and Nate would sorta separate and each one of you take charge of part of the men. I got the sheriff's only deputy holding down the middle, but you two've got more savvy about things like this than he has."

Hill and Webster started moving before he'd quite finished speaking. Longarm threw a leg over Tordo and settled into the saddle. The attention of the defenders was concentrated on the chamizal. The hoofbeats from the Mexican side of the river were loud and distinct now. Longarm nudged the dapple's sides and guided him into the ford. In midstream, he pulled up and waited.

His wait was short. Seconds after he'd gotten into position, the chamizal erupted rurales. The strip of shingle at the water's edge was filled with them, it seemed. Longarm saw Molina near the center of the rurale line, but there was no sign of Ramos. He was about to hail the sergeant when Ramos burst through the brush and rode down to the river. He didn't pull rein until his horse's front hooves were in the water.

"Qué pasa?" he demanded of Molina. *"Porqué no—"* He stopped when the sergeant pointed to the line of rifles and shotguns aimed at them from the sandspit. Then Ramos saw Longarm.

"Maldito gringo cabrón! Hijo de puta!" he shouted. He turned to his men. *"Adelante! Conmigo!"*

Along the rurale line, the men brought up their rifles.

"Ramos!" Longarm shouted. "Hold on! If you don't

want to start another war, you better tell your men not to shoot!"

Ramos didn't reply, but he did not give his men orders to fire. Though the rurales' faces were in the afternoon shadow, Longarm could see the struggle that was going on in Ramos's mind. He waited, not sure what the decision was going to be.

Ramos finally decided. *"Quedarse!"* he ordered his men. *"No tiran!"*

Along the line, the rurales slowly brought their gun muzzles down. On the sandspit, the motley band commanded by Longarm did the same thing. For the moment, at least, Longarm relaxed.

Chapter 19

"Now you're being smart, Ramos," Longarm said. He watched the rurales as, one by one, the men rested their weapons across their sadles. "Sorta surprises me. It's the first thing I seen you do that's halfway bright."

"Cuidado, gringo!" Ramos warned. "You keep make to me the insults with your dirty tongue, I come with my knife and cut it out of your head!"

"Now, that ain't your style. You're soft as a pig's turd without a bunch of your men to back you up."

"I don't tell you again, *hombre!* You go on, I tell my brave rurales to shoot!"

"You do that, Ramos! Mexico's never won a war yet. Texas beat you once, the U.S. beat you once; it'll be easy to do it again. So if you want to start the next war, just tell your men to let off one shot!"

"Now you insult my country and my men too! I do not warn you again, *cabrón!"*

"Oh, you got a right to be proud of them chickens you call men! Shit! They couldn't all of 'em hold on to three of us, even when they had us locked up! How the hell you think they could stand up to my men over there?"

"You play a *gringo* trick on us!" Ramos retorted. He was beginning to tremble with repressed anger. "Why you don't fight like men, not like old wrinkle-up *viejas?"*

"It wouldn't take more'n three old women to send your bunch off yelping," Longarm said. He was beginning to wonder how much longer the rurale captain would hold onto himself. "You had just one woman, but you couldn't keep her from walking away!"

"Bastardo! You are steal *mi rubia!* I make you pay for this!"

"I didn't steal her, Ramos. She couldn't wait to get shed of you. She told me you got no *cojones."*

"That is all!" Ramos shouted. He turned to his men,

who'd been growing increasingly restless as their captain talked endlessly and angrily with the *Norteamericano* on the dappled horse. Ramos ordered, *"Tome sus fusiles!"*

Eagerly, the rurales brought up their guns again.

Longarm lifted his rifle and let off a shot in the air. Ramos swiveled quickly in his saddle. His men awaited the order to shoot.

Longarm used the phrase he'd been working on in case he needed to use it. *"Parase! No tiran, o empeza una guerra!"* The rurales hesitated, and some of them began to lower their weapons. In a low voice Longarm said to Ramos, "You better listen to me, hombre. We got a platoon from Captain Hill's cavalry halfway here by now. If just one of your men pulls a trigger, them soldiers will chase your outfit clear to Mexico City. How'd Porfirio Diaz like that, Ramos?"

Ramos's face showed that he had no taste for a fight with the cavalry regulars. At the same time, he couldn't afford to let this gringo shame him in front of the rurales.

Longarm sensed that the time had come to press him. "Act like you have some brains, Ramos! Get them billygoats of yours outa here before we knock the shit outa them!"

"No! My men do not retreat!"

"That's all they know how to do! All you know, too! Like the blonde said, you got no balls!"

"This is too much insult! Now you pay!" Ramos's hand started for his pistol, but stopped when Longarm twitched the Winchester's barrel. Staring into the muzzle, Ramos froze. He said, "You talk big, *gringo federalista*. What kind of *cojones* you got? Enough to fight me, *mano á mano?*"

"Well, now," Longarm tried to put uncertainty in his voice and hoped he was succeeding, "I ain't so sure that'd prove much."

"It will prove I am better man than you! You are afraid, no?"

"No." Longarm drawled out the word. "But there's not much of anything for either one of us in it." He added thoughtfully, "Unless we make a deal that'll settle this thing."

"You want a bargain, no? I will make you one,

then. Listen to me, *gringo!* We fight. If I kill you, I get the other two *gringos* and *la rubia,* they come back with me. If I am lose, my rurales don't start the war. They go home. *Es agradable?"*

Hesitantly, Longarm said, "I guess I let you talk me into it. All right. What kind of fight you want? Fists? Knives? Pistols?"

"Fists are for *gringo* pigs! Knives are for *peones!* We fight, you and me, like *caballeros, como soldados!* With pistols, hombre!"

"Suits me." Having gotten what he wanted, Longarm decided to try for some frills. "You tell your men to pile up their guns on the bank and stay away from 'em. I'll tell mine to do the same thing. If you and me're going to settle this by ourselves, there ain't no use in taking a chance some hothead'll turn it into a free-for-all."

Ramos thought for a moment, then nodded. *"De acuerdo."*

"Now, then. Where're we going to do it? On the sand, over there? It's a good clear space." He pointed to the wide expanse of river-sand on the spit below the ford.

"Is as good as any place," the rurale agreed.

"Let's get on with it then!"

"No!" Ramos jerked his thumb over his shoulder in the general direction of the setting sun. "It will be too dark by the time we are ready. *Otra cosa,* if we fight now, you have the advantage over me. I have ride hard today, you are fresh and rested. No, *hombre.* Tomorrow, when the sky is bright, before *la salida del sol,* the light will favor us equally. *De verdad?"*

"If that's how you want it," Longarm shrugged. "It don't matter to me whether I kill you today or wait till tomorrow."

"Ay! Qué fanfarron! We will see, *mañana!"*

Ramos turned his horse in the shallows at the edge of the bank. His men clustered around him, and Longarm could hear them excitedly questioning the captain. He stayed in the middle of the ford until the rurales drew away, into the chamizal, to camp for the night. Then he turned Tordo and walked the gray to the sandspit. Hill and Webster reached him first.

"That was some hell of a long talk you had with Ramos," Webster said. "What was it all about?"

"Couldn't you hear?" Longarm asked.

Hill said, "I was down at the far end on one side. All I could get was a word now and then, when you two were shouting."

"About the same with me," Webster nodded. "I figured you must've had some pretty strong things to say, to get him to pull his men back. They gone for good?"

"Oh, I imagine they'll be around a while, yet."

"Well, tell us the whole story," Hill said impatiently. "I'm as curious as Nate to find out how you made him withdraw."

"I lied a little bit. Told him a platoon of your troopers was on the way here, to take on him and his bunch. He didn't like that idea very much." Then as as afterthought Longarm added, "Oh, and I agreed him and me'd shoot it out, man to man, just before sunup tomorrow."

"You did what?" Hill exploded.

"Now, we're right close together here, John. You couldn't've missed hearing me."

"You sure you can take him?" Webster asked soberly. "Some of the rurales are pretty good with a sixgun."

"Now, Nate, a man never does really know about a thing like that, does he?" Longarm asked. "But I'll take whatever chance there is."

"I'm not sure I approve of this," Hill frowned. "I'd rather get my troopers here, even if it means a night march. Let them handle things the army way."

"And maybe set off a war?" Longarm asked. "That's what we been trying not to do, John, remember? But I'd take it as a favor if you will back up my bluff, find somebody to ride to the fort with an order for 'em to come on. Then we'd know for sure there wouldn't be any trouble tomorrow."

"You're right. A show of force can stop most trouble before it gets under way," Hill replied. "I'll get that fellow Ralston to pick me out a messenger."

"We'd best set up a guard here at the ford tonight," Nate Webster suggested. "I don't trust rurales. Night raids are their style, you know."

"You do whatever you figure's best, Nate. Right now I'm mainly interested in a square meal and a good night's sleep in a real bed."

When Longarm got back to the sheriff's office, Tucker was nowhere to be seen. Longarm supposed he was back in the ell with Wahonta and decided not to disturb him. He went into the jail to tell the women it was now safe for them to go out. Lita was gone, but Flo was stretched out on the bunk, dozing.

"I thought I'd hear shooting if there was trouble," she said, "and I needed a nap. Lita left right after you did; she said something about having to help her mother serve supper. I tried to keep her, but she just wouldn't stay."

"No harm done, Flo. You must be about as starved as I am. Tell you what. Let's go out to where her mama cooks, and get supper."

"Before I eat, I want to clean up," Flo replied. "I'll enjoy supper a lot more if I get rid of a dozen layers of Mexican dirt first."

"That's easy. Lots of rooms vacant over at the saloon, and the porter'll get you a tub of hot water to bathe in. Rooms there ain't fancy like the hotel you got in New York, but the beds are better'n sleeping on the ground like we did last night."

Flo grinned at him. "I enjoyed it. Not so much the sleeping, but the lullabyes were wonderful."

"We'll have some more of them, for sure," he promised her. "I figure we better get to bed early. I got a busy day tomorrow."

Flo smiled again. "If that's an invitation for me to tuck you in, you already know I'm planning to do just that. I'll enjoy going to bed early too, under the circumstances."

She didn't ask him why his day was going to be busy, and Longarm didn't elaborate.

While Flo bathed in the room next to his, Longarm asked for a pitcher of boiling water and a bottle of fine oil to be sent up to his room while he waited for the tub. It was a common enough request in any frontier saloon that rented rooms. While he waited for Flo to finish her bath, Longarm stripped his Colt, poured boiling water through barrel and cylinder, swabbed the metal dry, and applied the lightest possible film of oil to the hammer and trigger mechanism. When he reloaded, he chose each cartridge with meticulous care, inspecting it carefully before sliding it into a chamber. He sipped from his bottle of Maryland rye while he worked, and wished again for a cheroot.

He made quick work of bathing. Apologetically, the *mozo* who served the rooms told Longarm that he'd taken the liberty of taking the dirty shirt and longjohns that Longarm had left in the room "to *la lavendera, señor, si no obedece*," and was surprised at the size of the tip he received for the unsolicited service. When Flo tapped at the door, Longarm was ready. He'd shaved in the tub, donned fresh underwear, and though he hadn't been able to do anything about the rips his coat had gotten during the past few days, he'd shaken the dust out of it. Flo had brushed off her coat and jacket. As she remarked, "We'd be taken for bums on Fifth Avenue, but we don't look out of place in Los Perros."

Longarm escorted her to the stall where Lita's mother was cooking. Lita served them, her dark eyes flashing with suppressed anger every time she looked at Flo. The food was as tasty as Longarm remembered but the atmosphere was distinctly cool. Lita didn't talk with them beyond the most necessary remarks, and none of Longarm's mild jokes brought laughter to her lips. They hurried through the meal and started back to the hotel.

As they crossed the plaza, Flo said, "I guess I'm not the most popular person in the world with your little friend. Isn't she a bit young for you, Custis?"

"I was a little bit leery of her at first, but when push comes to shove, Lita don't act as young as she looks. Not that she's the woman you are." He looked at Flo curiously. "You ain't a bit jealous, are you?"

"No. I suppose it's not in my nature to be. Maybe because I've learned not to fall in love, I can see jealousy as a waste of energy. Don't worry about your little Mexican girl, Custis. I won't mind her one bit, as long as you give me all I want of you while we're together."

"You know I'm going to do that, honey. Fact is, I'm

ready to start just as soon as we get by ourselves again."

"I can't wait, but I will. It'd attract too big a crowd if we let ourselves go right here in the middle of town."

As soon as Longarm locked the door of his room, Flo reached for him. "Now show me you meant what you said."

"We both got too many clothes on for me to prove it real good."

"You help me, I'll help you."

Longarm delayed following her suggestion only long enough to hang his gunbelt in its regular place at the head of the bed on the left-hand side.

They made a frolic of the undressing game, but it became something else when Longarm stood naked. It was the first time Flo had seen him undressed in a lighted room, and the scars he'd earned in scores of brushes with those on the wrong side of the law drew a gasp of dismay from her.

"My God! How can a man take so much punishment and still be healthy?"

"Oh, some of 'em slowed me down awhile. Didn't put me down for good though."

"I can see that." Her hand crept to his groin. "At least, I can see you're not down. Just the opposite." She stroked him gently. "And no scars where they might really have damaged you."

"And you haven't got a scar on you, have you?" Longarm ran his hands down Flo's lush body. He lingered over her breasts awhile, then stroked his hard palms down her waist to the satin skin of her hips and pulled her tightly to him, his erection between them, hard against her belly.

She wrapped her arms around him and began pulling him toward the bed. Just before they reached it she swung around so that Longarm toppled backward, with Flo on top of him. She raised her hips high to get him inside her and fell forward heavily, gasping with unconcealed delight as she felt him going deeper and deeper until their bodies were locked together and there was no more depth that he could seek. Squeezing tightly with the muscles in her buttocks, she began rotating her hips very slowly.

Longarm lay back and let Flo take her pleasure.

She prolonged it as much as possible, stopping her hip-rotations more and more often for shorter and shorter periods as she fell into the urging of her mounting ecstasy. Then, her blonde hair streaming down to enclose Longarm's head and shoulders in a golden tent, she rocked herself up and down until the flood of joy poured hot and wet. Longarm did not let her rest. While she was still limp and trembling, he pulled her higher on the bed and rolled on top of her.

"Not right away!" Flo protested. "I just came more than I ever did in my life before!"

"It ain't too soon. You'll like it better, now your edge is off."

He was already moving, thrusting with full, slow strokes, not hurrying, using only part of his weight and strength. For the first few minutes Flo could only lie quiet and receive him, panting from her own exertions of moments earlier. A little at a time she came to life. Longarm felt her inner muscles responding to his measured churning and began to move faster and drive harder. Flo's eyes were squeezed shut and her lips were opening and closing as little birdlike cries escaped them in rhythm with the movements of his rising and falling hips.

Longarm built to the final moments as fast as Flo did. The time came for him to let his body set its own rhythm, and he did. He pounded with fast, repeated drives until he could hear Flo's clear, small ululations only dimly as they became a single treble note. He could feel her body's pulsing as it drew him into her with force added to greater force until the gushing he could no longer hold back drained him and he dropped spent upon her.

When their breathing had quieted, Flo said with a sigh, "I didn't think anything could be better than last night. My God, was it only last night that we fucked under the trees?"

"That's when it was."

"Well, last night was good, but tonight's better."

"We didn't feel like taking our time then. Too many worries on our mind."

"Yes." Flo lay quietly for a moment. "You know, Custis," she confessed, "I like to think about fucking almost as much as I like to fuck. Especially when I'm around somebody like you."

"Most folks do, I guess. Only damned few of 'em are honest enough to admit it."

"People are such damned fools. Sometimes I think—"

Whatever it was Flo thought was lost in an insistent rapping on the door. Longarm glanced at his Colt to be sure it was in place before calling, "Who is it?"

"Is me, Coos-tees! Let me in! I got to find out is true, what I am hear!"

"What'd you hear, Lita?"

"I will tell you when you let me in!"

"Damn it, I can't. I'm busy."

"If is *la rubia* in there, I don' care, Coos-tees. Is you I wan' to talk to!" Lita said insistently.

"Oh, let her in," Flo told him. "I don't care if she sees what I've got; I've shown damn near as much on the stage. Might do her good to have something to compare herself to. And unless I'm a bad guesser, she's seen what you've got more than once."

Reluctantly and somewhat suspiciously, Longarm got off the bed, slipped his Colt from the holster, and opened the door just wide enough to let Lita enter. Her eyes widened when she saw Flo's pink and gold nakedness lying relaxed on the rumpled bed, but she ran to Longarm and grabbed him in a tight embrace.

"Is true, Coos-tees? Is true, this thing I hear?"

"You tell me what you heard and I'll tell you if it's true."

For the first time, Lita saw that he was holding his pistol. She cried out, "Is true, or else you don' got to be so careful not to let me in until you get *la pistola!* You think I bring somebody to shoot you, yes? Ay, Coos-tees! You don' trust me!"

"Sure I trust you, Lita. Now settle down. I let you in, didn't I? What did you hear that's got you so wrought up?"

"Down in the plaza, they talk about how you make the fight with *el capitán rurale* tomorrow, the fight with *pistolas*. Is true? You do this, Coos-tees?"

"Sure it's true. But that's not much to get worked up over."

"Maybe she's worked up because I'm here," Flo suggested.

"Is not so!" Lita objected. "I don' care if Coos-tees make *chinga* with you, *rubia*. But I rather he do it with me!"

"Come on to bed with us, then," Flo laughed. "He's man enough to handle both of us. And I want to find out more about this gunfight you've got set for tomorrow, Custis. You didn't say anything to me about it, any more than you did to Lita. Honey," she said to the girl, "it looks to me like we're in about the same boat. You might as well get off your clothes and enjoy the voyage."

"You mean this thing?" Lita asked. A corner of her mouth twitched in the beginning of a smile.

"Sure I do. We both want the same thing from the same man. No reason for us to fight, is there, when we can share?"

"Coos-tees?" Lita appealed to Longarm. "Is all right if I stay?"

"If you feel like you want to," he told her. He was thinking of the last time he'd shared a bed with two passionate women. That was in Cripple Creek, with the Stowers sisters. "If Flo says you're welcome, I sure do, too."

"Good! Then I stay!"

Lita's fingers flashed nimbly at the waistband of her skirt and it dropped to the floor at her feet. Longarm remembered that, like tonight, she'd worn nothing under it the night on the sandspit. She pulled at the neck-string of her low-cut blouse, shrugged it off her shoulders, and let it slip down her body to fall atop the skirt. She went to the bed and lay down beside Flo. Longarm felt himself getting hard just looking at them: Flo's soft white skin, pink breast rosettes and blonde hair and brush; Lita's perfect contrast of smooth brown skin, her dark nipples budding in anticipation, her groin a mystery of midnight.

Flo looked at Longarm and started chuckling. "You see, Lita? I told you it'd be all right. He's thinking about you right now."

Lita was smiling, too. "Then come here, Coos-tees. *Dame su grifo magnifico! Dame todo!* Maybe I show you *las trigueñas tienen mas deluce como las rubias!*"

217

Longarm didn't wait for her to ask a second time.

Darkness still filled the room when Longarm snapped awake. At once, his mind jumped ahead to the appointment that was waiting for him at daybreak. Then memories of the night came back, a confusion of warm, seeking mouths and hard-tipped breasts, of legs and thighs brown and white upraised and clamped around him, of clutching hands and wet inner recesses flowing hot while he strained to fill them. At some time, quite early, Lita had shed her anger and jealousy. She and Flo had become friends of a sort, joining together to please Longarm, lying side by side while he moved from one to the other, from brown to pink to brown and back to pink, sustaining their frenzy while increasing his, and never knowing who'd be partners during the instants of the final spasm.

While all three had lain exhausted for brief interludes of recovery, he'd told them of the duel that was to take place at dawn, and both had kissed him tenderly, their eyes shaded with a fear that all his calm assurances couldn't drive away. It had been Flo who'd ended the night, persuading Lita to leave when she did, so that Longarm could sleep. And when they'd left, he'd slept the deep, sound sleep of exhaustion after pleasure.

A light gray tinge was marking the window of Longarm's room. He held his hands up and studied them in silhouette against the faint light, watching for a twitch or tremor. They were both rock-steady. He stretched. He didn't feel tired, just pleasantly relaxed. He rolled out of bed and dressed quickly, wishing he had a fresh Prince Albert coat to put on. He took one wake-up sip out of the rye bottle, and savored its warmth and bite. Then he collected his possibles, distributing them in their accustomed pockets, and gave his Colt a final quick inspection after he'd adjusted his holster to the exact position where he wanted it to rest.

There was already a crowd waiting at the sandspit when Longarm pulled Tordo to a halt. Apparently, all of Los Perros had come to watch. Across the river, he saw the glow of dying fires where the rurales had made camp. He tilted his head to look at the sky. It was cloudless and brightening rapidly to pink in the east. The chamizal on the Mexican side of the river stirred and Ramos and his men pushed through.

As though their appearance was a signal, hooves thudded from the direction of Los Perros and a detachment of the 10th Cavalry rode up in squad column. Captain Hill rode at the column's flank. The troopers' faces, ebon black to mulatto, were set and serious, their eyes trained straight ahead. Longarm knew they'd been in the saddle all night, but anyone who didn't know it would have thought the group was fresh from the parade ground. The crowd parted to let the troopers through. At the edge of the sandspit the riders turned alternately right and left, to form a fence of horseflesh across the sand and keep the spectators back.

Hill rode up to Longarm. "You feel all right?"

"Fine. Be indecent if I felt any better."

"We'll be keeping an eye on Ramos's men." Longarm nodded, his eyes on the rurales, who were beginning to string across the ford. A bit diffidently, the cavalryman said, "Well, good luck, Marshal."

"Thanks." Longarm nudged Tordo through the line of troopers and stopped just beyond them. A hand touched his knee. He looked down and saw Nate Webster.

"That sergeant from the rurales, Molina, was over here a while ago," Webster said. "Maybe I butted in, but I took it on myself to work out some rules with him."

"Like what?"

"Everybody'll stay back outa your way. I'll walk up with you, and Molina'll come out with Ramos. Molina swore they wasn't fixing up any monkeyshines, but I still don't trust 'em."

"All right, so far. What then?"

"Me and Molina will draw a middle line. Then we'll step off fifteen paces in both directions from it, and draw deadlines. You and Ramos start out back to back from the middle. You can walk or run or bellycrawl, however you want to do it, long as you don't draw before you get to the deadline. Then you turn around and face it out."

"Sounds fair enough to me," Longarm told the

ranger. "Captain Hill says his troopers'll be watching the rurales to see they don't cut no didoes."

"I'd say everything's covered then." Webster studied the sky. The pink was fading in the east, a harbinger of sunrise. Above them, the air was bright and the sky clear. "Guess me and Molina better get on with it. I'll wave you out, when it's time."

Longarm lounged in the saddle and watched the ranger and the rurale pace off the deadlines and mark them with furrows scraped by bootheels. Behind him, the babble of the crowd grew louder as the onlookers observed the preliminaries. Webster and Molina walked back to the center line after marking the deadlines. Webster waved to Longarm, who dismounted and walked leisurely to the furrow from which the duellers would start. From the cluster of rurales at the river end of the spit, Ramos was walking toward them.

An argument developed between Webster and Molina. It was brief, and not especially heated. When they left the line and went over to the crowd together, Ramos and Longarm both stopped to watch what they did. The ranger and the sergeant were searching the faces that stared from behind the line of cavalrymen. Finally, both nodded and simultaneously signaled one of the spectators forward. There was a brief three-sided discussion and the trio returned to the center line. Longarm and Ramos resumed their approach.

"This hombre's going to start you off." Webster put his hand on the shoulder of the man he and Molina had picked from the spectators. "He'll count, then he'll run like hell to get outa the line of fire. You can see he's Mexican. He lives in Los Perros and he swears he don't hold sides for either one of you. That all right?"

"How many numbers will he count?" Ramos asked.

"Three," Webster replied.

"Uno, dos, tres," Molina supplemented.

Ramos nodded. So did Longarm.

"Might as well go ahead then," Webster said.

Longarm and Ramos did not shake hands as they walked to opposite sides of the center line and turned to stand back to back. Webster and Molina moved away. The tension that had slowly been building now began to make itself felt; the air was charged with unseen currents. The only sound was the bubbling of the Rio Grande's opaque water.

His voice high-pitched and strained, the man chosen from the crowd began to count, *"Uno—dos—tres!"* His heels scuffed softly in the sand as he ran from the line.

Behind him, as he started walking, Longarm heard the muffled crunching of Ramos's footsteps. He tuned his ears to the rhythm of the sound and tried to match his own pace to that of the rurale. Ahead of him, the deadline grew more sharply defined with each step.

Longarm divided his mind. Half of it counted the paces he must take to reach the furrow, the other half concentrated on translating the almost inaudible scratching of sand on bootsoles into the length and speed of Ramos's steps.

A jarring note in the rhythm of Ramos's paces warned Longarm. The rurale had begun to run. Longarm leaped forward over the furrow of the deadline. In midair, he curled his body. He landed prone and rolled, drawing as he landed. He saw Ramos over his sights and fired. Ramos dropped before he could trigger the revolver he was raising.

While the echo of Longarm's shot was dying, two more reports that sounded almost as one broke the disturbed morning air. Longarm, still lying on the ground, saw the spurt of sand raised by a pistol slug rise like a tiny geyser, a foot from his shoulder. He looked around. Molina was crumpling. Webster was standing with his revolver still extended.

"Bastard drew when he seen Ramos drop," the ranger called to Longarm.

There was a murmur of agreement from those in the crowd who'd seen Molina's move, of surprise and doubt from others. The rurales started forward as if on order. The cavalrymen advanced, closing into platoon front, their carbines resting on their thighs. The rurales stopped, clustered around the bodies of Ramos and Molina. When the Mexican force stopped, the troopers halted as well. In sullen silence the rurales picked up the dead men and draped them across horses. They turned and rode off the sandspit into the water, splashed across the ford, and disappeared into the chamizal.

Only after the conical tops of the rurales' sombreros could no longer be seen above the brush did the crowd let go its breath in a great collective sigh. The onlookers began to trickle back toward town. The cavalrymen held their position, watching for movement on the Mexican side of the river.

Longarm walked over to Webster. Both men were still holding their pistols, so brief had the interval been after the first shot.

"Thanks, Nate," Longarm said. He fished a cartridge out of his pocket and looked it over carefully before putting it into the Colt's cylinder. Then he told Webster, "I got to go back to the sheriff's office now and finish up the job I came here to do. I'd be proud to have your company, if you want to come along."

Webster nodded. Both men mounted and rode side by side back toward the shanties of Los Perros.

Chapter 20

As he and Webster rode into the plaza, Longarm said, "We'll need to stop by the saloon before we go to the sheriff's office. Both of us could stand a drink about now."

"Looking for Baskin?" Webster asked casually.

"Yep. You heard what Lefty said there in the jail before they killed him."

"It's not something I'd be likely to forget. But it's been your play, mostly. I'll let you call it."

Longarm tilted his glass of rye quickly and left Webster at the bar while he went upstairs and tapped at the door of Flo's room.

"Who is it?" she called. Her voice wasn't cheerful.

"Who'd you think it'd be?"

He heard her footsteps running to the door. It swung open. Flo said, "I didn't stay after the gunfight. I didn't know whether you'd feel like talking."

Longarm kissed her. "Don't fret over what's past. I just got a minute, but I'll be back when I'm done."

"You mean you're almost ready to leave here?"

"Pretty quick now. If you got any getting ready to do—"

"I'm ready any time." She sighed with relief. "I wasn't sure you were going to ask me to go with you."

"I'm asking, but only if that's what you feel like doing."

"You know I do. Where?"

"We'll talk about that later, after I get back."

He rejoined Webster at the bar. The ranger asked, "Want to tell me what you've got in mind?"

Longarm poured another glass of rye and sipped it before he answered. "Well, we got what my boss would call overlapping jurisdiction. Only I figure you got a better claim than I have, not that I want any at all, Nate."

Webster frowned. "Trouble is, I don't know how

much of a case I could make against the sheriff. Now Baskin, he's sure to go up a long time for rustling. But even if he turns evidence against Tucker, I don't know that a jury'd go hard on him, since Baskin's been his boss."

"Tell you what. You take Baskin. Let me worry about Tucker."

"Fair enough," the ranger agreed. "But it's still you who'll call the turns."

"If that suits you, it's good enough for me. Come on."

Longarm led the way back to Baskin's office. They entered without knocking. Baskin was kneeling in front of the big office safe, pulling out papers, ledgers, and money bags and stuffing them in a disorderly jumble into saddlebags that were already bulging. He leaped up when Webster and Longarm entered.

"Sorta thought you might've waited till you seen whether me or Ramos come out winner before you got ready to hightail," Longarm said mildly.

"Now, don't shoot me, Custis! If it's money you're after—"

"What the hell's he talking about?" Webster asked.

"Baskin's clock's running a little late," Longarm explained. "He's still got me tagged as a hard case on the dodge." He pulled out his wallet and flipped it open to show his marshal's badge. The saloonkeeper's jaw dropped. Longarm said, "I guess your friend the sheriff didn't introduce you to this gent here, when he passed through town before. He's Texas Ranger Nate Webster. I don't know how many federal laws you broke, Baskin, but Nate can damn sure make a good state case against you, so I'm letting him have you."

"Let's see now," Webster began. "There's rustling, which is about all I need. It'll get you a good long sentence when your part in the new Laredo Loop comes out. You don't look like you got guts enough for murder; I'd say you had your killing done by the sheriff and his boys, but you'll wind up as an accessory. And there'll be more before it's over, when Tucker starts talking."

"You don't have to wait for him to talk," Baskin said eagerly. "Just tell me what you want to know. Maybe you'll take it light on me if I—"

Webster interrupted. "I don't need you to make my case. No deal, Baskin. You'll take your chances with the rest of your bunch."

"As a favor, Nate, you might haul him with us when we go see the sheriff. Tucker still ain't caught on that this crook's kingdom he's set up has been busted to hell."

"Sure. If you're ready, we'll get on with the rat-catching," Webster grinned.

With Baskin in tow, they went out the back door of the saloon and walked the few steps to the sheriff's office. Ralston was sitting behind the desk. He leaped up and ran forward when he saw Longarm, stretching out his hand.

"That was the neatest piece of gun handling I ever saw, this morning—" Something in Longarm's eyes stopped him and his grin faded away. "What's the matter?"

"That's what we come to find out," Longarm told him. "Where's the sheriff?"

"He's still back in his rooms, him and Wahonta."

"Guess you better get him out here. We got a little business that needs to be settled."

Ralston hurried through the door into the ell. Tucker hadn't been in bed, for he returned with the deputy almost immediately, fully dressed even to his ivory-handled revolver in its tooled holster.

"What the hell's so important that I get roused out before I finish my breakfast?" he demanded. He saw Baskin then, and Webster standing beside the saloon-keeper. His florid face paled, but he tried to bluff things through. "Glad to see you got back from that trip to Mexico, Ranger. I hope them tips I give you panned out."

"You might say they panned out better than I thought they would." Webster's tone was carefully neutral.

Baskin's anger had been growing faster than his fear and caution. He blurted, "Damn it, Ed! Where'd you hide out last night and this morning?"

"I felt sick, Miles," Tucker answered. "Real sick, all night. Still don't feel too spry."

"You're a fool!" Baskin snorted. "You were blind drunk last night, if I know you, which I sure as hell ought to by now! Drunk, and wallowing in bed with your Apache whore! Do you know what happened in Los Perros last night and today at daybreak?"

"Well, I guess if it'd been somethin' important, I'd've heard about it," the sheriff said defensively.

"You've got shit where your brains used to be," Baskin said contemptuously. "I guess it's partly my fault. I knew you were getting past your time, but I didn't realize you'd gone so far."

"Now, you got no right—"

"I'd say he's got every right," Longarm broke in, "seeing as he's been your boss all these years. What Baskin's trying to tell you is that you're finished, Tucker."

His pig-eyes narrowed and Tucker said, "What're you doing, Custis? Trying to take Los Perros away from me?"

"You still ain't thinking straight. First off, Custis is only the first half of my name. The rest of it's Long. I'm a Deputy U.S. Marshal."

"He's dealing it to you straight," Webster said, when Tucker looked to him for confirmation. "Marshal Long was sent down here to find me and Captain Hill, after you hared us off into Mexico, and for all I know, tipped off the rurales to be on the lookout for us. And I don't think the Marshal would want Los Perros, even if you could hand it over to him."

"Damn you, Custis, or Long, or whatever your name is! You been trickin' me all along! You sneaky son of a bitch—"

Longarm's voice was steely as he cut Tucker short. "Mind what you say! Up to now I ain't held no personal grudge, so don't give me a reason to!"

Ralston volunteered, "The marshal outdrawed that rurale captain up on the sandspit at dawn today, Sheriff. Best gunplay I ever seen. If it was me, I'd apologize right quick."

"Well," Tucker grunted, "I guess I oughtn't've said that."

"No. You oughtn't," Longarm agreed. "I was aiming to turn you over to the rangers with your boss—"

This time it was Tucker who interrupted. He looked at Baskin. "Is he tellin' me the truth, Miles? You standing so close by that ranger because you're his prisoner?"

"If you hadn't been such a constipated jackass, you'd've seen that first thing!" Baskin shot back. "And it's mostly your fault. I'm going to see that you spend just as many years in jail as I do!"

"You didn't let me finish what I started to say," Longarm went on, his voice almost casual. "Now, the rangers could stand you up alongside of Baskin in a Texas court, but you might just get off too light. When you flapjawed at me, I decided you need a good, long sentence, so I'm taking you in on federal charges."

"You got no federal charges against me!" Tucker blustered. "I was real careful not to get crossways of that damn Reconstruction gov'mint we got now! Once it come out I rode with Quantrill—"

"They'd put you away for life, wouldn't they?" Longarm asked.

"They damn sure would, and you know it! That's why I was so careful—"

Again Longarm interrupted. "You wasn't careful enough. That Apache girl, now. She's a federal ward, like any other reservation Indian. She can't consent to lay up with no man, white or Indian, till she's legally married to him."

"You can't—"

Longarm went on as though he hadn't been interrupted. "But that's not the worst I'll charge you with, Tucker. You confessed to me that you bought that girl. Now, there's an amendment to the U.S. Constitution that makes buying a human being a federal crime. That's the big charge they'll keep you in jail for." He turned to Webster. "Sorry to take him away from you, Nate, but—"

Something in the ranger's eyes alerted Longarm. He whirled as he drew and faced Tucker just as the sheriff's hand closed over the ivory grips of his pistol. Longarm's slug went to Tucker's heart.

In the silence that followed the shot and the thud when Tucker hit the floor, Webster said, low, in Longarm's ear, "You really think he'd've gotten life for monkeying with that Indian girl, Marshal?"

"No. He'd have been tried in Texas, and I ain't

betting a jury here'd stick him a long term on both them charges."

"If you didn't have that badge in your pocket, I might be taking you in for inciting to murder," Webster said, unsmiling. Then he added, "But I can't say I blame you. I get mad when a man calls me a son of a bitch."

"Who don't?" Longarm asked as he slid his Colt back into its holster.

Late the next morning, Longarm helped Flo aboard the Butterfield stage that he'd flagged down at the river crossing just outside Fort Lancaster.

"Wish I could ride with you," he told her. "I got a few loose ends that still have to be tied up in Los Perros, and then I got to take my horse back to the remount depot in San Antonio."

"I've got a feeling one of those loose ends is named Lita," Flo smiled. "I halfway wish I'd decided to ride with you instead of taking the stage to San Antonio."

"You'll be more comfortable on the stage," he assured her. "And I'll beat the stage there. You take a hack to the Menger Hotel. It ain't grand like New York, but it beats Baskin's saloon. We'll have a few days there before you go on East."

"I've changed my mind about taking the train from San Antonio," Flo said. "Captain Hill told me I can get an express train from Denver that'll get me to New York quicker than the one I'd take from San Antonio. We'll have a few days, and then a few more."

Longarm watched the dust of the stage settle as it lurched down the rutted road. He'd have a day or two in San Antonio before the stage pulled in. He wondered if Cynthia Stanley—whose best friends called her Cyn—would get along with Flo as well as Lita had.

That's going to be something interesting to find out, old son, he told himself as he nudged Tordo with his knee. The dapple moved off.

SPECIAL PREVIEW

Here are the opening scenes
from

LONGARM AND THE AVENGING ANGELS

third novel in the bold new
LONGARM series from Jove/HBJ

Chapter 1

It was a Monday morning and it wasn't raining. The high, clear air of the capital of Colorado seemed reasonably fresh and invigorating as Longarm stood by the open window. Of course it was early in the morning, before the horse manure of a new day was pounded into its golden essence by countless hoofs, sending its pungent fragrance into the heavens to mingle with the coal smoke and soot that was already blackening every new building in Denver. But that was Denver after twenty-odd years of existence as a city—horseshit and coal smoke. And always from someplace—he wished to hell he knew where for sure—there came the smell of burning leaves.

As he peered down at the narrow streets, Longarm heard the bed springs squeak behind him and knew the girl was waking up. He was naked and did not want at this moment to turn and face his guest. After all, he had to report to the chief in less than an hour.

He sneaked a quick look over his shoulder and saw that she had just turned over, drawing the sheets up around her naked shoulders, the luxurious spill of her auburn hair tumbling down over the coverlet. She was breathing steadily, which meant she might well be asleep still. But then, he thought, you can never tell.

Longarm left the window and padded across the threadbare carpet to the dressing table and peered at his reflection in the mirror. He was a big man, lean and muscular, with the body of a young athlete. But there was nothing young about his face. It was seamed and cured to a saddle-leather brown by a raw sun and cutting winds, both of which he had experienced in abundance since lighting out from his native West-By-God-Virginia. His eyes were a gunmetal blue, his close-cropped hair was the color of aged tobacco leaf, and he wore proudly and kept well-trimmed a drooping longhorn mustache that added much to the ferocity of his appearance on those few occasions when ferocity as well as firepower might be decisive.

As he loomed above the dressing table in the early morning dimness, he heard another squeak of the bed springs behind him—and this time knew it was for real. He turned easily, catlike, aware as always that his movements had an almost hypnotic effect on others.

The girl—her name, she had told him the night before, was Emily—had a foolish little Allen pepperbox in her hand. It was a relic, at least twenty years old and of such an ancient and uncertain design that as often as not it would fire all six barrels at once. As Longarm loomed closer, she raised the pepperbox and aimed it at his naked chest.

"I'll fire!" she cried in a frightened voice. "I warn you!"

Longarm smiled and sat his naked rump down on the edge of the bed. "Ain't it some late for you to be protecting your honor, Miss?"

"But . . . I didn't *mean* that last night! I didn't mean that to happen!"

"Didn't appear to me like you was acting, ma'am. Leastways, you sure put your whole heart and soul into it." He grinned at her past the wavering pepperbox. "Fact is, what happened between us was mighty nice."

She scooted up angrily in the bed and propped her back against the brass bedstead, the little gun still trained on Longarm's chest. "It was my body that betrayed me, Mr. Longarm! I assure you. My heart and soul had nothing to do with it!"

"Why don't you put that little toy down now, Emily? You got my attention, all right."

"No!" she cried firmly, steadying the weapon. "I am going to shoot you, Mr. Longarm! I am going to send you to your Maker!"

"Mind if I ask why? I didn't think I was *that* bad last night. And by way of apology, I might remind you of the number of drinks you insisted on buying for me."

"That's not the reason!" she fumed. "What I mean is, you were . . . fine." She became intolerably flustered at this point and her face went dark with embarrassment. *"That's* not the reason!"

"And what is the reason?"

"My brother! Merle Bond! You're the one that sent him to prison! You testified against him. I heard your testimony. I was in court. When you stepped off that stand, the judge had no choice but to sentence Merle to all those years! You did it with your testimony!"

"Why, thank you, Miss Bond. I'm glad you think so."

Her eyes widened in fury. She brought up a small, pink hand to steady the weapon and seemed intent on pulling the trigger. "How dare you say that!"

"That's easy, Miss Emily. I believe in using the most direct route to wherever I'm going. Sometimes I might seem uncommonly blunt, but I don't mean no harm by it. I'm glad my testimony gave that jury the backbone to convict your brother. He is one mean son of a bitch, Miss Emily, if you'll pardon me for saying so."

"Oh!"

"I can't help it." He smiled sadly at her. "It's the truth and that's the long and the short of it. Wish it weren't, I surely do."

Tears welled into her dark blue eyes and began to roll down her fresh, round cheeks. There was nothing hard about her, he remembered from the night before. She was as soft and cuddly as a kitten—until she caught fire. And then it was all hands to battle stations and hang on! The pepperbox trembled. She seemed determined to pull the trigger.

Longarm got up casually and looked down at her. Convulsively, she brought the weapon up again so that it was still trained on his chest. "I *am* going to shoot you!" she cried between clenched teeth.

"Then do it, Emily, and get it over with."

She closed her eyes and squeezed the trigger. As the tiny hammer came down on an empty chamber, Longarm reached down and gently but firmly took the weapon out of the girl's hand. She collapsed onto a pillow, her head buried in it, sobbing.

He watched her for a moment, then turned and walked over to the dresser and dropped the Allen beside the pile of tiny rounds he had taken from it the night before. He poked through the rest of the clutter atop the dresser, found his bar of soap, and brought it over to the wash stand. Pouring water from a pitcher into a china basin, he dipped a washrag into it, soaped it, and began washing himself about the face, neck and shoulders. He was in the midst of rinsing off his face and neck when he heard the sobbing subside rather abruptly, and heard the bed springs jounce.

Reaching for a towel to dry himself, he looked back at the bed. Emily was sitting bolt upright, staring at him. She was still paying no attention to her nakedness, and this time he found it difficult not to notice her breasts. What was it that fellow Solomon called them, *like two young roes that are twins*? Well, maybe. And then he saw that she was looking at him.

"Longarm?"

"Yes?" He finished with the towel and tossed it onto the foot of the bed.

"Would you come over here?"

With a sigh, Longarm crossed to the bed and sat down facing her.

"You knew—about that gun, I mean."

"I found it last night while you was sleeping."

"You were just toying with me."

"I wasn't sure what you wanted."

"You weren't sure? You mean you suspected who I was?"

"I knew I'd seen you before somewhere and that it would be a good idea for me to remember. But like I said, I wasn't sure."

She closed her eyes, as if determined to keep her temper and remain composed. Opening them again, she said, "Those were terrible things for you to say about my brother."

"I just said he was a mean son of a bitch. And he was."

"He was just a high-spirited boy!"

Longarm nodded. "That's right. A high-spirited boy who robbed three stages, killed a driver and a shotgun on his third attempt, and later shot up a saloon, killing one of the bar girls. He resisted arrest and the posse that chased him to his hideout lost three good men. When they sent me after him, Emily, the price on his head was fifteen thousand, dead or alive. I brought him in alive. I didn't have to, but I did."

"And I should thank you for that, I suppose!"

"You can if you want. But maybe you already thanked me. Last night."

She tried to generate a head of steam over that comment, but couldn't quite manage it. And then her eyes dropped to that portion of Longarm's anatomy that made the most sense at times like this.

She looked back at him, her eyes softening. The memory of last night clouded her eyes, softened the anger she had tried so hard to retain. "Oh, Longarm," she whispered. "I'm so—confused."

Longarm stood up. "Let's put it this way, Emily. You're a woman—one hell of a woman—and that's nothing to be ashamed of. I can see what you planned, all right. You'd ply me with drinks, get me to take you up to my room, and then you would avenge your brother's life sentence. You been reading too much of that Ned Buntline crap, if you'll pardon my bluntness."

She closed her eyes and shook her head. "Don't keep asking me to pardon your language, Longarm. I'm used to it by now. But of course you're right. I guess I was being overly romantic."

"And foolish. But I guess you loved your brother. And I guess that excuses it some."

"I tried so hard to raise him properly, Longarm. But when mother died, he just went wild. I followed him out here, but he was determined to go his own way. And that meant guns. And robbing. And killing." She bowed her head and began to weep softly.

Longarm stood where he was, watching her, waiting. After a little bit, her crying slowed some and she glanced up at him. "Aren't you going to . . . comfort me?" She managed what she thought was a seductive smile, but it just didn't make the grade.

"Is that what you want, Emily? Comfort?"

She wiped her eyes. "I don't know. Last night we—"

"Forget last night, Emily. You had a reason for coming up here and trying to tire me out." He grinned quickly at the thought. "How did you know I'd be the one to tire *you* out?"

She blushed and wiped tears from her eyes hopefully. "I tired you out *some*," she insisted. "But you were so nice."

"You had a reason last night, Emily. What would your reason be now? I think you just better get dressed and go home and start thinking like a good girl again, and stop reading Ned Buntline."

"You mean you don't—"

"I mean I got a job to go to and you don't know me well enough to start bedding down with me on a regular basis. Not unless you're trying to gain instruction in a new line of work where the only rest you get is standing up."

"Oh! You're so cruel!" She snatched up the bedclothes and covered her lovely breasts. "If you wouldn't just stand in front of a girl like that with nothing at all in front of you . . . !"

"Beg pardon, Emily. Guess that *did* sort of cloud the issue some at that," Longarm reached for his knit cotton longjohns. He pulled them on while standing up and then reached for his brown tweed pants. They were a size too small and he had his usual struggle getting them on. At last he cursed his fly shut and straightened, the pants as snug as a second skin.

"That's much better," Emily said. "I don't feel so threatened now." There was a hint of deviltry in her voice, and glancing quickly over, he saw the gleam in her eye.

"As soon as I leave here," he said, "I'll expect you to dress and go back home, wherever that is. Understood, Emily?"

"You're not married, are you, Longarm?"

"No."

"Engaged?"

"No."

"Well then, why do you want to get rid of me?"

"How old are you, Emily?"

She hesitated. "Twenty!"

"Closer to eighteen, I'd say."

"I'll be nineteen next March!"

"I'm close to forty," he lied. "You're old enough to be my daughter. Come to think of it, I must have some daughters around your age at that."

"What's age got to do with it? It didn't seem to be such a terrible nuisance last night."

Longarm sighed, bent, and fished under the bed for his boots, then sat on the edge of the bed and tugged them on. They were low-heeled cavalry stovepipes more suited for running than riding, which was just what Longarm wanted. He spent as much time on foot as he did in the saddle, and with these boots he could outrun almost anyone.

But how was he going to outrun this girl? He stood up and turned to look down at her. She was still sitting up and holding the sheet over her breasts, but much of her shoulders were bare and her face was flushed, her eyes . . .

"Damn it, girl! I don't want any! You got that?"

"You don't have to shout!"

"Yes I do, it seems like. Now listen here to me. I'm a lawman. That means I go most anywhere they send me. I'm here today, gone tomorrow. I find my loving where I can, and I don't look back. I'm not interested in paying for it, which means I can go without if I have to. What I don't want and what I will never want, as far as I can see, is a wife on my neck—or a girl sitting in some hotel room waiting on me! Now if you don't make tracks, girl, back to wherever you came from, I'll haul you in for attempting to shoot a peace officer. I got your weapon here as evidence, and my testimony will be accurate. That means, Miss Emily, that I won't leave out a thing!"

"You wouldn't!"

He grinned at her. "If it would knock some sense into that pea-brain of yours, I would. Yes, I would."

"Oh!" she glared at him. "Oh!"

He turned his back to her, put on his gray flannel shirt, and fumbled with the string tie, fastening it into a tolerable knot, then tucked the shirt into his pants. His gunbelt he had stashed under some clothes in the second drawer of the dresser. He pulled it out now and strapped it around his waist, adjusting it to ride just above his hips. The rig was a cross-draw and he wore it high. He reached over, lifted up the mattress at the foot of the bed, and pulled out his Colt Model T. .44-40. Then he leaned back against the dresser.

Aware of Emily's eyes on him, he proceeded to inspect this most important tool of his trade. The barrel was cut to five inches and the front sight had been filed off; he didn't want it to catch in his open-toed holster. Moving then to the bed and still apparently ignoring the girl, Longarm emptied the cylinder on the bedsheet, dry-fired a few times to test the action, easing the hammer down with his thumb, as always. Then he reloaded. Before thumbing each cartridge home, he held it up to the window for a quick, minute inspection. He loaded only five cartridges into the cylinder. He had no intention of losing a foot when he jumped off a train or a horse, so he kept the firing pin riding safely on the empty chamber.

Satisfied with the condition of the Colt, he holstered it and looked at the girl.

"You had a gun there," Emily said, hushed, "under the mattress."

"That's right. I would have had it under my pillow, but I wanted to leave you room for that pepperbox."

Emily took a deep breath. "I've been very foolish, haven't I?"

"Yes."

"And this—isn't the beginning of anything, is it."

Longarm shook his head. "Nothing personal, Emily. It's just the way I'm built. Some men are for marrying, some men are for—" He shrugged and smiled at her. "For other lines of work. No hard feelings?"

She considered the question seriously for a moment or two, then looked him squarely in the eyes and shook her head. "I guess not. Just tell me one thing, Mr. Longarm."

"What's that?"

"Why is it that the men who want to settle down are so much less fun than the others?"

Longarm laughed and reached for his vest. "Maybe it seems that way now. Just give yourself time. You'll find a guy who's fun and who also wants to settle down. Just keep looking."

"That's what I've been doing."

He turned and looked at her. "You got some time left, you know."

"I suppose."

Longarm finished dressing swiftly. He took the change and his wallet off the top of the dresser and pocketed them, ducked into his frock coat, dropped the pepperbox and its cartridges into the right side pocket, then inspected critically his Ingersoll pocket watch. It was on a long gold-washed chain, the other end of which was soldered to the brass butt of a double-barreled .44 derringer. He placed the watch in the left breast pocket of the vest and dropped the derringer into the matching pocket on the right, allowing the chain to drape innocently across the vest front between them.

Positioning his snuff-brown Stetson carefully on his head—dead center, tilted slightly forward, cavalry style—he turned to face the girl. He smiled.

"You need a shave," she said.

"I plan to get one from the barber," he told her.

"And you want me to dress and leave as soon as you are gone."

"My landlady—an understanding soul—will be up here in less than thirty minutes to make sure. She knows I'm a lawman working for the government and she is a great help." Something occurred to him. "Do you need any money?"

"No. Didn't you say you never had to . . . pay for it?"

"That's not why I asked," he said, with a gentleness that surprised even him.

She ducked her head. "I'm sorry. A train ticket back to St. Louis would cost me more than I have left right now."

He nodded, reached into his pants pocket, and dropped a double eagle on the bedspread. "I know the train schedule," he told her. "I'll have someone at the depot watching to make sure you're on that train for St. Louis this afternoon."

"Thank you," she said, reaching for the gold coin. "This is more than generous of you." She turned her face up to his, fully expecting a goodbye kiss, he realized.

He bent swiftly and kissed her lightly on the forehead, then swept past her and to the door. Pulling it open, he turned to look back at her.

"Remember, I'll have someone watching that train. Be on it, young lady!"

There were fresh tears running down her cheeks as she nodded. Longarm pulled the door shut and hurried down the stairs to find the landlady. It was curious; he should have felt twenty dollars poorer and more than a mite irritated. But he didn't. He felt good, in fact.

Longarm's shave took longer than he had expected it would. Glancing at his watch as he passed the U.S. Mint at Cherokee and Colfax, he turned the corner and started for the Federal Building. Once inside, he strode through the lobby as swarms of officious lawyers hustled their legal briefs in one door and out another, talked excitedly in groups, or hurried upstairs and downstairs, sweating themselves into such a fine frenzy that their oil-plastered hair was already coming unstuck. At the top of a marble staircase, Longarm came upon a large oak door. The gilt lettering on it read: *United States Marshal, First District Court of Colorado.*

Longarm pushed the door open and strode into the outer office. The pink-cheeked clerk was playing with his typewriter; the newfangled piece of machinery was raising a fearsome clatter.

"The chief in?" Longarm asked the clerk above the clatter.

The fellow turned. "Oh, it's you, Mr. Long!"

"That's right." Longarm grinned at the clerk. "You don't have to announce me. You just go ahead and play that thing. You sound great." Longarm started for the inner office.

"Just a moment, Mr. Long," the clerk said, "I believe Marshal Vail—"

Vail appeared in the doorway. There was a harassed look on his face. He growled, "Can't you ever make it in here on time?"

"It's this damn clerk," Longarm said. "He makes me wait out here."

Vail glared at the clerk, who began to sputter indignantly. When he saw Longarm's sudden grin, his shoulders slumped and he waved Longarm past him. "Get in there, Longarm," the man said, "and stop upsetting the clerical staff." As Longarm moved past him into his office, Marshal Vail closed the door and smiled sardonically at him. "You're not going to like this."

Longarm slumped into the leather armchair across the desk from his superior and tipped his head slightly as he regarded the marshal. "They want me to rescue Sitting Bull from the Wild West Show?"

Vail's eyebrows shot up a notch. "That wouldn't be such a bad idea, at that." Then the man moved behind his desk and began pawing through a pile of paper. "It might be a lot easier than this little job." He found what he was looking for and squinted at Longarm. "Ever been to Utah?"

"Sure. Remember that jasper I caught up with in Provo? Tried to get lost in a band of them Mormon night riders. What the hell did they call themselves?"

"Avenging Angels."

"That's right. Sounds like a Ned Buntline joke."

"They are no joke, Longarm." He looked down at the dispatch he had retrieved as Longarm took out a cheroot and stuck it into his mouth. He didn't light it, just began chewing on it. "Seems a bunch of Mormon fanatics somewhere in Utah have kidnapped a Mormon girl from Salt Lake City. The Mormon authorities have requested federal help in getting her back." Vail leaned back and looked at Longarm, just the trace of a smile on his pasty, indoors face. "I'm sending you. Washington wants the best man for the job." Vail shrugged. "What choice did I have?"

Longarm shrugged. "Who do I contact in Salt Lake City?"

"Wells Daniel. But you won't contact him. He'll contact you. Stay at the Wayfarers—a new hotel. I understand it's reasonable."

"Who is this Daniel?"

"A high muckymuck in the Mormon Church. That's all I can tell you. But you work through him."

"I got the feeling you know a lot more you ain't telling."

"And if you notice, none of it's written down. This is a political hot potato, Longarm. As I understand it, there are members high up in the Mormon church who are sympathetic to this kidnapping—or at least to the fanatics behind it."

"I see," said Longarm dryly, working the cheroot about in his mouth. "So the federal government is called in to do the dirty work. I don't know if I like this so awful much. What can you tell me about the kidnapping?"

Vail shrugged. "I don't even know the girl's name. She was taken from her home at night and hasn't been heard from since. A note was left by the fanatics, but nothing from them since. She's supposed to be a very pretty young thing who'd make a fine addition to some Mormon's harem."

Longarm frowned. "From what I hear, those women are supposed to make a choice about joining one of them households."

"They are. This one, it seems, wasn't given that choice."

Longarm nodded and got to his feet. The thought of a young girl hauled off like that didn't sit right with him. "You got my expense vouchers? I'll need a railroad pass, too."

Vail nodded. "See my secretary." He looked up abruptly at Longarm. "Oh. I almost forgot. You remember that punk desperado, Bond? Merle Bond—the jasper you caught up with last spring?"

Longarm grew suddenly alert, his teeth chomping down hard on his unlit cheroot. "I remember."

"Did you know he had a sister?"

"Not until recently."

"Well, according to Deputy Wilson, she's in town looking for you."

"That so?"

"Well, she's armed, according to Wilson. Armed and dangerous."

Longarm interrupted Vail with a wave of his hand. Then he took out the old Allen pepperbox and the cartridges and dropped them on Vail's desk. "Miss Bond is no longer armed. And tell Wilson to check the train depot tonight. I've already seen the young lady and told her to be on tonight's train for St. Louis."

Vail got to his feet. "You mean you've already tangled with that girl?"

"I guess that's what you'd call it."

Vail's face got pale. "And you let her go?"

"She's just a kid, Chief. A foolish young thing with romantic notions about paying back those that testified against her brother. I disarmed her and got her promise. She'll be on her way back to St. Louis tonight. Relax."

"For God's sake, Longarm! Before that foolish kid

landed on your doorstep, she killed the poor son of a bitch in Cedar Creek who testified at her brother's trial—Amos Beedle, the stagecoach driver. He was number one on her list. *You* were number two!"

Longarm took a deep breath, his teeth clamping down hard, cutting through the cigar. He spit it out into the wastebasket, then looked at Vail.

"I guess she won't be on that train to St. Louis, then. Just the same, it might be a good idea for Wilson to check it out."

Without a word, Vail nodded. He was still standing, thunderstruck.

"By the way," Longarm asked, "what did she use to kill the stage driver?"

Vail slumped back down into his chair and nodded to the pepperbox. "She used all six barrels." He sighed. "At least you didn't give it back to her."

Longarm stuck what was left of his cheroot back into his mouth. "I'll go see about them travel vouchers and the railroad pass."

He turned then and made for the door. As he pulled it open, Vail cleared his throat. Longarm turned. Vail leaned forward onto his forearms.

"You take care of this business in Salt Lake City with a minimum of fuss, Longarm, and I just might forget to include this business with Miss Bond in my report to Washington."

"Chief?"

"Yes?"

"Have I ever asked you to wipe my ass before this?"

"Hell, Longarm, I was just—"

"Well, I ain't asking you to do that for me now. You hear? You want to include that there business with that little tramp, you go right ahead."

Longarm left then, slamming the door firmly behind him.

Longarm sat morosely on a faded red plush seat at the rear of the passenger car of the Union Pacific's *Hotel Express*. There had been nothing luxurious about his accommodations, and Longarm's tall frame was more than a little weary of the tedious ride. The coach was noisy, filled with smoke and with the stench of unwashed humanity. Looking about him, Longarm found it difficult to keep his temper at times. What he saw and what he heard made him stir restlessly in his seat.

His fellow travelers were not elegant, not by a long shot. They were dressed carelessly, sloppily, many times in ragged garments and more often than not clutching dirty bundles. Most of the men had revolvers stuck carelessly in their belts, a piratical gleam in their eye. They were unshaven, usually. Their talk was loud and filled with profanity that took no note of the women and children forced to endure their company. Those men with wives tried not to notice the language or the insolence of the single men's stares, lest they be forced to stand up to them and possibly lose their lives in the bargain.

Salt Lake City was the next stop. They were only a few hours away, having passed through Provo less than an hour ago. It was close to three in the afternoon and the heat inside the coach made Longarm's skin crawl. Babies were bawling and the voices of mothers scolding their restless children were a constant irritant to the coach's occupants.

The door to the coach opened and Longarm saw a bearded desperado enter. There was something particularly offensive about the man as he lurched down the aisle, found an empty seat alongside a drummer and slumped heavily down beside the man. The drummer had been dozing. He awoke with a start, began to protest the abrupt manner in which his new companion had joined him on the seat, then immediately thought better of it as he looked the man over. His voice trailed off apologetically. But the bearded fellow did not let well enough alone, and after he had directed a few well-chosen oaths at the drummer, the poor man shriveled noticeably.

It was an unpleasant scene, but Longarm saw no reason to get involved. He lit a sulfur match with a single flick of his thumbnail, held it to the tip of a fresh cheroot, and turned his attention to the landscape streaking by the train window. They had left the Utah Lake behind and Longarm could see the towering, snow-clad peaks of the Uinta Mountains to the east. The grade was now steadily downhill, and he realized the heat would get progressively worse as they neared the Great Salt Desert. Pine-covered ridges swept up to and fell away from the train as it racketed along. Great stretches of barren, uninhabited land met his gaze. Used to the long arid stretches of the West, Longarm was nevertheless mildly depressed by this glimpse of Mormon country. Only a band of religious fanatics, he supposed, could make a land like this bloom. Or would want to.

A woman entered the coach. She seemed very tired and just a mite desperate for a place to sit. She was a gaunt but attractive young woman, her head enclosed in a severe, dark blue bonnet, her dress heavy and extending down to her feet, which were encased in heavy black shoes, laced high and tight. She appeared to lose her balance for a moment, then began to move hopefully down the aisle toward Longarm.

She must have gotten on at Provo, Longarm realized, and had not yet been lucky enough to find a seat. He moved closer to the window and touched the brim of his hat as she met his gaze, and smiled. With enormous relief, she hurried toward him and the seat he offered her beside him.

As she passed the jasper who had entered the coach just before her, however, she let out a tiny cry. Longarm craned his neck to look and saw that the man had reached out and grabbed the woman by the wrist. She tried to pull away but the fellow just increased his pressure on the girl's wrist and pulled her back toward him. The man got to his feet as he pulled the girl to him and smiled. It was not a pleasant smile.

"Well, if it ain't Annie Dawkins!" the fellow exclaimed, a leering smile freezing the girl's feet to the floor, it seemed.

"Jason Kimball!" the girl managed. "You leave me be! I ain't a Mormon no more and you can't collect no more tithe from us!"

The fellow's leer deepened. "Why sure I can, Annie. You is in arrears, you is! We'll just collect you and even up the books! How's that?"

The girl Annie tried to pull away, but the fellow had a firm grip on her arm and wasn't about to let go. Still holding on to her, he looked down at the drummer, who all through this had been trying to ignore the ruckus completely, his head turned resolutely while he contemplated the grim Utah landscape.

"Get up, drummer," the fellow told him in a harsh, grating voice that allowed for no argument. "Me and my friend here wish to sit down in the same damn seat. Git!"

Longarm would never go looking for a fight. He would, in fact, leave an unfriendly bar rather than provoke a confrontation. A peaceable man who liked his solitude, he preferred always to mind his own business. But he was sorely tried at this juncture. The sight of this walking carrion manhandling the terrified girl caused his stomach to rumble dangerously. The fellow was nothing but a murderous, loud, profane old blackguard in an unclean shirt. His laugh was a demented horse laugh, and his walk was a buccaneer's swagger.

Glancing quickly about him, Longarm noticed that there was not a single male in the coach who did not have his eyes averted. The children were all being forcibly made to look elsewhere and they were all uncommonly hushed. The sight of this universal cowardice caused Longarm to grind the end of his unlit cheroot, and at last when he saw the quivering drummer sidling out of his seat to make room for the blackguard, he got reluctantly to his feet and started down the aisle.

The drummer was in the aisle when Longarm reached them. At the sight of Longarm's empty seat, his eyes lit up and he tried to move past Longarm to get to it. Longarm restrained him with a hand on his left shoulder and gently pushed him back and out of the way. Then he turned to the girl. Tears of anger and frustration were rolling down her youthful cheeks. She looked at him with wide, hopeful eyes.

"May I be of assistance, ma'am?" he asked her, lifting his Stetson slightly. "I saw you were looking for a seat."

Before she could answer, the fellow who had been bullying her spoke up roughly. "Here now, what the hell are you about, mister? You leave Annie be. She's with me now!"

"Why don't we leave that to her?" Longarm inquired, his voice gently conciliatory. Longarm turned his eyes to the girl. "Would you care to join me, Miss . . . ?"

"Dawkins," the girl said eagerly, wiping away her tears quickly with the back of her hand. "Annie Dawkins."

"Hey, now!" protested the bully. "You just stand back there, mister! Who says you can interfere, you dirty gentile!"

Longarm smiled at the man. "That's right. I'm a gentile. And what are you—a Mormon?"

The girl pressed anxiously toward Longarm. "He's —he's an Avenging Angel! Maybe you better not get mixed up in this." Longarm's quiet, almost gentle aspect had about convinced her that he was no match for this Avenging Angel.

"You heard her!" blustered the man, pulling himself up to his full five-feet-ten or so. "That's what I am, all right. So you better mind your own business."

Longarm smiled at the man. "You don't smell like an angel."

The fellow's eyes went hard. He reached his right hand up and began to tug on the handle of a big Colt he had stuck in his belt. Longarm slapped the fellow in the face with his left hand, drew his Colt with his right, and brought the gun's barrel up swiftly, catching the fellow across the side of his head. The Avenging Angel slumped back into his seat, glassy-eyed, his jaw slack, a broad red welt rising swiftly across his cheekbone.

Holstering his weapon, Longarm swiftly disarmed the man, then frisked him expertly for any hidden weapons. Finding none, he looked up and nodded to the drummer.

"You can have your seat back now. When this fellow wakes up, keep him amused with dirty jokes." Longarm grinned at the look of pure terror on the man's face.

Straightening, Longarm turned to the girl and tipped his hat. "My seat is this way, Annie."

Her eyes still wide—and a look of pure, undiluted gratitude filling them—she nodded, did a quick curtsy of a sort, then preceded him down the aisle to his seat. Longarm allowed her to get in first so that her seat would be next to the window. Longarm took from her the little carpetbag she had clung to all through this unpleasantness, and placed it in the rack over their seat. Then he sat down beside her and smiled at her kindly in an effort to quiet the young girl's thudding heart. Her face was flushed and it was obvious she did not really know how to account for her good fortune.

For his part, Longarm did not know how to explain his own lack of good sense. Twice now within two days he had allowed a pretty face to obscure his role as a law officer. He should have brought in that sweet little murderess when she pulled that weapon on him, ridiculous as it appeared to him at the time. And this most recent bit of gallantry did nothing at all to insure his quiet entry into the case of the missing Mormon girl. Every Mormon and gentile in this coach—and soon, he had no doubt, throughout the train—would be discussing in hushed tones the way he had rescued the Fair Young Maid from the Avenging Angel. Longarm might as well have entered Salt Lake City wearing a sign announcing his profession and his intent.

He sighed, stretched his legs as much as was possible, and took from his inside breast pocket a fresh cheroot. This one he was tempted to smoke, despite his vow to quit the filthy habit.

He spat out the stub of his previous cheroot and poked the fresh one into his mouth, then turned his head to nod at the girl. He didn't want his preoccupied silence to make the woman feel unwelcome.

"You can light that, if you want," she suggested. "I won't mind."

He smiled in appreciation of her consent, took out a match, and lit it with his thumbnail. As he sucked the pungent tobacco smoke into his lungs, he leaned back, placated somewhat.

"Perhaps I should explain," the girl said softly.

"That ain't necessary, ma'am," Longarm said.

"Call me Annie," she insisted quietly.

He smiled at her and took a deep drag on his smoke. "Annie, then."

Frowning, he leaned back in his seat. What was the matter with him? He could use any information he could get on the Avenging Angels, and this girl beside him might very well be a fund of such lore. Maybe he was getting old. He had never heard of senility setting in at his age, but he sure as hell wasn't acting very bright lately.

"Of course," he said, turning to look at her, "it did seem strange for a man to do something like that in front of so many people. Did he know you from somewhere?"

She nodded quickly. "My father drew a terrible farm in the lottery years ago. Southern Utah, it was in. Brigham Young told my father and the others to grow cotton there. But we couldn't, no matter how hard we worked. The soil was alkaline, and the grasshoppers and crickets were everywhere. We were lucky if we could grow enough food for our table."

She sighed and looked away from Longarm, her gaze following the shifting contours of the semi-arid landscape. She was seeing it all again, Longarm realized, in her mind's eye. Talking about it had upset her.

"You don't have to tell me about it if you don't want," Longarm suggested gently.

She looked back up at his face. "But I do. I owe you an explanation. You see, we did so poorly that we couldn't pay our tithes. So Brigham Young sent the Avenging Angels after us. And even then we couldn't hardly gather enough to satisfy them. So my father left the church."

"Did that help?"

She shook her head sadly. "They said he couldn't leave the church. They said they were excommunicating *him*. And so we lost everything."

"I'm sorry, Annie. What happened to your family?"

"I don't know what happened to my father. He rode out one night—to talk sense to those Avenging Angels, he said. He never came back. My mother just gave up after that and died soon after. My sisters, like me, have become fallen women." She bowed her head in her hands and wept softly.

Longarm said nothing and did not try to comfort her. Instead he quietly, patiently puffed on his cheroot, being careful not to blow any smoke toward her. At last she recovered her composure and looked at him.

"So you see, Mr.—"

"Long," he told her, smiling. "Custis Long."

"So you see, Mr. Long, you seem to have saved from that terrible man only a piece of soiled goods."

"Guess you got a right to be ashamed if it makes you feel any better, Annie. But I always thought soiling came from inside."

She raised her eyebrows in surprise and appreciation at Longarm's comment. "Yes, of course, Mr. Long. You're right. But there aren't many people in the Mormon community—or anywhere else for that matter—who would agree with you. You have no idea how difficult they make it for a woman without a family or a husband. I tried to get a job as a seamstress in Provo and Salt Lake City, but since the Saints own all the establishments that use seamstresses and since my family and I were excommunicated—" She shrugged. "So I went to work for Ma Randle at the Utah House."

"A saloon?"

"Yes—among other things."

"I thought Mormons didn't drink."

"There are many gentiles living in Salt Lake City, Mr. Long. And many Mormons do drink. Have you ever tasted Valley Tan?"

Longarm shook his head.

"Wait until you do." Her eyes danced mischievously. "It is a kind of whiskey. Only the Mormons make it and we're the only ones who can drink it, seems to me."

"Annie," Longarm said, noting that the girl had recovered her composure well enough to handle tough questions, "what was that fellow going to do with you? He said something about collecting you and evening up the books. I assume he had some plan—some way of using you."

She shuddered involuntarily and nodded. "Yes he did, Mr. Long. He would take me as his wife—or as one of his wives."

"I thought the Mormons could only do that if the girl was willing." He watched her narrowly.

"That's the way it *should* be, and that's the way it is, usually. But not for them—not for the Avenging Angels." She looked back out the window of the coach. "They're out there. Everywhere. Waiting. Small colonies of squatters." She shuddered. "One of my sisters is with them. I haven't heard from her in a year." Then she uttered a bitter laugh. "Celestial marriage, Joseph Smith called it."

Longarm leaned back in his seat. He had almost finished his cheroot and he had just glimpsed a portion of the Great Salt Desert through the coach window. He was almost to Salt Lake City, and Annie to the Utah House.

Not long after, the train creaked to a stop. As Longarm got to his feet and lifted down Annie's carpetbag, he saw the Avenging Angel she had addressed as Jason Kimball getting to his feet as well. Once in the aisle, he glanced in Longarm's direction. The look on his face would have curdled the heart of an Apache. Longarm just smiled at the man and nodded briskly.

Jason strode angrily down the aisle to the door of the coach, not at all gentle with those he brushed aside.

"You have made an enemy there, I'm afraid," said Annie, watching the man go. "But I thank you from the bottom of my heart."

"I wouldn't say any day of mine was entirely wasted, ma'am, when I gained an enemy of that stamp. When carrion like that starts thinking of you with any kind of charity, you maybe ought to wonder what you're doing wrong."

The train jolted to a stop. He stepped back and let the girl precede him down the aisle while he followed, carrying her carpetbag and his own canvas gladstone. He could not help noting her trim figure and the thick curls that coiled on her slim shoulders. Despite her severe dress, there was no doubt in his mind that Annie was all woman and he did not wonder at Jason Kimball's eagerness to take her into his harem to settle past debts.

Hell, Longarm thought, I wouldn't even need that much of an excuse. *But hold it right there, old son,* he told himself somewhat sheepishly. *Just you back off. You already muddied the waters enough. The chief told you to keep low, not to spend the taxpayers' money to spark a fallen woman with pretty ankles!*

With a sigh directed at the unsought complexities of a lawman's life, Longarm followed the girl from the train and was immediately engulfed in a tide of gushing femininity.

Three shrieking, delighted young ladies had darted across the platform to welcome Annie, and she was reciprocating their greeting heartily. His face reddened at finding himself in the midst of all this feminine clatter. Longarm put down Annie's carpetbag and tried to sidle out of the crush. But Annie reached out before he could get away and caught his arm.

Squeezing it fondly, she called out above the happy babble, "Thank you so much, Mr. Long. You are very kind!"

Longarm nodded his goodbye to her, aware suddenly of the curious, approving appraisal of the three young women, and pulled away. A tall, imposing woman in her mid-thirties, with a handsome face and magnificent dark eyes, stopped before him. She didn't seem to have the bust her size would have deserved. Indeed, she was almost as straight as a razor. But her waist was slim, her hips ample. This was obviously Ma Randle, the owner of the Utah House.

As the girls moved off across the platform, chatting gaily, the madam's dark eyes regarded Longarm coolly. "Thank you, sir, for escorting Annie from the train. I trust you are under no misapprehension concerning Miss Dawkins?"

"You mean do I know where she works?"

"Yes, that's precisely what I mean. I own the Utah House and the adjoining facilities, and Annie is one of my nicest girls. I am very fond of her."

"Yes, I can see that," Longarm remarked. "She must be great for business."

"That is not my only concern."

"If you'll excuse me, ma'am." Longarm started to move past the woman.

"Just a moment. You don't understand. I simply wanted you to realize that if you do come to visit Annie at the Utah House, you are most welcome. Only I would hope you won't make a fuss if you find she is occupied with other . . . customers." She sighed. "Annie is very popular, and sometimes men who are taken by her make a fuss when they find her already with someone."

Longarm smiled in spite of himself. "No chance of that, ma'am. My expense voucher don't cover that expense, and besides, my interest in Miss Dawkins has just about evaporated." Longarm caught sight then of Jason Kimball standing with four other cutthroats on the far edge of the platform. They were dressed in the same nondescript fashion, falling somewhere between that of a pirate and that of a highwayman. They were all uncommonly interested in Longarm. He turned back to the woman. "But you better keep those sharp eyes of yours peeled. One of them Avenging Angels over there—the good-looking one with all the hair—put in a claim for Miss Annie on the train. But I lost my head completely and went to her aid. Shoulda known better. Now if you don't mind, ma'am, I've got business."

Frowning, Ma Randle turned quickly to note Kimball and the men with him. Then she turned back to Longarm, restraining him with a gloved hand on his arm. "You mean that man was on the train? The one in the middle? And you tangled with *him?*"

"I just told you, ma'am," Longarm said patiently. "Now would you please unhand me? I really do have work to do—and you have four young ladies to escort back to your place of business." The five men, he saw, were walking toward them.

She let go his arm, as if she had touched a hot stove. "Of course," she said, stepping back. "Please forgive me for detaining you."

Longarm smiled, touched the brim of his hat to the madam, then crossed the platform to the few remaining hacks waiting and climbed into one rather beat-up old carriage. He gave the name of the hotel the chief had mentioned to the driver. As the man cracked his whip over the backs of his horses, Longarm leaned out the side window to look back.

He was in time to see the five piling into another carriage. In a moment it had started up and was following Longarm's. Longarm leaned back in the seat and frowned thoughtfully. He was sorry he had been so short with that madam, but he had seen at once what was happening. As the crowd thinned out after the train's arrival, the five men became encouraged to make a move. Kimball, it seemed, was not a man to let a grudge simmer for too long. With a small army at his back, he liked to take immediate action.

Longarm took a cartwheel out of his wallet and handed it out to the driver. "Take this. There's a carriage following me. Go down the next side street you come to and keep a steady pace. I'll be getting out the first chance I get. Don't slow down. Keep right on going, back to the station. Do you understand?"

The man shouted back that he did.

Longarm hung on as his carriage wheeled suddenly down a side street a few moments later. Looking out the window, he saw that the carriage was still following. Then Longarm's carriage turned on to another street. The hack following was out of sight around the corner. Longarm opened the carriage door and jumped out. The heavy canvas gladstone almost cost him his footing, but he kept his balance and darted into a tobacco shop, almost toppling the massive wooden Indian standing in the doorway.

Looking out around the Indian, he saw the hack racing after his carriage, the horses straining mightily to keep up with five men to haul. As soon as the hack had left the side street, Longarm walked back to the main thoroughfare and hailed another hack.

As he climbed wearily into the carriage he had an ominous feeling in the pit of his stomach. And his stomach, over the years, had never been wrong.

AS A STAR SHE WAS ONE-IN-A-MILLION... AND SO WAS HER CHANCE AT LOVE.

THE GIRL WITH THE GOLDEN HAIR

LESLIE DEANE

Darla Dawson had a million dollar smile—and a mane of golden hair that gave her a style all her own. Her ambition set her apart from all the other girls in Hollywood. She knew she had what it took to make it.

And she did. From low-paid model to superstar—the dreamgirl of millions of men.

But she didn't want other men. She wanted her husband—a man she couldn't have—a man she refused to give up.

THE SAGA OF A STAR, AND OF A WOMAN DETERMINED TO LOVE AND BE LOVED!

$2.25 12048070
Available wherever
paperbacks are sold.

NT-30

Are you missing out on some great Jove/HBJ books?

"You can have any title in print at Jove/HBJ delivered right to your door! To receive your Jove/HBJ Shop-At-Home Catalog, send us 25¢ together with the label below showing your name and address.

JOVE PUBLICATIONS, INC.
Harcourt Brace Jovanovich, Inc.
Dept. M.O., 757 Third Avenue, New York, N.Y. 10017

NAME_____

ADDRESS_____

CITY_____STATE_____

NT-1   ZIP_____